Praise for So

So Rare a Gift is just that, a delicious offering of romance, intrigue, and conflicting loyalties that spans two tumultuous continents. Drawing the reader in with heart-racing action, Anna and Henry are endearing, layered characters journeying down a memorable path of faith and freedom during America's founding. Amber Perry's passion for colonial history and romance is never more apparent than in this novel, sure to please new fans!

-*Laura Frantz, Christy Award nominated author of The Mistress of Tall Acre and The Ballantyne Legacy Series*

So Rare
A Gift

Book 3
Daughters of His Kingdom Series

By, Amber Lynn Perry

So Rare a Gift
By Amber Lynn Perry

Copyright 2016 Amber Lynn Perry
ISBN-13: 978-0997895209

Cover Design, Indie Cover Design and Tekeme Studios
Cover Photos, Danyell Diaz Photography
Formatting by PerryElisabethDesign.com

Published by Liberty Publishing

Author/publisher contact information:
www.amberlynnperry.com

Dedicated to those who strive for
a righteous cause.
May you always have strength to live fearlessly.

Chapter One

"You know why I have called you here, do you not?"

Mouth tight and hands daintily knit at her middle, Anna Rone measured every intake of air as she stared at the man who had fathered her. She had not returned to Wellhaven but thirty minutes past and already he had summoned her. "I do, sir." The very thought made her stomach coil.

"Then we shall make this brief." Rush Martin rose from his chair and rounded the large desk, the hazy afternoon sun casting forlorn shadows across the book-laden shelves. "Charles Worth has asked for your hand in marriage."

Rush shifted his mouth side to side, as if he chewed on the words he prepared to speak. Never once moving his gaze from hers, he brushed past all formalities or any fatherly sentiment. "I trust you have learned from your past mistakes." He stopped only inches from her, not even the hint of a smile on his worn face. With a patronizing tap on her shoulder, he loomed over her, the afternoon meal on his breath souring his words. "You have another opportunity before you. Do not disappoint me again."

Bleeding sincerity through her smile, Anna masked the hatred. He had not seen her in three years and these were the first words he chose to speak? But then, why should such a thing surprise her? "Forgive me, Father, but I do not recall that I had done any wrong. I did as you wished."

"Only after much trouble." The dark mahogany bookshelves and exotic trinkets that lined her father's study oozed an unwelcome aura that matched well the dry brown of Rush's eyes. He dropped his hand from her shoulder, that familiar rise of disgust clouding his features. "Do not feign ignorance. Enough shame has come upon this family in the past ten years because of you and your brother. I will not have any more of your actions further tarnish our reputation."

A sharp laugh burst from her lips, but she could produce no words. He would imprison her again, would he? She would not submit. Not this time. But the means of escape, the way in which her heart's desire would be granted had yet to enlighten her mind. *Lord, I pray thee, show me a way.*

Only his lips moved while the rest of his face remained vacant when he answered. "I expect a Martin to know their place. It seems you have never known yours."

"Perhaps I was simply discontent with my

allotment. Or should I say, my *assignment.*" She stared at him, but she didn't see him. Instead, that night, so many memories ago, consumed her vision and crashed upon her like a mountainside of earth. Cool air rushing past, ribbons of moonlight, budding hope, the heaving breath of her mount as she raced to freedom. A shock of fear and the sudden prison of knowing what might have been and would never be when her flight was discovered. And thwarted.

She snapped from the past and lifted her chin. "What father, truly caring for his daughter, would subject her to a marriage devoid of all that would provide the necessities of life. And I no more than a child."

"You were sixteen, hardly a child! And after ten years of marriage you ought to know how fortunate you are. Even in death your husband thought of your welfare, just as I always did, though you choose not to believe it." Voice booming like a crash of thunder, Rush gestured to the door. "Edwin Rone gave you everything you could ever desire. Every necessity he provided."

"Aye." Anna answered as calm as if they discussed gardens over afternoon tea. "Physical necessities to be sure, but not love. Not caring and devotion and companionship. Not kindness and sincerity. Not those *necessities* that a happy marriage would gift to both husband and wife." Slowly, her grasp of composure began to slip, her tone pitching upward.

"I was his ornament. Someone to hold his arm at parties and converse with across the dining table." Volume rising, courage spinning, Anna met him gaze for gaze. "Do I not have a say in my future? Can I not craft my own destiny? Samuel advised against such a marriage then, as I am sure he would advise against it now."

Face suddenly crimson, Rush stepped back and pointed a crooked finger. His voice scraped so low it rumbled the floor at her feet. "You will not mention your brother's name. We are not speaking of him. We are speaking of your future and nothing else." A cloud drifted past the sun, shading the opulent study with heavy gloom. "If you think for a moment you can augment my intentions for you by reminding me of times past, then you are more ignorant than I believed. Anna, can you not see? My actions are securing a way that your barren womb will not be a hindrance to your finding a companion. If I did not do so you would have no one to care for you—no roof over your head, no food in your belly."

Throat too thick to speak, Anna stared down at the Persian rug beneath her shoes. Closing her eyes, she found the ever-ready place in her memory where happiness lived and clung to it as he continued. "Anyone who knows the family—and here, that is nearly everyone that matters—knows the illnesses you suffered as a child. They know you cannot bear children. What man wants a woman who cannot provide a son?"

Glancing up, she soothed the tender parts of her that shrunk back in his presence, before nudging them behind her growing resolve. "I am well aware of what hinders my securing a husband. But perhaps if you allowed me to find someone of my choosing—"

"Do not begin to suggest you do not need my patronage. Without me you would be nothing. 'Twas I who gave you your pleasant looks and without that no one would have you at all." His eyes trailed her face as if he were inspecting a piece of fine china for cracks. "You have grown older. Still pleasant enough, but at six and twenty you are lucky to have any man interested in you at all." He stepped nearer. "And listen well. I will not abide any more of your—"

"If you are worried that I shall once again attempt to flee, then worry no longer. I have no intention of doing so." She lied as big as the heavy sun in the sky. But her years with Edwin had taught her well when to mask the truth of her words. "Despite my misgivings I accept the arrangement."

No emotion to be seen on his face or in his eyes, Rush stepped back and moved around the desk. Once again seated in his high-backed chair, he blinked. "Then perhaps you are not as foolish as I believed." He reached for the quill and dotted it in the silver inkwell. "You will make Lord Worth a fine wife, as you did your first husband. And the fortune you take with you will give added stock to the Martin name for Charles Worth is nearly as rich as the King of France."

Anna clutched her hands tighter. *As if I care for such things. The trappings of wealth have never held interest for me.*

He scrolled something across the paper at his desk almost as if she were no longer standing merely feet away. Anna's chest threatened to collapse, but she inhaled, searching out those happy childhood memories that brought smiles to her sorrowed past. Across the room on the wall, a portrait of Samuel dominated the space above the shelves. Young and handsome, wearing his red officer's uniform, her brother remained as she remembered him—strong, vital. Alive. Not as he had left them, in the shame of self-inflicted death.

"Do not think it." Rush looked up and folded the paper. "Do not even *begin* to think it."

"I'm sure I don't know what you mean." Her acting skills had so sharpened over the years that even she almost believed the surprise in her voice. Though she knew exactly what he meant and had every intention of thinking of nothing else.

"I know that look in your eye." Rush twirled a stick of emerald wax over a flame before circling the melted tip against the folds of the paper. He glanced briefly at the portrait and shook his head. "Too long you have wasted precious funds in your vain attempt to exonerate your brother." He removed his ring and pressed it into the wax before pausing to stare at her.

"He killed himself, Anna."

The words burned. "You do not believe that. I know you do not. And neither do I. Samuel was not like that. If you will only—"

"Silence!" Rush pushed up, the chair grinding across the floor. "I refuse to honor his demise by attempting to discover anything at all."

The fresh wounds that throbbed in her heart pressed the words from her mouth. "If your pride hadn't been so quick to accept the news you might have thought to—"

"He was not the man you remember, Anna."

"I do not believe it!"

"Believe what you will, but that will not change the facts." He moved around the desk and waved the paper in the space between them. "Your new husband will be here in three days, at which time the marriage will be performed."

Suddenly numb, Anna stared at the green seal on the paper. The figure of a dragon, tail up and mouth open stared back at her. So much like her father.

He opened the door and motioned for her to exit. "Thomasina will see you to your room."

Even if she could have answered, she would not have. The man did not deserve any more of her energy, even for the slightest of words.

Eager to be rid of the foul heaviness that surrounded her, Anna made for the stairs. Must she live a life of painted smiles and empty laughs until the day she exhaled her last breath? Was there truly no way to be free from such a fate? *There must be a way out, Lord.*

"And Anna," Rush said.

She paused, not looking back.

"You are wrong to think you cannot make your own destiny. After your marriage you shall have enough wealth to do anything you wish."

Gazing at him over her shoulder, she noticed the light from the window behind his desk resting on one of his many trinkets—a model ship—and a flash of genius enlightened her mind.

"Thank you, Father." She dipped her head and masked the frenzy of excitement with an illuminated smile.

But I shall not have need of it. I shall be in America.

Rush stared after her, his pride cracked. Anna's mouth had spoken the words he'd wished to hear, but her eyes belied all else.

You shall not go against me. Not this time.

A figure appeared beside him from the shadow of the hall. "You summoned me?"

Rush turned, staying silent only long enough for the servant to come beside him. "I would speak to you, *Warren*."

The head gamekeeper's gaze narrowed. He

stepped beside Rush in the doorway but no further. The man's height brought him nose to nose with Rush, and his indignant timbre matched the ire flaming in Rush's chest. "Speak your business here or speak it not at all."

Pricks of anger heated Rush's back. He curled his fingers and relaxed his grip, glancing up the stairs where Anna had gone then back again at Warren. Pressing out a bitter breath as he accepted the irony, he sneered. Why was it that this man was the only one he could trust—and at the same time, the only one he couldn't?

Warren tilted his head, impatience oozing from his eyes and arrogance from the breadth of his shoulders. Rush's eye twitched. Of what did a simple gamekeeper have to be so proud?

"You feel yourself equal to me." Rush glared, keeping his voice void of the hatred that surged.

"Nay." The man stood straighter, the knife in his voice stabbing Rush clear through. "I feel myself above you."

Warren turned to go, but Rush gripped his arm. "You will not leave until I have said my piece."

Arms bent, fists round, Warren sneered.

Rush pushed him inside the study and slammed the door. "She plans to run again. I see it in her eyes."

"Can you blame her?" Warren stood still, expressionless. "What would you have me do about it? That *is* why you have called me here is it not?" He paused, the muscles in his face hardening. "How can you be sure I will do your bidding? Might I not as easily steal her away from you?"

A cloud moved in front of the sun, darkening the room and Rush's soul as well. Unable to stand his enemy's presence without the abiding desire to strangle him, Rush made his purpose impossible to misunderstand. "Do not think me ignorant of the vow you made to *my wife*." Still Warren stared, unmoving. Rush continued. "You may not wish to follow my orders, but I know you would not wish to break your tender promise to Catanna, even after her departure from this life."

A vein in Warren's neck bulged.

Seething, Rush spoke through his teeth leaning near enough to feel Warren's breath on his skin. "I want only what is best for her."

"You want money."

"I want the Martin name not to be sullied as it has been since the day I married Catanna Bello."

Warren lunged, snatching Rush's throat, his nostrils flaring, spit flying as he spoke. "Do not speak of her that way."

Air refused to enter, but Rush cooled his straining lungs. Warren wouldn't get the satisfaction of knowing his grip was so strong. He spoke, though strained. "I speak only the truth, as well you know it."

Warren's face twitched as if he wished he could kill with his eyes alone. He released his grip with a shove. "I know more than you ever will."

Gasping, Rush corrected his cravat. Jaw twitching, he straightened. "You owe me everything, Warren Fox. Without me you could never have lived such a life, and now I require something in return. If you decline, I will find another, more willing party. And...I venture to guess you would not be pleased with my choice."

That produced the desired effect, even if it was only in the slight pinch of Warren's mouth. "Go on."

Rush stepped closer, his voice low enough to rumble the earth. "Wherever she goes, follow her. And bring her back to me."

The angry throbbing in Henry's arm pulled a groan from his throat as he tore across the clearing. Running nearly blind from the consuming pain, he fixed his gaze on a grove of trees twenty yards ahead. His salvation. Breath surging, heartbeat drumming loud in his ears, all other sounds seemed merely an echo. *They shall not have me.*

Yanking the red coat from his shoulders, he growled at the burning in his flesh as he wrenched free from the one thing that would most easily identify him to his pursuers. He left it where it fell and pushed harder toward the wood, daring a glance across the field at the wagon from whence he'd escaped. 'Twas only a spec on the horizon now, but the yells and barks of his hunters made it seem they were but inches from his heels.

He could almost taste the sweetness of freedom when at last the trees encircled him. He stopped, gasping. Scouring the unfamiliar wood, he gripped his arm and ground his teeth, a warm stream of blood oozing between his fingers. To the left, a cabin, barn, and water-well rested like weatherworn gravestones, crumbling and forgotten. The sounds behind him grew louder, and he dashed to the shelter only to stop seconds later. Those dogs would find his scent no matter where he went.

Henry's muscles cramped. *They shall not have me.*

The barking intensified and he raced for the well, the only place he might remain hidden from sight—and smell. Clinging to the rope with his one good arm, he carefully lowered himself to the water below. Before long the hollow sounds of his boots scraping against the wall bounced off the standing liquid. Pushing against one side with his back and one foot against the other, he tested the depth of the water before releasing his position. Only inches deep. One small blessing in this tangle of misfortunes.

"Brown, check the shack! You, Ward, look inside the barn."

Henry's breath died at the sound of Paul Stockton's deep tone. Blood seeped stronger through Henry's fingers while his pulse charged with hate. Nay. Hate was too kind a word.

"You're sympathetic with their cause, Donaldson," Paul continued. His volume grew as he drew nearer. "You helped that woman escape. I know it. Otherwise, you would not have run."

The wound on Henry's arm throbbed, slandering the bullet that had left the seeping gash. Memories of that night surged to the front of his mind. Kitty running. Nathaniel whirling to shoot the enemy. The crack of gun shots and clouds of white smoke. Blinding pain. Shackles. And now, the bottom of a well.

His enemy continued the tirade. "You knew she was guilty, and yet you let her run—nay, you *aided* her in fleeing the punishment she deserves."

Paul's accusation pressed Henry's hatred deeper.

Guilty only of acting with courage in the defense of that which she believed to be right. Naught else. Henry glanced up, praying the darkness would deepen farther and fully shield him from view of the one who wished death upon him.

Up and across, down and backward, the jangle of sword and bayonet moved across the yard and echoed down the well as they searched the forsaken homestead. The dogs sniffed and barked. Paul shouted at Brown and Ward to check the barn again while he searched the yard one last time.

Henry clutched the rope so tight that liquid could have dripped from the brittle fibers. Footsteps approached. 'Twas as if Paul knew where he hid.

Surely he must. For though Paul was only a year behind him in age, his skills as a soldier were second only to his own. But pride had always weakened the strength of Paul's abilities. The selfsame pride that had led to Captain Samuel Martin's death.

Henry strangled a groan in his throat, the face of his despised superior rearing to life from the graveyard of memory. His stomach turned and he breathed out. Samuel could no longer plague him. God willing, in time, neither would Paul.

Just then, Stockton neared the well and Henry ground his teeth. *Lord, do not let him find me.*

Paul's shadowed figure peered in and Henry stilled every muscle. Closing his eyes, Henry prayed as if his salvation depended upon it. For certainly his earthly salvation did. At once the figure turned back, yelling. "Anything?" Paul's silhouette disappeared and Henry allowed his lungs to drag in slow, quiet breaths.

"No, sir," Jimmy Brown answered. "Only his coat." The young soldier sounded more distressed than pleased.

Such a good boy you are, Jimmy.

"Could you worthless dogs not smell him out?" Paul cursed. "Blast it all! He could not have vanished. Brown, I need you and Ward to continue south until you reach the river. Return to camp before nightfall then report to me—tell no one else of this. We must be sure we've checked all avenues of escape. I refuse to return empty handed."

"Aye, sir."

"Be quick about it!"

The pathetic message hidden in Paul's words gave away everything. So, Ezra Stockton hadn't ordered them after him? This was Paul's doing, and asking for more men meant alerting his father of what he planned to do. Henry allowed a smile to breach his lips while he enjoyed the sweet taste of upsetting the enemy. Then that *was* how he'd risen in Ezra Stockton's favor and how Paul had fallen. Following orders was a soldier's duty. Somehow, Paul had never understood that.

Receding sounds of boots and dogs lasted only a moment until finally all was silent. At long last Henry allowed his starving lungs to indulge fully in the stale air that surrounded him. He might have gagged at the stench if his relief hadn't overpowered every other sense.

He stood straighter and looked down at his boots now covered to the ankle in muddy water. The sun rested high in the heavens, the heat of summer reaching down to find him in the pleasant shade of the earth. He need only wait until nightfall. Then, if he could negotiate with his unwilling arm, he might make it back out, and God willing, journey the last twenty miles to Sandwich. His arm throbbed until his teeth nearly cracked from keeping his jaw clenched against the pain. If only the wrappings hadn't unraveled in his attempt to escape. He looked up again, the blood on his fingers suddenly forcing him to reevaluate his plan.

He debated the alternatives while his arm pled for mercy. Climbing out now, even if to bandage his wound, could bring the end upon him. Paul might even now be stroking his pistol in the shadows of the wood. He couldn't have missed the drops of blood that no doubt dotted the ground. How the dogs had missed them Henry would never know. Tender mercies of God no doubt.

Henry peered up. Revealing himself was too much of a risk. His arm throbbed, forcing the final decision. Emerging from this blessed hiding spot could mean the noose, but staying here much longer meant certain death.

A prayer at his lips, Henry grasped hold of the rope, pressed his back against one side, his foot against the other and started upward.

The closer he inched to sunlight, the more fervent he prayed. *Lord, let me emerge to find no one waiting.*

Henry slowed when the warmth of the sun crested his hair and he peered over the ledge just enough to allow his vision to comb the trees. Green leaves, brown tree trunks, bushes, dirt. Nothing else. That he could see...

With a giant heave, he hoisted his legs over the edge and fell to his knees, his muscles cramping. Bathed in the yellow light of mid-day, Henry grimaced as he peeled the red-soaked cloth from the gash in his arm. A thousand curses collided on his tongue. This was no minor wound. He needed a doctor. The wrap from two days ago had stayed the bleeding temporarily, and it seemed the wound nearly closed on its own, but after today's maltreatment, it would need to be stitched.

A crack echoed in the woods and Henry spun. The click of a weapon preparing to fire stopped his blood. He hurled to his feet and dashed for the cabin, lunging against the floor beneath the clouded window. Dust from the ground billowed around him in the shafts of sunlight. Henry suppressed a growl in his throat, working his jaw back and forth as he counted the ways his enemy had wronged him. But such thoughts only heated—and wasted—his precious blood.

When he'd scanned the room and found nothing to use as a weapon, he stilled, training every thought on the sounds outside the walls of his battered fortress. No brushing of boots against the ground, no heaving breath. Only the music of birds and wind-swept branches played on the breeze.

Henry pushed up and propped himself against the wall. Was he a coward for running? In that moment his mind played tricks upon him as his vision landed upon a pair of pale green eyes, worn and tired, but so full of maternal love his spirit tore within him. What did it matter if he were killed? Now that his mother and sisters were freed from their crippled bodies they no longer needed his pay—no longer shed tears for what he'd done.

He stopped there. The recollections threatened to yank his beating heart from his chest. Yet, somehow, the memories refused to be ignored. He rubbed the few smallpox scars on his face, recalling Julia's bright smile and Jane's song-like voice. If not for him, if not for his foolishness, they would have lived. Or at least, they would not have died alone.

Senses ever alert, Henry froze as the anticipated footsteps drew near. He pushed himself to his feet, keeping his back against the wall. Fists clenched, stance wide, the pain in his arm receded as he prepared for the attacker to become the attacked.

"Donaldson," Paul yelled. "You're a fool. You should have known I would wait for you."

Just then he dove through the door. Henry lunged and rammed his shoulder into Paul, at the same time clutching the wrist of the hand that gripped the ready pistol. Paul pushed against him, but the chorus of recent ills pumped iron through Henry's veins. He slammed him against the opposite wall and wedged his forearm just beneath Paul's jaw.

"I *did* know you waited." Hot breath seethed from Henry's mouth. He pressed harder, enjoying the way Paul's throat worked for breath against his arm.

Paul's face turned red, then crimson, then edged to purple. Henry eased his pressure just enough to allow the man a thread of air.

"You came after me alone," Henry seethed. He knew, but wanted to hear it from the mouth of his enemy.

"Father is an idiot for not killing you when he had the chance." Paul's face contorted. "I would never let a patriot-sympathizer desert."

Henry restored the full force of his arm and Paul gasped, but Henry spoke over his fight for breath. "You know nothing about me."

"Gah..." Paul tried to answer, tugging on Henry's arm. He eased the pressure and Paul blinked as he gained a small breath. "I know enough."

"I did what was *right*." Somehow his muscles hardened even more. It seemed the army cared less and less about what was honorable. Which is why he left.

"You're a deserter—"

Henry slammed Paul's wrist against the wall, forcing the gun to drop from his enemy's fingers. He kicked it away and grabbed a fist-full of fabric at Paul's throat then yanked him out the door. Teeth clenched, Henry all but lifted him from the ground as he spoke to him nose to nose. "There are reasons your father trusts me and not you."

He released with a shove and Paul stumbled back, barely staying on his feet. With a swift move of his arm, Paul reached for the dagger at his side and jabbed. Henry sidestepped. The incoming blade sliced through his shirt. A roar bellowed from Paul when he swiped again. Henry dodged and planted the heel of his boot in the center of Paul's ribs. He dropped to the ground with a wild groan.

One hand on his chest, the other still wielding the blade, Paul gasped for air through contorted lips. His eyes turned black as hatred etched itself into the lines of his mouth.

A quick brush of the breeze calmed the rage that threatened to force Henry's hand. He stepped back and stared at the man, who of a sudden seemed more like a scared boy than a seasoned man of war.

"I don't wish to fight you, Paul." Every letter of the sentence held more veracity than the man would ever know. But he had to go on. "I cannot continue in something I don't believe in."

Paul peeled himself from the ground, the blade and his gaze never once dropping. "Your charade of goodwill will not shadow the truth." He took a step back. "I know who you really are." This time, his eyes faltered and his throat bobbed. "As does my father, make no mistake."

The two held their stance. Henry glanced at the knife, the sunlight glinting off the red stone in the hilt. He readied his fists. "You will not take me, Paul."

"Will I not?" His knife-hand thrust forward until it waited only inches from Henry's face.

Henry refused to move his stare from the enemy. Paul's frame might have matched Henry's in height, but his strength was not near equal. And Paul knew it.

Paul's neck muscles worked, and the twitch in his face revealed the war within him. "You're a traitor." His hand trembled. "You're a rebel traitor, you son of a—."

"Get out." Henry barely contained the urge to lunge and strangle. He opened and closed his fists to stem the aching for Paul's throat.

Still facing him, Paul stepped backward toward the wood, face contorted. "You cannot hide forever. Do not doubt I will find you and give you the justice you deserve. I *will* find you, Donaldson."

Blinding fury turned Henry's vision red. "And *I* will be ready."

Chapter Two

The familiar smell of tobacco smoke stung Paul's throat as he inhaled, but it was the bitter stare in his father's eyes that stiffened his back. "Sir, I believed you would wish him found. I took it upon myself to—"

"You pursued your own directive, is that it?" Ezra Stockton didn't look up as he walked from the window to stand in front of Paul. Beads of sweat formed on his forehead while the familiar cloud of discontent shadowed his face. Paul's muscles went hard. It would be a blessing if the perspiration stemmed from the oppressive summer heat and not anger. But Paul knew better.

Empty but for the desk and chair that rested woefully in front of the window, the room seemed to breathe apologies in the stale, humid air. Even nature felt pity for Paul's misbegotten plight. All the while his father inhaled his pipe and piled looks of ill-will upon his offspring.

When Ezra refused to speak, Paul labored to ameliorate the poisonous silence. "We looked everywhere—"

"Did you? *Did you?*" The flash of black in Ezra's glare slapped Paul like a hand against his face. "If that were the case, which I know it is not, then would not Donaldson be standing in front of me now?" He paced the room then stopped with such a start his shoes scraped against the floor. "You deliberately went against my orders. Again!"

More than a slap this time. The words slugged Paul in the chest and suddenly Donaldson's hateful words buzzed in his ears. *There are reasons your father trusts me and not you.* "I did what was right—"

"Silence! Your actions were a blatant dereliction of duty," Ezra barked. "You sought your own interest. As usual." He sneered, as if the words tasted bitter. "Donaldson is too clever. Smarter than you, and aye, smarter than even myself."

Longing waved behind the dark gray of Ezra's eyes as he stared into the corner of the room. "He took to soldiering like a horse takes to running." He gestured to Paul. "You, on the other hand, despite my endless and careful training, have never learned to follow orders. You have never learned that your place is not to question, it is to obey. Aye, I have been hard on you, but only because I see your potential for greatness. A potential that you have never embraced. Your actions bring shame upon me and upon His Majesty's Army, and I will have no more of it."

Paul ground his teeth, back rigid, arms at his sides. His father was a blind fool. Pursuing a man who aided the colonists and bringing him to justice was not something to be slandered. But Ezra wouldn't see it that way no matter how truthful. "If you would only—"

"Nothing will change you into the kind of man I should have for a son. You are slothful, ignorant, and self-centered." His father stopped in front of him. Another plume of freshly exhaled smoke soured the air around Paul's head. "Donaldson was loyal, determined, fearless, and—"

"Loyal?" The rage that he'd bottled shot skyward. Somewhere Donaldson raced to freedom, a freedom he didn't deserve. A freedom he'd bought with his devil's nature. Yet here his father said Donaldson had been loyal? "He is a traitor to the crown. He has aided numerous colonists in escaping capture. You favor him."

"I favor no one!" Ezra's face reddened as he stomped forward. Paul's stomach clenched. So did his fists. He opened his mouth, but his father cut him off.

"How dare you slander me! I am your superior officer as well as the man who gave you life. Your behavior is insubordinate."

"Do forgive me, Father."

Shock and rage weaved through Ezra's expression at Paul's mocking. Instantly, the still-hovering words clashed with the greater need that swirled in Paul's chest. His father would never accept the truth of what must be done. Though it pained him to the very core, submitting now might be the only way to attain the higher goal. "I...I beg you to...to please indulge me one last word."

Ezra stared, blinking long and slow. "Well?"

"I know a man—a mercenary of sorts—who could track a field mouse in a blizzard." Paul stepped forward. "Allow me to send him a message, to let him know of our plight. I *know* he would find Donaldson and bring him to us. It would take only as much effort as giving him a few coins."

With an audible exhale, Ezra stepped back and leaned against the desk. He folded his arms around his sturdy chest. "So, you would spend the king's money to hire someone to do the job you took upon yourself but were too incompetent to complete?"

"I would only wish to see Donaldson brought to stand trial for what he's done."

Ezra's brow folded and he breathed in and out, one eye twitching. The even tone of his voice said as much as his words. "Let it alone, Paul."

"Let it alone?" Paul's volume heated. "Donaldson must be found and punished for desertion—"

"Do you know how many soldiers have deserted this army?"

"Aye. Which is why we should pursue him. We must show what will be done to those who do not fulfill their duty to the crown."

Ezra set down his pipe and closed the distance between them. He reached out and cupped Paul's shoulder, the sudden calmness in his face lurching

Paul's suspicion. "Let the man go, son. We have more important things to occupy our time than chasing someone who will never be found."

Ezra dropped his hand and the tender moment faded, allowing the ever-present color of disdain that lurked in the back of his eyes to peek out from behind the pretended kindness.

Paul fought the disgust that worked its way from his chest to his face, the truth blasting through him like a musket at close range. His father cared for Donaldson. Cared for him so much he was willing to overlook the law and a soldier's commitment to duty to let the man get away with crimes for which he should be killed. He stared at Ezra as the man walked around his desk and took his seat, a signal the conversation was over.

Years of resentment turned Paul's chest to granite. The confrontation at the cabin lunged from his memory and refused to vanish. The incompetent dogs, the vacant home, how he'd been trapped and forced to run when all he'd wished to do was fight. He seethed, inhaling the hot air deep into his lungs. Only a coward would choose to hide instead of accepting the consequences of his actions like a man of honor. Nay. Honor and loyalty had no place in Donaldson, despite what his father believed. Donaldson lied. He had said Ezra trusted him only as a way of cutting where he knew it would wound Paul the deepest. They'd labored side by side since their first days in America. They tolerated each other as soldiers but hated each other as men.

The more Paul thumbed through the ills his enemy had handed him, the more his neck heated. Lost commissions. Denied praises. Subjected to hearing the many ways Donaldson was superior. It could not be borne.

"I'm sending you to Virginia." Ezra's sudden words yanked Paul from his thoughts.

"What?"

Ezra pulled a folded paper from the drawer and extended it to Paul. "The colonists there are nearly as belligerent as those in Massachusetts."

Paul stepped forward and took the note, immediately opening it and pouring over the words. A volley of curses readied for firing.

Heart pounding, he swallowed before he spoke. "With all due respect, sir, my work here is not finished."

Ezra rose from his seat. "You are going south, and I am leaving for Boston within the hour."

Rage turned his muscles to steel. "How can you—"

"Out of my sight." Ezra turned and waved him away as if he were the errand boy.

Turning, Paul stomped from the room, still gripping the paper in his hand. The shock of what transpired stabbed with the thrust of a blade. How could the man hate him so? After all he'd done for him? Paul growled aloud and exited the house through the back door, grateful for the sounds and constant motion of the city.

He plodded toward the street, gripping the handle of his dagger, circling his thumb along the red jewel at its base. A smile bled over his lips. There had been fear in Donaldson's face. Fear that Paul would kill him. And he would.

Halting his step, he stared down at the cobblestone as the sun baked the red coat on his back. He snarled at the painful truth and moved to the shadow of the building. Leaving for Virginia in the morning would destroy his opportunity to follow through on his vow. If only he had some way to get a message to Barrik. The man could find anyone in a matter of days. He gripped the dagger's handle tighter. The tantalizing prospect wet his mouth like the scent of sizzling meat, but just as quickly he grimaced. He could send no messenger. He may be a captain, but the soldiers were too loyal to his witless father and could not be trusted with secrecy.

He cursed under his breath and moved from the shadow of the building to the sun-blasted street. There had to be a way to get a message to Barrik. If there was, he had only hours in which to do it. If there wasn't, the decision he must make was too difficult for his mind to produce.

All the same, he would keep his vow no matter the cost. Donaldson's days were few in number.

The foul air drifting up from the wharf seemed a pleasant dream compared to the nightmare of aromas that consumed the underbelly of the ship all those long days across the sea. Anna gripped the bag in her hands, crunching beneath her feet every remaining fear as she stepped from the dock to the bustling streets of New York.

Head high, she strolled beside the other travelers, mindless of the heat that threatened to blister her back and the anxieties that threatened her resolve. A few queer looks from fellow travelers almost made her belly twist. Was it her imagination or did their stares whisper, "He knows you have come." Several steps forward and the questions she'd attempted to ignore continued to plague. *Did* her father know? Had his years of paranoia and greed made him follow her as he'd done before? Could she really blend in amongst the people of the colonies, or would the truth betray her?

A hard thump against her leg jolted her and the man whose cart she'd bumped scowled, the spray of words hitting her like rain. "Watch where you're going! Are you blind?"

She corrected her balance and offered an apologetic smile. "Forgive me, sir."

He growled at her apology as if it had splattered over his goods. "If you don't plan to buy then move on."

Resisting the frown that pulled at her mouth, she nodded and continued on, sidling beside the others as they continued through the crowded street. Would all the people of New York treat her in such a way? Hardly a good omen, but she'd never been one to allow such a thing to buckle her knees.

Far across the miles her father's voice whispered, the hairs on her neck pricking. *Foolish, foolish girl.*

The bark of a dog and whinny of a horse knocked her from the fatal thoughts. What would Mother have said? Anna dodged sideways seconds before stepping in a large pile of horse manure. She lifted her skirts an inch and gazed more intently on where she placed her feet. Mother was the one who instilled in her spirit those things that mattered. Faith, kindness, confidence. Then again, ten years of marriage to a man she hadn't loved, to a man who cared only for her face and the attention she awarded him, had done plenty to etch away those precious parts of her. She stopped and held tighter to the small bag that carried everything she owned. Edwin was gone. Here was a new chance at life. A new land, a new way of thinking.

Closing her eyes, she inhaled. With this blessing, this new-found freedom, she could make her own choices and plan for her future without the dictates of the man who wished to use her for his gain. For the first time in all her six and twenty years, she would discover who she truly was.

She started her feet once more, this time her stride longer, her back straighter. A smile tickled one side of her face. Mother would be proud—nay, she *will* be. For she watched from heaven. She'd promised she would.

As Anna continued to the center of town the face of

her dear brother—his kind, soft eyes, same in shape and color as her own—consumed her mind. Samuel had been here. America had been his last home. It would be hers as well. The mere thought of being where he had been for so long brought strength to her weary limbs.

I shall discover what happened to you, brother. You may depend upon it.

A loud volley of laughter jumped at her from the front of a large two-story building. She turned to the right and inhaled a delighted breath. Three buildings from her, in the center of the street, a crowd of soldiers gathered.

She strode forward, hardly feeling the hard cobblestone beneath her shoes. Surely this was a sign from God. Of course she'd thought of what she might do, who she might question in her attempts to gain the knowledge she sought. But here, most clearly was what she *must* do. And why hadn't she thought of it before?

Not far from the crowd, a young soldier, not much older than a boy, turned to her and bowed his head ever so slightly. The others, four in total, hushed and turned to her, nodding in unison.

An older one spoke. "May we be of some assistance, miss?"

She grinned, waiting a beat until she was sure her sudden nerves wouldn't add a tremor to her voice. "I'm...I'm looking for someone."

The same soldier spoke again, with a gleam in his

dark eyes that wormed an uncomfortable sensation to the pit of her stomach. "And who might that be?"

"My—" she stopped. If she divulged she sought her brother, and perchance her father *had* followed her, or sent someone else to follow such information could bode ill. She cleared her throat and tried again. "I'm looking for someone by the name of Captain Samuel Martin."

Only vacant looks. A few shoulders bobbed. Perhaps one or two heads tilted in thought, but that was all. But of course they knew of him. Hadn't he been a captain? Did that not mean he had earned such a rank with his bravery and obvious intelligence? Did that not earn him prestige and celebrity?

Sighing, she tilted her head. "He was stationed in Boston last I heard."

They only stared. Of course she would have gone into Boston directly had not the strains between the colonies and the king closed the harbor.

Good heavens! Was this the treatment she was to expect? She raised her chin and added a notch of force behind her mostly reserved tone. "It is imperative that I speak with him. If you would inform me of someone who may know his location I would be most grateful."

"The name is familiar..." A tall one in the back inclined his head toward the brick building at the right. "You'll want to speak with Major Stockton. I believe he was Martin's superior"

Finally some cordiality. "I thank you, sir." She

bobbed a quick curtsy and strode toward the house—or what looked like a house. Two guards, one at either side of the door, stood rigid with muskets at their sides, white wigs and hats atop heads that peered forward, faces void of expression.

The one on the left, whose white wig looked freshly powdered, addressed her first. "May we help you, miss?"

"Aye, thank you." She smiled, attempting to flick the irritation that began to buzz like the flies that seemed to find the narrow street so pleasing. "I should like to see Major Stockton."

Both sets of eyebrows suddenly pressed to their noses, and Anna ground the frustration at her feet. They were only yards from the group she'd just left. Had they not heard the conversation? She blamed her rising annoyance on the plagues of fatigue, hunger, and if she admitted it, fear.

With a breath, she attempted the request a second time. "I need to speak with your superior on a pressing matter." She paused, inspecting their quirked mouths and narrowed eyes. "Please?"

Like the others, they regarded her as if she'd spoken a language completely foreign.

She cleared her throat, caressing her voice with both charm and confidence. "I am looking to discuss a matter of great urgency."

The other soldier shook his head, his eyes squinting, as if he still endeavored to understand her meaning. "Forgive me, miss, but has Major Stockton asked to see you?"

"Well, no, but—"

"I thought as much." The soldier shifted his weight over his feet, impatience bleeding from his eyes. "Major Stockton doesn't see anyone unless he wishes to see them first."

"Well, of course. I do understand." She offered a slight smile. "But I'm sure if you knew the reason for my coming and how desperately I must speak with—"

"You are welcome to wait inside, miss, but I won't make you any promises."

She breathed out a sigh and grinned. "Thank you."

Gripping the door handle, she stopped when he spoke again. "You might be waiting for some time."

With a nod, she opened the door. "I appreciate your candor, but I assure you I will wait as long as I must."

Anna placed herself just inside the doorway of the regiment headquarters, keeping her posture straight despite the insecurities that threatened to weaken her. One soldier stood in front of another door, behind which erupted several heated voices. He acknowledged her with a scowl, as if she were a stray dog the army had taken to feeding with reluctance. She took a quick, sweeping look around the room. A lonely chair rested in front of the entryway window, and she quickly determined to keep it company by putting its vacancy to use.

Voices continued to bellow from behind the closed

door and she imagined the deeper-toned one must be Major Stockton's. A word here or there wedged through the barrier, but Anna kept her attention on the outside, praying that her audience with the major would not come near the level of discord of the current exchange.

Staring through the window that overlooked the small street, her mind drifted to the recent memories that clung to her spirit like the scent of stale smoke. She tapped her fingers against the small bag in her hands. Had she done right? Leaving all she owned—all but her Bible with Samuel's likeness tucked in the pages, her beloved sewing kit, the clothes on her body, and the treasured ring and chain around her neck—to come to this rough land in search of something that she might never find? Nay. She shifted her head to tilt away the misgivings. Leaving had been her only choice. Another marriage like her first—loveless and empty— would have been the death of her. If not the death of her body, then indeed the death of her spirit.

As she watched the crowd of soldiers she fingered the ring that rested on her chest, her mother's words singing from the past. *I want only happiness for you, child. Marry for love alone, not for status or money or rank. We are come to this life to have joy, though sorrow will be ever present, that is true. If you are joined with the one who truly fills your heart, you will never wet your pillow with tears of regret.*

A familiar figure in the road jerked her from her

memories and Anna leaned closer to the window, clutching the bag as her pulse took flight. She blinked and tried to clear her vision. Nay. Her mind but played a trick. She scowled. Her breath quickened and she leaned closer to the glass. Across the road, beyond the soldiers and past a resting horse and cart, a man stood. Staring at her.

Spinning from sight, she pressed her back against the wall of the entry, hoping the distance and commotion of soldiers had made her invisible. The thumping in her chest told her otherwise. She blinked, rifling like mad through her mind to locate when and where she had seen those eyes. England perhaps? On the ship?

"Miss?...Pardon me, miss."

"Oh!" Anna jumped and spun, her cheeks hot as the sun that beat the side of the building. She cleared her throat and took a breath to calm her embarrassment. "Do forgive me, I'm afraid I was lost in thought."

The soldier nodded slowly, a questioning tilt to his mouth. "What is your business here?"

A hopeful excitement burst from her chest, but she clamped it down and answered with practiced calm. "I should like to speak with Major Stockton on matters of—"

"I'm sorry..." The man shook his head. "I fear he is preparing to leave and hasn't time to speak with anyone."

Anna stood motionless. She squinted, trying to

make sense of what he said. "You don't understand I *need* to speak with him on matters of extreme—"

"As I said, miss, I'm deeply sorry, but there's nothing I can do."

She lost a measure of her posture. "You are in earnest." The truth began to take root, and her stomach twisted.

Any hope she'd borne wilted like a plucked flower. Reaching for the reserves of determination that waited within, she looked toward the door then to the man in front of her. Undeterred by his one raised eyebrow, or the way he continued to look behind her as if he wished she'd find her way from the building, she smiled.

"Then I should like to know to whom I may speak in regard to a Captain Samuel Martin. I understood that—"

"I beg your pardon, miss."

Anna contained a retort behind pursed lips. Must he continue to interrupt?

He lowered his chin, as if preparing to speak some unpleasant news to a pleading child. "You are not enlisted in His Majesty's Army and have no previous appointment. Therefore, there is nothing that I can do for you." His eyes widened and his mouth pinched, indicating he was more than finished with her.

Anna's skin prickled as shame dripped down her back. Her father's voice laughed from across the sea. *Vain attempt.*

She glanced down at the simple homespun gown. In place of her usual silks and lace, this rough, plain fabric contributed to her newly espoused identity. An identity that had yet to change as easily within as it had without. In years past she'd needed only to request something for it to be granted. Money often had a way of speaking louder than words or connections ever could. Not that having wealth ever became the desire of her heart, as it seemed to do with others. Simply, such had been her way of life. But no more.

What now, simpleton?

She gave herself the reprimand she deserved before she met his gaze and offered a humble half-smile. "I do understand fully, and I thank you for making that clear."

Anna straightened. This was merely a slight impediment, something to be expected and certainly nothing she couldn't remedy. If Major Stockton had known Samuel, then she'd do whatever it took to find him. With a grin she hoped would inform the impatient soldier she was not one to be easily deterred, Anna turned and opened the door. She paused and widened her smile to indicate she wouldn't ease his obvious pains without first making this slight setback worth her while. "Seeing as how Major Stockton is unavailable, perhaps you would be so kind as to tell me—"

"You don't seem to understand."

An unladylike grumble waited for release in her

throat. Why must he be so rude? The man deserved a scolding. She refrained from stomping her foot, however desperately she wished to. "I simply wish to know if there is anyone else—"

He cut her off again, this time with volume raised. "There is no one else—"

"What seems to be the trouble, Gaiters?"

Both Anna and the soldier turned to see another man standing just below them on the stoop. Tall, commanding, and with features that spoke as strong as his deep voice, he removed his hat and bowed. His red coat appeared freshly laundered and the sword at his side gleamed from the beam of afternoon light.

The man he'd addressed as Gaiters stood straighter and answered, nudging his elbow toward Anna. "This woman claims she must speak with Major Stockton on urgent business. I've just informed her that he is not available for an audience."

"Indeed." The new stranger replaced his tricorne. "I should be grateful, miss, if you would apprise me of your business so that I may assist you, forthwith." He bowed at the waist, keeping his eyes upon her. "Captain Paul Stockton, Major Stockton's son, at your service"

Anna curtsied and stopped herself from staring at the man's sky-blue eyes. Her unexpressed prayers must have made it to God's ears before she'd even had time to contemplate them. Surely the son could be as helpful as the father. Perhaps more so. "I would be most grateful, indeed, sir."

Paul motioned to the man who seemed perpetually irritated. "I shall escort her outside. Return to your duties."

He gave a curt nod. "Aye, sir."

Paul cocked his elbow and offered it to Anna, which she took without hesitation, stepping down the few bricks to the street.

She inhaled deeply for the first time in days. "I cannot begin to thank you for your consideration, Captain."

"I am grateful to be of service, and pray, do not feel you must use such formality. My name is Paul." His voice was as deep as the waters she'd just crossed. "Would you be so kind as to tell me your name?"

A warning bell chimed in the back of her mind. What gentleman offered the use of his first name with such flippancy? Certainly she would not ignore propriety.

"I am Miss Whitehead." Anna craned her neck to peer up at him, reading his response to her answer. The lie seemed to be believed. She squinted against the sun. "I do hope you will be able to help me."

"I'll do whatever I can." He smiled at her in a way that made her pulse jump. He wasn't handsome, not to her way of thinking, but the mere thought of being gazed upon in such a way by someone her own age created a smile of her own that started deep within.

They walked slowly to the side of the house, away

from the commotion of the street, but she soon stopped, grateful for the added privacy but uneasy at the thought of being too alone with him. "I do not wish...I do not wish to make my business widely known, which is why I had hoped to speak with your father. Seeing that he is in a position of trust, I believed he would keep my confidence."

Paul's features relaxed and in the same instance turned serious, calming the sudden bubbling nerves in Anna's chest. Could she trust him? Even if she couldn't, who else would help her? *Lord, guide me.*

"You may put your confidence in me, Miss Whitehead."

She glanced around again and lowered her voice. "I am looking for Captain Samuel Martin."

Paul's head tilted, an unmistakable knowing in his eyes. "Samuel Martin."

"Aye. Do you know him?" For a moment the possibility of her deepest hopes breathing back to life stopped the very blood in her veins.

"I *knew* him." Paul's mouth tightened. "I'm sorry to say he's passed on."

Frozen, Anna stared, allowing the words to fall into the holes that waited to receive them. She breathed deeply to coax the blood to move again. So. He *was* dead. A coffin lid slammed shut in her mind as she buried forever the dream she'd clung to. 'Twas a foolish thing to even consider the report had been false. She met Paul's gaze. "Do you know how he died?"

"I'm afraid I do not." His long face expressed more emotions than Anna could clearly detect. The softening of his eyes suggested compassion. However, the tightness of his mouth made her re-examine her decision to confide in him.

She glanced to the crowd of soldiers not twenty feet away. "Is there no one else? I understand Captain Martin served under your father, and I'd hoped—"

"You needn't speak with my father."

Startled by his sharp reply, Anna took a step back and prepared to answer, but he continued without pause.

"There isn't much anyone knows about what happened to Martin." He glanced away, eyes squinted, as if he struggled to recall a memory. "He died outside of Boston, it seems to me. But no one else was there to—"

He stopped cold, his eyes suddenly round and motionless.

Anna leaned forward. "Captain?"

"Forgive me." He shook his head and touched her elbow, nudging her farther away from the group. "I have remembered something that may be of use to you."

"You have?" She clutched the bag harder. "Sir, I will do anything that must be done to discover what happened to him. Please tell me what you know."

He nodded lightly then looked directly into her eyes. "I cannot tell more, because I know nothing more.

But I do know someone who does."

The beautiful, mysterious woman gazed at Paul with wide, pleading eyes. The way she stared up at him, hands clasped at her stomach and forehead creased, reminded him of a poor street urchin. And she might have been, from the way she was dressed. The gray petticoat she wore, frayed at the bottom and stained, looked as though it should have been discarded long ago. That is, if she had anything else to wear. And yet, her hair wasn't matted and she smelled clean, unlike the sorry lot that littered the streets. What relationship had she had with Martin that created in her such a need to know the story of his death? Who *was* she?

He studied her face. Lovely, no doubt of it. Black hair, gentle features and cool blue eyes. Aye. This kind of woman would have suited Martin's tastes. Perhaps she'd been a favorite of his? Perhaps she'd had his child...Nay. Martin had talked of a young woman he'd loved and hoped to marry. He'd never been one to use women the way so many other soldiers did. Paul tossed the theory away and focused his energy on the plan that unfolded within him.

Forcing as much tenderness to his features as he could muster, he took a step closer. His soul was still raw from the lashing he'd endured from his father only minutes past, but the wounds urged him to fight on, not abandon the irrepressible need to find the man who'd flaunted his abilities and skills, ensuring his father would find pride in one and not the other.

The scheme that had sprung to life was nothing short of sheer brilliance. Donaldson had been the only other soldier there when Martin had died. And here, with this pleading woman, perhaps Paul could reach Barrik after all—and thereby, capture the man whose life he would end.

Using the well-toned charm he'd perfected over the few, but productive years of his career, Paul lowered his tone and stepped an inch closer. "I am well acquainted with the man you must find. He was there the night of Captain Martin's death and was privy to all that transpired."

Her crystalline eyes widened and her gentle smile stretched across her face. In a near breathless voice, she pleaded. "Please, sir, tell me where I may find this man. Is he here, in New York?"

Paul opened his mouth then snapped it shut and glanced around him. The regulars crowded on the street would more likely dull their hearing than strain to glean his words, but he couldn't take the risk. Offering his arm once again, he motioned up the road.

She hesitated before offering a tentative bob of her head and took his arm once more.

He sighed before speaking. "This conflict with the colonies has been difficult on us all." He gave her a quick glance, but her gaze was on the road ahead. "Many soldiers are deserting their posts, leaving that which is right and honorable to feed upon the slop of *liberty* the colonies fling from every direction."

At this the woman peered at him briefly, her dainty eyebrows folded in question, but she said nothing.

He exhaled before continuing. "Henry Donaldson is one of those men." Speaking his name heated the resentment that simmered deep within. "For several years now he has aided the colonists in resisting the king's benevolent hand. He has at last run from us, fearing he will be punished for his actions." Paul stopped walking at the corner, grateful for the sudden calm in the road. The summer heat blistered his back as the unadulterated rage for his enemy did the same to his stomach. He took a calming breath to mask every emotion but sincerity. "But that is untrue. He is simply misguided. We only wish to speak with him and help him find the error of his ways."

At this Miss Whitehead pulled her hand from his arm and looked away, her lips pressed tight. Did she not believe him? He chewed the inside of his cheek. The lie was plain, but such a woman could not be acquainted enough with the ways of war to understand what kind of punishment awaited anyone who deserted. He could only hope that adding more cushion to his report would soften whatever it was that made her question him.

"He was Samuel's good friend," Paul continued, "and I know that he would be most glad to tell you what he knows, if only we could find him."

She stayed silent for a moment, keeping her expression from his view. "So, the man I must find is missing. And is there no one else?" At this she turned to face him, her expression firm.

"I am afraid there is not."

"There must be a way..." The rest of her words trailed off.

Had she said what he thought? He cleared his throat. "I beg your pardon?"

She faced him fully and straightened her posture. "I said there must be some way to find him, is there not? Surely you have tried?"

He looked down at his boots, not needing to feign the blast of anger that rushed up his back. "We have." He paused and looked up. "Perhaps if you would...forgive me, I should not suggest such a thing."

"Pray continue." She raised a hand. "You must know how desperate I am. If there is anything I can do to help, I wish to know."

Paul nodded and studied her face, giving just enough silence to imply he still struggled with the suggestion. "Perhaps you would like to help us in our search?"

"How?"

"I know a man staying at the Rockport Inn, five miles south of Providence." He pulled out a slip of paper from his pocket and handed it to her. "Give him this and tell him you are assisting the army in appreh— I mean, rescuing Henry Donaldson."

"Rescuing?"

"Aye, do not all misguided souls need rescuing?"

Again her expression darkened, as if she were not fully convinced. "How will I know the man when I see him? Can you tell me his name?"

Paul shook his head. "That I cannot do. There is much of secrecy and spying and those of us who play such games must keep the upper hand."

She turned away again and Paul held his breath. Would she take the bait? The miracle in finding this stranger to help in his cause could only be an act of God—the very confirmation he needed that his father was wrong.

The woman circled her finger against the bag in her hand. She then touched the ring that rested against her chest and pulled her lip between her teeth.

Stemming the desire to speak further, his gut knotted with anxiety. *Say yes.*

Suddenly she turned to him. The set of her feminine jaw and the confidence in her eyes struck him like a cool breeze.

"I shall do it and I should like to leave immediately."

He bowed, holding his exuberance behind a wide smile. "Allow me to hire you a carriage."

Chapter Three

A second full day of travel with hours upon hours of bumping and jostling. Anna leaned back against the worn cushion of the carriage and peered out the open window wondering, not for the first time, how it was that she'd come to be traveling alone. Strange, was it not? Yesterday's carriage had been so jammed with travelers she'd come to know her companions far more intimately than she ever would have wished. She snickered to herself, remembering the young mother and child who sat beside her on one side and the ancient man on the other, hips and elbows so near it seemed as if she could feel the other's bones against her own. Not to mention the three others opposite them. How they had all managed to fit, she still couldn't fathom. Anna rested her bag beside her and took a long inhale of air void of the perfumes and body odors that pervaded the previous day's journey. So this was how the other classes traveled. She'd never known anything but a fine carriage of her own. There was much of the world she had yet to understand, but this adventure was tallying her daily lessons at a rapid pace.

Anna reached her legs out and circled her ankles, relishing in her quiet little cocoon, when the peace of it began to crack as if the subconscious parts of her struggled to bump free. Why *was* she alone? She dropped her feet back down as her muscles went taut. Surely she couldn't be the only person on their way to Providence. Then again, perhaps she was simply lucky to have left at a time when no others were prepared to travel. That was a possibility, was it not? She peered out the window at the passing trees, attempting to dispel the niggling worry. Perhaps her concerns were futile. Her energies should be put to far better use in considering the blessing of an empty carriage and giving thanks for it.

She propped her elbow on the small notch beside the window and rested her chin in her hand, studying the landscape as it passed, like an adventurer discovering a new world for the first time. She smiled to herself, for that's what she was—or at least what she felt like. A gigantic tree loomed, and she stuck her head out the open window to grasp the scope of it as it passed. She gasped in awe at the expanse of towering branches, a covering of green leaves the hue of which she'd never seen.

With a huff of amazement, she leaned back in but didn't take her eyes from the landscape. How majestic it was. So wild, so inviting. In all her travels she hadn't seen anything so free. Not that she hadn't experienced untamed lands in the travels she had taken throughout

Europe, but there was something different here. Something in the colors and the scent of the air, as if the sentiments of those who called it home seeped into the very soil on which they tread. More, perhaps the liberty she felt in her solitude—traveling alone, following her heart—made the beauty in her surroundings that much more enchanting.

She reached over and touched the bag when her mind went back to Edwin. Heaven be praised for God's tender mercies, for He alone knew how much longer she could have endured such a life. Her mind trailed away, backward into the black, not-yet-receded memories. Glittering Paris halls, women caked in powder, perfume and smoke stifling the air while men and women, drunk on their own pride, nursed overpriced wines in goblets trimmed with gold. She rubbed her head and her face began to coil as the painful memories flooded from the dark place she'd shoved them.

A rustle in the bushes beside the road snapped her back to the present. A doe and her two fawns leaped from their hiding place beside the road and raced to the freedom of the wood. Once again away from the shadowed past, she forced herself to remain in the empty carriage and enjoy the surrounding beauty, not retreat back to the days of old. That life was no more. Her dreams of joy were within her grasp. No matter how poor or how desolate she lived, she would have joy, so long as she could choose her own future. She stared again out the window, then looked to the bag beside her. Once the truth of her brother's death was revealed, then and only then would she have the overwhelming serenity she craved.

Captain Stockton's numerous instructions replayed in her mind like a motherly list of to-do's. *Make it as far into Connecticut as you are able the first day before securing a room at an inn. Make the trip in two days if possible. You will find the man who needs the note at the Rockport Inn in Providence. He is always the tallest in the room. You would be hard pressed to miss him.*

She pulled the note from her pocket and ran her fingers over the top of it. Curiosity pricked and she was helpless to curb the desire to read the secretive note. She peeled apart the folds with tentative care and read.

Find Captain Henry Donaldson and a large reward will be yours. Bring him to me. Alive.
P.S.

She scoffed and folded the paper back together before tucking it next to Samuel's likeness in her Bible. A deserter. Was that all? Somehow she'd expected to discover something truly scandalous, though indeed desertion was no small crime. Anna leaned forward and rubbed the ache that began to inch through her head. She prayed the man had good reason to leave his post. For what little she did know about the army, she understood well that no matter what befell a man, leaving his company for any reason was met with exacting punishment. Her brother would have done the same as Captain Stockton. Bring him in, certainly, and make him pay his due. She could only hope the captain would be as lenient as he stated, but she wasn't a fool as she'd allowed the man to believe. She was willing to help locate the fellow for her own reasons, but believing this Henry Donaldson would be treated as merely "misguided" was laughable. War was a terrible thing. For everyone.

"Whoa!"

The carriage jerked to a halt. Quickly, Anna replaced the likeness in the Bible and stuffed it in her bag.

She peered out the window. "Is everything all right?"

"Aye, miss." The driver got down and spoke to her without looking in. "Got to check the horses."

"Oh, of course."

"You are free to get out and stretch your legs if'n you like."

The mere thought of it made her limbs twitch with the need to straighten. Tightening the strings of her bag and clutching it against her lap, she waited. After a moment, Anna scowled and peeked out the window. The driver would not expect her to open the door for herself would he? She unlatched the door and peered both directions. Well, apparently he would. Was this what it felt like to be of such low status? No one to help you, no one to even assist you in exiting a carriage? Of course, she'd hoped to be seen of low status when she'd taken the tattered dress and left all her worldly goods in England. She glanced at her clothes again, almost grinning to herself. *You wanted a new life, Anna, and here you have it.*

She pushed the door open, feeling as if she'd stepped into a new world, one with less confinement and more power. Her spirit lifted and somehow she could breathe deeper. Once outside the carriage she walked around the back of the large wheels to reach her arms wide without being seen engaging in such unladylike behavior. She couldn't stem the grin that widened her mouth as she gazed at the sky, stretching her arms. When had she ever felt so uninhibited? Edwin would have been horrified to see her so recklessly ignoring propriety.

"Excuse me, miss."

Anna jumped and twirled. "Aye?"

"Forgive me, I..." Mouth parted, eyes scanning her head to foot, the driver stared breathlessly. "Forgive me. You look so much like your mother. I nearly called you Catanna."

Anna's heart lurched at the sound of her mother's name. "I beg your pardon?" She stepped back and pressed a hand to her chest. When she next spoke her voice was so low she hardly recognized the sound of it. "Who are you?"

He moved toward her, hand extended. "Do not be alarmed, I beg you. I simply..." His brow furrowed. "You don't remember me."

"Why should I?" The man took another step forward, and Anna hurried backward, bumping into the wheel behind her. "Get away from me."

"I won't hurt you."

Despite the sincerity in his soft eyes, Anna's breath came in and out in short bursts. "Then tell me who you are and how you knew my mother."

The man opened his mouth, then closed it and rocked his jaw back and forth. His gaze lowered to her necklace then moved back up to her eyes. "That I cannot tell you." He continued toward her and Anna's pulse jumped.

"You will not?" She hurried around the other side of the carriage, the stranger at her heels. "That is fine. I wish to continue to Providence." She opened the carriage door, trying to keep her quivering fingers from revealing her fear. "I will overlook this upsetting interlude if we continue immediately."

He grabbed her arm. "You do not belong here, Anna."

"How do you know my name?" Fear cascaded through her, blood leaving her head and limbs yet pulsing wildly at the same moment. "Let go of me!"

She struggled against his grasp, but he held firm. "I would see you returned to England where you will have safety and security."

Nay! The truth knocked her so hard she nearly choked from the impact. "My father sent you." Her blood chilled.

Without releasing his hold, the man's gentle tone mirrored the pleading in his eyes. "'Tis only the best he seeks for you. Though I understand why you have run, you cannot know what calamities await you here. 'Tis folly to believe—"

"Nay!" 'Twas then his eyes took their place in her memory, and she gasped. He was the one she had seen from the window of the officer's house. Father had known she would leave. He'd sent this man to collect her, but never would she let him claim the prize.

"I will not go back!" She all but yelled. Jerking from his grasp she whirled and stepped toward the woods. "I refuse to be forced to live a life of bondage. I would rather die here than endure the rest of my days in such a prison."

Anna spun around, scanning the dense wood for some place, any place, to escape. The blowing branches beckoned her to the safety of their shadows. Blood racing, she clutched tighter to the bag in her hands. There was the wood, aye, but nowhere to hide. Nowhere to run and no one to hear her cries. *Lord, rescue me!*

"Please, Anna, forget this foolish venture and return with me to England."

She breathed hot and hard as indignation surged in her chest. Turning to him, she growled. "Never! I will never go back!" Anna paused and her jaw ticked. "Father cares only for the material means another such union would provide and I will *not* be his pawn."

The man blinked and turned his head as if somehow he didn't understand a word she'd spoken. "Your father wants to see you well cared for, Anna. Can you not see that? That is why I followed you here. To bring you home."

Like the doe she'd seen moments before, Anna dashed into the wood, the low bushes scraping her stockings as she lifted her skirts to run.

"Anna!" The man called after her and seconds later his heavy footfalls were directly behind.

His hand grabbed her shoulder and she tripped, falling to the ground with a scream. "Get off of me! Let me go!" She kicked and clawed, but her struggle did nothing. He was too strong. In a swift, smooth movement he scooped her up and carried her over his shoulder. "I wish you could understand. What I am doing for you is the best." His voice sounded unstrained as if he carried a small child.

She screamed again. "Help me! Someone help!" But she knew there was no one.

They reached the carriage again, and her muscles cramped with surging panic. She yanked his queue, and he groaned as his neck arched back.

He dropped her with a growl.

"Help!" She scrambled to her feet, but he grabbed her around the shoulders from behind with a grip of iron. He whispered into her ear with heated breath. "You are coming with me. There is no other choice."

"Please..." She calmed herself, tugging on his arm. "Please, I beg of you, sir. Do not do this. Let me go. If you knew my mother then you knew she wouldn't want me to marry into a life so void of happiness."

He stilled and the hard grip loosed. "She would want you to be safe, Anna. You will not find safety here." The tightness returned. "Which is why I must insist that you come with me."

She screamed and writhed with every force within her.

"Stop your screaming, I beg of you."

"Never!" Scratching and kicking she fought like a trapped animal.

With his one free hand, he produced a large handkerchief and shoved her to the ground. "Forgive me child, you must believe I do not wish to do this."

He pushed her to the ground, and Anna let out a piercing wail before he tied a gag around her mouth.

Inside the cabin that had become his solitary confinement since the day he raced to the safety of its walls, Henry rested on one of two chairs in the room and fooled with the fresh bandage on his wound. The continuous throbbing and periodic shots of pain that raced up and down his arm took most of his attention. At least the flow had stemmed somewhat. He still needed a doctor's care...

Henry glanced to the shelf above the fire then to

the loft where he'd found the trunk, and the sheet he'd used for bandages. 'Twas adequate for now, but he needed more—he needed food. He'd eaten the bit of pemmican he'd hidden in his pocket, and now his stomach groaned with every passing hour.

With a flick of his gaze he eyed the small pot resting beside the fireplace. Having checked the contents the first night, his imagination bloomed and his mouth salivated. There was flour beneath its wooden lid. Ash cakes were simple and would fill his aching middle, yet taking what was not his would go against the very center of his being. He rubbed the wound on his arm. While the sheet had been a necessity, eating could wait. Though he feared he could not wait much longer.

He stood and went to the window. This sanctuary had served its purpose, but staying hidden from the world wasn't possible even if he wished it. Which he did not. The regiment was far from here by now, and if he did happen upon another he would be unknown to them. He hoped.

Henry put a hand to his head and rubbed the pain that radiated from the back of his eyes. Every plan he'd devised fell flat when compared to the one that continued to rise to the top of his mind. He must go to Sandwich. Not only for the doctoring that his friend Nathaniel Smith could provide, but also for the sanctuary he would find among friends.

The breeze stiffened and he peered from the

window, noting how the branches of the trees swayed deeper against the wind. A storm would be here before nightfall. God willing, it would pass by morning and he could travel the twenty miles to the small seaside town.

Just then a cry struck the air and Henry stilled. A voice. He turned in the direction of the sound, squinting and straining his ears. After another moment of silence he shook his head. Nay. He'd imagined it.

When his stomach growled again he turned to the pot and gnawed on the inside of his cheek. He could find a way to pay back what little he took, should the owner return, couldn't he? He almost laughed. From the look of things the likelihood of their return was minimal to none. Better to use it than let it go to waste—

A woman's scream shot through the walls of the cabin and Henry jerked. It had not been imagined. Another wail struck the air. Henry's instinct consumed him, and he raced for the wood. She yelled again. Anger surged and his training hurled to the forefront of his mind. How many were there? How were they armed? Could he defend himself and the victim should they be out numbered? Suddenly a thought assailed him so hard his pace slowed. This could be a trap. Paul knew him well enough to know that should any person cry for help he would come to their aid.

When the woman cried out again Henry put all his force in his legs. That was a risk he must take. Jumping over branches and dodging bushes, he followed the sound of her cries until he burst from the trees, whipping Paul's unused pistol from his side.

"Get up now!" he roared, the weapon pointed at the attacker's head. He shot his gaze to the pinned woman, her eyes round and expression gripped with fear.

The attacker froze. He dropped the gag he'd held against the woman's mouth. "I am not a criminal. This is not as it seems."

In the half second it took to take in the scene, Henry interpreted every emotion in the woman's face. "Move away from her or I will shoot you where you kneel."

Scrambling to his feet, the man patted the air in front of him as if Henry were a wild animal and he the tamer. "Listen to me. This woman is in my care and I am trying to—"

"Quiet!" Henry yelled. The thundering of hoof beats rumbled against the ground and Henry's pulse thumped like a war drum. He paused and turned toward the road. Soldiers? Had this been a trap after all?

The stranger jumped forward and grabbed the woman, pulling her against him. "Leave now, and let me take the woman. I promise no harm will come to her."

The woman's tear stained face crumbled, and the fingers of her fettered hand strained. "No! Please don't make me go with him!"

Racing against the approaching riders, Henry

lunged and jammed the butt of his pistol against the man's skull. He dropped to the ground and rolled on his back, a trickle of blood streaming past his ear to the ground.

"Come with me." Henry grabbed the woman's arm and dashed to a large bush three yards from the road just as the riders came into view. He slid to the dirt and pulled her in front of him, whispering into her hair. "Do not make a sound."

She nodded and her body tensed. The sound of her breathing stopped.

His heart began a savage beat and threatened to break from his chest as the riders halted beside the carriage. Their red coats and white breeches told Henry all he needed to know.

A trap.

He squinted and moved his head down and to the side to catch a better glimpse in the slots of light between the round leaves.

All privates. None familiar. But from what regiment?

"What's happened here?" The first soldier jumped from his mount. "A man's been hurt!"

"Quickly, Baker, retrieve your sack and pull out the napkin."

Henry tried to follow their movement. Flashes of red and white and brown were as much as he could make out.

Two of the men crouched beside the attacker.

"What's happened to you?"

Henry tensed. The man was conscious?

The woman shook her head and pressed her back into him as if she feared the same. He tightened his grip around her and spoke so low he wondered if even she could hear him. "Pray."

The man began to speak. "I was traveling with my daughter when a man came and took her from me."

"What man?"

"Where did he go?"

"I...I don't know. He hit me and vanished."

Another barrage of questions followed.

"How long ago was this? Was he traveling alone?"

"Was there anyone else with you in the carriage?"

Henry whispered into the woman's ear while the others continued talking. "Is that man your father?"

"Nay," she whispered back, a waver in her voice. "I've never seen him before today."

From the way her petite body trembled, he believed she feared the man whether she spoke true or not.

Again, he answered in a tone so quiet his voice barely carried over the sound of his pulse. "I will not let them harm you."

"Baker, Winslow—you check the woods to the left, Marcus and I will check here."

"Aye, sir."

The woman pressed against him, her tense body going rigid. Her chest pumped as if she prepared to scream.

Henry clapped a hand to her mouth and tightened his grip around her quaking shoulders. "Stay silent and I promise they will not see us behind these branches."

A soldier stomped in their direction, and Henry held his breath at the same moment her chest stopped its movement. The man called to his companion. "Baker?"

"Aye?"

"Do you see anything?"

"Nay. You?"

"Eh." The soldier grunted and came closer, his boots only inches from their eyes.

Henry willed his blood to stop, fearing the sound of it running wild through his veins would reach the soldier's ears. *Move away. Move away now.* He prayed the soldier was not a skilled tracker, for Henry's footprints littered the ground.

The other soldier called from afar. "I see nothing. They've gone, whoever they were."

"Aye," said the man closest to them. "Let's get on with it." He turned and made his way back to the carriage.

The woman dropped her head against Henry's shoulder and he relaxed his arm. *Thank you, Lord.*

The group of soldiers huddled around the man who claimed to be her father, speaking in low tones. If it weren't for the jangle of swords and muffled stomp of horses' hooves, he might have been able to make out their conversation. The first soldier offered his hand

and helped the man to his feet.

"Follow us," the soldier said.

The man, still bleeding, dotted his arm against the side of his head. "At your heels."

The soldiers mounted and raced from the scene in a blur of color. Seconds later the carriage jolted and with a sharp "Yaw!" the attacker followed.

Soon, all but the sounds of birdsong and the rustle of trees met Henry's ears. He could finally breathe, but still kept his volume minimal. "Are you all right, miss?" He scooted back and sat upright. "Did he harm you?"

The woman pushed up and propped herself against her arm. "Nay."

He scooted from their spot and offered his hand. She took it and fumbled with her skirts as she rose to her feet.

"I thank you." 'Twas then she looked at him, her large eyes wide and brimmed with emotion as her words seemed to yearn for a way to relate the depth of what she felt but couldn't quite express. "I am forever indebted to you, sir."

Henry's tongue welded to the top of his mouth. He stared, blinking, unable to answer. Her large eyes, full mouth, and raven hair made her appear more like a heroine from a painting than a stranger in the wood. Giving his head a shake, he found his voice. "Not at all."

The small smile she'd borne faded, and she turned her pale blue gaze away from him. "How could I not have known? How foolish I was."

"The man?"

She looked at him, brow creased. Her mouth opened but she snapped it shut again. She darted a quick look to the road then toward the trees. A scowl darkened her face seconds before her voice met his ears once more. "Who are you? Where did you come from?"

'Twas then his earlier fears resurfaced, but this time without the threat of veracity. It was no trap. Or so it would seem. This woman had indeed needed him just as he'd feared. What a blessing, then, that he'd been able to come to her aid.

He offered a polite bow, scrambling to locate a name he could use in place of his own. "They...they call me William Fredericks." Studying her expression, he paused, praying the way he spoke the name he'd appointed slipped from his tongue as if he'd said it for the full twenty-eight years of his life. The accepting smile she offered buoyed his confidence, and he determined to take that as a boon.

William Fredericks. He grinned on the inside and it grew until the smile painted itself on his face. His boyhood friend—taken by smallpox during the same epidemic that took William's father—had carried the name Henry had always envied. Why not christen himself with it in honor of such a good soul? His friend would be happy to have shared it, that much was certain.

From this moment he must think, feel, breathe William. Henry must stay in the past.

The woman turned away, her hands clasping her bag against her middle, eyes scanning the road as if she believed any moment her attacker would return and snatch her away.

He shuffled his stance. He must pry from her some information, to know better how he may help her from this point on. Such familiarity was hardly proper, but there was nothing else to be done. "May I be so bold as to inquire after your name?"

She flashed a glance over his shoulder and the clear color of her eyes made his heart trip, but he squashed the sensation before it had a chance to feel through him.

Turning away, she answered to the ground. "I am...I am Miss Whitehead."

William refused to allow the scowl on his forehead to grow as deep as it wished. She lied. But why?

He shrugged off his question when a strong wind pushed against them, allowing his mind to focus on matters much more pressing. "Where will you be safe? Is there anywhere I may take you?"

The woman who called herself Miss Whitehead shifted toward him. Her mouth tightened and her hands smoothed across her bag. She stared into the forest, shaking her head as if she were lost in a vast field, unsure which direction to go.

His eyes went to her busy fingers as they played with the tie of her small reticule. He allowed the scowl a slight release. Was that all she had? 'Twas then he took note of her dress, how it frayed at the bottom and was so threadbare in places he could nearly see her white petticoat beneath the pale gray.

Her face reddened when she caught his gaze upon her. She brushed a hand over her skirt then clutched the bag to her chest. "Forgive me...I believe, I mean I fear...to be honest, sir, I do not know what I am to do." The way her voice changed in the few words she spoke, beginning with inflated courage and trailing away to fragile breaths as she stared across the road, wound strings of compassion through his chest.

She carried secrets. And wounds. As did Henry. He was no stranger to the weight of a burdened soul.

"Well, perhaps you can—" The rough *clomp, clomp* of a horse's hoof beat drummed against the ground, and his hands reached for his weapon. Another soldier? Paul? The attacker returned to find her?

The woman paled, and he grabbed her arm. "Run."

Anna held tight to her rescuer's firm hand, gripping her skirts with the other as they charged through the trees. At the middle of the wood she flung a glance over her shoulder just long enough to see the one from whom they fled. Black tricorne, blue jacket whipping behind him, eyes on the road. A root caught her toe and she stumbled, but her rescuer caught her before she fell flat against the ground. The halt in speed must have allowed the man at her side a look at the rider as he helped her stand, for the urgency in his eyes dulled.

He remained unmoving, his vision pointed like a weapon to the rider that raced past. His muscled chest pumped, pressing against the fabric of his shirt. His broad shoulders refused to shed their tension and his arms remained flexed. Anna lowered her attention to her feet, trying to loosen her mind from its focus on the gentle, protective touch of his hand against her arm.

"He's passed," the man breathed. "We are safe. For now."

She inhaled deeply and released a pained breath, praying with the rush of air from her lungs. *Lord, I thank thee for sending this man to me.*

He cupped her elbow and urged her onward. "I should like to help you to a place of safety. Where is your family?"

His words jolted Anna, forcing her to meet his gaze. Strong, and yet, behind the courage that first gave her pause, his blue eyes seemed to twine through her spirit.

She stared and toiled against her tied tongue. *Where is your family?* Such a question.

Anna licked her lips and flung him a look before studying the path, grateful for the steady wind that beat upon her back and cooled the fears that burned beneath her skin. Suddenly she stopped. The man from the carriage—the one who'd attacked her—knew who she was. He would not stop looking for her, not when Father had sent him. So why must she keep her identity a secret from this man? Would such a thing bring her greater safety or greater peril? Braving a look at her rescuer, Anna tried to untangle the knot of confusion that coiled within her when the thread of thought lay straight. No matter how her secret strained to be revealed, no one must know her true identity.

The man...William...spoke before she could form a single thought. "If it..." He stopped and glanced skyward. "I fear a storm will be upon us. There will be no traveling tonight. If...if you are comfortable, there is a cabin just beyond this small wood where we may take shelter and in the morning I will see what can be done about taking you to your family. Or wherever it is you wish to go."

A rumble thundered high above them. He was right. It would not be long before the heavens gave up their tears. She glanced at his hand still upon her elbow, allowing her vision to travel up his muscled forearm until she halted, startled by the tear in his shirt and the blood-stained bandage that circled his bicep.

"You're hurt."

He stalled, quirking his head as if he hadn't understood what she'd said before following her gaze to his arm. "An old wound that is healing, 'tis all."

He gestured forward and Anna began walking again, watching every footfall so she would not need his assistance a second time.

She glanced up from her footing. There before her, waiting like a lost child begging for notice, a little cabin rested at the far side of a clearing. Small, but not as run-down as she'd thought on first hearing the word "cabin." The rustic nature of the dwelling stirred the youthful cravings for adventure that had always lured her heart. Peaceful, inviting. A sense of wilderness. A far cry from the spacious estate she'd resided in these past years, but far more *real*.

William's fingers brushed against her elbow as he walked past. He stopped a few paces ahead and turned back. "This will suffice, I hope. Just for the night, of course. I will stay in the barn."

"Nay." She answered on top of his words. The man was a stranger and yet the fear of being left alone was greater than the fear of sheltering with him.

He tipped his head to the side, his expression peaked in polite questioning. She met him at the edge of the wood and stared at the small home just as heavy drops of rain began to fall. "I would be most grateful if you would...that is to say I do not wish to be—" Thunder rumbled in the clouds above them, and she put her lip between her teeth, looking away.

"Not to worry," he said.

Anna flung him a glance, her tension softening as the gentle smile in his face widened.

"I understand." He gestured forward. "Sheltering together is a prudent course of action." He nodded and motioned for her to continue walking to the cabin. "As promised, in the morning we will discuss what is to be done, but for now, ash cakes."

Ash cakes? She stepped forward, ignoring the

foreign phrase, words hardly befitting the gratitude that swelled. "Thank you, Mr. Fredericks."

They reached the cabin just as the drops began to flick harder against the dirt.

"Not at all." He entered behind her, and closed the door before setting his attentions to the fire.

Anna took measure of the dank room. Very little furniture—only two chairs and a small bed frame, no tick. She lifted her chin to follow the stairs. Was there anything in the loft?

She stepped farther into the room, holding her bag tight against her to calm the growing disquiet. Was this his home? The man must be poor indeed. With his back to her, Anna tilted her head. He didn't appear to have anything at all. The questions cascaded from her mind like a waterfall in spring. How old was he? Did he have a family? What was his trade, or was he simply a farmer? She watched as he gathered the logs and arranged them in the fireplace, making such a menial task look ruggedly appealing.

William Fredericks.

She tilted her head and mused. A strong name for a strong man. Yet somehow, the name didn't seem to fit him at all.

Chapter Four

Anna pulled her cloak around her shoulders, squinting as she gazed through the cabin window when another flash and crack consumed the heavens. Large drops plunked against the glass and she rubbed her hands up and down her arms, pondering the question she'd kneaded for the last half-hour since their arrival. Who had her father hired to find her? She could still smell the man's breath and feel his rough hands on her arm. The way he'd spoken her mother's name and the familiarity of his declaration that she resembled her mother made her squirm within her stays. So why had she detected a glimpse of tenderness in his eyes before he tried to force her away with him?

Thunder boomed again and her thoughts changed direction. She stole a glimpse over her shoulder at the man now hunched over the fire. A stranger. Yet, he had saved her. Why? To what purpose? Could someone truly be so sincere for the mere sake of Christian goodness? She turned back to study the wooded darkness and pulled her arms tighter around her. That kind of genuine kindness was not something she had often experienced, at least not from a man. But then, there had been Samuel...

Another boom of thunder shook the ground. Caustic memories tugged at her mind, chilling her soul as another storm crashed within. Cold rains of loneliness and winds of despair threatened to topple the newly constructed hope of a better future. Anna squinted hard and pressed the destructive thoughts away.

"It isn't much but should fill our bellies."

Anna spun and glanced at the man who crouched beside the glowing embers.

Using a straight stick he turned over several gray circular objects that rested beside the red embers. "Supper is nearly ready."

At the mention of a meal her belly grumbled, but another celestial boom covered the unladylike sound. Blessedly. She didn't wish to bring more attention to herself than her circumstance already provided. Whatever he offered, how little that may be, she planned to eat as daintily as she could. The ravenous hunger would fight to be satiated, and she couldn't bear for him to look on her with any more pity than he already did.

Coming toward the fireplace, she reached for the nearest chair but he darted up and pulled it for her, settling it near the warmth. The hidden smile in his features snipped the remaining thread of apprehension at being in such proximity with someone she hardly knew. A mysterious, *male* someone. He stepped aside when she sat and she nodded her thanks, too shocked at his genuine chivalry to attempt a verbal response.

The orange glow from the embers radiated little brightness, but what did reach him shadowed his face in perfect chiaroscuro. A magnificent contrast of dark and light. A realness with an alluring contrast of mystery.

Again Anna looked around the empty cabin then pinned her gaze upon the man. Such a dreary place to live. Had he been here long? This house was far too bare to sustain one's needs, not to mention lacking in basic up-keep. But then again, perhaps a man needed far less than a woman.

His gaze met hers and she stilled at the clarity in his eyes. A half-smile tugged at his mouth then vanished when he looked away. Had she been staring? Her cheeks burned. *Gather yourself, Anna. For shame.*

"Your supper." He plucked a cake from the embers and reached out, holding a flat, gray disk in a handkerchief. "Be careful not to burn your mouth."

"Thank you." She took it, cloth and all, careful that her fingers didn't touch his.

He pulled the other chair to the opposite side of the fire and sat. Removing another disk from the heat, jostled it in his hands before pulling off a piece, blowing on it, and popping it into his mouth.

Anna fingered the warm, round cake and sniffed it. Another bolt of lightning illuminated the morsel in her hands. She froze and shot a look to the man who sat opposite her. Did he know it was covered in *ash*? Of course he must. She glanced again at the food in her hands. Calling them "ash cakes" as he had, she should have understood. But this?

Licking her lips, she gave him a side glance, squirming. Ash! Never in her life had she eaten anything so primitive.

She stared, gathering the frantic parts of herself that chased around her mind like screaming children, and heartily scolded every one. Who was she? The kind of woman who scoffed at anything not presented on china plates? Although in England she may have eaten only from the finest dishes, she was not that kind of woman. And this life—this new life—was one she welcomed with every portion of her being. Ash and all.

She lowered her head as the reprimand nestled in her middle and the largest portion of her humiliation fell on its back. How ungrateful could she be? And then, the largest shame upon her ingratitude slashed her remaining dignity. *He* had cooked it, had not even implied that such was a woman's job as so many other men might have done. She flicked a gaze at him as he took another bite. He could have easily assumed she knew how to cook. And why not?

She lifted the bread to her nose and sniffed as she prepared for a bite.

"You don't care for ash cakes?"

Startled, Anna pulled back, flinging a smile to her

face. "Nay—I mean, I do. Forgive me, I...I simply haven't had—I mean to say I haven't..." The words slowed and dropped away as Anna retreated into her seat as far as it would allow, praying the darkness masked the sudden heat in her face. "I mean to say, I haven't ever been so grateful for such a meal. Thank you."

He chuckled lightly. "Such a meal, hmm? Well, I shall take that as a compliment. We soldiers have a lot of practice preparing ash cakes."

"Soldiers?"

Instantly still, as if he'd been turned to stone, the man didn't move. His high eyebrows and tight mouth masked a fleeting emotion before he shook his head and smiled brighter than before. He cleared his throat. "Forgive me. Every town has its own militia, and with the conflict with England at such dangerous heights, every worthy patriot considers himself a soldier now."

"Oh, of course." Anna turned the cake against the handkerchief. She was in a war-torn land now. How could she have forgotten?

He took another bite, swallowed, then pointed to the fire. "I really should have let you cook them for I have no doubt that in spite of my practice, your skills are superior to mine."

Her blood stalled so quick it rendered her motionless.

He continued. "My mother could create a feast out of anything, even if we had but flour paste and fat. I fear I didn't inherit her talent." He pointed to her untouched cake. "I would repent and let you make the morning meal if we had flour remaining, but I fear we do not."

She exhaled to ease the rise of panic in her lungs. *Thank goodness for that*, she thought, and took a large bite. The instant bitter palate melted into a bland taste of unsalted flour. Not unpleasant in the least. For her screaming belly, it was in fact far better than anything else she could have asked for. When she swallowed, she finished her reply. "You do not do yourself enough credit, sir. These are excellent. I hope you do not think me ungrateful."

That familiar half-smile returned to his mouth. "I think you should eat your fill and prepare for the night." He glanced to the window then the loft. "You may sleep there if you wish, though I fear there is no bed."

No bed? She glanced to the tick-less bed frame, reminding herself she'd slept in worse conditions on her voyage across the sea. "Not to worry." She tilted her head with a slanted grin. "I am tired enough to sleep on cobblestone."

Just then, a boom of thunder rattled the rickety cabin. Anna turned in her seat and glanced to the window, taking a large bite of cake. Then another. And another.

"You were more hungry than you let on, hmm?"

Anna peeked up and halted. He stood, a flash of amusement in his face.

She jerked a hand to her mouth to cover any crumbs. That first bite had unleashed the hunger she'd tried to suppress, but now the mere scent of food, even a meal dusted in ash, made her abandon her primary manners.

Embarrassment heated her core. Anna dotted the cloth against her mouth as she finished the last morsel. She cleared her throat, praying her voice would reveal that she still was a lady, not an ill-mannered child. "I suppose I was."

He peered sideways, his eyes darting to the empty cloth in her hands. Without asking if she wished for more, he bent over and plucked the last cake from its perch on the stone nearest the heat. "Here."

Reaching across the warmth, Anna took the remaining piece. "Thank you—" Her words fumbled when the tips of her fingers brushed against his.

She pulled her hand away and stared at the small round cake, the sudden awkwardness drenching her skin in heat. She took another quick bite.

"Tomorrow I must finish my journey," he said, the deep, masculine ring of his voice reminding Anna of both silk and stone.

She swallowed. "Your journey?" Perhaps some of the mystery behind her fearless rescuer would finally come to light. "Where...to where are you journeying?"

His mouth pinched then relaxed as he studied her, but he looked to the fire when he spoke. "I am on my way to...to a town twenty miles from here. Sandwich."

"Ah." Was that all he would share? Then again, why would he share with her anything more personal? She was just as much a stranger to him as he was to her.

His expression flashed with something she couldn't name before his eyes clouded. "Where will you go?"

The question circled her like a ghost. She stared at the partially eaten cake nestled in the handkerchief. "I don't know." The words flung from her lips and she nearly covered them to be sure nothing else escaped, but she clasped her hands tighter around the last few bites of her dinner. She hadn't expected to answer so truthfully, but she allowed the reply to rest in the air, heavy and dark as it was.

His eyebrows folded down and he glanced to the window. "You fear that man will seek you out again?" His stare pinned on her as he finished the question.

Once again, the thunder crashed.

Her stomach churned and suddenly she wished she hadn't eaten. "I do."

Lip between his teeth, he looked away, resting his elbows on his knees. "Is there anywhere you will be safe from him?"

Without warning, the emotions she'd suppressed since the moment her father had delivered the unthinkable news welled behind her eyes. Unable to answer in words, she gave a quick, sharp shake of the head.

A beat of silence rested in the air before he spoke. "You may come with me if you like."

Jolted by his offer, Anna blinked. What had he said? She opened her mouth, grasping for words, but there were none. Was he in earnest?

His gaze rested upon her, as if searching the response in her face. He must not have liked what he saw, for his expression dropped and he spoke again, the words coming faster. "'Tis not a demand. I do not wish for you to feel I would take you against your will. 'Tis simply that I must go tomorrow, and if it is safety you seek then you shall find it in Sandwich."

Truly?

She turned the dusty cake in her fingers, her throat thick. The tears welled again, but this time, from gratitude. By grace alone she kept them from falling. *Thank you, Lord. Thank you for all you have done.* "I would be forever grateful, sir."

"It is the least I can do." He smiled then looked to his arm and grimaced.

Anna lowered the cake. "Does it pain you greatly?"

He gave a quick shake of the head, clearly ignoring the question. "What will you do once we reach Sandwich?"

She heard him but let the question rest wearily in the air. Her focus on the man's wound secured ever more of her attention. She didn't wish to press the matter, but it niggled. It surely pained him. How could it not? Should she offer to tend it? If she did, would she even know what to do? The red she'd noted on his bandage had turned a muddy brown. At least the flow had stopped. However if infection were to—

"Miss?"

"Hmm?" She met his gaze.

"I asked, what will you do once we reach Sandwich?"

"Oh..." She stared ahead then scrunched her mouth and studied the uneaten morsel in her fingers. "I...I cannot say." She pressed a hand against the note in her skirt pocket. She had promised Captain Stockton she would get the vital message to the man in Providence, but now, all that was changed. Her need to find the truth of Samuel's death must wait. *But not forever, brother.*

Her companion stared at her, she knew, though she didn't look up. The heat of his gaze radiated against her like the fire between them, as if somehow he had seen the emotions she'd tried so hard to hide. "Should you wish to stay with my friends, I am sure they would be happy to have you until you have decided on the best course for yourself."

She turned, her gaze colliding with his. She stilled, all thought leaving her mind as the sight of him consumed her. The scruff that shadowed his jaw, the strength and gentleness in his eyes...Anna forced her face forward, praying he didn't see the heat that bled color into her cheeks.

She inhaled to dispel the momentary lapse in sanity and focused on the matter at hand.

"Miss?"

That warm, inviting sound turned her head around. Anna tried to look away, but his stare pulled against her own and hardened, as if he tried to discover what she might be thinking.

She blinked. Did he mean it? Could she travel with him—trust him? Who were his friends? Would they truly be kind enough to allow her to stay until she determined what she must do?

Anna reached to her chest and felt for the ring that somehow always gave her peace, like a child's well-loved toy. Her fingers found nothing but skin. The cake fell from her fingers. She whirled from her seat and searched the ground around her chair, but the darkness refused to restore what she'd lost. "Nay, it cannot be gone!"

Panic surged and suddenly the anxieties and fears she'd borne since the moment her father told of his intentions weeks ago fell from her eyes. Tears as large as the drops that continued to fall against the house wet her cheeks. She put a hand to her mouth and bit her tongue to keep the sobs in the cage of her chest.

Warm hands grasped her shoulders. "What cannot be gone?"

Shameful tears trickled over her hand which covered her mouth. She fought to breathe through her nose which thickened with the cries she refused to release. If she opened her lips to speak, even to breathe, she would prove herself the weak, senseless female her father professed her to be.

"Miss?" He bent in front of her, the outline of his figure blurred by the constant rise of moisture. His head tilted and he reached for her shoulder, but stopped just before touching. "I wish to help. If you would tell me what you've lost."

Anna's spirit crushed with more emotions than she could name—thanks for his kindness, grief at the loss of something so dear, despair that her need for understanding her brother's death would elude her, despite the efforts she'd given. Foremost, fear that the future of freedom she dreamed for herself would never be realized.

What little courage pulsed from her spirit, she clung to, looking up. "I..." Her voice squeaked from her throat. She looked down, accepting the wave of truth as it crashed against her. "My ring."

She struggled to her feet. He stayed at her side, one hand cupping her elbow, the other resting against her back as he helped her into the chair.

"I am so sorry." Not a hint of disgust in his voice. Not a shadow of mockery. He could not possibly be so sincere. But if he was...

Oh, how she wished she could shrink away, fall back into the shadows and forget this terrible display. But her mind refused to cease its obsession over the thing she'd prayed would never occur. Her mother's ring was gone forever. How could it be otherwise? It had broken from her neck and fallen in the woods during their escape, covered forever by mud and rain.

Just as her mother's grave had been.

Numb, the tears retreated, leaving Anna's lonely soul exposed. She stared at the fire. The few drops still in her eyes caught the light from the embers and flayed spikes of orange. No Samuel. No ring to give her hope for the future. *Lord, I am lost.*

"You are married then?"

Anna looked up. What harm was there in sharing this bit of truth? "I am a widow."

He pulled back, so slight a nod from his head she hardly noticed it. "Forgive me. If I had known I should have addressed you properly."

She shook her head. "You did no wrong, as I did not tell you." For truly, what did formalities mean, when the hope of her future had vanished? She stroked the skin where the ring had rested for so many years. What she'd come to America to find—freedom, and the knowledge of Samuel's death—she might never obtain. Mother had wished happiness for her. 'Twould not be reality, but merely the dust of her dreams. Easily collected, more easily blown away.

The rain trickled now, tapping instead of striking the house as it had done for hours. William rested in the chair, the woman having taken to the loft sometime past. He glanced upward, his elbows against his knees. Though he couldn't see her, he could imagine she slept fitfully. With only her cloak and the floor on which to rest, who wouldn't? He'd offered for her to sleep near the fire, but not surprisingly, she'd opted for solitude in place of comfort. The fresh memory of the well of tears in her eyes, the hard pinch of her lips, made his chest ache anew. Poor woman. After such an ordeal it was remarkable she was calm as she was. Still, there was an emotion, unrecognizable but clearly painful, that lived ever-present in her eyes.

Fiddling with the handkerchief she'd returned, he sorted the evening's events, its revelations and secrets. The soft fabric caught on his rough hands. She was a widow. Surprising in some respects, and in others not at all. She presented herself as "Miss". He understood her need to be cautious in what she shared, but wondered at the deeper secrets that shadowed her pale blue eyes.

William looked up to the loft once again. Whoever her husband had been, she had clearly loved him. The loss of her ring had been her undoing. Instantly, the sad tone of her voice crawled through him. The way she'd spoken the words *my ring*, was as if the pains of her spouse's death were still fresh.

Cold memories misted through him. He knew that pain. Knew it far too well. That unyeilding loss that opened a bottomless cavern in the heart. Yet the one he had loved, he had never wed. The one he had loved still lived, still breathed and spoke and smiled. But not with him. The cold within died, replaced by the heat of anger that needed only a spark of memory to kindle a blaze of hatred. *Never again, Henry. Never again.*

A whimper chirped down from the loft and he looked up. She wept. Helpless, he sat back against the chair, alternately looking up and down, wishing somehow the answer to what he might do to help would materialize and ease both their suffering. He squirmed, straining to hear if she wept again. She did not, or if she did, he could not hear.

William sighed, rubbing his thumb and forefinger against his temples. What was she doing traveling alone? Moreover, who was the man that wished to take her and for what purpose? She hadn't said, and naturally, he hadn't inquired. The fear in her eyes, the way her body had trembled against his as they'd hidden in the bushes, told him all he needed to know. Whoever he was, she didn't wish to see him ever again.

A faraway rumble of thunder drummed the skies. The storm would be passed by morning. He glanced out the window, his old friend fatigue pulling against his eyelids. He wiped a hand down his face, took a deep breath and stood. Pacing the room, he kept clear of the warmth of the radiating embers, knowing the cold would keep him uncomfortable enough to stay awake through the night's watch.

Hours passed. His head bobbed a time or two, but he kept his eyes on the horizon. The clouds drained their remaining drops and drew back like curtains on a stage, the sun bursting its rays toward heaven.

Resting his shoulder against the window frame, William marveled at the sparkling drops reflecting the brilliant light of morning. A dutiful bucket waited on the porch, full to the brim and begging William to come and partake of some of its contents. He was all too willing.

Once outside, William crouched and cupped his hands, washing the evening's weariness from his eyes. The chilled water splashed over his face and trailed down his neck. He rubbed his eyes with another handful, even sipped some to relieve the bitter taste from the night past.

He glanced over his shoulder. She would be up soon.

She.

He stood and shook his head, trying to purge the image of her pale blue eyes from his memory, but his mind refused to release its grip. He'd seen eyes like that before, hadn't he? That striking pale blue, so light they reminded him of sparkling crystal. Nay, no one had eyes so clear. He glanced toward the sun, squinting as it rose ever higher in the sky, forcing away the bewitching thoughts to focus instead on what mattered most. He turned and looked north. They'd best begin their journey. 'Twas possible to travel the distance in a single day, but that meant journeying several hours in darkness. And with his companion no more than a slight-framed woman who would be just as fatigued as he...

He bit his cheek and turned to look behind him again. What a puzzle she was. Her tattered clothing bore witness to the hardships she'd no doubt endured. Hardship was a faithful companion to the colonists. But *she* was not a colonist, or at least not one of many years. Her accent gave that away. And there were her hands, so delicate, looking soft as rose petals. Those were not the hands of a woman who'd cooked and cleaned, gardened and laundered. His sisters' hands had been calloused and chapped, as well as Mother's, from the endless work just to survive.

Again he glanced to the cabin, sure she would arise any moment. The knowledge they must leave without so much as a crumb to calm their hungry bellies made him wince.

A rustle in the trees broke the silence. William spun and scanned the woods like a rabbit waiting for the fox to pounce. He reached for the ready pistol at his side, his finger caressing the trigger. A doe jumped from her hiding spot and William released a rush of air. He dropped his hand to his side, his body humming as the sudden anxieties both drained and filled his limbs. If he hadn't felt the urgency before, he surely felt it now.

Paul would return. 'Twas not a matter of if, but when. If William had learned anything from the years serving beside Paul Stockton, 'twas that the man kept his word.

He pivoted to return inside to wake her, but the brush of something hard against the bottom of his boot pulled his attention to his feet. Jutting his head forward, he blinked to be sure he didn't imagine the sight of the small ring and chain. He bent and picked it up, brushing away the bits of mud with his thumb. How delicate it was. How small. He studied the ring, touched by the simplicity. No stone. Not more than a simple circle of gold. The tiny inscription inside met his eyes before he could avert his gaze to honor their privacy. The loving words scrolled inside found their way to his heart and etched themselves upon it. *Forget not he who loveth thee.*

"Sir?"

He whirled to see the woman standing just the other side of the threshold.

"Good morning." Instantly, he thrust out his hand. "Look what I have found."

She gasped and cupped her mouth. Coming forward, eyes rimmed with moisture, she lifted the ring from his hand. Clutching it to her chest, her gaze met his. And there, in those sparkling depths, he saw an expanse of gratitude that coated away a portion of the anger that lived like a monster within the wounds of his heart. Perhaps a woman could feel gratitude and express it.

Breathlessly, she spoke through a smile. "Where did you find it?"

He pointed at the ground. "'Twould seem your ring would not wish to be far from you."

She sighed and glanced heavenward, the unspoken

prayer read easily in her eyes. Then she faced him. "I cannot thank you enough, sir."

With a smile of acknowledgement he motioned behind him. "We best hurry if we are to reach Sandwich before tomorrow."

"Of course." Within seconds she'd secured the chain around her neck. She glanced toward the trees. "Shall we leave straightaway?"

He nodded, praying the few bites she'd eaten last night would sustain her through the day's journey ahead.

They began walking side by side, leaving behind the house that had shielded both of them from capture. Surely God had led him there. He turned to glance behind, offering a prayer of thanks, and a prayer of need. For without a doubt, danger was at their heels.

The trees were thick, their robust foliage just as dense, and ever ready to abet the enemy. Nature didn't take sides in matters of war. Though the yellow sunlight lit the world around them with exuberant rays, the shadows at their feet whispered ill-will. His senses were at their height, his fingers twitching, ready to grab for the weapon at his side. If only he'd had his sword or even a dagger, any additional weapon. But his fists and one round in the chamber of his gun would have to be enough to protect himself and the woman.

He glanced over his shoulder at his companion. Her arms were around her middle, her eyes at the ground then at the trees. He raised his head and considered the silence. The sounds of nature were pleasant, but the lack of conversation could not continue for the entire trip, could it?

He flung another look at her, but she didn't seem to notice. Should he say something? There were plenty of things he could inquire of her, but—

"The foliage is such a lovely shade of green."

Her voice chimed in the quiet wood like a bell on a hill. William looked across his shoulder to her. "Different from England?"

Her dainty brows folded down. "How did you—"

"Your accent. Most colonists have a different sound."

A small smile toyed with one side of her mouth. "Do they sound like you?"

He grinned, shrugging a single shoulder. "I suppose." Had he lost his accent after only three years?

The momentary relief from silence was quickly washed again in awkward quiet. He cleared his throat, hoping he could organize a thought—any thought into words, but she rescued him by speaking again.

"How did you come by that injury?"

He exhaled the emotions that breached the bounds of their hiding place within his chest. "A hazard of farming."

Would she buy it? He darted a gaze toward her, gauging her acceptance of his impetuous answer. He breathed again when she nodded, ready to continue his story but once more she questioned him.

"Will you be in…in…this place you are going to…"

"Sandwich?"

"Aye, will you be in Sandwich long before returning to your farm?"

The sudden realization hit him square in the gut. "Nay, that was not my farm, only an abandoned place to take refuge. I am…I am returning…" He swallowed, squirming at the sound of his stuttering. Lying had never come easily to him, though 'twould seem that would have to change if he wished to keep his head attached to the rest of him. "I have no farm of my own at present. I was traveling from New York to Sandwich when I happened upon you."

"I see." Myriad questions dashed through her eyes before a veil of sorrow draped her features. "I don't know what would have become of me if you hadn't been traveling through."

"You haven't any idea who that man was?"

"Nay." She gripped harder around her middle. "But my father sent him. That much I do know." She stopped, her mouth pinched. "That is all I really need to know."

Her answer begged for more questions, but William bit his tongue and nodded.

"I cannot go with him. I cannot be found. I do not care what happens so long as—"

With a yelp she tripped and fell to the ground. William lunged for her, but was a moment too late.

Instantly, he crouched beside her, then helped her

to her feet. "Are you hurt?"

She ducked her head, red staining her cheeks. "I should have watched where I was going." The slight laugh in her voice assured him she was neither hurt nor so embarrassed she could not be at ease with him.

He allowed a full smile to rest on his mouth. He stopped and glanced at her neck. "Your ring is still in place, I see."

Her head flung toward him, eyes wide, lips parted as if such a pronouncement were both unexpected and reassuring. She touched the ring and looked away. "'Twas kind of you to think of it."

A mournful smile passed her lips as he helped her to standing, one hand on her shoulder, his other at her elbow. She turned toward him and William stilled, his pulse rising. He gazed down at her, his gentle grip still anchoring him in place. Something about their nearness arrested his senses. Her pink cheeks and clear eyes, the heady scent of late summer, and the sound of their breath sparked a yearning he hadn't felt for years.

Dangerous waters, Henry.

Yet, he couldn't move.

She blinked and he noted the long lashes that framed her eyes like black lace. *Move, you fool!* His muscles rebelled and he stayed motionless a moment longer. She closed her lips as her eyes darted to his mouth and instantly down to her feet.

Forcing his hands to release their hold, he broke the trance, keeping his movements slow to prove he hadn't been affected.

He offered a light bob of the head and found a way to make his legs start moving again. How many years had passed since he'd been so close to a woman? He pulled his shoulders back, keeping a steady pace that his companion matched step for step.

There had been Kitty, of course, though she had been more like a sister to him—gentle like Julia and fiery like Jane. Kitty's closeness hadn't muddled his thinking, hadn't doubled his pulse or caught his breath.

He looked forward, the phantoms rising before him once more. *Her* shoulders had been just as delicate. *Her* eyes just as sweetly framed. The tone of *her* voice like birdsong. But the deceit in her soul had been black as the night she'd carried away his heart. The night his actions had all but killed those he loved most.

The tainted parts of him resisted the boyish inclinations to steal another glance at the lovely stranger, reminding himself that women were not to be trusted, were full of lies and ready to use a man for their own pleasures. He would be wise to remember that, lest he suffer the same pains again.

Somehow, from the windows of heaven a whisper niggled his conscience. *Your mother was not as she, nor Julia or Jane or Kitty.*

With another quick look to the lady, he clenched and released his fists, desperate to ignore the clash of emotions that warred within. What was so innocent about this stranger? What made her seem so sincere?

He knew nothing of her, and somehow that fact failed to caution as it should. With a rough breath, he put his feelings in their rightful place, far from the reaches of his memory.

Sandwich was a hard day's journey, but well worth the pains. 'Twas a chance to get to safety, and a chance to leave this woman—and his phantoms—behind.

They were nearly there, he'd said, but his statement had been uttered when the sun still graced the sky. Now, darkness had cloaked them for more than several hours. Anna rubbed her hands up and down her arms and looked toward the sky. 'Twas only a half-moon, and therefore half the light, making their passage more treacherous, more tedious.

Fatigue cut to her core, but she refused to let a single whimper escape her lips. She was strong, and courageous, and capable—no matter what her father believed. And if William's word proved trustworthy, she would have a place to stay protected. That is, at least until she discovered what to do next.

Their conversation was polite but clipped. Though he'd seemed ever watchful and kind, William kept careful distance since that startling moment at the beginning of their journey. For that, she was grateful. Though now, with the pains of their tireless journey scraping her very bones, speaking would be a blessed distraction.

Heaven's mercy! How much longer?

"Mr. Fredericks?"

The pale light cast shadows on his face as he turned to look at her. "You may use my Christian name."

She offered a polite smile, before studying the dark path. Though she had begun to think of him as William, speaking it aloud was far too intimate. "Have you any family in Sandwich?"

He halted mid-step, turning to her with questioning creases around his eyes.

His falter caused her to stop as well. The crickets and frogs filled the night air with their croaks and chirps. But William said nothing, only stared, his silhouette mingling with the shadows.

Finally, he broke the crushing silence, his voice low and deep. "I have no family, Miss Whitehead."

He turned and stared again without another word, leaving Anna behind him. Inky ribbons of regret twisted around her. She should never have asked, for clearly he hadn't wished to speak of family. Whatever his reasons, they pained, or his tone would not have carried so much sorrow. And here he continued to use a name that wasn't even hers.

Stupid, ignorant girl. Carrying on with her need to keep her identity secret seemed a vain attempt. Why continue the charade when her rescuer could likely do more for her if indeed he knew her true identity.

"Mr. Fredericks."

He stopped again and looked over his shoulder,

questioning her with only the lowering of his chin.

She swallowed and cleared her throat, his acute expression unsettling the ground she stood upon. "I feel I should tell you, I have not been completely honest. My name...is Mrs. Rone." Shame coated her voice so thick she feared she couldn't speak the rest. "I...I used Whitehead in hopes that I would not be found. But it seems it made no difference. I hope you can forgive me."

The dusting of light that rested over him showed little of his expression, but his stance softened. "I understand."

Two simple words, but spoken with such raw depth that the air warmed around her.

William motioned in front of him. "We are here."

Praise the Lord. Engulfed with pleasure at their arrival, her body began to give way with the knowledge that rest was nearly within her grasp.

She reached for the tree beside her and held fast, as her limbs cramped.

Darkness shrouded his face, but the tenderness in his voice coated her weakening limbs. "Forgive me for making you walk so much today. I wanted to reach our destination before nightfall."

She squeaked out the only words she could manage, the reserves of her strength at risk of depletion. "Not at all."

He must have detected the weakness she tried to mask, for in a moment he was at her side. "Take my arm."

Ashamed at how much she relied on his strength, Anna was careful not to linger on the thickness of his muscle. She kept her eyes on the ground then ahead as the trees cleared and the side of a house came into view. How he'd been able to find this place in the dead of night, she would never know.

When they reached the house, he stopped and Anna gratefully released her grip and clung to the wood siding.

"I'll go to the door first, to be sure I've found the right home," he said. Almost as an after thought added, "Don't go anywhere."

Anna grinned, feeling light-headed thanks to the exhaustion that weighted her down. "Where else would I go?"

He stared, his dark blonde hair looking black in the shadows that covered him. A flash of white behind his smile was all she could see before he finished the few steps to the door.

Chapter Five

A single light glimmered in the upstairs window. Was someone awake? Staring up, William raked a hand over his head, catching a quick but pungent scent from beneath his arm. A bath could not come soon enough. He sighed. It must be near midnight.

William glanced to the woman who clutched the side of the house. All those miles and she hadn't breathed a word of complaint. He knew from the hobble in her step that her feet pained her, and she must be as starving as he, if not more.

Pushing out a firm exhale, he knocked twice.

After a moment with nary a rustle from within, he reached to knock again, but the door creaked open a crack then flew back wide.

"Hen—"

"Good evening, Thomas. 'Tis I, William Fredericks."

Thomas scowled, analyzing William's expression, before reaching out his hand. "Of course. 'Tis a pleasure, old friend. Come in, quickly."

"I have someone with me."

Thomas's expression dropped. "Aye?"

William looked to where the woman stood. "I happened upon a woman...she is in need and I assured her you would be willing to help."

"We are happy to assist however we can."

William finally inhaled a deep breath, though he hadn't even known he'd stilled his lungs. His friends would help her, just as he'd promised. Thank the Lord for people such as these.

He motioned to her at the same time that Thomas called to Eliza to come down quickly, and with a blanket.

Eliza hurried down the stairs, flinging a shawl around her shoulders. Her mouth opened and she rushed to the door, but Thomas slowed her with a gentle touch to her arm.

"Eliza, you remember William."

With a quick look to her husband then back to William, the question in her expression dispelled in place of a smile.

"Why of course, William, how good it is to see you. I—" Her gaze fell upon Anna. "Have you both journeyed here through the night? You poor dear!" She reached a caring arm around Anna's shoulder and led her toward the kitchen. "You'll want to soak your feet. I can attest to that from experience." Eliza turned and spoke to Thomas as he shut the door. "There's bread and cider on the table. Be sure he gets some."

"Of course." Thomas pointed toward the table and chair. "Refresh yourself. I'm going to fetch Nathaniel.

That wound on your arm looks like it needs care." He flung his cloak over his shoulder and snatched his hat off the wall. "Then you will tell us everything."

William satiated his need for nourishment, and not a quarter hour later Thomas burst back through the door. "Nathaniel will be here promptly." A grin flooded his face as he hung up his hat and coat. "Kitty as well. She refused to be left behind."

William frowned. "Kitty is at Nathaniel's home?"

Thomas angled his head. "I should have guessed that would be obvious."

The realization clapped William on the back, and his mouth dropped open. "They are married."

"You are surprised?"

"Nay..." He chuckled lightly. "Not at all. I am pleased."

Grinning, Thomas nodded then looked in the direction of the kitchen. "I suppose Eliza is still seeing to your companion's needs?"

"Aye."

Thomas went to the fire and added another log before lighting two more lamps. "I would hear more of what you know about her, but first to the matters most pressing." His timbre deepened. "I am pleased you came to us. We have always hoped you would trust—"

The door creaked and Nathaniel Smith pushed it open, his doctor's bag in hand, but 'twas Kitty who entered first, her large eyes wide and full of worry.

"Are you all right?" She rushed forward and reached

for William's wounded arm just as Nathaniel came behind her. "This was all my doing." Her pinched voice and the drop of her features pulled at William's heart.

"Nay, 'tis the army which is to blame for all of this. For all that we have suffered."

Her gaze still did not leave his. "I am so pleased you came to us."

The sight of her lifted the weighted pieces of his soul, making the loss of Julia and Jane easier to bear. He glanced at Nathaniel. "I understand congratulations are in order."

Nathaniel's smile expanded, brightening his entire frame. "Did you think I would have waited another moment?"

"You'd have been a fool."

"I'll say amen to that." Thomas lifted an amber-filled glass and took a drink.

Kitty gently patted William's arm. "I shall see to the woman in the kitchen."

The three of them watched her go before they fully relaxed, the meat of their conversation waiting to be spoken.

Nathaniel rested his bag on the table beside the largest upholstered chair and motioned for William to sit. "You couldn't bear to be so long parted from us, I see."

"I was only curious to know whether you would make good on your debt."

With an answering laugh, Nathaniel pulled another

chair beside William. He reached in his bag and retrieved a pair of shears, a vile of salve and a roll of bandages. "Let me have a look."

When both men were seated, Nathaniel's face grew solemn and with Thomas standing close behind, he upended the cup of curiosity. "Thomas tells me you are no longer Henry Donaldson. Rather, you're calling yourself William Fredericks."

"'Tis true." Though the name offered an element of safety, a shield to hide behind, and though he could make himself think such a name were his identity, his soul would always answer to Henry.

Thomas answered before William had a chance. "He's defected."

Nathaniel's eyes shot open then narrowed as his brow dipped in a deep V. An unvoiced inquest circled in his face, just as it had in Thomas's.

"When was this? Immediately after?" Nathaniel asked.

William looked between them, knowing exactly to what "after" Nathaniel referred. The battle in the woods, the frantic flight to safety...

He lowered his voice. "Three days ago. After you and Kitty escaped, I returned to camp as planned. Stockton believed my story. Most of it..." He cringed at the memory then grunted as Nathaniel prodded at the wound on his arm. "But his son did not, insisting that this was not the first time I had sided with the colonists."

Though such was true, no evidence could prove it.

Thomas leaned his shoulder against the fireplace. "His son?"

William nodded. "Ezra has a son, Paul, and his company joined our camp the next morning. He convinced his father I had planned Kitty's escape. I was able to send word to Higley about your plight that morning, but only hours later I was on my way to trial in New York. I then constructed an escape of my own— have mercy!" He half-scowled, half-chuckled at Nathaniel. "Are you trying to torture me?"

Nathaniel's expression held little amusement. "This wound is greatly infected."

William ground his teeth. "Can it be healed?"

"The tear, yes. The infection, I believe so, with care."

"No stitches?"

"Nay. With proper wrapping I expect it will heal well." Nathaniel reached for additional bandages in his bag. "What will you do now?"

Rubbing his head, William exhaled. "In truth, I have thought of little beyond coming here."

"You did right in coming," Thomas said. "You may stay as long as needed."

"I cannot do that." William kept speaking as Nathaniel rubbed an ointment around his wound and wrapped it anew. "I have already placed you in considerable harm. I must leave by morning."

Nathaniel and Thomas exchanged looks.

Still leaning beside the fireplace, Thomas put his

hands in his pockets. "If you truly wish to defect, you must assimilate somewhere. Why not here?"

The pointed question struck William as if it were a blow to the head. "You are not serious."

Nathaniel tied the bandage in place. "Do you know any other people so foolish as to stick their necks out for you?"

"I cannot live here." A weak chuckle leaked out through his words. "You know what kind of suspicion that would cause. I have been in town before, so I could be recognized. Besides, if you have regulars here...I can't take that risk."

Again, Thomas and Nathaniel eyed each other.

Thomas looked toward the kitchen, the soft voices of the women not quite reaching beyond the open doorway. He lowered his tone. "You could convert. The local Quaker population is high, and many wish to stay out of the conflict. If you did the same, perhaps we could find you a place—"

"I cannot ignore this fight, Thomas. I'm a soldier. I've simply been fighting for the wrong side."

Nathaniel stood and began replacing the shears and unused bandages back in his bag. "'Twould be foolish to think you could hide somewhere else." He crossed his arms and leaned back against the table, his gaze narrowing. "Kitty has worried over you."

William examined the fresh bandage and relished in the soothing sensation from the ointment that coated his wound. "As I have worried over the two of you. But now that you have joined your lives, I supposed I need worry no longer."

Nathaniel chewed the inside of his lip. "You know, *William*, if a man remains a bachelor for too long he runs the risk of being a menace to society." He stopped almost before he'd finished his words and narrowed his eyes. "How do you feel about marriage?"

The last word blasted like an icy wind, freezing him where he sat. "I am afraid I don't understand." Though he did. Fully.

Again, Nathaniel and Thomas exchanged a glance. Thomas tilted his head and Nathaniel nodded.

William lowered his voice breathing a threat through his teeth. "Speak aloud or I leave this instant."

Nathaniel ignored him, directing his communications to Thomas. "You heard the Atticks family passed."

Thomas shook his head, his expression falling. "All of them?"

"Aye." Nathaniel nodded. "The fever took them all despite our best efforts to save them. Their home is now empty." He turned to William. "In need of care."

Thomas continued the thought. "The farm is small but provides plenty. A husband and wife would do well there. Could make a good home, just as the Atticks did. Custer and his wife had no family to take the land. It may as well go to someone in need of a fresh start."

Nathaniel smacked William on the back. "All we must do is find you a good woman."

"Absolutely not." His muscles burned. "I'd sooner take the noose."

"Come now." Thomas leaned back against the table and crossed his arms with an annoying grin on his face. "A woman can do great things for a man."

Aye. Such as betray him and leave bare his heart to be trampled by the painful memories of what would never be.

William exhaled a rough laugh as he stood and poured himself another glass of cider. "You may do as you like for yourselves, but marriage could not be further from my thoughts." He downed the amber liquid. "Do not press me."

"Of course, if you did marry," Nathaniel continued, sitting in the chair next to the fire as if William had issued no warning, "you would have to keep your identity a secret from even your wife...at least until the conflict with the crown is ended."

William grimaced, the stench of the conversation permeating the room like rot. "I will say it again. No."

Thomas motioned with a finger toward town. "There are plenty of fine women—"

"Gentlemen, please." William clutched the glass in his hand, fearing it might break from the pressure. "I do not take my plight lightly."

"Neither do we." Nathaniel glanced at Thomas without moving his head before nailing his gaze on William, his expression every bit as heavy as his tone. He stood and rested a hand on William's shoulder. "We would not wish you to think we are anything but deadly serious."

Thomas neared. His volume dropped and the earnest caring in his voice soothed William's ruffled pride. "If you mean to defect, we will help you in any way we can. If you mean to stay hidden, then taking on a new life, far from the one you have been living, is the best way to ensure the least amount of suspicion."

William stared at the bottom of the glass in his hands as a chill crept up his spine. It was true. If he took not only a new name, but a new life, the risk of being found would plummet. He swallowed and shut his eyes against the vaporous memories—her smile, the cushion of her mouth, the scent of her hair—and the way she patted his arm with a grin and turned her back on him forever.

"Fredericks."

William jerked at the sound of his new name.

The half-smile on Thomas's face said more than words. "You cannot do something you do not believe in. We won't press it upon you. We simply mean to help."

With another forced breath, William exhaled through clenched teeth. "I thank you for your sincerity." He set the glass down. "I do believe in marriage..." The words stuck in his throat. What was he thinking?

Nathaniel tipped his head. "Then you would consider it?"

Rubbing his temples, William groaned his answer before he could reconsider. "I suppose."

Such a stark silence followed he jolted up to be sure he wasn't suddenly alone. Thomas and Nathaniel both stared at him, their expressions knit in thought. Thoughts clearly occupied on the very subject he didn't wish to discuss but had willingly become a party to.

His friends' expressions shifted, their eyes thinning, mouths quirking sideways. William's muscles tightened, ready to snap like the lock of his pistol. He took the open seat nearest the kitchen and slumped back, voice bare of expression. "Do not look at me as if you were fitting me for shoes."

"Fitting you for shoes? Nay." A chuckle sparkled in Nathaniel's eyes. "But if we are to find you a wife then we must consider the options."

"What's this?"

The men jumped at the sound of Eliza's melodic tone. She and Kitty stood wide-eyed in the doorframe of the kitchen.

Thomas reached for his wife's hand and she neared, taking his fingers in hers. He seemed to relay the entire conversation to her in a single, solemn look. "Fredericks is in need of a bride."

Kitty's mouth dropped open and she flung a glance to her husband. "Nathaniel?"

"'Tis true." Nathaniel answered with such seeming delight William fought the urge to smack the mirth from the man's face.

Kitty's eyebrows shot up and she pinned her gaze on Eliza, who nodded slowly and brushed a hand over her rounded belly. After a moment of quiet thought a smile grew on her face and she turned to Thomas. "I know you gentlemen mean well, but if we are to find Fredericks a wife, you cannot simply choose a woman and be done with it."

"True." Nathaniel sat back in his chair and rubbed his jaw. "What would you suggest?"

William's stomach turned to granite. Was he in some terrible dream where moments from now he would awaken, covered in sweat and heaving breaths of gratitude that this conversation had been only in his mind?

"A girl must be courted." Eliza turned to Thomas, a cant to her smile. "You and I did not officially court, but that was different."

Thomas flicked his eyes to William, then to Nathaniel and back to Eliza. "'Tis obvious Nathaniel and I are unfit for planning such matters."

Kitty stepped forward. "We could always begin by arranging meetings, and attending dances and other social events. If 'tis truly your intent to marry then there are proper ways to find women who would be more than willing to court."

"Aye," Thomas said. "Caroline Whitney is a staunch patriot and always attends Cooper's gatherings."

Nathaniel shook his head. "She is an excellent choice, but I feel we need to give William the respect of choice he needs in this matter."

"I haven't time to court." William growled and leaned his head back, glaring and speaking the next words under his breath. "Why did I say I would consider this?"

Eliza moved closer to her husband, the four of them forming a semi-circle in front of the fire as if William weren't in the room. "I fear we are taking too much upon ourselves."

Thomas gestured to William but spoke to his wife. "He knows no ladies in town, and did we not promise to help him?" He exhaled and looked to Nathaniel. "Elizabeth Curling?"

Eliza shook her head. "She's left for Georgia."

"Katie Pickett?" Nathaniel said.

Both women refused with sharp eyes.

Shoots of nervous energy buzzed through William's limbs, forcing his knee up and down so hard he feared the heel of his boot would pound a hole in the floor. More and more names drifted in the parlor air. His entire future rested upon whether they could concur on a complete stranger to suit him for the rest of his life. He shouldn't allow it. He should stand and demand they put an end to this fruitless and embarrassing display.

Yet, he stayed quiet. Why? Only God knew. And if God would ever impart a portion of His wisdom, now would be a most welcome moment. William tried to work his jaw from its motionless position, to allow his voice to speak in his behalf, but it wouldn't move. He closed his eyes and gripped the arms of the chair. Surely this foolish notion would dissolve soon enough and he could resume his journey in the morning.

"Martha Curry?" Thomas suggested, clearly determined to continue. "She's just returned from Salem to live with her brother, and from what I hear she is quite lovely."

"You mean you've never seen her?" William shot from the chair, his heated blood rising to his neck. "Though I know your idea is well meant, it is folly. For this new life I've undertaken to be believable, a marriage must be made quickly." He raked his hand through his hair with a growl before moving around his seat and clutching the back of it. "What woman would accept a man she hardly knows?"

Alone in the kitchen, Anna struggled to close her ears to the conversation that ensued in the connecting room. Poor William. He needed to marry? Why? Having missed much of what the gentlemen had said previously—when Mrs. Watson had so kindly seen to her needs—Anna fumbled with the few facts she'd gleaned. Something dreadful must have happened to force him to such a decision. One he seemed none too keen to accept.

The voices stretching into her quiet kitchen

sanctuary rose, edged with frustration. Name after name tossed upon the air, and every one refused. William's irritation thickened like a seaside fog. She bit her lip and toyed with the ring at her neck. She knew that feeling—that sense of falling, dropping into an abyss, an empty dark future that you must accept despite the yearnings of your heart.

William's voice carried above the rest. "What woman would accept a man she hardly knows?"

Anna looked to the door and answered silently. A woman would be a simpleton indeed to refuse the hand of someone so kind and generous. Never had she met a man with whom she felt so...safe.

Suddenly, a silent melody danced upon the air, like a song from an unseen angel chorus. *He needs to marry someone...but whom?* The answer hummed over her skin in delicate harmony. *You.*

She bolted upright. *What in heaven's name?* Breathing long and deep, Anna tried to shake the thought from her mind but it refused to release its hold. A flurry of questions she'd forced from her mind started a quick and violent quarrel. What would happen to her now? They had made it this far, but where would she go tomorrow and the day after that? Father would stop at nothing until she was found and returned to him. William was the only person she knew, and strangely, the only person she trusted. He needed to start a new life, and so did she.

Perhaps...

Anna swiveled in her seat and glanced toward the parlor. Her pulse drummed wildly, and she pressed her palm against the ring that rested against her skin. What if she offered—

She laughed quietly to herself. Nay, she couldn't. Silly notion.

Could she?

Anna stared at the orange glow from the kitchen fire. What about love? Had she not promised her mother she would only marry if her heart directed her? Though if she did offer, she would be the one choosing her future and no one else. *Why am I even considering this?* She blinked, but the action failed to dislodge the rooted thought.

Would William even accept her if she offered herself? How foolish she would feel if he refused her. Then again, should she not at least try? Sacrificing a marriage of love for one of safety seemed the best way to ensure her future in America—a future away from her father's dominant hand. For now, though discovering the truth of Samuel's death was ingrained in her spirit, 'twas paramount that her feet never again tread upon London soil. William was a good man. How she could be so sure of it, she didn't know, but she was. She could be content living the rest of her life as his companion, if he would have her.

Propelled to standing by a weight of courage that drove through her middle, Anna stepped toward the parlor, hands quivering, stomach turning. Pressing away every quaking fear, she fixed the singular purpose in her vision as she stood in the doorway of the kitchen and steadied her eyes on William. His back to her, he still debated with the others as they circled the fireplace, all of them oblivious to her presence.

"Pardon me?" Hardly more than a whisper left her mouth. She cleared her throat and tried again. "Pa—pardon me?" Not any more volume than before. *Gather yourself, Anna.*

"William?" Finally, the needed volume.

The group pivoted toward her, and before her fears submerged her determination she spoke. "I...I would marry you."

Pressing her hands against her middle Anna measured every inhale and exhale. William blinked as if he tried to interpret what she'd spoken, and instant regret dripped down her spine. The words remained on the air, echoing back and forth in the space between them, growing louder with every second that passed.

She offered a smile, however small she could muster, to show the sincerity of her statement and mask the way she quivered from head to foot, lest he believe she made light of his serious troubles.

William didn't move. His gaze drove through her like a sharp spike, every unspoken word preaching from the folds in his brow.

He thinks I am mad.

She cleared her throat. "Forgive me, I—"

"What did you say?" he said.

She swallowed and gripped her fingers harder, straining with every thread of strength to keep her voice from shaking. "I...I said I would marry you." Her throat clenched and she hardly found the strength to speak again. She prayed her plea would soften the hard lines of his jaw. "If you would have me."

He scowled deeper then turned to look at the others as if seeking some kind of counsel. They thought her a fool. Likely she was. What had she done?

Mrs. Watson stepped forward, arms outstretched until she reached Anna, taking her hand. Her gentle grasp tightened as she undoubtedly felt the tremor in Anna's fingers.

Her voice was low and wound around Anna like a comforting blanket. "Mrs. Rone, you needn't offer yourself. I am sure you are very grateful to..." She turned around briefly. "To Mr. Fredericks. But you mustn't feel the need to—"

"But I don't—I mean I do, I mean..." Anna looked down, feeling the heat of every eye and the oppressive weight of her declaration. Her breath raced. What else could she do? No doubt that man from the carriage still sought her. If her rescuer did not accept this proposal, where would she go? She had no one. No place of refuge. Could it be possible God had arranged such a moment— for her? For both of them?

Mouth pressed together, she looked at the man who once again stared. He'd been so kind. Was it foolish to think such generosity would be continued through a lifetime? The past cried from her memory like a prisoner just freed from the shackles. *You fool! Have your years of bondage taught you nothing?*

Then, as if the hand of God Himself stroked her very spirit, the quivering ceased and she looked up, meeting the kind gaze of the woman in front of her as the fear drained from her spirit. "I do wish to, Mrs. Watson."

With a quick squeeze, Anna released her grip and stepped into the parlor, stopping several feet from the man who could be her husband.

Meeting his stare, she lifted her chin, unsure how she was able to stay upright, let alone meet his questioning gaze. "I do not know your reasons, as well I know you do not know mine." She stopped, screaming a silent prayer. "But I do know if we are both committed to God, and to one another, we can make a happy marriage."

She bit her tongue, fighting the urge to keep speaking and fill the itching silence.

Still he said nothing, but the pique in his features melted and the slope of his mouth seemed to ask if she were in earnest.

Anna pleaded with God to quiet the remaining fears, holding tight to her abiding faith. Gaining William's gaze, she gifted him a half-smile, his endless blue eyes swimming with questions and fears, and perhaps, even hope.

The painful silence continued.

Would he say nothing? Her mind whirled. Had she spoken when she ought not? Her cheeks turned hot. Her stomach twisted as she fought the memories of Edwin— his forceful hand, jealous eye and demanding nature. Consumed, she lowered her eyes. Nay. Not again. Not ever again. *Dear Lord, what have I done?*

She took a step back when William reached out. "Mrs. Rone."

The tenderness in his strong fingers eased her rising anxiety and she stopped, studying his fingers as they tenderly gripped her arm.

He continued and moved his hand to hers, that deep resonating voice now a thick whisper. "You would do this? You are under no obligation."

"I know." She waited, expecting the fears to rise to threatening levels, for her throat to close and her vision to blur. But her pulse stayed even and her eyes remained clear. The longer she stood with her hand in his, hope, weightless and warm, circled her spirit.

She found her voice. "I would do this."

The smallest grin lit his eyes only and he released her hand then turned to the men behind him. "Well, gentlemen, I believe I have been blessed with a willing bride."

"Excellent." Nathaniel came forward and cupped his shoulder. "The moment the sun rises, I shall ride for Reverend Charles."

Chapter Six

William stood in front of the kitchen fire, gazing at the dancing flames. After only a few hours of sleep, the sun had crested over the horizon, awakening him to the strange future he'd accepted. All that had transpired in the last three days seemed so surreal he'd half expected to awake and find himself in his quarters, ready to begin his daily routine of drills and reports.

He peered toward the stairway where Eliza and Kitty had whisked Mrs. Rone away to prepare her for the speaking of vows while Nathaniel had gone for the reverend.

Could this really be? *Should* this be? Too many questions warred within him to allow clear enough thought. He breathed out a laugh. In battle, when decisions must be made, when lives were at stake, those decisions came easily. Here, the decision to marry having clearly been made, his mind and spirit fought like bitter rivals. Marriage was not to be taken lightly. This was a commitment made before God that one would love and care for a spouse until death, in all tribulations of life. Was he ready to make that vow? He

SO *rare* A GIFT

ground his teeth. He had been once. Had been willing to risk everything for such a life, only to have his heart left to canker in his chest.

The memories burned and he blinked them away as Thomas entered, a brush and mirror in one hand, a fresh shirt tucked under his arm. In his other hand he carried a bucket of water and a cloth. "You best clean yourself up, or she might change her mind."

William grinned and pulled at the ribbon in his hair, eager to wipe away the stench. "I suppose if she's willing to marry me looking like this, she's a better woman than most."

"That she is." Thomas offered a light chuckle then quickly turned somber. "Are you certain this is what you want?"

William's jaw ticked and he pulled off the soiled shirt. "We both know the alternative." Dipping the cloth in the cool water he wiped his arms and chest. "I could head west, but to what end?"

The fresh scent of the soap almost cleaned away the dark anxieties that coated his lungs. He dried himself and slipped the crisp linen over his shoulders, the clean fabric feeling light against his cool skin. He placed the mirror on the mantel and focused on tying the neckcloth before turning to Thomas. He bound his hair behind his neck, sighing. "There's nothing else to be done. I shall marry a woman I've known for barely two days and become a farmer." It made his stomach turn the way his mouth could form the words as if he were merely discussing the weather.

Thomas's expression dipped. "You do not have to give up soldiering forever."

William scoffed. "Do I not?"

"You must know they will tire searching for you. The siege on Boston and continuing skirmishes are more than sufficient to keep the redcoats occupied."

He pulled himself straighter. "Is it not cowardly of me to take up such a life when I could make myself useful to Washington?"

"You can make yourself useful by becoming a patriot. There are countless ways for you to be of help to our cause, and no doubt God will make sure your particular skills are put to use." Thomas joined him in front of the fire. "And I have a feeling we shall discover those ways soon enough."

A knock at the front door, followed by Nathaniel's immediate greeting, pulled William back to the place his mind tried to escape.

Nathaniel peeked his head around the kitchen door. "I've brought the reverend."

Thomas left with a nod and William stalled, taking one last look in the mirror. He pushed a hard, loud breath through his mouth. The face of a husband, was it? Hardly. The face of a fool, more like.

Never since London had he considered marriage. Not since her—since Anna. There. He'd thought her name. Allowed it to unearth from the graveyard of his memory. That name carried the dregs of hell with it. He shook his arms at his sides to rid the nerves from his tightening muscles and marched to the parlor to shake hands with Reverend Charles, and to forever forget the woman who had used him so ill.

Perhaps God had found a way to heal him after all.

Even if such a remedy were a hasty marriage to a stranger.

Anna could hardly breathe, hardly swallow.

She stared at herself in the mirror, blinking, grasping desperately for a semblance of reason. What had she done?

Seated in front of the dressing table, Anna resisted gaining Eliza's gaze in the mirror. She stood behind her, brushing and finishing Anna's hair with a delicate pink ribbon. The dear woman, who had insisted Anna call her by her first name, seemed able to read Anna's thoughts with a mere glance. Kitty had gone home to retrieve a gown she insisted would be perfect for such an occasion. The gesture was so kind it lured tears to Anna's eyes.

She swallowed and cleared her throat again, dropping a quick glance to Eliza's growing belly, her own stomach suddenly hard as stone. Should she tell him she could never bear children? If she did it may change his mind and then what would she do? Be forced to surrender to her father's will? Nay. This time, she was making the decisions for her future—for the good or for the bad.

"Mrs. Rone?"

Anna looked up.

Eliza stopped brushing and rested her hands on her shoulders. "You have done a brave and generous thing."

Allowing her mouth to lift on one side, Anna attempted a smile. She was neither brave nor generous. Rather, selfish and fearful. Anna looked down at her hands. "I thank you for that." For though the words were meant to strengthen, they ripped open the vulnerable parts of her spirit and flayed them for all to see.

Eliza continued. "I want you to know that Hen—" she stopped and smiled briefly. "That he, William, is a good man."

Was he? She'd known him not even two days. And yet, she'd offered her life to him. She raced back through the memories of her brief time with the handsome stranger. Not once had he raised his hand or his voice despite the perils they'd endured on their short journey together. On the contrary. He'd risked his life on her behalf—saved her from that which she most feared. She shivered at the thought. *I shall never return to England.* She reached for the chain at her neck and closed her eyes. *Never, Lord, I pray thee.*

Anna played with the treasure that rested against her chest as Eliza tugged at her hair. Her eyes misted. Mother had wished more for her, had she not? And here, with a new chance at life, in a new land, she had chosen to bind herself to a man she hardly knew.

"There." Eliza stepped back and grinned so wide her face beamed, eyes twinkling in the light of the sunrise that shone through the window. "He would be a fool indeed to turn down such an offer from one so beautiful. And so kind."

Anna's chest tightened. How generous of her, truly. But what man would marry a woman who is barren? Her father had made that clear from her youth.

The door burst open and Kitty rushed in, her cheeks ruddy and her breath shallow as if she'd run every step. "I've found it."

Eliza whirled, her hands clasped beneath her chin. "Oh, it is so lovely, Kitty." She turned to Anna. "This color will be stunning for you."

Anna turned and clasped her hands at her middle. The gown draped the bed. Light blue, embroidered with white flowers, the neck and sleeves of the gown were edged with the most delicate lace. 'Twas stunning indeed. Though she had owned gowns at the height of fashion and far more decadent, this gown was lovelier than anything she had ever worn, not for the needlework or design, but for what it meant. For who had ever thought of her in such a way? Who had ever offered something so generous? No one.

She glanced at the two women, their eyes round and hopeful. How could she repay such kindness? "I am more grateful than I can express, but I cannot receive such a gift. I have nothing with which to repay such kindness."

Eliza lowered her head disapprovingly. "Come now. You cannot be married in your homespun."

Anna squirmed and looked down at her dress. Bringing attention to herself was the last thing she wished to do. Her face burned. But wearing such a tattered dress would hardly make her a fitting bride.

Eliza neared and rested a hand on her arm. "Forgive me, but...I should not wish to speak of things that are not mine to mention. However, I feel to say it is my hope and belief that this union will bring more joy than your last."

What? Anna stilled. Too shocked to pretend otherwise, her eyes darted between her two companions. When she answered, her words were crowded and hoarse. "How did you know?"

Eliza's large, brown eyes grew soft. "A woman who has loved deeply, and lost, would not speak about their departed as you have."

"But I have said nothing—"

"*That* is how I know."

Anna quirked her head, brow down.

"Eliza has always been able to discern such things," Kitty said, seating herself on the edge of the bed. "Her compassion for others allows her to see through the shields we erect in order to help when help is needed."

Eliza threw her sister a loving smile. "As do you Kitty, in your way as well." She motioned for Anna to rise from the chair then turned to Kitty, who stood and readied the gown as Eliza began unfastening Anna's dress. "If you had loved him, had been happy with him, you would have said as much. Or at least your eyes would have, when I asked about your necklace when we were in the kitchen."

Anna touched the ring before Eliza helped her off with the bodice. "This wasn't mine—I mean, it is mine, but..." She stopped. Was she really about to expose her entire life to strangers? She couldn't. Yet these kind women had a way of making it easy to speak of memories that cut.

"You won't tell William," Anna said.

Eliza shook her head. "Nay, I will not."

"We will keep in confidence anything you wish," Kitty said.

"I thank you." The cramping in Anna's muscles eased. "I simply do not wish him to know anything until I can tell him myself."

Eliza reached out and gripped her hand. The tenderness in her large eyes coated Anna's middle like a warm sip of tea. "You have our word."

Kitty stepped forward from the bed. "We wish ours to be a true friendship, for we shall see you as our sister as we see William as our brother, and we wouldn't wish to betray something so precious."

Anna's throat ached so, she could hardly speak. "Thank you."

Kitty's eyes narrowed as her smile grew wide. "We must hurry. Reverend Charles is already here."

Anna stepped out of the gray, mud-laced skirts and petticoat and pulled her arms from her sleeves. Eliza offered a moist cloth and Anna grinned, relishing the feel of the cool wet as it wiped away the dirt from her skin. Once refreshed, she turned to the bed to reach for the gown, but stopped when Eliza and Kitty both stared open-mouthed.

"Is something wrong?"

"Anna!" Eliza motioned to her. "I've never seen such lovely stays."

Kitty came forward and touched the laces that criss-crossed up the back. "The needlework is exquisite. Wherever did you get such a thing?"

Swallowing, Anna paused. Never in her wildest imaginations had she thought any person would see her stays. She hadn't thought to change them as she had her gown. And since she'd made them herself, she could hardly part with them. They *were* lovely. She dropped her gaze, tugged away by the memories that had only recently begun to wilt. Edwin had refused to allow her to do anything so lowly as sew clothing. Embroider cloths, yes, but nothing that she would wear. That was for the lower classes, he'd said. But she'd gone behind his back and learned despite his protests. The thrill of such secrecy made her insides buzz even now.

Facing her friends, she dusted her hands down her stomach. "I'm pleased you like them. I...I made them."

"You made them!" Both girls answered together.

"What a talent you have. I could never dream of creating something so beautiful." Kitty blinked breathlessly. She turned to the bed and helped Anna step into the petticoat. "I can't imagine where you came upon such lovely material, and the thread...'tis so delicate."

Eliza touched her rounded belly and sat back against the bed. ""Forgive me, ladies, but I must sit a moment. I fear this babe takes much of my strength these days, and I find myself sitting more often than I'd wish."

Kitty peered over her shoulder and winked. "I am all too pleased to help. So long as I may hold your dear baby whenever I please."

Eliza's dark eyes twinkled. "I am sure it won't be too long before you have one of your own."

A giggle burst from Kitty's mouth. "I am married but a few days, Liza."

"It only takes once."

"Liza!" Kitty dropped her hands, her face crimson.

Eliza pulled her lips between her teeth and shrugged with a mischievous gleam in her face. "Anna knows all about—" The mirth slipped from her features. "You haven't lost any children, Anna? I fear I may be speaking unkindly without knowing it."

"Do not worry." She answered quickly, before the truth of her pain would reveal itself in her eyes. "I have never had a child."

At this, the ache in Anna's throat grew. She would

never have the opportunity to experience such a joy. The emptiness in her womb suddenly filled every part of her until she feared she could no longer breathe. Would William despise her for what she could never give him? Should she reveal the truth before tying him to a wife that couldn't bear him the children he wished for?

A knock tapped at the door.

"Are you ready? The reverend is waiting." Thomas's voice floated through the wood.

The two sisters glanced at Anna, their eyes trailing her up and down as if to be sure they'd tied every bow and cinched every knot. Her heart lurched to her throat. *Lord, give me strength.*

"We'll be right down," Eliza said, rising from the bed. Then to Anna she whispered, "You look so lovely. William will be awestruck."

"Without a doubt." Kitty grinned wide and opened the door, motioning for Anna to exit first.

Lord, give me strength. Trying to recall how to place one foot in front of the other, she started down the stairs to speak vows with a man who was little more than a stranger.

The sound of swishing skirts and the light tapping of shoes made William whirl toward the stairs. He gripped the mantel, allowing his eyes to linger only a moment as Mrs. Rone entered the parlor. A moment was all he needed. His pulse surged. He'd known she was lovely, but dressed in such a gown, her hair pinned up, and that smile...was she smiling? At him?

He cleared his throat. Attempting some kind of greeting, he opened his mouth but no sound emerged. He closed it again. Choosing instead to offer a nod, he motioned to the opposite side of the fireplace and looked immediately at the reverend. This was all happening so fast. Too fast.

She neared and the scent of lavender alerted his senses. With her head bowed in reverence, William spied the pink ribbon in her hair and his chest squeezed. Pink. He'd always had affinity for the color. Ever since his sister Julia had insisted he learn to tie her own pink hair ribbon—the only one she owned—when their mother was too ill to do it.

If only I had not been such a fool, they might still be living...

Pain pinched and he focused again on the woman who would become his bride, her head still lowered. Good heavens, but she was lovely. Like a strand of silk caught in a sea of black, the pink ribbon wound and twirled between the curls. 'Twas then she looked up and his chest stopped. That same beautiful pink dusted her cheeks.

Reverend Charles stood in front of them, his back to the fireplace, Bible in hand. The Smiths and the Watsons took their seats, varied expressions painting their faces, all of which William decided he would not try to interpret. Had they more time they might have waited for banns to be read and for a more proper celebration to be planned. But as it was, the marriage needed to remain quiet, his existence as hushed as possible. He only hoped his bride didn't begrudge the hastiness of their union. Though since she had been the one to offer the arrangement, he figured she was content. Hoped she was so.

He peeked again at Mrs. Rone. She peered at her folded hands, allowing William a perfect view of her long, black lashes. She looked up and inhaled a quick, delicate breath when their gazes met.

"Have you a ring?"

The reverend's question struck him. William swallowed a growl beneath an apologetic smile.

Reverend Charles nodded. "None is truly needed. The vows before God are all that really—"

"I have a ring." Mrs. Rone's quiet voice came between them, her hand at her neck. "You may use this."

William reached out and touched his fingers to hers as she prepared to remove the ring from its chain. "You needn't do that."

Her dainty mouth slanted up as she reached behind her and unfastened the chain. With the ring in her hand, she met William's pointed gaze with her own. "I know." She handed it to the reverend. "Will this be sufficient?"

The reverend took it thoughtfully and nodded. "It

will, my dear."

William's heart tipped. Knowing what this ring meant to her, how it had pained her at the thought of losing it, he could hardly believe she could wear it again—with him—a man she hardly knew and didn't love. The scrolled engraving glowed in his memory. *Forget not he who loveth thee.* Now, this woman would marry him. A man who must keep the truest parts of himself hidden from her. Not of desire, but of necessity.

Lord, forgive me. Help her to forgive me.

The reverend began. "Dearly beloved, we are gathered together to join this man and this woman..."

William tried to think, to focus on the words the reverend spoke. He couldn't. His mind raced. What was he thinking? She was beautiful, no doubt of that. Kind and generous to be sure—

"William?"

He looked at Reverend Charles, feigning grave attentiveness. "Aye?"

"Repeat after me. I, William Fredericks."

He shifted his feet and met her eyes. "I, William Fredericks..."

"Take thee," The reverend stopped. "Forgive me, I didn't ask your full name."

She licked her lips, barely speaking aloud. "Anna Fairchild Martin Rone."

The blood in William's veins halted. His lungs no longer took in air. Anna? *Dearest Lord in heaven, was that truly her name?* He shook his head to force some circulation back into his brain. He hadn't heard correctly.

Reverend Charles spoke again, waiting for a response.

In the seconds that followed, William lectured himself. He couldn't back down, not over a name. That's all it was. She knew nothing of Anna Muhr and would be nothing like her. Would she? Nay. *Show your backbone, Henry.*

He raised his head, repeating the words he'd been given. "I, William, take thee, Anna, to be my wedded wife..."

And so they continued. Though to William, 'twas more a dream. Lights and colors. Sounds and scents. Movement and shadows.

All would be over soon. It must.

Then the words, "You may now kiss your bride."

Chapter Seven

Kiss?

Anna choked on her breath. She shot a pleading glance to the young reverend. Surely they could forego that part of the ceremony. His bright eyes and smile said otherwise. Her blood charged and she sent a look to her new friends, skillfully avoiding the glance of the man in front of her. Both women exhibited partial grins and raised brows, as if unsure whether to cheer or reassure.

She tapped her toes in her shoes. Well, they were husband and wife now. No turning back time. Forward with courage. She lifted her eyes and her face instantly heated. Her mouth went dry. William looked directly at her, emotions flashing through his eyes faster than she could name them. Angled jaw ticking, his gaze went from her eyes to her mouth then up again. The blue of his gaze turned a deep navy and he cupped the back of her head before he descended, his warm mouth closing over hers.

Anna sucked in a quick breath, suddenly weightless. The soft, tenderness of his lips, the fresh scent of his breath...

As quickly as it began, he pulled away, taking the fleeting warmth and wanting with it. Eyes hooded, his gaze lingered, searching, while reverent congratulations began to usher through the room. Her lungs tried to work. How did one breathe? She stared, mouth partly open, her heart beating a furious rhythm.

He blinked his eyes wide and looked away. The two other fellows neared her husband, all smiles and slaps on the back.

"Anna!"

Behind her, Eliza and Kitty took her by the shoulders and turned her to face them. They wrapped her in a firm embrace then released her, talking at once.

"I'm so happy for you."

"Mrs. Fredericks. The name suits you well."

"Come." Thomas motioned to the kitchen. "Let us enjoy some refreshment in honor of our newly wedded friends."

Kitty neared, her husband by her side. "Anna, I would like to introduce my husband, Nathaniel Smith."

He bowed, his handsome face brimming with happiness. "'Tis a pleasure to meet you, Mrs. Fredericks."

Anna curtsied. "The pleasure is mine."

Kitty smiled up at her husband, love shining in her countenance as he continued to speak. "I surely speak for everyone when I say we are pleased to have you join our little *family*."

The emphasis he placed on the last word brought the ever-present moisture to her eyes once more, but blessedly it stayed in place. The generosity so sincerely offered moved her beyond words.

He took his wife by the hand. "We will soon have you and your husband to our home for supper. But I believe Kitty has brought some delicious vittles for us to enjoy here."

Kitty looked at her husband and nodded. "True." She grinned then took Anna by the hand and led her to the kitchen. "I always manage to have some baked goods waiting to be eaten."

At the doorway, a hand brushed her arm. "Mrs. Fredericks?" That now familiar timbre tickled the air at her neck. She turned, her chest instantly tightening. Her husband's kind features rose. "I would speak to you." He paused and looked to the others gathering around the table in the kitchen. "Only for a moment."

"Of course."

He gestured to the parlor, ushering her to the place they'd stood moments before.

"I hear..." He lowered his voice and turned to face her. His jaw tightened and loosened before he spoke again. "I hear there is a farm we may look after."

She slanted her head. "Farm?" She heard him but failed to listen, instead allowing her vision to trace his hair, his eyes, his lips, remembering all too well the pleasing sensation of his mouth against hers. The pleasure tickled her memory, begging to be savored, but she forced away the vain imaginations and raised her head, fully determined to keep her eyes and thoughts away from anything but the business he wished to discuss.

William shifted his weight over his feet. "An entire family has passed, leaving their farm in need of care."

She forced both her breath and her pulse to stay calm. "Oh?"

"Doctor Smith says no other relatives have come forth to claim the property, and to this point it has remained vacant." William stopped, his eyes studying her face. "Would that...would that please you?"

Would it please me? She blinked and gripped the skirt of her gown. No one had ever asked that of her. This had to be a dream, for how could reality bring such a man into her life? She shook her head lightly, believing the action might clear away the hopes she wished not to be dashed, but instead, it clarified them. In the light of the fire his honey-colored hair looked darkish brown, his eyes glimmering with a kind of sincerity she'd never known. Could this be real? Would this feeling of being wanted, cared for, continue when the sun rose again the next morning?

The words jumped from her lips. "You would ask me such a thing? If it would please me?"

He tilted his head, his eyes thin, as if her question were so foreign he could not interpret it. "Of course. If we are to work together, should we not be equal partners and have equal say in such decisions?"

His response rendered her mute. She looked down. Never had a man, or any person besides Mother and Samuel, expressed to her their desire for such an open and honest relationship. Edwin had never discussed anything with her—had cared only for those things which furthered his interests. As did her father.

She peered at him. "Are you in earnest?"

"You do not like the idea." He pulled back. His words inquired more than accused.

"Nay." Anna opened her mouth in a softening laugh. "I do. 'Tis a fine idea." She looked away briefly. "You must forgive me. I find myself startled by the abundant generosity so freely offered."

"You are not alone in those feelings." He touched her arm. "Your generosity is...humbling indeed."

The way his eyes roamed her face, around her hair, and down to her lips made her mouth go dry. The intensity of his gaze became too much, and she turned toward the fire. "I fear you do me too great an honor." She found her courage and looked up. "As I said. We both have our reasons."

His gaze narrowed. "You wish not to return to England."

"That is true." She turned the ring around her finger, noting not for the first time, how easily her new husband had slipped it onto her hand. How perfectly it fit. "Pray do not think ill of me."

"Nay." His hand came under her chin, nudging her

face upward. But still she couldn't look at him, for fear it might undo her.

"Look at me." The gentle command in his silky baritone forced her eyes to meet his. Her breath caught when the clarity of his gentle blue eyes wove through hers.

"I would not think ill of you," he whispered. "I could not think ill of a woman who offered her life to a stranger as you have done." He lowered his hand, and the lack of his warm touch on her face left her wanting.

He continued. "No matter what transpires, know that I will give my best to you. This I promise."

Anna's vision clouded. She blinked to keep the mist from forming tears. *Lord, what kind of man have you given me?*

She swallowed, only speaking when she was sure her voice wouldn't waver. "I believe you, William." She stepped forward, reaching for his arm. "And I will do my best. Though I fear I am not...am not...as skilled as I should like to be. I will do my best to provide you a happy home."

"I thank you for that. And believe me, I have no expectations." William looked up and released a quick chuckle. "I am simply pleased you are not the kind of woman who is accustomed to fine linens and gowns, fancy meals at your beckoning, and servants to dress you. For I fear that is not the kind of life I can provide."

He motioned to the kitchen and she walked beside him, pressing her hands against her stomach to hide the glistening sweat on her palms. How little they knew of each other. She breathed out a long exhale. Perhaps she should tell him of her past?

She stopped mid-step. That was not the only thing needing to be spoken. But it was too late, was it not? Speaking the truth of her barren womb would destroy the only lovely moment her life had known. She could not taint it with such sorrow. Not now.

"Mrs. Fredericks?" William said, stopping a few paces in front of her. "Is there something else?"

She stalled, scrambling for a way to answer. Tilting her head, she offered a crooked smile. "You may call me Anna."

He stopped, his stare suddenly cold. He looked down, then toward the group in the kitchen before giving his attention back to her. The sudden darkness that shadowed his expression made Anna's chest tighten.

"I thank you." He looked down again then back at her, his mouth pressed so tight it seemed he couldn't speak at all, and he didn't. Only nodded.

Was it her name? She'd seen the shock in his eyes when she'd spoken it, his distress so apparent she'd almost feared he might refuse her altogether.

Whatever it was that pained him, whatever memory he carried, it was not hers to inquire. She buried the unpleasant sensation with a long, slow inhale. They both had secrets. But his, she believed, were far more painful than her own.

'Twas four days later when William entered the Watson's parlor declaring the Attick's' home officially their own. The lining of Anna's middle tickled with nerves. Their first days as husband and wife they'd spent at the Watson's as there had been nowhere else for them to go until William had secured the farm. Congratulations were exchanged and Eliza promised to visit the following day. If only she knew how Anna needed her help and guidance, but saying so would only prove her worthlessness. Though it was true as the sun was yellow, Anna still refused to admit such.

Gathering their few belongings had taken only a handful of minutes, and now, as Anna walked side by side with her husband, the quiet road enclosed them in a canyon of large trees, their heavy shadows blanketing the road while the brilliant blue sky shown bright above them.

She clutched her small bag to her chest and looked down at the ring on her finger. Would she ever become accustomed to the sight? Someday, perhaps. She glanced beside her. William carried a basket full of garments their friends had insisted they take, as well as the items every female needed for her toilette. As it had since the moment she arrived in Sandwich, Anna's spirit swelled with gratitude. Indeed she would find a way to give back to them the kindness they had offered. God only knew what it had done for her ailing heart.

William cleared his throat and jolted Anna away from the closet of her thoughts. "You are nervous."

"I am?" A sprite giggle bubbled from her, one she forced more than felt. She relaxed her grip around the bag. "Nay...well, I suppose I am...a little."

"If it is any comfort I am not in the least bit nervous."

She glanced up. Only the lines around his eyes shifted, and she tried to read his face, straining to understand his meaning. Had he been genuine or had he—

"I am only joking." His face bloomed.

Anna lowered her head and clutched the bag harder, releasing a laugh that took pressure from her chest. "I'm pleased to know I'm not a fool for feeling so."

"Perhaps we are both fools."

The statement was in turn tender and far too true. Perhaps they were both fools.

She voiced the questions that ate her from within. "How could we be given such a place? Complete strangers with not so much as a half-pence between us."

"Doctor Smith said he vouched for our characters. We will care for the property, work the land, and soon be able to provide the money necessary to purchase it."

The scowl on her face formed before she could stop it. She hadn't any idea how to work land. She pulled her lip between her teeth. At least William did. And perhaps if she kept close enough to him to study how he worked, her deficiencies would be less discernible.

Walking side by side in silence as they did, reminded her of the first days they'd spent together. And the first nights. Even now his nearness created the same delicious tingles that she'd tried to ignore, for why should she feel this way? She allowed herself a quick peek at him and her pulse struggled to find a regular rhythm. His dark blonde hair seemed to glow in the sunlight, his freshly shaven jaw.... She stopped mid-thought and squinted. Aye, those were scars on his face. Few and faint, but visible. She looked away before he could catch her staring. Small pox. Those tell-tale scars were not to be mistaken. When had he endured it? How had he survived?

The sounds of their shoes against the ground and occasional song of a bird were the only disturbance in the expansive silence, bringing her once again to the place her mind seemed far too willing to venture. Those nights beside him in the Watson's spare room...Anna blushed at the memory. Though they'd shared a bed, that was all they had done. He had not forced himself upon her. Did he not think it his right? Was he simply being chivalrous in allowing her time? Then again, considering they were not in their own home, perhaps he prepared to wait for tonight.

The thought fell so heavy from her mind she almost careened against the wall of it. *Tonight.*

William shifted the basket in his grasp, and blessedly stole her from the impassable thoughts. "When I surveyed the property yesterday, I found it more than fitting for our needs." He offered a quick look before keeping his sight on the road. "There's food aplenty. In fact, more than we can use. The vegetables are ready to harvest, and the apple trees are so laden the branches are near to touching the ground."

He stopped and pointed to a small home at the end of the road. Behind it, a barn rested beside an expansive garden.

Beautiful.

She felt his heated gaze upon her. "What do you think of it?" he asked.

Think? She could hardly place two thoughts together. It looked like something out of a storybook. Quaint, cozy. In fact, 'twas what she'd dreamed for herself as a child. Far different from the opulent life into which she'd been born. 'Twas in such a place she imagined happy families lived and worked side by side, where parents cared for one another and bore children who thrived on the love of mother and father.

Anna's hands shook when the truth arrested her hopes. Children would never be part of their future.

The air pled for an answer. She shifted her feet and inhaled, hiding the fears that bellowed within. "'Tis lovely. 'Tis perfect, really."

With a single nod, a testament that he approved of her answer, William started again. Anna could not.

Panic gripped her. She didn't know how to harvest or bake, cook or preserve. She hadn't any idea how to keep a house, to clean and launder. The only thing she could do was sew. A pitiful skill considering what necessities required proficiency. The realization of her lacking abilities seized until her legs cramped, holding her rigid, like a frightened animal in the road. She stared at the peaceful-looking home. Her home. Sweet, inviting and too dream-like to be described in words, and she, not worthy to sweep its floors. *What have I done?* She would fail him. Then he would regret his decision as powerfully as she regretted hers now.

William stopped a few paces ahead before coming back beside her. "Are you unwell? You look ashen."

Anna took a deep breath, but hadn't the strength to look at him when she answered. "I am well. Simply, overcome."

His hand came to her elbow and she looked up, the understanding in his eyes dispelling the dark misgivings in the corners of her spirit. "Overcome in a pleasing way, I hope."

She flung him a quick look, pulling her lips into a smile she prayed would bleed into her heart. The heat from the sun somehow gave her the strength she lacked as she forced her heavy legs to move again. This time he stayed beside her, matching her stride as they neared the welcoming cottage. It grew larger with every step forward. Its windows, like eyes upon a face, grew wider and brighter as if expressing its joy at their arrival.

"You are tired, no doubt." William made conversation more easily than she was able. "Do not feel the need to begin chores today. This is new to both of us and certainly some rest is in order."

He finished speaking just as they reached the door, and Anna gazed upward, looking over and around the house that would be hers—and his.

The red siding peeled in places, but the front step was swept clean and the air smelled of sun-kissed herbs.

William switched the basket to his other arm and reached around to open the door. "Welcome home, Mrs. Fredericks."

William clenched his chest so tight only the tiniest breath could squeeze through his lungs. His wife stood motionless at the threshold, peering into the house as if she were making a mental inventory of everything she could see without moving a muscle.

His hand around the woven basket gripped harder and a twig snapped. Was she waiting for him to carry her in? Wasn't that a tradition? Is that what her departed husband had done for her the day they married?

Just when he thought his chest would burst from lack of air, she stepped in and he released a silent breath. Either she hadn't expected it, or he'd waited too long. Thankfully, the moment had passed and he could move on to the next inevitable blunder.

As he would have expected, she walked straight to the kitchen fire, depositing her bag on the table that rested in the center of the room. Small as the house was, the kitchen, dining room, and parlor were all the same space, reminiscent of the dilapidated cabin they'd shared that first night. Only this place was clean, well kept, and larger. The loft space was sufficient for a full bedroom, complete with a fireplace directly above the one downstairs. Another room, most likely where the Mr. And Mrs. Attick had slept, rested behind a door adjacent to the fireplace on the main floor.

"Mrs. Fredericks?" He used the name he intended for her to temper his tongue to the taste of it, as well as allow her to get used to the sound. Saying her first name would take time.

She didn't look but went to the cabinet beside the fire, opening doors and drawers, inspecting the contents.

He tried again. "Mrs. Fredericks?"

Still, she didn't hear him.

He ground his teeth then spoke the name he loathed. "Anna."

She jolted and slammed the cupboard shut as if she'd done something she shouldn't. "Aye?" Her eyes were wide and her cheeks painted red.

He set the basket on the floor beside the table.

"Allow me to show you the property and then you may have all the time you need to discover what tools are available for your needs."

A quick, tight smile darted across her face before a solemn expression darkened the hue of her eyes. "Of course."

She hurried to him and he debated the wisdom of questioning the sudden change in countenance, but thought better of it. They were both nervous, scared, and walking on a bed of eggshells that would surely crack any moment, exposing the truth they'd concealed in a mess of foul reality. Neither of them were ready for that.

He followed the short hall to the back door and led her toward the garden. The scent of dirt, manure, and vegetables drifted on the air.

William peered over his shoulder. All the color that had moments ago dusted her cheeks was gone. She stared, mouth tight, at the garden. Her hands clutched her skirts. Worry niggled a hole through his gut. Perhaps all this, though more than provided for him, was insufficient in her eyes. He knew nothing of the home she'd had before. And although she'd been poor, perhaps she'd had more at her disposal.

A thought struck him across the face, pushing a question to view in his mind. Perhaps it was not the house or the garden...*perhaps it is me*. She had married someone she didn't love and therein lay the reason for the sudden changes in her color, the hard line of her mouth.

Her mouth.

In a single thought the anxieties dissolved. He allowed his vision to trace her as she walked around the garden. He'd never thought her lips could be so incomparably soft. The tiny breath she'd taken as he'd pressed his mouth against hers had sparked a sudden need to hold her tighter. Thankfully, he'd heeded greater wisdom and pulled away before the impression of her lips was forever branded on his memory.

"Is that water I hear?" she asked.

Grateful for her question, which distracted him from the precarious cliff he had perched himself on, he motioned sideways. "Aye, there's a creek to the right of us. I'll show you."

Her sculpted eyebrows rose, and she lifted her skirts as she stepped out of the beans and cabbages. "Is that where we shall fetch our water?"

The question stalled him. Had she not seen the well? He motioned behind them. "Nay, there's no need for that. The well will serve fine enough. Though of course the creek will be helpful for washing and laundering in the summer months."

Instantly, the color returned to her cheeks. "Oh, of course." She turned away, once again gripping her skirt.

The small trail at the back of the garden led down a path no more than thirty feet to the creek.

He stopped at the rocky edge and she beside him. The breeze toyed with the black strands of her hair that freed themselves from their pins. A fragrance he'd noticed since their wedding teased the air around him. He couldn't name the scent, but could detect the slightest lavender, fresh and inviting.

Bending down, he gave his hands something to do other than wish for the feeling of that black curl against his skin. He plucked a rock from the ground and stood, rubbing it in his fingers.

He followed her gaze to the water. "It doesn't race much now, but come spring it will be quite full."

A faint breath eased from her mouth, and her shoulders dropped. "'Tis a lovely place. So calming."

The sentiment took him aback, and he permitted his eyes to roam the scenery. Trees banked the river on the side where they stood, tall grasses on the other. No more than ten feet wide, the water belied a depth of three feet or more.

"On days when the water flows heavy, you should keep far from the center."

She faced him. "To where does it flow?"

"The ocean."

Nodding, she turned to the trail and started back. "How far away is the ocean?"

"A mile and a half."

The sun blazed against her hair, the black tendrils shimmering. He lengthened his stride, for standing beside her made it more difficult to study her profile and the perfect way her small ears framed her head. Any allowance he made in that arena—memorizing her—would only fashion problems he would later regret.

Once again at the garden, she lifted her chin as she gazed at the house. "'Tis a far better house than I could have asked for."

William stalled. Did she speak in truth? "I am pleased you approve."

She continued past, tossing him a blithe but reserved expression. "I should like to see more of the inside now, if I may."

"Of course."

After a quick tour of the one large room below stairs and the loft above, William stumbled upon the glaring absence of a second bed. He'd not noticed before, but now, the thought consumed him. After sleeping side by side and not having touched more than the lace of her sleeves, he began to wonder if he could endure sharing a bed—and nothing more. He shook his head. It made perfect sense that they hadn't *been* together, seeing as they'd had little privacy at the Watson's. But now that they had their own home, did she expect it? Certainly not.

The circle of questions made him dizzy. Physical attraction was no worry where he was concerned—he'd rarely met anyone so lovely—but such a union should be enjoyed only when both parties were wanting. Though they were clearly civil with one another, intimacy was a different realm entirely. He could never force such a thing upon their relationship.

Suddenly he couldn't feel his limbs. He needed space and a wealth of fresh air.

"I'll let you have a moment while I make sure we've enough wood for the fire."

He started for the door when she called for him.

"William?"

He stopped in the doorway, half of him wanting to return to the painful but bewitching thoughts, the other wanting nothing more than to run to higher ground. "Aye?"

"Do you think...do you think we will be safe here?"

Like a flood, every other worry escaped in his next breath, replaced by the sting of shame. These were the thoughts that consumed her. How selfish could he be?

Fighting the instant battle to stay by the door, or risk nearness by comforting her, he remained motionless. He ground his teeth. He should go to her, take her hand at least and speak the reassuring words at her side.

But he couldn't.

"We shall be," he said from the safety of the doorway. "I promise."

The answer brought a smile to her face and loosed the tight knot of her fingers that clutched her skirt, if only a little. "Thank you."

He nodded and escaped the house before warning drums could beat him into submission. He'd let the lie live.

For he knew, as well as he knew the sun would rise

in the morning, they would be found. It wasn't a matter of if—it was a matter of when.

Chapter Eight

"Captain Stockton?"

The call came from behind and Paul pivoted away from the soldier beside him to see a young errand boy hurrying toward him. His boyish cheeks were red from heat. Sweat dotted his forehead. "Major Stockton has asked for you, sir."

Paul returned the musket to the new recruit he'd been assisting and turned to the adolescent.

"I'm sorry?" He must have misheard. Ezra was traveling to Boston and not expected back within the month. "You must have me mistaken with someone else."

"Forgive me, sir, but I know exactly who you are, and who your father is." The boy, far more confident than Paul had been at his age, motioned behind him. "He's waiting in the drawing room of the officer's quarters."

Blast it. A low, guttural groan rumbled in Paul's throat. "I'll be there presently."

The boy hustled away, wiping his sleeve against his hairline as he rounded the corner. Paul leaned his head back and gazed heavenward. Of all the times to be discovered. When Richards had requested he stay on another two weeks to train the new arrivals from England, he'd been only too pleased to assist him and procrastinate his transport to Virginia. Paul rested his palm against the sword at his side and intentionally slowed his step. The heat in his chest matched the heat of the early-autumn sun. If only he'd had a few more days. The woman he'd hired to carry the message had surely made it to Barrik by now. He need only wait a few days longer.

Paul swore under his breath as he turned the knob and went into the house. To the right, the drawing room—and his fate. The boy looked in the direction of the open door and motioned with his eyes for Paul to enter. His spine went rigid as it did every time he was forced to encounter the man whose name he carried.

"Why are you not in Williamsburg?" Stockton whirled as Paul crossed the shadow of the doorway. Venom seeped from his father's eyes. "Close the door."

Paul obeyed then stood at attention. His newly cleaned coat and freshly polished scabbard dimmed in the light of Ezra's scrutiny. "I can see you've taken pains to clean yourself up. Did you think it would soften my anger when I discovered your infraction?"

"You always told me a soldier must look the part as well as play it, did you not?"

Stuffing his pipe, Ezra refused to look up, that ever-present undercurrent of disgust sitting heavy in his voice. "Pray, tell me why you would do something so foolish as to go against my orders?"

Face forward, Paul didn't measure the words before he spoke them. "I thought you were supposed to be in Boston."

Ezra looked up, his face red. "My affairs are none of your concern." He stared, his expression bleeding hate. "Why are you not on your way to Virginia?"

Paul straightened. How much longer must he be forced to answer for his actions when everyone above him needn't? "I stayed behind to help Richards. He requested that I assist in training the new men in his regiment and since my assignment was—"

"That was not for him to request and certainly not for you to accept!" Ezra slammed his pipe on the table. Slowly, the red color slipped from his cheeks and his tone evened. "My trip to Boston was altered when we discovered that the patriots are smuggling goods to the few civilians still inside the city." He stood and walked to the other side of his desk. "I've returned to prepare the regiment for deployment on the frigate *Braynwaithe* with the mission to block off all means of travel by ocean and bring to justice any and all who go against the wishes of the crown."

At last. A chance to prove himself. Paul stood taller. "When will we make ready?"

Ezra's eyes flashed black while his body remained motionless. "*We* will not make ready."

Paul scowled in question. "If the regiment is

preparing for—"

"*I* will make ready." Ezra rounded the desk, finger extended to Paul's shoulder. "Remove your epaulette."

No.

Paul's hand went to his sword and he stepped back. "You would not."

"Don't act the fool." Ezra's eye twitched. "You never learned, son. I hoped I would not have to do this, but I am forced to remove you from your position."

Reeling back from the sudden revolt in his gut, a bitter laugh burst from Paul's throat. "Never learned what? I have done what should have been done but you never had the—"

"It was never your place to resolve what must be done." The small lines around Ezra's mouth deepened as he once again pointed to the indication of Paul's station that decorated his coat. "Those that lead others into battle must be worthy of their rank."

"And I am not?"

Ezra inclined his head, hate in his eyes. "Your epaulette, Lieutenant."

"No." Paul barreled forward, pointing a rigid finger at his father's chest. "I've made one mistake. One! Yet you allow Donaldson to go free when he's betrayed the crown?"

"You're obsessed."

"Obsessed to prove that I am right and you are wrong."

"I will hear no more of this."

Rage, thick and hot, singed Paul from the inside and he refused to release his father from the heat of his gaze. "I will not be treated as lower when there are far greater *failures* than I and their situations were bought or granted by connections."

Ezra straightened, his broad shoulders not as intimidating as he may have hoped. "I wanted to grant you more, but you continually disobey and I cannot offer anyone something for which I believe they are unworthy."

"Unworthy?" Paul leaned into his words, inches from Ezra's face. "I have worked my way to this rank and I will work my way higher. I will prove to this army that I stand by my claim to uphold the crown no matter what you say about it!" He whirled and marched to the door. "I will do what needs to be done and I will not be stopped."

Ezra called from behind him. "If you pursue this course you are no longer my son!"

Paul stopped just as his fingers gripped the handle. His father meant to injure with those words, but instead they inspired. Gripping the handle hard enough to leave the prints of his hands, he spoke over his shoulder. "So be it."

Charging from the room, Paul marched from the house, his boots afire. Once in the street, he raced to the road that led out of town. Flinging a look behind him to be sure he wasn't followed, he ran to the safety of the trees.

In the shadows he yanked off his hat and unbuttoned his coat, eager to be rid of the vestiges of his misery. He dropped the sword and bayonet, his chest pumping and hands sweating. Here he would do it. Here he would leave behind all he'd known and prove to himself, if to none other, that he could do and *would* do the very thing no one believe him capable of.

If that woman couldn't find Barrik, so be it. The man didn't have his soul invested in the hunt like Paul did.

Donaldson was his alone to find, and his to bring to justice.

The occasional pop of a log burning in the fireplace was the only sound. Anna sat at the kitchen table on one side, William at the other, his elbows on his knees as he polished the grip of his pistol. The clock had long ago struck ten o'clock and the sky was draped in black, yet sleep was miles from her mind.

She twisted the ring on her finger over and over, staring at the fire and straining against the deafening silence. They'd managed to stay an easy distance from one another during the day, but after finishing the supper Kitty and Nathaniel had dropped by as a warming present for their new home, they'd had nothing else to do but be near one another and talk. And avoid the topic that Anna could only assume consumed both their minds, but which neither wished to discuss.

The marriage bed.

Should she say something? Casting a quick look to him, she endeavored to surmise the distant look on his stoic face. Was he waiting for her to announce she was ready to retire? If she did, would he assume she meant *more* than simply sleeping?

Nay. Silly notion.

Thick tendrils of reality wound around her neck. Then again, she had been married before—though not, she supposed, the kind of marriage William believed it had been—and perhaps thought she expected?

Her palms began to sweat, and she rubbed them against her stomach both to erase the wetness and calm the rise of butterflies. The fire popped again and her nerves popped with it. They'd shared a bed at the Watson's and though the awkwardness had thrived, their new arrangement launched her disquiet to unchartered seas.

The droning tick of the clock grew louder with each minute that passed. She spied in his direction, hoping she could skirt her eyes away before being seen, but it was too late. Their eyes met and she turned away, scrambling to gather her emotions that scattered like a set of children's marbles.

He sat back, placing his pistol on the table beside him. "I suppose we ought to retire." William's rich timbre spilled through the air and brought a warm prickle to her skin.

Anna gripped the arms of the chair and pushed to her feet, praying her legs would perform their duty. Once sure of her stability, she reached for her bag that rested on the table. "Aye, of course." Her voice came out high and pinched.

William stood as well and motioned to the bedchamber door at the side of the fireplace. She tried to remember how to walk. Oh, that was it—a simple *left right, left right*. So why did the elementary task take outrageous amounts of concentration?

At the door, William stopped her with a hand on her elbow. "Anna." His eyes were pointed and his tone deep.

She answered only with a tight smile to let him know she listened.

"I would have you know that I do not expect anything from you."

She tilted her head. Did he mean what she thought he did?

Either she uttered the question aloud, or her expression spoke for her, for he answered immediately. "Since we are still not more than strangers, though we've spoken vows, we need not...we don't..." He stopped and cleared his throat.

Relief flooded and Anna's once-liquid knees found their strength. She gripped her fingers around the top of her bag and squeezed, releasing the anxieties into the fabric. She offered a smile, unsure quite how to respond. "That sounds...fine."

"Though, I fear this is the only bed." He paused, his brow twitching ever so slight. "You are comfortable sharing, are you not?"

No. Yes.

Her mind bounced back and forth between her emotions. Nothing could be less comfortable. Being so close to him—someone so deathly handsome and gallant—she would hardly sleep. No different from the previous nights. Yet, for those same reasons—and because he was brave and genuine and kind—nothing could be more natural in the world than sharing a bed with such a man, when such a man was her husband.

She swallowed and nodded. "I am."

He made a slow bob of the head, his gaze seeming to gauge whether she spoke true. After a quick blink he pushed open the door and Anna entered. The lovely, vibrant quilt draped over the bed, two large pillows propped at the headboard. Other than the bed, a small chest of drawers, and a writing table the room was bare. No art on the walls, nor paper or paint.

"What do you think of it?" William entered behind her, bringing the light of the candle.

Once illuminated, the room cheered, and so did Anna, though pride brought to mind her bedchamber in England. The large feather bed and perfectly soft bed sheets, the large curtained windows and armoire for her gowns. She flicked away the memory and grounded herself in the present. What this simple home lacked in opulence, it made up for in things that mattered.

A folded paper at the head of the bed caught her attention and she went to retrieve it as William placed the candle on the writing table at the side of the bed.

She cracked the seal and read silently at first. "Oh, 'tis from the Watsons." She read aloud. "May this quilt be with you throughout your many years together. Thomas and Eliza."

Turning, she jumped at William's closeness. Had he been reading over her shoulder? Or had he simply wished to be close to her? She scolded herself for the last thought. But it couldn't be helped. The musky scent of him, the way he stared down, his eyes trailing her face, made every bit of her attention converge on him.

"I knew they'd been by," he said, stepping back and moving to the other side of the bed, "but I hadn't known they'd left a wedding gift." He sat and began removing his boots. "You will never find more genuine people."

Anna retreated a step, resting the note beside the candle. "I must agree I have never met people as kind as they."

He stood and removed his jacket and waistcoat, retiring them to the top drawer of the dresser. Anna's face heated at the sight of his muscles so visible under his shirt. The past nights he'd slept in shirt and breeches, for her comfort, she surmised. Would he allow himself more ease now?

Pulling back the quilt and sheet, he paused. "Would

you like help with your stays?"

The question socked the wind from her lungs. He gazed at her from across the room, his expression so unaffected he could easily have asked if she would blow out the candle. Though it had nearly made sleep impossible, she'd refused the urge to remove them since their wedding—excepting the times she'd washed—to keep her curves well reserved.

She licked her lips and tried to find the strength to loose her tongue from the top of her mouth so she could respond. "Nay, I thank you. I can manage."

William nodded and lowered to his knees beside the bed. Anna froze. Was he praying? She dared not move while he clasped his fingers and closed his eyes. After what seemed like a quarter of an hour, but in truth must have been only a minute or more, he rose and crawled into bed.

He rested his head on the pillow and offered her a wayward grin. "I'll give you some privacy."

With that he turned aside and Anna's lungs began to take in a bit more air, but still only a thread. Why did his nearness do such curious things to her?

She rested her bag on the writing table and began to unfasten her bodice and petticoat, careful not to make a sound. Ears strained, Anna struggled to hear whether William's breathing had grown soft and deep as in the nights past, indicating he slept. Aye, there it was, that slow in and out.

Fussing with the stays, she craned her arms behind

her and found the knot, untying with ease and pulling the lace through the first few holes. Eliza must have pulled them extra tight that morning. A quiet groan escaped her throat before she could stop it and she held her breath, turning to glance at the bed. Thank heaven. He still slept.

She rubbed her cramping shoulders before reaching back and trying again. The last few laces at the top eluded her, laughing, it seemed, with every failed attempt to loosen them. A light perspiration started on her brow, both from exertion and fear that he'd somehow awaken and come to her aid. But her heart betrayed her.

That is what you would like, is it not? She bantered back with a huff. *Not in the least.*

"Stuck are you?"

A high-pitched laugh popped from Anna's throat and her muscles seized. She glanced over her shoulder, her arms still wrenched behind her. She did her best to strangle the distress in her voice. "I've nearly got it."

A knowing half-smile bloomed on his face as he peeled back the quilt and rose from the bed. "Here, let me help you."

Her skin burned even before he stood behind her. And when he did, his nearness turned her blood to fire. Thank heaven for her linen chemise, so she needn't feel completely exposed. For even though her skin was mostly covered, she had never felt more bare.

A spray of gooseflesh covered her skin when his calloused fingers brushed the tender place between her shoulder blades. Her lungs started again, working so hard she knew he could hear. She commanded them to calm. They refused.

"How do I...?" William paused and he peered behind to see his hands hovering just over the laces she couldn't reach. He released a light laugh. "Is there a proper way to do it?"

A smile twitched at her lips. He was nervous? The notion eased her own anxieties whether or not 'twas true.

She forced a calm depth to her voice. "There is no proper way. However you do it will be fine."

He cleared his throat and once again she felt his fingers on her skin. "Simple enough."

Anna trained her vision on the candle's yellow flame and forced her pulse to ease.

"There," he said, stepping back, his low resonating tone circling her like silken ribbon. "I hope that's helpful."

She pressed the loosened garment to her chest and turned to speak over her shoulder. "Thank you."

He nodded and moved again to the bed, never once looking back as he at last retired.

Anna sat on the edge of the bed, soothing her frantic breath as one would a frightened child. She only needed a few moments. Once he slept she could easily crawl under the sheets and...

And what? Sleep beside him? She clamped her teeth to keep back the laugh that crowded in her throat.

She pulled the stays away from her chest and hid them under her petticoat, both reveling in and tensing at the sensation of her unencumbered breasts.

Flinging a look his direction, Anna waited. Aye. This time she was sure he slept.

Keeping her movements so slow she hardly moved, Anna lifted the covers and slipped her legs into the cold sheets, careful to keep her body a good distance from his. A feat to be sure, when the bed was scarcely large enough for the two of them.

She rested against the straw tick, surprised at its comfort. Though not the feathers she was accustomed to, 'twas fine in its own way. She settled her head against the pillow. Aye, very fine indeed.

Sleep tugged at her mind and she succumbed, allowing the luring black of the night to own her mind. She turned, rose up on one elbow and blew out the candle. Black shrouded the room.

"Good night, Anna."

Dear Lord. He was awake.

Lowering herself back to the pillow, she stared at the ceiling she couldn't see. "Good night, William."

And from that moment, she prayed for morning.

William woke to a loud clang and sprung from his pillow. Blinking the sleep that held to his eyes, he looked to the bed. Anna was gone. He squinted, looking to the east window. A sliver of orange against the horizon signaled the full rise of the sun was only moments away. He wiped his hands over his face, flung the covers from his legs and walked to the chest at the end of the bed to retrieve a fresh set of clothing. He should have been up long ago. He looked to the bed again then to the door when another clang sounded from the kitchen. Anna must be preparing the morning meal. A clash of metal followed by a faint response sounded through the wall.

William hurried on with his clothes and pulled a brush over his hair as a fleck of worry niggled his stomach. Was that smoke he smelled or just his imagination?

This time the voice he heard was louder.

"Cieli! Cosa ho fatto?" A growl-like huff followed and then another clang.

It sounded like Anna's voice, but that certainly wasn't English she spoke.

'Twas then the scent of burned food met his nose, and he rushed from the room to see a cloud of black billowing in the fireplace.

"Anna?"

She yelped and jumped to her feet beside the fire. "William!"

Her face, flecked with flour and red from heat, nudged a chuckle to his throat but he refused its exposure.

The smell stung again and he scowled in concern. "Is everything all right?"

She struck her hands back and forth against her apron and looked from him to the fire. A circle of biscuits, as black as the charred wood beside them, rested inside a casket of iron. "Oh, I uh...I'm just preparing your morning meal." Anna turned back to the embers and wiped her forearm against her head, mumbling something under her breath.

Now knowing she was well, and that only the food was charred, he allowed his gaze to study her round, worried eyes and the determined set of her mouth. Endearing that she would try so hard and be so obviously concerned with pleasing him. Far too entertaining to seek the moment's premature end, William stared a moment longer. "May I be of help?"

Kneeling, she used a folded cloth to remove the skillet from the fire and rested it on the brick beside the embers. She shot a quick glance over her shoulder. "Nay, I thank you." She poked at the food then jumped back, and flicked her finger before sticking it in her mouth. She didn't look up. "It appears I have burned these, but I will make more."

William surveyed the table. Flour everywhere. Egg shells in a bowl next to a thick lump of what looked like batter. "You gathered eggs this morning."

"Aye," she said, still fussing with the black biscuits. "But I could only fetch three before the rooster shooed me away."

He pressed his lips between his teeth to bite back the laugh that inched ever higher. She acted as if she'd never done a minute of work in her life. Simply nerves perhaps. He understood that all too well and standing there wouldn't help matters. He moved to the door. "Allow me to fetch you some more water. I'll return in a moment."

Anna looked up only long enough for him to see a flash of gratitude and distress. She nodded quickly then stood and rested the now empty skillet on the table.

Plucking the bucket from the floor, William hurried to the back door as another stream of foreign words drifted to his ears, though their whispered tone made him believe she didn't think he could hear them.

"Perché hai dovuto bruciare?"

A soothing melody, the words drifted like a song, despite the frustrating nature of the phrase. Not that he understood it, but her tone was unmistakable. Where had a poor English woman learned Italian? He returned moments later, bucket full, to find smoke once again chasing up the chimney. Anna bunched her apron and removed the pitiful meal from the embers, resting it on the brick. She lowered her head and rested it against her knee.

"I don't care for biscuits anyway."

She spun and dotted her eyes, but couldn't mask the red that rimmed them. His heart tipped. She was crying. Strands of black hair frayed from underneath her cap and more flour dotted her nose and forehead. Turning away, she rose to her feet, and went to the table brushing her apron across her face to clean away the white.

"Forgive me." She looked behind her. "I have yet to familiarize myself with this fire."

How was this fire different from any other?

The color in her face deepened to an even darker crimson and she avoided his gaze. "But I did boil you a bit of salt pork."

Boiled the salt pork? He looked at her then to the pot he'd failed to notice at the back corner of the fireplace. Salt pork must be soaked of course, but boiled? He ignored the thought and neared, hoping his smile would massage the worry from her features. "Aye, of course. Thank you."

She released a quiet sigh and motioned to the table. A charger was set out, a mug and a fork. He sent her a quick glance. Anna's gentle face beamed, her eyes crowned with hope as if she were a child waiting for praise. His heart turned to mush. How desperately she wanted to please him. Why? The reason didn't matter, only that she did. And the mere thought nourished a seed of joy he hadn't known was planted.

He glanced down at the watery mass of grayish-pink already on the plate and kept the words flowing to avoid thinking what knocked at his mind. He took the fork in hand. "I shall be in the garden most of the day."

Taking his fork to the meat, he stripped off a piece and put it in his mouth. Instantly his reflexes gagged, forcing him to spit it back onto the plate. He reached for the mug and cleaned his palate of the writhing intensity.

"Is something wrong?" Anna's woeful tone forced William to look up. Straightway he regretted what he'd done. Her dainty eyebrows pinched up in the middle as tears gathered in her eyes.

"Nay." William braced himself for what he must do. How could he not when her pleading expression slayed every need but to bring a smile to her face. "I should have allowed another moment for it to cool."

"Oh," she breathed, a portion of concern easing away from her eyes—eyes that would not move from him.

With such an audience, William summoned what pitiful theatrics he could and took another fork-full, putting it to his tongue. Her gaze didn't waver, but grew more intense when he closed his lips around the fork. The same gag lurched, but he kept his teeth moving, offering a hum of pleasure as he chewed the salty mass. Anna's shoulder's relaxed as if she'd been holding her breath, and a look of relief consumed her sweet face.

"I'm so pleased you like it."

After chewing only as much as necessary, William nodded his answer and reached for his mug once more, flooding his throat with liquid.

He set the mug down and met his wife's gentle gaze, praying the truth of his words would wipe the tears from her eyes. "I appreciate your efforts more than I can say, Anna."

She sighed. "I wish there was more for you, but I'll have something prepared for mid-day. I promise."

"The more you become familiar with this house the easier it will be. The same could be said for myself as well." He pushed up from the table. "We have much with which to grow accustomed." He scoffed inwardly at the irony of such a statement. A soldier posing as a farmer? He knew nothing of sowing or harvesting. God help them.

Anna motioned to his plate, her expression nipped with worry. "But you've hardly eaten. One bite will not sustain you."

He reached for his hat and placed it on his head as he started for the door. "Not to worry." Offering her a kind smile and bob of the head, he winked. "I'll be fine."

The lines of concern around her eyes didn't ease as he'd hoped, but her lips bowed at the ends. She didn't speak but nodded quickly before spinning away.

He stood in the open doorway, one foot in and one out. Should he say something? Had there been more tears in her eyes or had he imagined it? He shook his head and went out, closing the door behind him. They were both overwhelmed, struggling to find normality in a life so new and foreign.

After two steps toward the garden he halted, his advance arrested by the mounds of dirt and rows of plants. Tangles of vines and vegetation in various shades and colors taunted him as if they knew he was as unskilled in a garden as Anna apparently was in the kitchen. He looked behind him, allowing that chuckle to finally break free. Kind woman. She'd looked devastated that he hadn't eaten more, but he couldn't have forced another bite no matter how hungry he was.

He looked back at the garden and his own faults washed over him anew. He lowered his head, rubbing his finger and thumb against his eyes. What had he done? Marriage? Had that really been the wisest choice?

It had seemed so at the time. Without bidding, Anna's coaxing smile, her courage and determination, rallied what remained of his own. They'd shared a bed. Not for the first time of course, but for the first time alone. The memory of last night consumed him as the rest of the bright world dimmed. Her petite body, so warm and perfectly curved had rested only inches from his. He hadn't wished for her, not like that—at least not *quite* like that. Did she expect it perhaps? Was that not what a husband *should* do?

He finished the short distance to the garden and lowered to his haunches, fingering the green stalks in his hands to determine what vegetable lurked beneath the soil. Ah. Carrots. Exactly which was a vegetable and which was a weed quickly became apparent, and he went to work, his mind laboring as much as his body.

If she could marry a stranger, accept life in a new land with no thought of ever going back, then certainly he could do the same. William leaned back against his heels and trailed his gaze over the land. It would not be the same as soldiering. His chest ached at the thought. He was made for firing a musket, for taking orders and issuing them, for determining and executing plans of action. He was made for battle.

An audible sigh, deep and cleansing, pressed out of his chest and he stared once again at the weeds. He could only hope he'd find farming more simple than he believed, for if breakfast was any indication, he might need to take up cooking as well. Poor, sweet Anna. *Anna.* Her name became easier to speak with every hour it seemed.

A grin pulled his mouth upward. If eating plain meals was the darkest of his worries where she was concerned, then he was a lucky man indeed.

Chapter Nine

Hands dusted in soil, William leaned back on his knees and used his sleeve to wipe his forehead as he rested between the beans and cabbages. The sun bore down heavy. And he thought the daily drills he'd endured as a soldier were fatiguing. A week of farming, and already he wanted to give up and join the rebels in Boston. He tinkered with the idea for the hundredth time. Though now, as every time before, a dissatisfying pit welled in his middle. It wasn't right for him. Not now. Why, he didn't know. But he'd learned never to distrust the whisperings of the Spirit.

He peered behind him at the house, wondering if Anna was at the fire. Kitty's kind assistance over the past few days had helped his wife some, but still his belly ached for a hearty meal. With a sigh he turned back to the garden, and gripping hard against a large cabbage, he yanked it free. If he could only care for the garden well enough he might be able to give Anna more help. A laugh escaped his chest. He'd never seen anyone boil bacon—just as she'd done with the salt pork—but she had. As he pondered the possibility of another supper of hard biscuits and bland beans, his stomach gurgled. How had she sustained her previous husband on such meals? As William reached for another cabbage, his mind toyed with the memory of her gentle nature, soft smile, and the way she refused to let something difficult conquer her spirit. It must have been her nature that sustained her first love. And that was likely enough.

"William!"

Thomas's familiar voice called and William turned. The length of his stride and hardness in his eyes brought William to his feet. He brushed his hands against his breeches and rushed to meet his friend.

"What's happened?"

Thomas's red face and hard mouth made William's shoulders tighten.

"Redcoats were spotted three miles south of here." The way Thomas seethed the message with fire behind his breath, 'twas clear there was more that needed telling. But William feared he already knew.

"How many?" William's fingers ached for a weapon.

Thomas looked behind him then to the house as if to be sure they were alone. "Three hundred."

"Three hundred!" An entire regiment? Impossible.

"That is the report. We will need to see for ourselves if we are to know for certain."

"I will come with you."

Thomas raised an eyebrow. "That's not exactly staying out of harm's way."

"I refuse to hide like a coward." Instinctively William reached for the sword at his side and ground his teeth when he felt nothing. Curse this new identity.

"I tell you to warn you." Thomas glanced around again. "Staying safe so you are not wrongly hanged is not cowardice."

"I am a soldier, Thomas," William said. "Now that I am free to fight for the right cause, I will do so with all that is in my power. I am not afraid."

A rustle along the path hushed their conversation before Nathaniel appeared. He nodded when he reached them, out of breath as though he'd run all the way. "You've told him?"

Thomas dipped his chin. "He'd like to take a look himself."

Nathaniel's eyes rounded. "Is that so?" A smile widened his face. "I always knew I liked you."

"Am I the only one thinking sense?" Frustration latched to Thomas's expression. "I came here to warn him, just as I remember you did for me once, need I remind you?" His expression narrowed. "You would encourage him to do something that could put him in further danger? Has no one thought of his wife?"

His wife. William pivoted to look toward the house. He had forgotten. Not about having a wife, but how it might affect her if in fact he was caught. He scowled, putting together a dozen reasons why doing nothing could be equally as dangerous as discovering why such a number of soldiers had gathered so close to town.

"Your point is well taken, Thomas. However," William said, "if we do not discover what they aim to do here, we could all be in more danger than if we do nothing."

Nathaniel eyed them both, mouth pressed tight, eyes hard. The message in his expression was clear.

William's body sparked with energy. "Thomas?"

Grinning, Thomas started toward the wood, speaking over his shoulder. "Up for a bit of adventure?"

William followed. "Always."

"William?"

William's heart lurched and he jerked to a halt at the sound of the lilting voice behind him. He spun to see Anna in the doorway, a towel in her hands. The question in her wide eyes pricked the feelings of duty that grew each day that passed. Should he go? Nay, 'twas not a matter of whether he should go. He had to. Having been on the other side, he knew more than any of them what kind of danger awaited.

Nathaniel and Thomas touched their hats in greeting to Anna.

William jogged forward to meet her by the doorway. "Thomas and Nathaniel have some business they wish to discuss in town." He silently groaned at the ridiculous sound of such an excuse. Business? "I won't be long."

Her delicate throat shifted and her gaze dropped. He reached for her arm, knowing the fears that hovered always near the surface. "Stay to the house and you will be safe."

She looked up, and the lack of light in her eyes bit into his conscience. She licked her lips and turned toward the house. "I have plenty to keep me busy here." One hand on the door, she stopped. "Will you be home for supper?"

"Long before."

Her gaze brushed over him and like a breath of air to aching lungs he savored it, however short it was. And with that, she was inside once again.

Hastening to his companions, he clapped them both on the back. "The redcoats are waiting."

The inlet hummed as soldiers worked like red ants, trudging back and forth along the sand and between the trees. On his stomach, William's pulse exploded as he spied them through the dry, grassy reeds. He stared at the mumbling crowd as they relieved the small boats of their supplies not fifty feet away.

"That's an entire regiment." He turned to Thomas, also on his stomach, whispering through clenched teeth. "Did your source say anything else—why they are here, how long they will stay?"

From the other side of William, Nathaniel whispered as he stared forward. "That is all we know."

Mind reeling, William combed through the files of his memory. What intelligences had he heard before being cut from the ranks? He bit his cheek. Those two days in shackles he'd heard more about the siege in Boston, but that was all.

"Well?" Thomas said.

William shook his head at the puzzle. "They don't have any cannon, but they've plenty of munitions."

"Can you recognize anyone?" Nathaniel asked the question for the third time.

Squinting, William trailed his vision over the soldiers as they moved about, setting up tents and starting campfires. He jerked forward, raising to his elbows.

Thomas touched his arm. "What is it?"

William leaned another inch forward, the hum of excitement seeping deeper into his chest. "Jimmy Brown." He lowered back down, speaking side to side. "Brown served under me from the time I was made Captain, but I've known him for even longer, almost three years." He looked up again and spoke more to himself. "I wonder what he's doing here?"

"Could you trust him?" Thomas asked.

"Trust him?"

Thomas tipped his head and the unspoken question sunk deep into William's muscles. He pinned his vision on Brown once again. Tall and thin, the man—who was no more than a boy of nineteen—had long wished to return home. Army life suited him like a pan suits a fish. William put his head down and rubbed his eyes. Could he trust him? Aye. In the years William had known him, Jimmy had performed every duty, met every task with exactness, despite any inclination he may have had otherwise. Nay. William could not think of anyone he would trust more. But any contact would put them both in grave danger...

A shout rose from the boat at the shore, and the three of them lay flat against the hard ground, the loamy scent of moist leaves making William's nose itch. He faced Nathaniel. For the first time he understood how Thomas and Nathaniel spoke so clearly with their expressions alone. The message in Nathaniel's eyes mirrored William's thoughts. He nodded slowly then shot Thomas a quick glance.

"I'll return shortly."

In a flash he was up, racing toward the far end of the camp, legs charging, lungs heaving. He slid against the base of a tree, keeping his back to the camp. His blood fired through his veins like a well-trained army. How to draw Brown from the group? He stole a glimpse behind the tree but spun back when a soldier glanced his way.

Then it came to him. This regiment wasn't likely to know him or to even be aware that the companies to the south had been searching for him. Spies crawled back and forth along these routes like spiders. How were they to know if he was a spy...or not? He looked again and blinked, unable to discern what he saw. After another moment, his cramping muscles eased a measure of their tension as Brown and another soldier made their way toward him, gathering sticks and griping about their menial chore.

Providence at work, no doubt. *Thank you, Lord.*

He clicked his tongue three times. Brown looked up, expression sharp. William clicked again and both soldiers dropped the sticks.

"What was that?" the other one asked, glancing to the side and behind.

William's pulse stormed as he peered out, snatching Brown's attention. He put a finger at his mouth and raised a surrendering hand with the other. "Shhh!"

Brown's entire frame jerked and his face rounded in shock. "What the devil?"

The soldier scowled. "What is it?"

Brown pointed to camp. "Go back and wait for me there."

Jogging to the tree where William still crouched, Brown looked like a boy who'd found his lost brother. "Captain Donaldson, where have you been?"

William tugged on Brown's arm and pulled him out of sight. He lowered his voice, indicating Brown should do the same. "Good to see you, Brown."

He threw a glance to William's arm. "How is your wound?" He shook his head and repeated the previous question with more strength. "Where have you been? We couldn't find you, though of course I was pleased we couldn't find you. I'm surprised to see you here. You know if they find you they'll hang you."

They'll do more than hang me. William paused, grinning inwardly at the speed of Brown's mouth. The boy had always been too young, too kind for the army. And certainly too trusting.

"'Tis true that I meant to be undiscovered. It was all a ruse." William formulated the plan only one word ahead of the next. "That's what we hoped everyone would think—what the colonists would think." He lowered his voice and cupped Brown's shoulder, the boy's eyes growing wide. "I'm a spy."

"A spy?" His expression crunched.

William glanced back at the regiment. "My mission is to gain the confidence of the patriots and learn of their plans. They do not suspect I am still a valiant man of the king." He kept his vision clipped on Brown. Would he believe him? The boy didn't flinch so William continued. "How many soldiers are here?"

"Three hundred."

As suspected.

He kept the strain behind his hard exterior. "Who is in command?"

"Randall." Brown looked toward camp then back again. "Stockton's on his way back to Boston from New York we hear. Expected sometime today. Rumor is, fifty men will remain at this camp, and so on every twenty miles to somewhere south of Boston, but no one knows for certain."

The news filled his muscles with blood. He asked the question that seared through his chest. "What is your mission here?"

Brown shrugged. "Billy says he heard we're

supposed to watch for smugglers. We aim to stop them, I suppose." Jimmy looked toward camp then back to William. "If we can snuff out the fervor in Boston, the rest of the colonies will follow suit."

Fully masked in his new character, William nodded, though within he laughed as loud as the sky is wide. Snuff it out or fan the flames?

"Brown?" Another soldier called from camp.

William swung back and pressed against the tree.

"What is it?" Brown jumped up and pulled at his breeches.

The soldier neared and William stopped his lungs, his blood chilling in his veins.

Jimmy moved forward, away from the tree. "What do you want? Can't a man take a piss?"

"Apparently not." The soldier chuckled. "Randall wants three patrols to go looking about. You're one of the lucky ones."

Jimmy hurried his step and the other soldier followed. "We'd better get a move on then."

When the sound of their footsteps turned to whispers against the ground, William leapt from his spot and ran to where his friends waited. He lay flat on the ground between them, sucking in huge gasps of air.

Thomas pushed up. "Well?"

"They're about to send patrols to search the area." Panting, William spoke between breaths. "We need to leave now. I'll give details when we reach town."

Careful not to rise too quickly, they crawled several

yards on their bellies to a thick grove then bolted, refusing to slow the entire three miles.

William's lungs were on fire. When they neared the house he stopped and gripped his knees, explaining between exhales what he'd learned from Brown. "Who knows if they will come this way, but the chances sound likely." He stood straight. "Is it true? The smuggling?"

The men shared a quick look before Thomas answered. "We heard of the movement ourselves only two nights ago." He looked to Nathaniel. "But we plan to take part."

With such boldness in his answer William could do nothing but smile. "I'm pleased to hear it."

"I am pleased that you are pleased." Nathaniel removed his hat and wiped his forehead. "I shall warn the others on the committee and call a meeting to decide what is to be done to secure the smuggling effort." He started toward town. "I shall require your help, Thomas."

Thomas nodded and followed.

William stepped after them. "You've an army in Sandwich?"

Nathaniel halted. "Our militia is small, but we are fearless." He turned, a light in his eye. "I shall return here tonight and give you what information I have." At William's nod he and Thomas started toward town.

"William?"

Anna.

He whirled, dread robbing him any clarity of thought. The soldiers could come here. And if they did...

"I thought I heard your voice." Her head cocked to the side. "Are you unwell?

William shook his head and pulled back his shoulders, constructing a barrier that would conceal the war that waged inside of him. "I am well, I thank you."

He glanced back the way he'd come then looked up at the sky, thankful for the way it was just starting to darken. If any soldiers came to town they would likely check the farm and if they found him... *Blast*. He had to take her somewhere. Staying at the house would be too dangerous. They'd have to find a place the soldiers would be less likely to look.

A thought burst to light and he started for the house. "Shall I help you carry the wash to the creek?"

Her shoulders dropped. "Now?"

He jogged the rest of the way to the house, feeling as if the soldiers were at the very edge of the wood though he knew such a thing was improbable. He cupped her elbow. "We must hurry. We have little daylight left."

Whether she sensed the urgency he strained to disguise, he couldn't tell. She dashed to the kitchen and grabbed the laden basket, but he plucked it from her arms. "Follow me."

After a few paces he glanced to Anna before

focusing on the trail, with her only steps behind. He'd have to find a reason to stay longer at the creek than they had clothes to launder. What if he was found? He flung a look to Anna, praying that his earlier belief that the soldiers of this regiment wouldn't know him was well founded. But if they did know him, and he were apprehended, would they take her as well?

He flicked away the rancid thoughts and hurried his pace toward the creek.

Nay, he would not think it. In time they would be home and enjoying a meal of boiled meat and burnt biscuits. Suddenly, such a meal had never sounded so inviting.

Anna tried to keep her eyes ahead, not on her husband's broad shoulders or how his biceps strained the linen fabric of his shirt as he hefted the laden basket. The light evening breeze carried scents of late-blooming foliage mixed with salt air from the sea. Inhaling, she focused on that.

She raised her eyes to the sky. Was William really so concerned about the washing? It would be dark soon. She opened her mouth to voice the question but snapped it shut again. Nay, better not to ask when he'd so willingly offered to assist in a woman's chore. The other men she'd known in her life would have scoffed at the mere thought of participating in such a task.

Well, perhaps not Samuel.

A niggling worry pierced her stomach. She shook her hands at her sides to release the building nerves. She'd never washed a thing in her life. Seen it performed, aye, but never participated and certainly never watched from beginning to end. Did she need soap? How would they dry the clothing? She'd nearly attempted the task days ago, but her worries over cooking had consumed every thought, every moment.

Anna bunched her skirts in her hands. Why must he be so kind? It would have been better to learn such a chore on her own rather than shame herself with an exhibition of her failings. He'd notice first hand her lack of domesticity and solidify any regret he may have in marrying her, if her humiliating meals had not already done so.

"Did anyone come by the house this afternoon?"

Anna almost tripped over the commanding sound of his voice.

She cleared her throat. "Nay. No one."

He glanced over his shoulder, a slight dip in his chin. "You are certain?"

"Aye."

He stopped so sharp Anna nearly careened into him. "We're here."

Stooping, he lowered the basket and glanced the way they'd come, then to the right and left. He scowled. "We should begin. The sun won't be up much longer."

Anna's stomach rose to her throat, but she forced a smile and took a shirt from the basket. Whatever he did, she would do. That wouldn't give too much away, would it?

He grabbed a pair of breeches and stepped to the edge of the water. He crouched and soaked the pants before rubbing the fabric together in his hands. Anna neared and lowered beside him, doing the same with a shirt she'd grabbed. Relief coated away the tension in her muscles. How had she imagined it to be so difficult?

After a minute of silence, she peeked at him briefly, allowing her mind to enjoy more pleasant things, such as trying to decipher if his hair was always so light or only happened to be so in the sunnier months.

He must have sensed her gaze and looked up. "No soap, but this should be sufficient."

"Of course." She allowed a quick smile to light her face before focusing on the wash in her hands, her cheeks burning. Had he known she was staring?

He remained mute, dipping the breeches fully under the water then ringing them out. He gave her a brisk look and stood to rest the cleaned breeches over a nearby branch. His deep voice floated like a leaf on the water. "There is something I've been wanting to speak with you about."

Anna's stomach churned. "Oh?"

He walked over and snatched another article from the basket then returned to the water. His gaze narrowed before again turning his attention to the wash. "As you mentioned before, we both had our reasons for marrying."

"True."

Too nervous to focus on what he might say, Anna trained her thoughts on the wash, her tongue against her teeth. She attempted to wring out the sopping shirt for a third time. With a long exhale, she rested it over her knee and massaged her aching fingers until she realized he'd stopped talking and was looking directly at her.

His mouth tilted up in a half-smile that made her insides flip. He motioned to her. "Let me."

She froze. He extended his hand and wiggled his fingers as a boyish smile lifted his mouth. She offered it, embarrassment singeing her face.

With one large twist he wrung it until it no longer dripped. But her shame did, falling from her like the very water on her hands. Was she really so incapable?

"There." He handed it back and his fingers brushed against hers, however briefly, igniting a heat in her hand that traveled up her arm. She turned and focused her jumbled energy on opening the fabric and laying it over the nearest branch. The quicker they finished, the quicker Anna could find her place of solitude in front of the fire with needle and thread in her hands.

"Anna?"

She spun round. "Aye." He'd taken to using her first name most of the time now, though 'twas still as if he disliked the taste of it.

He stood and flapped the newly rung-out sheet then placed it over the next available branch. Nearing, he released a soft sigh. "We both have secrets, that much is clear."

She swallowed and the muscles in her neck tensed. His eyes roamed her face. Anna stared down at her hands as he continued. "There are some things you must know. This land is crawling with spies—redcoats and otherwise. Do not talk to anyone unless you trust them." His timbre dropped and carried such a weight it pulled her spirit with it.

She looked up, brow folded. "What do you mean?"

"We know someone is looking for you. And the fact that you're married doesn't mean they will let you stay if they find you." His blue eyes darkened, mirroring the evening sky. "If ever you feel threatened, the rifle is above the hearth, loaded and ready. Don't be afraid to use it."

Anna bit her lip and looked toward the creek. Did he really think it would come to that? She glanced at him again, startled by the sternness in the cut lines of his face.

He stepped closer, putting a hand on her arm. "I will do my best to keep you safe, but you must use caution."

"I understand."

"But there is more." He dropped his chin and his volume. "To others, speak about me as little as possible." He lowered his voice even more and Anna's skin shivered. "You are not the only one being hunted."

The revelation jarred to life a thousand terrifying questions that culminated in one. Who was he hiding from?

When she didn't respond, he must have felt the need to soften his statement. "Nothing to worry over, really. 'Tis simply best to keep to ourselves for a while, that is all. For both our sakes."

Anna nodded, a blade of relief cutting away only a sliver of the rising anxieties. "What should I do if—"

He sliced the air with his hand and cut off her words. His features hardened and his eyes searched. Chest pumping, he lunged for the path then stopped.

Quickly crouching, he raced back to her. "Someone's coming."

Her breath stalled. "What?"

Holding tight to her hand, he led her behind the trees to the edge of the creek, the cold water pulling on her skirts.

He grabbed her shoulders. "Whatever you do, do not come out from this spot until I come and get you."

She nodded, her tongue welded to the roof of her mouth. Her pulse thumped in her ears. How had he known someone was near? She hadn't heard a thing. She gripped the trunk of a tree and crouched as low as she could, almost kneeling on the slippery stones beneath her feet as she watched him go.

Minutes passed in clutching silence. How many, she

couldn't tell. Her muscles shivered both from fear and the cold water that swam past her legs. She glanced up, noting how the first few stars twinkled above and the full moon promised a blanket of milky light. Her feet tingled and her toes ached with the beginnings of numbness. Should she look for him? Perhaps something had happened? Her body gave a quick tremor. Where was he?

Just then, voices shot back and forth some paces away. More shivers shook her limbs. She strained to hear over the gurgling of the water when footsteps neared and halted.

Chapter Ten

The pistol William had hidden at his side burned against his ribs, begging to be relieved of the ball within. Silent, he widened his feet, the muscles of his back tensing with every intake of breath. Had they been followed, or were the soldiers discharging the duties he'd heard that soldier profess to Brown?

The sound of shuffling feet was quickly followed by the man that owned them.

A young soldier hurried to the water then stopped with a lurch when his eyes landed on William. His expression fell, his eyes wide as if he'd seen an apparition. He flung his weapon against his shoulder, the nose of the musket aimed at William's chest.

"State your business," the young soldier commanded.

The muzzle quivered. William allowed only the slightest tick of his eyebrow. Was the weapon too heavy for the lad or was he frightened?

William took a step forward, his biceps pulsing. "State yours." Playing the part of a patriot came easy. For truly, he was one. "What right have you to burst

So *rare* A GIFT

upon my property and raise your weapon?"

The boy's eyes widened, and he moved back before another wave of courage took its place and he lunged forward. "I..." He shook his head. "State your business!"

"I'm laundering, what does it look like?"

The boy tilted his head to peer past William where the basket rested at the water's edge. The fictitious courage in his face dropped, as did his weapon as he spied the few articles hanging on the bushes.

Eyes shifting, voice strained, the soldier took a step back. "Are you friendly to the crown?"

"Are you lost?" Answering with a question of his own might provide William with additional knowledge. He moved toward him like an animal stalking prey. "I've not seen any troops here for some time. So either you are lost or you are looking for trouble you'll be sorry you sought."

The soldier's throat shifted and he glanced left, once more raising his weapon. "Have you seen any suspicious activity? We're looking for smugglers."

There it was. The truth he'd been waiting for. A laugh stacked in William's chest. Was this one of the newly enlisted soldiers the crown had to depend upon? If that were the case, the British army was doomed indeed. "I cannot say I have."

He continued to press forward and the boy continued to step back. Fear rose in his eyes as William neared, and so did his weapon. Finally the boy stopped, speaking louder, the weapon still quivering. "How do I know you speak the truth?" Again he glanced left. "Are you alone?"

William's chest went solid, his eyes narrowing. The soldier kept looking in the direction of Anna. Had he seen her? Suspected? Impossible. She was too far from sight.

A sudden thought struck his head like the back of a pistol.

Perhaps the soldier wasn't alone...

"Get out." William's patience vanished. The last thing he wished was to be forced to show this inferior soldier all the ways he could best him.

Gripping the weapon tighter, the boy shifted his feet. "Answer me."

William's fingers twitched.

The boy looked left again and William lunged, snatching the weapon from his grasp and slamming the end of the weapon into his belly. Arms flailing, the boy fell to his back with a groan. He gripped his middle and scooted against the ground, eyes squinted and mouth contorted.

William neared and stood over him, tossing the weapon to the ground. "Get out. Now."

Scrambling to his feet, the boy lunged for the gun and darted back down the trail.

With the soldier now gone the angst he'd suppressed burst from its bounds and flooded William's legs. He ran into the water and hurried to the place where Anna waited.

She was gone.

Whirling around, William looked across the creek then back again. The water was too shallow for her to have been taken in a current...

He raced down stream a few more steps, his stomach twisting as the sound of voices reached him from the bank. He leapt through the trees and jerked to a stop.

Blinking, he tried to calm the wild pace of his pulse so he could comprehend the placid scene before him.

Anna stood on the bank, her skirts wet all the way to her waist, speaking with another man as easy as one might a friendly stranger in town. Only this man was neither a friend, nor a stranger. He was a soldier.

The redcoat saw him first and immediately replaced his hat and with a nod of his head, turned and walked out of sight.

Anna spun, the corners of her mouth lifting the moment her gaze landed on him. She rushed forward and reached out. "Are you all right?"

The concern in her lyrical voice soothed the dying panic another measure. "Are *you*?"

"I was so worried when you didn't come back right away..."

He gripped her shoulders, asking again, slower this time, and with a slight downturn of his head. "Are you all right?"

Her gaze darted back and forth between his eyes. "I am well. Why? Did something happen?"

"Something could have." William neither shifted his look nor altered his grip. "What did he say to you?" Their encounter had looked blessedly benign, but the motives could have been more than a simple search for smugglers. They could have been looking for him.

"He found me in the water where you'd left me and asked if I was in need of help." She stopped and looked to where the soldier had gone, then back. "I told him my husband and I were laundering and that I'd gone looking for a neckerchief that had floated away and that I'd slipped on a mossy rock."

Clever. William lowered his hands. "Is that all?"

"He helped me from the water and...and he was so polite I asked what he was doing here."

Brave. And foolish. "What did he say?"

"Nothing. He asked if I lived near—"

"You didn't tell him did you?"

The insistent question must have appalled her for she pulled her head back with a quick shake. "I said that I was from town, that is all."

William looked behind. He should allow her more credit. The sky, having been relieved of most of its light, reflected its deep blue in the gurgling stream. He stared at the water, sorting through the report. Her accent must have prompted the soldier's question. Distrust, the serpent of past experiences, slithered at William's feet. Was she telling the truth? Or was she hiding something?

He gave himself a much needed mental slap. He

could read one's eyes well enough and hers held no guile.

"His smile reminded me of my brother's."

Anna's soft-spoken words made William turn back to her. "You have a brother?"

She looked to her hands. "I had a brother." Her face lifted and her mouth tightened as if she wrestled with the thought of sharing more. "He was a soldier, too."

Such a revelation tore down his spine and suddenly the thousands of unknown facets of his new wife's past loomed like a coming storm. He brother had fought among the king's men? When? Was her father in uniform as well?

Quickly executing the thoughts before they could plunge too deep, William motioned forward, acknowledging her comment with only an understanding nod. "We should gather the laundry and return before the sun leaves us completely."

They did so in minutes and were once again within the safety of their home. William lit a candle, then another, granting a quaint glow to the darkness before securing a place for the wet clothes to dry. Anna retired to the bedchamber to change from her sopping clothes and returned to the parlor soon after. She draped her damp skirts over a chair in front of the fire. He swallowed. Against the firelight her figure looked far too pleasing. Round in all the right places, and slender in all the rest. The memories of the nights she'd slept beside him, that sweet, soft sound of her breath, the inviting scent of her hair. The warmth of her body just inches from his...

He licked his lips and forced himself to focus on the three remaining articles of wet clothes under his care. Theirs was not a traditional union and therefore certain things might never be. *Remember that, Henry.*

Once the clothes rested on the pegs by the door, William turned back, stopping silent as he did.

Bible in hand, Anna stood in front of the fire and opened the pages of the book she'd peered at every evening since their wedding. Her Bible. But this time, unlike the times before, she turned to the back and pulled a small likeness from the weathered pages, unaware that he watched her from the opposite side of the room. Fingers tender, eyes equally so, she stared as if her spirit communicated to the image gazing back at her. William's heart thudded to a stop. *Her first husband.*

With a quick shake of his head, William turned away and tried to reassemble the mad scramble of his thoughts, but he was losing. Though he and Anna had spoken vows, though she had offered her life to him, she still grieved the loss of the one she loved.

The sudden, befuddling urge to go to her, to take her in his arms and promise all would be well, so conquered his thinking he gripped the chair to keep from surrendering. She wouldn't want his comfort. She wanted what was lost to her, what she could never have.

He gripped his head and settled upon a thought that would take him back to the reality he craved. "Do not worry yourself over supper. I must speak with Nathaniel and Thomas about what has happened."

Anna looked up, worry inscribed into the lines of her forehead. "Oh? But I don't wish for you to be hungry—"

"I am well." Truthfully, moments ago he would have been hungry enough to eat whatever she boiled, but now his appetite was dead. Thank heaven there were far more pressing matters that required his attention.

"I understand." She angled away from him, but not before he caught the slight downturn of her mouth. The visible pain in her stance, the way she gripped the book in her hands made him ache to reach for her. Should he ask what pained her? Should he delay and speak with Nathaniel and Thomas in the morning? William shook his head. Nay, he should go and give her the quiet reverie she likely sought in which to relive the memories of happier times.

"I'll not be long," he said.

He started for the door, but the thread of her voice pulled him back. "Do you regret me?"

The question startled him and William swung back around. "Regret you?"

She waved a hand and spun away. "Forgive me, I shouldn't have spoken it."

Wisdom preached to him from the pulpit of his mind. He should nod and say he'd return later. But he did the opposite. Before he could stop himself he was at her side, aching to touch her.

She took a step away, but he grabbed her arm. "Speak to me."

"'Tis nothing."

Did she mean it? He looked to the fire in front of them as painful memories, like tar, waited for him to fall into them and bind him in their sticky black. Was Anna using him as *she* had done?

The yearning of compassion bowed to suspicion. This was too dangerous. He knew nothing about her. She could be every bit the Anna he had known, not the Anna that stood before him.

The sudden urge to flee itched his feet but vanished when she spoke. "I am indebted to you, William." She cast him a glance over her shoulder, and though fleeting, it was enough to show the hundred unspoken feelings of her soul. Though he couldn't name one.

"I have been so..." She rested the Bible on the table and her lips thinned as if she tried to discover the word that evaded her. Finally, she dropped her hands to her side with a sigh of defeat. "I shall improve. I shall do better, I promise."

Whatever safety the walls of suspicion had constructed moments before, he scaled them. Her voice spoke not only in words but in the drop of her tone. She knew her failings and they berated her. Did she think he would regret his decision simply because she was not natural in the kitchen?

Again she turned away, and he was powerless against the urge to reach for her. Brushing his fingers at her elbow, he turned her to face him. Though her body came nearer she kept her gaze to the fire.

Slowly, he curved his finger beneath her chin and nudged her face upward. Her crystalline eyes met his and instantly his folly assailed him. He should have left, should have resisted. For now he was captured.

Her breath halted and his mouth went dry. Flecks of firelight beamed in her pleading eyes as delicate shadows shaded her lips. Pulse charging, William succumbed to the luring memory of their wedding kiss. That one short touch of the lips at their exchange of vows flourished. His body ached to feel it again.

A quick inhale allowed for a clear thought. Perhaps speaking would quench the sudden burn. He tendered his words and lowered his volume until it blanketed the air between them. "There is much for both of us to learn. Everything is new now, but in time we will settle into our roles." Her expression softened and the fire in his chest grew almost too hot to contain. Speaking had only flamed the fire. He leaned toward her. "I do not regret you."

Anna's lips parted and her chest moved quicker. The pulse in her neck flicked wildly. "You do not?"

"Nay, I do not." He dipped forward until her breath dusted his mouth. Oh, how he wanted it. That gentle brush of skin to elicit the same tickle of pleasure as before. And why not? They were husband and wife.

He leaned nearer and Anna's quick intake of breath tempted him to comb his fingers through her hair and angle her head to more perfectly accept his kiss.

Her lashes fluttered closed and she tilted her head when the door burst open.

They had a visitor...

Anna gasped and spun toward the door. Mind struggling against the un-carved marble of what had almost been so beautiful, she forced her lungs to take in long sweeps of air. He'd nearly kissed her. And she'd nearly allowed it. But 'twas not that she had simply allowed him to draw near—she had hoped, nay, yearned for the touch of his mouth upon hers. William's gaze, as it had dropped to her mouth, implied the impending kiss would have been far more passionate than their first had been.

"Thomas," William called out, rushing to the door.

"Forgive me for intruding." Pale moonlight outlined Thomas's tall, strong frame. "Nathaniel asked me to come in his place and see if everything was well."

William offered Anna a glance before meeting Thomas in the center of the room. "You could have knocked."

A smile peeked though Thomas's expression. "I did. But it appears you were preoccupied."

Anna's face ignited. She crouched to the fire and feigned business with an empty soup pot. The humiliation! To be caught in such a way—her lips ready to accept him. If only the planks beneath her feet would open and she could hide beneath the cold wood.

'Tis not unseemly. You are married... Somehow, the thought didn't alleviate the rake of embarrassment. Of course, if he wished to have her it was his right and her obligation. Not that he'd asked for anything more than a kiss, but she knew where it could lead. And if he had followed through, with nothing more than a husbandly desire to father a child, then the painful realities of her barren womb would be all too apparent. Then, most assuredly, he would regret her in full.

"I must go, Anna," William said.

She darted to her feet and strangled the fear that rose within. "Aye." She could squeak out nothing more. Would he really leave her again? With soldiers about?

He must have read the unspoken question for his eyes went soft, reaching across the small room to circle her shoulders with calm. "I have no fear they will return. I would not leave you if I believed you to be in danger."

Ushering the quivers behind her back, like a mother to a fearful child, she gripped the confidence he offered and grinned her reply.

Thomas nodded and stepped out, but William stopped at the threshold, glancing over his broad shoulder as he placed his hat on his head. "Keep the door latched. I shall return before long."

He waited only a breath before shutting the door.

Anna rushed across the small room and pushed the latch, her hands trembling. She put her back against the door and looked to the ceiling. *Lord, what have I done?*

She'd known the man little more than a week and already she was opening her heart in a way that would surely cause her pain. Why she felt such a powerful need for his approval, she couldn't tell. Perhaps 'twas the debt she owed him for saving her from a life of misery. Perhaps 'twas her consuming fear that if he found her wanting, he would forsake their vows and leave her to count the days before she was discovered once more and returned to England.

"I will not go back," she whispered to the questioning shadows.

Releasing an audible breath, she pushed away from the door and went to the table. With a sigh, she pulled out a chair and sat, drawing the Bible to her. She thumbed through the pages, speaking to herself inwardly to put in place the jumble of emotions that yearned for rest.

Of course William wished to take his leave, however pressing the need was or not. Wouldn't any man? He felt as if she had lured him to her with her self-pitying words. *Do you regret me?* How could she have spoken it? The thought made her squirm. In a moment of weakness she'd let slip the very thoughts that had made their way to her tongue.

She dropped her head against the crook of her arm

and squeezed her eyes to shut out the unyielding thoughts. But in the dark of her clamped-shut eyes, the beguiling memory of William's hooded gaze and tender touch made her stomach do tantalizing flips. She'd never been looked at the way William had looked at her, with a kind of desire that was tender and pure, hungry and wanting. Never had anyone traced her face with their eyes or spoken in a way that twined around her limbs like ribbons of warmth from a crackling fire.

She sat up and looked to the door, frustrated at the way she wished he would stride back in, pull her to him, and bring to life the girlish fantasies that tickled her chest.

"Foolish, Anna," she whispered again.

With another huff of air, she opened to the last page of her Bible and retrieved Samuel's likeness. The flickering light from the fire made it seem as if his smile widened at the sight of her and she smiled in return. Images of the kind young soldier at the creek pricked her memory. How much he had looked like Samuel. That same crooked smile and those same gentle eyes.

"I shall try to be brave, as you were brave, Sam." She caressed the edge with her thumb. "William is a good man, I believe. But my fears are so crossed with my desires for a happy future that at times I cannot tell the difference between up and down."

She stared, listening, hoping somehow her brother would share a bit of wisdom she could cling to, anything to help her endure the hardships and heartaches that awaited. Instead of hope, 'twas loss that struck her. Samuel would never speak to her again, never wink and smile at her from across the table, never make her laugh when she was sad, never come to her defense when father wished upon her things she did not wish for herself.

The sudden longing for his story—the truth of it—bit into her lungs, fighting for space along with her breath. "I have not given up on you, Sam. Pray, do not give up on me."

Nathaniel was waiting by the fire when William and Thomas entered. With a quick look, William glanced around. His first time at the doctor's home matched how he would have pictured it. Well furnished, clean and warm. He removed his hat and cloak. Different from the Watson's home. More formal, but equally inviting.

"Good evening," Nathaniel said, motioning to the chair that faced the fire. "Forgive me for not being able to come myself, William. Anything to report?"

"Aye." Thomas pulled a Windsor chair from the gaming table and spoke to Nathaniel. "William was...occupied." He sat and turned to William. "If I had known as much, I would have left well enough alone."

Instant heat burst in William's chest as he occupied the nearest chair but he kept his exterior cool. "I don't know what you mean."

Nathaniel removed his arm from the mantel as a grin swooped up one side of his face. "You and Anna are becoming better acquainted?" He leaned his back against the wall next to the fireplace and crossed one ankle over the other. "I told you marriage would be good for you."

William answered on top of his words. "I do not recall you ever said that."

He shrugged with a quick tilt of the head. "If I didn't I should have."

"I quite agree with Nathaniel." Thomas rubbed his finger against the cleft in his chin. "You seem to be handling the transition with incredible ease for someone who insisted against it so emphatically at the beginning."

"You are all goodness and kindness, I'm sure." William couldn't seem to add enough sarcasm to his voice or his smile. He pulled his expression flat. "May we discuss the matters at hand?"

"With pleasure." Nathaniel's eyes flashed as if William had divulged something secretive.

Instead of challenging the implied look, William let it evaporate untouched.

"We've alerted the patriots in town to be on the lookout," Thomas said. "Though I haven't seen any soldiers, Nathaniel believes he did."

"Aye," Nathaniel answered. "From a distance, but 'twas only one of them and 'twas difficult to tell if he was a part of the regiment we saw or a remnant of the redcoats in town."

"I happened upon two of them."

Both men froze, their eyes stern.

William sat up in his chair and went on, grateful to be freed from the suffocating conversation of moments ago. "I took Anna to the creek to hopefully stay out of sight." He stopped, pondering the instability of his logic. It had seemed like the right thing to do at the time, but looking back... "We were discovered and one of them approached me."

"Were you threatened?" Thomas didn't move, save the small twitch in his jaw.

"Not with anything but a show of boyish bravado."

Nathaniel pushed away from the wall. "You put him in his place I trust."

"In a way of speaking." William allowed a small laugh from his chest, remembering the encounter and suddenly flooded with compassion for the incompetent young soldier.

"Did he say anything to you—anything that could help us?"

"Not much." William sighed. "But he did confirm that the information I was told in the wood is correct. They *are* looking for smugglers."

"You said there were two?" Thomas asked. "Where was the other?"

The shock of panic he'd felt at the creek trickled over him again. How fortunate they had been that the soldiers who had found them were not like Samuel and Paul, ruthless and cold. If Anna had been so much as touched, William would have blood on his hands.

"I'd hidden Anna among the trees, but she was found by the other soldier." Their faces went white, and William hurried to finish before their disquiet escalated. "She was well. They simply talked with one another." He paused, crinkling his forehead in thought. "It seems she had a brother in the army and this particular soldier reminded her of him."

Nathaniel and Thomas shared a quick glance, eyebrows high.

"So they simply left without a fuss?" Thomas shook his head. "Too simple. They will keep watch here, I'm sure of it."

Nathaniel stayed motionless, his arms crossed over his chest, tone somber as the fire cracked beside him. "They would be foolish to weaken their numbers by stationing soldiers all the way from here to Boston. Sixty miles? Nay, too taxing upon their forces. They have enough to worry them in Boston itself."

William scrunched his mouth and shook his head. "I wouldn't be so sure."

"Why is that?" Thomas asked.

"You under estimate their numbers. And their tenacity." William took a long inhale and breathed out slow. "I know all too well their desire for the complete submission of the colonists and I fear any and all measures will be taken to ensure that end."

Nathaniel looked down, his head wagging for a second before he looked up again. "You believe we will be surrounded by the king's men from now until..."

"I cannot say. But if they believe colonists are smuggling goods into the city, then they will not relent until the conspirators are apprehended."

This time, the look the other men exchanged made William's spine brace. He knew their thoughts as if they'd spoken them aloud.

William finally broke the deafening silence. "You do understand that if you join in this venture you will be risking your lives?"

Thomas answered first. "Aye. But our fellow patriots are risking just as much, if not more as they wait upon the hills around the city." He looked off, as if seeing in vision the thousands of men who even now collected at the borders around Boston. "I told you once that I felt God needed us in some other way than joining the ranks. Though I do know the time for us to fight alongside our brothers will come, I believe that our mission has now been revealed."

William glanced to Nathaniel whose pointed gaze was upon his friend.

"Boston was my home since I was a boy," Thomas continued. "And though I have now made Sandwich the home of my heart, I cannot forget what I owe to those who taught me the inestimable value of liberty." He rose from the chair, stopping in front of the fire. "How can I sit back and do nothing? They helped me, and now I must help them."

Struck speechless by the willing sacrifice of such a man, William stared, motionless. Thomas had been blackmailed and abused by the British Army—Samuel Martin had treated him as chattel. Of all men, Thomas should know well the risks he took by making such a choice, and yet his desire to help was so powerful he would place his new-found freedom in jeopardy? Did Eliza approve? Did she even know?

"What does your wife say to this decision?" The question was out before he could debate its sagacity.

Thomas glanced over his shoulder then turned back to the fire. "She believes, as I do, that the pursuit of liberty is worth every sacrifice. As for now we do not fight, but until then, we will do whatever else we can to aid this cause."

William turned to Nathaniel. "And Kitty?" When Nathaniel didn't answer right away, William continued. "Gentlemen, your wives could be widows at the end of this. If you are caught, they too could be considered traitors."

Back still against the wall, Nathaniel blinked, his mouth a hard line. "They understand the risks."

"And they accept them?"

The silent answer of fearless resolve resounded in the quiet room.

William numbed. So. This was the indomitable spirit of the American patriot. His heart broke and simultaneously mended far beyond the feeble metal it had been constructed of before. Despite their uncertain futures, these patriots—their very necks in the balance—would not retreat into the shadows. His spirit soared. Here, at long last, was the courageous brotherhood he longed to be counted amongst. Here, with the patriots, was the unyielding quest for purpose in which his soul yearned to unite. Freedom. 'Twas no longer their fight alone, but his as well.

He pushed up from his chair and went to the table where an oil lamp dusted its light over a tray of hasty puddings and sweet cakes. His empty belly snarled at the sight of food. He turned to Nathaniel and pointed at the table.

"Please." Nathaniel moved from his position and gestured to the plate. "Kitty always manages to have enough food in the house to feed a small hamlet."

William chuckled. "Kitty is welcome to continue her cooking lessons with Anna any time."

Thomas joined him at the table and took a pudding. "She isn't skilled in the kitchen?"

Finishing the bite in his mouth, William shrugged. "She tries, and I am grateful for her efforts." He put the rest of the sweet cake in his mouth and finished before speaking again. "Anna is ever kind and willing, but...she lacks such basic skills I am beginning to wonder if she was ever really a housewife at all."

"You fear she was not forthcoming?" Nathaniel neared from behind and snatched a cake from the tray.

William turned with a slight cant of the head. He

tried to gather his thoughts in a way that wouldn't produce an ill picture of his wife, but there were actions and manners he'd noticed that made him wonder. "There are certain behaviors she exhibits that do not align with those of a simple housewife."

Thomas dotted his mouth with a cloth and took his seat once more. "Such as?"

"She—" William halted, second guessing the path upon which he prepared to tread. 'Twas precarious territory for him to explore, but his need for communication outweighed the risks. "Though willing to work, her attempts suggest she has never done a basic or menial chore in all her life."

"She was married before, was she not?" Nathaniel joined them, brow furrowed. "Since you didn't answer me before, I'll ask again. Do you fear she was untruthful?"

"I cannot say." A harsh breath passed his teeth. "Our meals have been barely edible and she...she tries *too* hard, as if she fears I will discover something she wishes to hide."

"Then she has misrepresented herself," Thomas said.

"Aye, but not in the way you think." Though the truth settled into the fissures of his broken understanding, still, William stood his resolve. "We both have secrets. And although she may not have been a woman skilled in keeping a house, I know she was married and that she deeply loved her husband."

The words soured his mouth. So much so, he refused to speak again. The memory of Anna's face, soft and draped in longing as she stared at the picture from her Bible, made his chest throb. But why he cared, he couldn't surmise. They had wed only a week before. There was time yet to learn the ways of her heart.

Then again, perhaps never learning such things would keep his own feelings locked behind the years of experience that had taught him to keep it from the warmth of feminine affection. That kind of thing only brought ruin upon everyone.

"'Tis a blessing that God gave you a woman who knows what it is to love." Nathaniel offered a soft smile. "In time, she will see the truth of you and offer that love again."

William's chest squeezed like the dripping laundry he'd cleaned only hours ago. "I do not ask that she love me, only that we remain equal partners. God knows I am hardly a man without haunting phantoms."

Silence enveloped them until Nathaniel spoke. "A woman would be hard pressed to find a man more worthy than you, Henry."

The sound of his real name made William stall. Worthy? Nay. Not when he'd accepted a new name and changed his life to cover a multitude of hazards that could endanger them both, should he be discovered. The reality he'd ignored since his wedding day bore down on him like a winter storm. His entire past, every bit of him he had to keep secret. How could he ever really be worthy of anything when the truth circled above him like a vulture, ready to pick him apart at the demise of his charade.

"But the two of you have kissed. That should reveal something of how she feels." Thomas's statement smacked William back to the moment.

Like a boy in school who'd been caught daydreaming, William stumbled for a reply. "Well...no...we were—"

"Come now, you can't tell me you haven't kissed her yet?" Nathaniel's sharp laugh bit the air. He shook his head, a look of disapproval in his face. "For shame, *William*."

Thomas waved his hand in the air. "Nay, I saw you when I came in, you were—"

"We were about to if you hadn't burst in the room." The pent-up frustration shot like steam from a kettle. "And may we cease this conversation? I'd rather not discuss my marital struggles with men who clearly have little more experience than I."

Nathaniel nodded, his hands in his pockets. "I understand." His solemn look lasted only a second. "But rest assured we will be asking until we are sure you have made her your wife in all respects."

He wouldn't.

The smile on his face said he would.

William bristled. "Don't do it, Nathaniel."

"I should not." Nathaniel chuckled as he spoke. "But the look of puerile embarrassment on your face when I do mention it is worth every moment I risk feeling your fist against my jaw."

That comment signaled the end of their evening. William gave a quick nod then spun toward the door.

Thomas was right behind him, his hand on his shoulder. He whispered in William's ear. "Now would be a good time to return home and finish where you were so *rudely* interrupted. She cares for you, that much is obvious."

William whirled. Thomas fought a smile that urged for release, one his eyes were all too willing to share.

Battling the irritation that scratched his stomach, William snatched his hat and flung open the door.

He didn't even turn around to see their looks of triumph. He could feel them burning into his back as he walked from the house. They'd switched conversations so easily it made his head spin. One moment they were discussing matters of supreme importance and the next, prodding him toward matrimonial bliss as if it were the most natural transition. The cool evening air soothed his burning skin. Had they so little regard for their own safety that they would push aside their pressing matters to discuss what had happened—or what hadn't happened—with Anna?

"William!" Nathaniel called.

He stopped but didn't turn until his friend was at his side. William answered with lifted eyebrows only.

Nathaniel lowered his voice. "We'll be making our

first exchange tomorrow night."

"Where?"

Nathaniel's eyes darkened. "You are not to be part of this."

"You knew I would want to help or you wouldn't have spoken to me."

Turning back to Thomas, Nathaniel gave a slow nod and a smile opened Thomas's face before he slipped back into the house.

He lowered his voice to a thin whisper as if the leaves on the trees were keeping watch. "We will hold you back from taking part in the exchanges. For now. We will need you later, should the rest of us be suspected. 'Tis not a matter of if, but when."

William nodded, a sudden buzz shooting through his limbs. "I will be ready at a moment's notice."

Nathaniel pivoted away then stopped and cupped William on the shoulder once more. "You're a true patriot now, Henry."

"William," he corrected. A familiar longing at the sound of his old name flickered then dimmed. "I am Henry no longer."

Nathaniel dropped his arm, his gaze firm. "Henry was a good man."

"I hope William is a better one."

With a smile and a nod, Nathaniel turned and started toward the house. "He already is."

Chapter Eleven

The disguise was easy to obtain, the horse equally so.

Sitting astride his mount, garbed in a pair of homespun breeches, a linen shirt, and heavy greatcoat, Paul's posture relaxed as he shifted his cocked hat. The scruff he'd grown around his jaw may be out of fashion, but it hid his face and made him appear more rugged, as he wished. No longer a soldier in the king's army. Nay. A liberty-loving patriot traveling up from the south to lend his efforts to the cause.

The breeze beat against the front of him as if it wished to bend Paul's inflexible resolve. A burst of fire lit through him. Nothing could stay him from his goal. Donaldson would be found. Of that there was no question.

He glanced down the road, loosening his hold on the reins. After days of travel he was now less than sixty miles from Boston, an easy three day's travel—two if he pressed it. If he knew anything of Donaldson—and he knew much—he knew the man had nowhere to go, nothing to do but assimilate in the patriot army. Since

Donaldson was such a seasoned soldier, it would be easy to distinguish him amongst the sea of New Englanders who couldn't tell one end of a musket from the other.

He glanced at the sky and gauged the remaining hours of sunlight. Five hours? Six? The need to increase his pace pitted in his stomach, but he resisted and swallowed away the ever-present frustration that Barrik was nowhere to be found. Paul groaned at the memory of finding the tavern in Providence well patronized, but with no sight of his cohort. Had the woman traveled there as she'd said she would, or abandoned her quest? Had Barrik found her to his liking and taken her back to the mysterious mountains from which he hailed? Paul gnawed on the inside of his cheek. Perhaps. It mattered little, though his pride dented at the thought of it. He should never have invested his energy in the thought of someone else doing the job that was truly all his own.

As the sun rose to the center of the sky, the air warmed and he stopped at the side of the road to remove his cloak and stretch the ache from his back. He reached for the small wooden canteen and leaned his head back, coating his parched throat. Wiping his sleeve against his mouth, he halted and whirled as the sounds of voices mingled with the rustle of leaves.

He prepared to mount as two young soldiers rounded the corner, ambling as if they were school boys avoiding work on the farm. Paul busied himself with his saddle and kept his head down.

"Good day to you, sir," one of them offered as they neared.

Paul barely looked up and waved a hand. *Get on, you fools.*

The soldiers stopped only a few feet from him in the center of the road. The other soldier spoke this time. "You look as if you are lost. Perhaps we may be of assistance."

Stunned, Paul stilled. He knew that voice.

Jimmy Brown.

Paul jerked his head up, instantly finding the source of the voice. He darted his gaze to Jimmy's companion, but the boy's round face called no recollection to mind.

But would Jimmy recognize Paul? Paul deepened his voice with a mask of accent. "Is this the way to Boston?"

Jimmy's eyebrows pulled close, a deep line creasing in the center of his eyes. "Aye." He turned to his companion. "Still sixty miles though, wouldn't you say?"

The boy, even younger than Jimmy nodded. "Aye, just about." His expression grew stern. "You one of them patriots? What's your business on this road, anyway?"

Jimmy shot his companion a warning glare, but Paul took the reins of the encounter. "I should like to talk to this one, if I may." He pointed at Jimmy then staked his stare on the other. "Alone."

The stranger balked and shifted his feet, chuckling. "Who are you? Giving orders to a—"

"Do as he says, Marcus," Jimmy commanded.

"But—"

"Just do it." Jimmy's voice cracked with more depth than Paul had ever heard from him. "Continue on and I shall meet with you soon enough."

Scowling, the round-faced soldier backed away, taking a last and lingering look at Paul before turning down the road once again.

Paul kept his eye on the receding figure, carefully crafting the method he must employ to obtain the information that evaded him. For surely this little minion, though he likely knew little of import, could surely tell him something of worth.

He released a full sigh, placing a half smile on his face, and allowing his usual sound to emerge. "So they've promoted you to nursemaid, have they?"

Jimmy's forehead wrinkled and his eyes flitted to the receding figure of his companion. He opened his mouth to answer, but snapped it shut, staring for a moment before speaking. He breathed out through his nose. "What do you want, Captain?"

Paul stepped forward, patting the horse and grinning to ease the angst in Jimmy's stance. "I was only jesting." He chuckled, summoning all the ease and useful charm he had trained so well. "Frankly, I don't understand why you haven't been moved up in the ranks. You were one of my best soldiers."

The compliment seemed to hit a mark. Jimmy's posture rose, but his eyes still questioned, so Paul continued. "I haven't seen you since we lost Donaldson that day. Who are you serving under now?"

"Randall."

"Ah, I see." Paul relaxed his stance. "What are you doing so far from camp? Where are you stationed?"

Jimmy shifted his weight over his feet, answering in quick clipped words. "We are headed to Sandwich to bring back a wagon of goods for camp. Food and so forth."

"Just the two of you?"

Staring, Jimmy's wary expression carried into his words. "What do you want, Stockton?"

Paul laughed again, hiding the pinch of irritation that started at his back. "Don't be so suspicious, Jimmy. I'm simply pleased to see you. I always thought of you as a brother, you know that."

Jimmy's expression flattened and his gaze turned back to the road.

Shifting tactics with all the talent of a well-rehearsed actor, Paul rested his elbow on his horse's mane and lowered his head. "Truth is, I'm on assignment."

At this, Jimmy faced him once again.

Paul continued, clouding his face with a grave expression. "Several of us have been given the task of infiltrating the patriot ranks."

"Oh?"

"Aye." Paul looked down then up again. "We've lost track of Donaldson, and we believe he might be in danger."

"Hmm." Mouth tight, Jimmy's fingers tapped against his leg.

"I'm headed to Boston to see if I can find him and bring him to safety before the patriots can hang him."

Paul looked up and noted the tick in Jimmy's jaw. Did he know something?

"I..." Paul lowered his chin and sobered his tone. "I only hope I reach him in time."

Jimmy looked away, then down before meeting Paul with a pointed stare. "I thought you hated him."

"Trivial differences matter little when such issues are at hand—when lives are at stake."

Unmoving, Jimmy's eyes penetrated, as if reaching into Paul's very soul. With a swift nod of the head, Jimmy stepped back. "I fear I cannot help you, Captain."

That was it? He really had nothing to tell?

Paul reached out and grabbed Jimmy's arm. "I know you cared for him. If you know anything at all—if you have heard anything that might save his life...I..." He paused and quieted. "If you fear what may happen to you if you tell, be assured that I will never divulge where I gained my knowledge."

The boy looked away, his lips tightening.

Patient, Paul waited before prodding further. "He could be walking into a trap. But if I can reach him first—"

"He is not in Boston."

Paul stopped. "How do you know this?"

Jimmy shook his head. "Do you really think he is so foolish to allow himself to be caught?"

"I want only to be sure he is safe. Tell me what you know."

With a sigh, Jimmy studied his boots. "He didn't say where he was going. Only that he was working with the patriots."

"When was this, Jimmy? Where did you see him?"

Blinking, the young soldier answered. "I saw him here. Yesterday morning."

"He didn't say where he was going."

"Nay, Sir."

Hang it all. He was on his tail but still a day behind. And a greater dilemma impeded him now. Should he continue to Boston or reverse his journey south? The harsh exchange that volleyed in his mind made his head swirl. Boston would provide a large number of men to hide among. But it would also mean more soldiers. Nay. The patriots were distrusting and Donaldson would risk too much suspicion. *I should have considered that before.* Donaldson would have to find someone he knew...

In the far corners of his memory, a tiny glimmer of light flickered. Hadn't Donaldson spoken of his encounter with a patriot in a small town on the coast? Captain Martin had gone there some years past and had taken Donaldson with him, but what was the name of the place? 'Twas the same family of the woman Donaldson had helped escape before his capture. Paul squinted, straining to rouse that small flicker to a blaze. He looked over the saddle tapping his hand against the seat when in an instant the name burst like the flash of musket fire.

Paul launched onto his saddle and yanked the reins left. With a nod he kicked the horse. "Thank you, Jimmy. You've been most helpful."

Hurrying backward away from the horse, Jimmy's face bunched in question. "Where are you going?"

Paul answered over his shoulder. "Sandwich."

A mere three days after being in their new home, Eliza had invited Anna and William for supper. "Once you are settled, of course," she had said. A fortnight had passed now, and the appointed day was upon them. Walking down the dirt-covered road, Anna welcomed the yellow autumn light on her back and the loamy scent of the air as she found her way to the mercantile in the center of town. She grinned wide. Of all the towns she'd seen in her travels, this might be the smallest. But size or population mattered little. She'd have chosen this lovely little place over the foul streets of London a hundred times over.

Reveling in the sun against her skin, she nodded at

a mother and daughter as they passed along the road, other travelers and shoppers dotting the street. 'Twas only a few hours before they were expected for supper at the Watson's and she had much to prepare. She increased her pace.

Blessedly Eliza hadn't asked for her to bring any food to contribute for the meal—Kitty may have suggested against it—but the thought warmed rather than frustrated. She could hardly feed her own husband, let alone prepare anything for their friends. A smile budded. Coming without food did not mean she would arrive empty handed. All she needed was a bit of ribbon.

She stopped and looked up at the shingle that rocked back and forth in the afternoon breeze. "Breets: Goods and Wares", it read. Wasn't that what Eliza had mentioned to be the best mercantile?

Mouth scrunched in thought, she stepped in, the powerful scent of spices tickling her nose.

"Good day to you, lass." The proprietor approached, his round spectacles sitting crooked on his nose. He touched them and squinted. "How may I be of service?"

Warmth radiated from his dimpled smile, allowing her to set her shoulders at a more relaxed slope. "I thank you, sir. Indeed I am in need of some ribbon, if you have it."

"I do believe I can assist you there." He hummed and pinched the bridge of his nose then wagged his finger in the air. Silent, he disappeared through the backdoor and reemerged seconds later. "My wife takes care of these things most of the time, but she's visiting down south." He held out his hand, his mouth pulled down in a disparaging smile. "I've got only four here. I do hope one of these will be to your liking."

She reached out, granting him a quick, thankful grin before examining the pieces. Two simple white strands, a thick blue and another light pink. Either of them would look lovely for the christening gown she had nearly finished for Eliza's baby. She looked up again and removed her glove, pointing. "Do you mind?"

"Nay, lass." He chuckled. "The feel of it makes all the difference."

She offered a pleasing hum as she dusted her fingers against the different ribbons. All were remarkably soft and of incredible craft. "Beautiful. I've hardly seen anything so delicate. From England, I suspect?"

"Aye." With a scowl both stern and cordial, he continued. "But no more. From now on I sell only goods produced in the colonies, lass. We do not take lightly to what King George has imposed and 'tis our duty to prove it."

Her cheeks heated as embarrassment crept up her face. She should have known. "Oh, of course."

"We do not need Mother England to care for us like a pudding-capped child." The words, deep with conviction, were soft, as if he wished to share with her, and perhaps even convert her to the deepest thoughts of his soul. "The king will soon see that we can provide for ourselves and that our lives must not be so unjustly forced upon. Unless he wishes to respect our needs, we shall force independence."

The set of his jaw and slight upturn of one eyebrow sent a spark through her. What courage. Had these brave colonists any idea of the trouble that awaited them if they continued to oppose the king? They must, surely. Not that she was opposed to it, only that the vastness of such a paradigm was impossible to grasp. And if this war did continue, she would undoubtedly feel the inevitable lashings of it. Was she prepared for such a future?

She brushed away the deep thoughts with a smile and quick breath and reached in her reticule. "How much for the blue?"

He waved his hand, mouth bowed down. "'Tis a gift to you."

"Sir, I—."

"Nay, nay." He put his hands in his pockets, eyes bright. "You've brought a smile to me this quiet afternoon, lass."

Her face lifted in a smile that started from deep within. "I cannot begin to thank you."

He blew out from his lips and wagged his hand at her again, then pointed. "No thanks is needed. I've just arranged a lovely stack of new fabrics—in the corner over there." His dimples made another grand appearance. "You are welcome to look over them and see if anything appeals to you. I shall be in the back if you have need of anything more."

"I should love to look at them, thank you."

He made his way to the far corner, and Anna only removed her eyes after another full breath. Such kind people the colonists were. If she'd have known as much, she might have gained enough courage to insist she and Edwin visit here years ago. And perhaps he would have wished them to stay. If so, she could have seen Samuel before...

She shook her head and forced her vision on the stack of patterned fabrics by the front door. A hard sigh left her lungs. Better to put her energies in the present than to wish for things that could never have been.

Lifting three thick folds of solids and stripes, she reached for the soft printed cotton. Undoubtedly, these were English made as well. The delicacy of the tiny dual-colored floral seemed to float before her, begging to be snipped and styled, to feel the bite of the cool needle in its weave. Such a lovely petticoat it would make, or even a waistcoat for William.

She held the fabric to the light, examining its length and breadth as two others entered the shop. The brush of air as they passed jostled the fabric and she pulled it tighter and lifted it up, studying the fine craftsmanship.

"Sheriff Bergman, what brings you to town?" the proprietor asked, his voice muffled from his position in the back.

"Good day, Porter."

Anna heard the conversation, but didn't look back, still considering the many uses for something so fine.

"We're looking for a missing woman."

The downy hairs at her nape went rigid.

"A woman you say?" The proprietor's tone thinned with concern. "What's happened to her?"

One of the strangers continued. "This man says someone has kidnapped his daughter, and he's employed me to assist him in finding her."

"I'm more sorry than I can say." The shop owner's genuine concern darkened his words. "How may I help you, sir?"

"I am wondering if anyone has seen her about town. She's six and twenty years—about this height, black hair, blue eyes. Very lovely, very sweet."

Anna's stomach lurched to her throat. *Lord, help me!* She'd only heard that voice once, but 'twas a voice she'd never forget. She rested the fabric back in its place and stepped from the store, acting as indifferent to the conversation as any carefree shopper.

One thought dominated. *Run.*

Darting left, she lifted her skirts and fled, her pulse thumping so hard her entire frame ignited with fear-induced heat. Finally at the house, she hurled herself through the doorway and slammed it behind her. Her throat scratched with every gasped breath and her lungs heaved, unable to intake the needed amounts of air.

Her hands shook and her knees threatened to

buckle as the sound of that man's voice roared in her memory. "...Black hair, blue eyes. Very lovely, very sweet..."

Had he seen her? Had she escaped in time?

"William!"

Silence answered.

"William!"

She raced to the back and flung open the door, staring at the vacant garden as panic shredded her remaining courage. Where had he gone?

Anna stepped back in and shut the door, failing to calm her racing breath. Rational thought escaped her, though she chased it with every inhale. *What do I do?*

The answer cleared the darkening clouds in her mind. Eliza and Kitty. They could keep her in good company until William was found. They expected her anyway, so arriving earlier than planned would not be harmful. She lurched for the door then paused. Not harmful nay, but perhaps suspicious. She put a hand to her heart as it raced behind her breast. She'd have to find a way to calm herself first. Revealing anything, even to them, could risk the very thing William had warned her of. But there was nowhere else to go. Remaining here, without another soul to keep her company, she might surely go mad. Taking the back way, through the trees and behind the neighboring farm could keep her from prying eyes.

Again she ran, stopping only when her shoes touched the step of the Watson's kitchen door. She knocked and glanced behind, skimming her vision across the yard, her stomach in her throat. *Lord, do not let them find me.*

The door opened and Anna whirled.

"Anna," Eliza said. "What a pleasant sur—my dear, what's happened? You look positively white." She reached for Anna's arm and led her in, speaking over her shoulder. "Kitty, will you fetch a mug of cider?"

"Of course." Kitty's kind features scrunched as she hurried to a pitcher and did as requested.

Eliza brought Anna to a chair. "My dear, what's happened?"

"Pray, do no not fuss over me." Anna gestured in the air, as if all her efforts to ease her fears had not failed. "I am well, I believe I have simply forgotten to eat today."

Her spirit groaned at the veiled truth. These women were sincerer and more worthy of her trust than anyone, and yet she feared revealing herself to them. For what they might think of her, aye, but more, for the consequences unknown and how the revelations could change everything.

A mug of amber liquid filled her vision and Anna looked up to Kitty. She took the drink and smiled. "Thank you."

Kitty's face beamed and her blue-green eyes smiled. "A woman must keep up her strength." She offered Anna a still-steaming slice of bread. "There is plenty more if you would like."

The tantalizing scent of the yeasty bread made Anna's mouth water. Her stomach growled and she chuckled before the melancholy returned to her spirit and chased away the mirth. She looked down at the white, fluffy piece and spoke in deep earnest. "I thank you." *More than I can say.* She picked at the bread and took a sip of drink. "I am looking for William. Has he been here?"

The girls looked at each other then Eliza spoke. "We haven't seen him. But Thomas is at the shop, perhaps he has. You could go into town and ask—"

"Nay." She answered too quickly. "I mean, 'tis not urgent."

"Of course." Eliza's eyes searched as if she were unsatisfied with the answer, but chose to postpone additional questioning. "Once your strength is recovered, we would be more than pleased if you would stay." Eliza looked behind from her position near the fire. "There is plenty to be prepared for tonight's celebration, and a third pair of hands would be of great help."

"I'd be delighted." She finished the food and drink, breathing deeply to quiet the few quivers that remained. Finding a spot to stand beside the littered table, she sighed, forcing serenity into her voice. "I didn't remember tonight's meal was a celebration. What's the occasion?"

"Eliza?" Kitty said, stirring something in a large pot hanging over the flame. "I believe you should have the honors of explaining." Kitty looked back at Anna with a sprite spark in her expression. "She tells it best."

"Oh?" Anna answered with a laugh.

Eliza peered up from the table, her fingers covered in dough. "Today marks the day we first came to Sandwich."

Anna grinned, her nerves beginning to ease. "When was this?"

"Two years ago," Eliza turned back to the pastry. "Each day has been a joy ever since."

A curt laugh shot from Kitty. "Well, you remember things a mite differently than I."

Eliza glanced behind again, a flash of warning in her eye, but it vanished the next instant. "Life provides trial, but that is to be expected."

Kitty's cheeks reddened as she lifted a cast-iron pot onto the hook above the fire. "Well said, Liza. I suppose I need to improve my outlook." She smirked at Anna. "You should tell her about how you and Thomas met." Kitty pointed to the carrots. "Anna, would you be willing to chop those?"

She nodded, infused with a kind of exotic excitement. She'd never chopped carrots. William had harvested a few of theirs, but she'd yet to use them as he had already hauled them to the cold cellar. Not knowing what to do with them, she'd left them there.

Anna moved to the table and retrieved the knife. "You weren't married when you came here?"

Eliza's face bloomed. "Nay, we hardly knew each

other."

"She was love-struck from the moment she saw him." Kitty leaned over the table as if she were tattling. "I knew they would be married."

Eliza's brows shot up then instantly plummeted as a happy-irritated smile graced her face. "You did not." She reached over and flicked flour from her fingers at Kitty's face.

A giggle shot from Kitty's throat. She looked at Anna, pointing an accusatory finger at her sister. "You see how I am treated?" She kissed Eliza on the cheek.

The strings around Anna's heart loosened as she watched the sisters banter. How genuine they were. She'd been so surprised by their kindness at her and William's wedding. It seemed unreal that a person could show so much love to a stranger. Yet here they were, including her in such an intimate way.

To have friends. A smile warmed from within. A joy she'd never truly known.

"Well," Eliza said, "if we are speaking of who was love-struck I think it only fair to say you were purely besotted with Nathaniel."

Kitty's mouth scrunched as she looked upward. "'Tis true, I cannot deny it. Though I did try to suppress my feelings, it was all in vain." She returned her smile to Anna. "Now, you must tell us...how are you enjoying married life?"

Putting her attention back on the carrots, Anna shrugged a single shoulder, fighting the sudden and alluring fog of memory. His scent, his tender hands, the husky sound of his voice. How he'd nearly touched his lips to hers...

"Anna?" Kitty asked. "Everything is well I hope?"

She gave a quick shake of her head to dispel the trance. "Aye, of course." She rested the knife, mentally surveying the little mountain of carrot rounds. "'Twill take time of course, but we are becoming more familiar and I should like to believe our lives will be happy."

Kitty leaned in. "Has he kissed you?"

"Kitty!" Eliza shot her sister a look. "Such a thing should not be asked." She turned to Anna, a sly tilt to her features. "Unless of course you should like to share any such news."

Anna's face burned. She watched intently as her knife sliced the shrinking carrot.

"He has!" Kitty giggled. "I can see it in your face."

Blood poured into Anna's neck and cheeks. She peeked up quickly. Both Eliza and Kitty were motionless, their eyes round as the plates on the table and mouths slightly open. Were they surprised? Happy? Their looks said they wanted to know more. Never having had a sister of her own, never having had much female companionship at all, Anna debated how much more to reveal. Unable to stifle the grin that urged for freedom, she acquiesced to the beckoning need to share with someone. "Nay, he has not kissed me. But nearly..."

Kitty tilted her head back. "Oh! Such delightful

tension." She plucked a sticky pan from a pile at the end of the table and dunked it into a large pot of hot water. "Well, when he has finally kissed you, I should hope you would tell us."

Eliza shot a loving but warning stare at her sister while her words were directed to Anna. "Not that we wish you to divulge anything you would prefer to keep silent, of course," she said. "We simply hope for love to bloom between you." She smirked. "And to be made privy to any romantic details you deem fit to share."

Anna grinned in reply and looked down, her face heating all the more as she hovered over the one word that filled her mind. Love. Such a word. If a lifetime of equal partnership were accomplished that would be more than she would have dreamed possible. But William *had* nearly kissed her...why? She blew away the thought with an exhale. Men had urges that needed to be fulfilled. That she knew. Perhaps that was all. For certainly she would be a fool to ever consider otherwise.

"Anna?" Eliza asked, thankfully drawing her away from such thoughts. "There's a pudding boiling at the back of the fire. Would you be willing to check and see if it is done? It should be about time to remove it."

Nodding, Anna started toward the fire then froze. Done? She hadn't the slightest idea how to tell if a pudding was done. Her hands began to sweat. Stooping to the pan resting on the ashes, she peered into the pot. A strange lump tied in a cloth rested at the bottom of the water. She licked her lip and turned behind her. Eliza was still focused on the bread.

She tapped her fingers against her knee. Perhaps she could retrieve it and then if it wasn't done, they could simply return it to the pot? She tapped harder. That might not do. From what little she knew of cooking, to do such a thing to a dish before it was completely finished cooking might ruin it altogether.

"Anna?" Kitty asked, turning to her from her place at the work-table. "Do you...would you..." She closed her mouth and smiled as if searching for what to say. "Sometimes it is difficult to know when a pudding is ready." Wiping her hands on her apron, she came and knelt beside Anna. "Let me have a look." After poking it with the end of a spoon, she shook her head. "It will need another hour or so."

Breathing easier, Anna followed Kitty back to the table.

Eliza pointed to the basin by the window. "If you're finished with the potatoes, Kitty, you and Anna could prepare the fish."

"Certainly." Kitty brushed her palms together in excitement, looking at Anna with wide eyes. "The crowning course of the meal."

Fish?

Kitty removed the rest of the dirty pans before bringing the wrapped fish to the end of the large cooking table.

Anna watched as Kitty unwrapped the creature,

revealing the white and silver scales, fins, and open mouth. Anna gagged and put a hand to her lips as the unmistakable scent of fish assailed her. The creature's large, glassy eye stared, as if to scold her for what she planned to do to it, daring her to come a step closer. Holding back another lurch of her stomach, she spun and stared at the yeast rolls that could not stare back.

"Anna, are you well?"

Now both nausea and shame swam in her stomach. "I'm perfectly well. Forgive me."

"Nothing to forgive," Kitty said, her hand at Anna's elbow.

Still, Anna couldn't turn around for fear the creature might rise from the table and snap its mouth at her.

Silence circled the room and Anna could only guess the conversation going on between her friends' wide-eyed expressions. And why shouldn't they be curious? Anna tried to make them believe that this kind of life was all she'd ever known. But the audacity of such a lie became more apparent every day.

Truth, girl. You should have told the truth.

"Never mind the fish. It can wait." Kitty took Anna's hand. "How would you feel about chopping an onion?"

Chopping, aye. That was simple enough. She released a breath through tight lips. "Of course. That would be fine."

Kitty reached for a vegetable-laden basket and retrieved a large, white onion. "You did so well with the carrots, I know this onion is in good hands."

The compliment, as small as it was, picked a few pieces of her shattered spirit from the floor. She felt like a child being praised for trying something new, and somehow the comparison hugged her drooping spirit rather than stung it. For she was young in terms of such things, and for that, she determined to be less ashamed and more adventurous, despite the facade she must try to keep believable.

Eliza rested both hands against the table and lowered her head. After a few deep breaths, she put a hand on her head then her stomach. "Forgive me, ladies, but I fear I must sit down. I think I've been standing too long."

Kitty hurried to Eliza's side. "Are you having pains?"

"A few. But not consistent."

Kitty shot Anna a look, her eyes large and lips tight. The expression disappeared when she turned back to her sister. "Well, your time will be here any day, we've known that for some time." She took Eliza's arm. "I'll set you in your bedchamber and help you put your feet up." At the door, she turned to Anna. "You'll be all right for a moment?"

Nodding, Anna brushed the air in front of her. "Take your time making her comfortable. And should you need anything, don't hesitate to ask."

Eliza glanced over her shoulder, thanking her with a nod, and for the first time Anna noticed the perspiration that lined Eliza's forehead. She shifted her feet, her stomach dropping. How selfish she'd been not to notice Eliza was unwell. Sending up a silent prayer for her friend, Anna turned to the onion.

She breathed in deep, releasing the air through her nose. Now, this was something she could do. A harmless vegetable. No scales, no menacing eye to stare at her.

With the crinkly outer layers removed, Anna sliced it in half and instantly the scent bit her nose. Not an unpleasant scent, but powerful indeed. She sliced again and again, marveling at the way the circular layers hugged so perfectly. She sniffed and her eyes began to burn. Blinking, she sliced once more and suddenly her eyes stung with such force, she was powerless to keep them open.

Sniffing more, she put down the knife and pressed her wrists into her eyes as tears rolled down her cheeks. What had happened? The stinging worsened and she pressed her apron against her face. *Come mai?* She blotted her eyes, a growl in her throat. *What a fool I am. What have I done wrong?* At least Eliza and Kitty were not here to see her dreadful display.

Not to mention William.

Chapter Twelve

William knocked on the Watson's door then tapped the dust from his boots against the step while he waited. When no one answered, he knocked again, this time following after Nathaniel's bold habit of opening the door.

"Hello?"

The parlor was empty. Only a few sounds shuffled out from the kitchen.

"Mrs. Watson?" Still no answer.

He followed the sound of muffled sniffles to the kitchen and halted in the doorway. Anna stood by the table alone, her face in her apron.

"Anna?" He strode forward, hand outstretched. "What's happened?"

With a gasp, she jerked her hands down then turned away to dab at her eyes. "Aye, I am...I am well."

Well? Nay. He reached for her, tugging at her elbow and asked again. "What's happened? Tell me." When she refused to look up, worry knit up his back. Was she hurt, sick perhaps?

More tender this time, he reached in front and took

her other arm, turning her to face him. "Why are you crying?"

The tears on her soft cheeks and the red rimming her crystal-colored eyes pricked his memory. A protective shield shot up, guarding from incoming fire. The former Anna had done this. Used her tears to get her way, and he'd met every pleading request. His neck tensed. *Do not give in, Henry. You know nothing about her.* But he cut down the advancing fears before they could scar him with their sabers. There was something too real about this woman he had married—something far too innocent for him to equate her with the Anna of his past. At least, not completely.

She glanced up, dabbing at her cheeks. "Forgive me, I don't know why I'm crying." Sniffing, she pointed at the partially chopped onion on the table. "I was cutting and—"

"You hurt yourself." He took her hands and turned them over, prepared to find a gash in her flesh, her fingers dripping red. But they were not, thank the Lord. Nay, they were not hurt, but they were...soft...and slender and warm. His thoughts slowed as he stared at her dainty hands in his. He gripped slightly stronger, moving his thumb against the silken skin between her knuckles. His heartbeat roared in his ears.

Looking up, his gaze twined with hers then slid to her parted mouth.

He cleared his throat and released his grip, attempting to clear the husky sound from his voice. But he failed. "You are not hurt then?"

Anna blinked, her own sweet voice almost a whisper. "Nay."

She stilled, her misty eyes staring at him. Those same eyes that had begged him nearer the night before. He wiped his hand against his leg, hoping to brush away the tingling in his fingers.

"If you didn't cut yourself, what happened?"

"I don't know." She shrugged and pointed to the half-chopped onion. "I was simply cutting when suddenly my eyes started to burn and I couldn't stop crying."

William thrust his head forward. He gauged her expression and looked from her to the onion and back again. Could she be serious? He choked a laugh that worked its way up his chest.

Anna stared, her eyebrows pressed down. "Why do you look at me like that?"

"This cannot be your first time cutting an onion?"

"Why would you ask such a thing?"

The words fumbled so quickly from her mouth and her face turned such a deep shade of pink, the truth was obvious. And delightfully funny. Boiling bacon was one thing, but never having cut an onion? A smile flourished over his face as he looked at the sweet, innocent, determined women he'd married.

Her full lips pressed tight, and the way her fists flew to her hips made the laugh he'd tried to suppress bubble to the surface. He put a fist to his mouth and ground his teeth, attempting to smother the amusement that would not be contained.

She straightened, speaking loudly as if it would drown out the merry chuckle. "Pray, what do you find so amusing?"

After a few attempts to clear his throat and press away his smile, his answer came out smooth. "A cut onion can make a person cry, Anna."

The tight lines around her mouth smoothed and her eyes went wide. She flung a glance to the offending vegetable. "You jest."

"'Tis a well-known fact." William stopped and ventured where he feared he ought not. "That is, 'tis well-known for anyone accustomed to work in a kitchen."

Her shapely chin popped up and her mouth formed a hard line. "You think I have no skills in the kitchen." She motioned to the door. "Unlike Eliza and Kitty, who are accomplished at such things."

Tread carefully. "I simply think 'tis...unusual for a woman, such as yourself, to be unfamiliar with performing certain tasks unless she was brought up in a class of people where such labors were not of her concern."

The suspicions he'd harbored now finally voiced, he waited, refusing to move his eyes from her should the language of her body bring credibility to his words.

Her throat shifted and her gaze dropped. She swallowed, and after a heavy stretch of silence, answered in a hushed voice. "I did tell you I would try my best, and I do."

The sight of her sorrow-filled eyes smacked him with guilt. He doubted her story of poverty, aye, and with the answer now clear, more questions beseeched their unveiling. But he could not force her to speak, and any more prodding would only make her pull further away from him.

"I know you do." He stepped forward and reached for her arm. "And you do well."

"I do not." She refused to meet his gaze and wrapped her arms tighter around her middle. "I see how little you eat. I am no fool." A hard, breathy laugh left her mouth. "My cooking is not fit to consume."

Blast it. Why had he brought it up? Had he known she felt her lack of skill so keenly, he would have bit back the words before they had a chance to leave his tongue. He shifted his feet, praying the levity he tapped into his words made it into her heart. "Man does not live on biscuits alone, hmm?"

A slight smile leaned on one half of her mouth. "Burned biscuits."

William tilted his head, allowing half a smile to play on his face. Did that mean she was in good humor and not ruminating over her shortcomings? He continued on, the truth of his words resting deeper in his spirit than even he thought they would. "I would rather enjoy your burned biscuits than any made by Eliza or Kitty."

She tilted her head, flinging him a quick look. "I

hardly believe that is true."

"Believe what you like." He moved his fingers down her arm until they twined with hers, and once again those pleasurable tingles sprayed over his skin. "But I will enjoy them whether burned or under baked or golden, because you are my wife and I care for you."

He may as well have said he loved her. Anna's gaze shot to his and held there, searching. Her lips parted as the questioning look deepened and it took unearthly strength not to let his mind wander where it wished to. He could not permit such thoughts. Not when his tongue had slipped and said something so foolish. Though as the words floated between them, their truth settled. He did care. How much, he couldn't tell. But 'twas certainly more than the day they spoke vows. And 'twas true—he did enjoy eating her biscuits, for the simple fact that she had baked them.

"William! I nearly forgot!" Anna gripped his arms, as the tenderness of moments before vanished in a flood of panic that consumed her face. "In town today I—"

"Oh! I'm so glad you're here." Kitty burst into the kitchen and rushed for the pitcher of water on the table. She snatched a cup and stopped beside William. "You must fetch Thomas immediately."

"Fetch me for what?" Thomas entered the back door and rested his coat and hat on an empty kitchen chair.

Kitty faced him, her expression so bright 'twas as if the very sun itself were glowing from within. "Eliza is having her baby."

William leaned his shoulder against the kitchen doorframe, chuckling inwardly at the scene that played out before him. Never had he witnessed a grown man go from fully composed to complete helplessness in a matter of seconds. Thomas's face had gone white when Kitty related the news of Eliza's labor, and dashed from the room as if the floor were collapsing at his heels. That was more than fourteen hours ago and even still, Thomas couldn't stop moving.

William rocked the empty glass back and forth against his palm. "Are you sure you don't want to try to get some rest?"

"Rest?" Thomas whirled from his place beside the window. One hand on his hair, the other at his hip, he shook his head. A muted groan drifted down from the room above. "Impossible."

Thomas tapped his hands against his legs as he paced the room from one end to the other.

William pushed away from the door and went to the chair nearest the fire, rubbing the throb in his temple. He glanced at the clock. Midnight. Again he rubbed as the thought of a warm, cushioned bed lured his eyelids shut. He blinked hard and took a deep breath through his nose. Anna was up with the women. If she could endure the work and fatigue, then so could he. He glanced again at Thomas, feeling for the first time a small thread in the tapestry of agony that draped the shoulders of the father-to-be.

Another shout of pain filtered down through the ceiling, and Thomas spun toward Nathaniel, a taut arm extending toward the stairs. "Can you not do something?"

"And what would you suggest?" Unfazed by his friend's outburst, Nathaniel strode to the table to pour another drink. He handed it to Thomas when he passed. "You know they insisted we remain below stairs."

"Why?" Thomas stopped moving and his face reddened as if it took every measure of strength he possessed to comply. "I cannot bear to hear her suffer and I not be at her side to give her aid." He rested the untouched drink on the table and marched to his perch by the window. "How can having a child possibly take so long? These hours of agony can't be safe for her—or the child."

"Fourteen hours is a relatively short amount of time for a woman's first labor, Thomas," Nathaniel said. "For some woman it can last days."

All the color drained from Thomas's face. "Days?"

Again, a cry came from the room above and Thomas spun, eyes so round with exasperation that the laugh in William's chest melted in place of the desire to find some kind of comfort to offer. He rose and joined Nathaniel in front of the fire, searching for any words that might alleviate Thomas's suffering, but Nathaniel spoke first.

"I know you're concerned, Thomas," he said, "but what would you have me do? Ask her to be silent so her husband can have a bit more peace?" Nathaniel tilted his head with a single raised brow that seemed to infuriate the father-to-be even more. "You seem to be in more pain than your wife."

Eliza cried out again and Thomas's neck corded. "You're a doctor. Demand to be let in."

"You're the husband. I think that weighs far heavier." Nathaniel sat in the chair, sipping his cider as if they had just finished a game of cards. "You seem to think I could alleviate her pain somehow. Childbirth is the most natural event in the word. Eliza will be *fine*."

Thomas recoiled, his face crimson. "My mother *died* giving birth to me. You cannot be certain she will be fine."

After a beat Nathaniel rose to his feet, the once relaxed expression now drawn as he went slowly to Thomas's side. "Forgive me." He cupped a hand to his friend's shoulder and spoke in a tone that matched the caring in his stance. "She will be well, I promise you. Kitty knows enough to call for me if there is serious trouble."

This time, William spoke. "I remember my mother bearing my youngest sister, Jane. She made quite a commotion, but in the end both mother and child were—"

"Thomas?"

A woman's voice plucked them from their huddle

and all three whirled toward the stairs. Kitty stood on the bottom step and tucked a thick auburn curl around her ear.

Thomas was frozen, mouth part-way open. "Well?"

Her face lit in a soft, reverent smile. "Come meet your daughter."

"Daughter?" Thomas regained composure by increments. He shook his head, the smile on his face growing until it surpassed the one on Kitty's. "'Tis a girl!"

"Daughters usually are." Nathaniel chuckled at his own wit, but Thomas didn't seem to hear. He rushed for the stairs but stopped before racing upward, his face sullen. "How is she?"

Knowing whom he specified, Kitty gripped his arm. "Your wife is healthy, Thomas. Healthy and happy." She squeezed his shoulder and motioned up the stairs with a quick tilt of the head.

Taking them two-by-two, Thomas raced out of sight.

Kitty finished descending and Nathaniel went to her, following her to the kitchen. He wound his arm around her waist and she leaned her head against his shoulder. William grinned and turned away. 'Twas good to see them so happy. Only weeks ago he feared they might never find the joy that awaited them, but God had a way of bringing souls together. Contemplating His goodness never ceased to bring a warmth to William's chest. A new marriage, and now—

for the Watson's—a new babe.

The fatigue William had battled finally breached his bastion of persistence. Once Anna descended he would whisk her away and indulge in what little sleep he could before once again starting in the fields. A few hours of blissful slumber was better than none.

"William?"

He turned to find Anna just behind him, curls of black hair escaping the confines of her pins. Her shoulders slumped slightly and her tight expression masked an emotion that wavered beneath.

"You should be home sleeping." She sighed, looking to the door then back to him. "Somehow I didn't expect to see you here."

He placed a hand at her back and led her to the door. "I couldn't indulge in sleep knowing you were...busy." When they came to the door, he stopped. "How are you? Were you..."

Voicing the question he yearned to ask might insult, but his curiosity refused to be gainsaid. "Have you helped with a birth before this?"

Her throat shifted. "Kitty had everything well in hand. I was simply there for support."

William grinned and reached for her cloak. "They know we are leaving? They don't need anything else?"

"Nay." She pulled the fabric tight around her. "Kitty and Nathaniel will be staying the night." She covered her mouth as she yawned then her eyes went wide. "There is something I must tell you. I—"

A knock pounded on the door only inches in front of them.

Anna jumped back and William's muscles jerked. Who would be calling this time of night?

"Who goes there?" he asked through the wood.

"'Tis Joseph Wythe. I am looking for Nathaniel."

Nathaniel appeared from behind, reaching around William and pulling open the door. "Joseph, what's wrong?"

The tall man entered, his blonde hair wild under his hat, his expression hard. "We have trouble," he bellowed.

Kitty rushed in, hushing him. "Eliza and the baby are sleeping."

Joseph looked between Nathaniel and Kitty. "Baby?"

Nathaniel lowered his tone as he neared. "Eliza's just given birth to a girl."

A swift glance toward the stairs then back to Nathaniel told William the man wasn't about to postpone what he had to share on account of a newborn. But he did quiet his voice. Removing his hat, he entered, speaking with his gaze pointed. "'Twas my evening to make an exchange, and a redcoat was waiting for me. I was able to appear innocent enough, but he followed and I was forced to hide three hours."

Nathaniel's jaw went tight and he stared forward, his nostrils flaring. "They suspect." He turned first to Kitty. "Darling, could you ready the bed in the spare room below for Anna? I fear this meeting is too vital to defer until morning and I shouldn't wish her to be over tired."

Kitty nodded, as if she understood her husband's unexpressed need to speak to the men alone. She hurried to Anna's side and took her arm. Anna flung only a fleeting glance to William, her face awash with exhaustion. He nodded and she turned moments before the two women entered the room behind the fireplace.

Nathaniel's jaw ticked sharper with every second. "Someone has been slothful in their post, but I doubt 'twas one of us." He looked up to the stairs then back to Joseph. "The patriots in Plymouth are headstrong and without much practice in stealth."

Joseph went to the fire, lowering his voice another rung as he stared into the flames. "We must find a way to be more covert." He tapped the hat against his thigh. "I feel the need to join the men in Boston." With that he turned back. "I know your work is here, that the smuggling you do is every bit as helpful now, but I must fight."

Nathaniel said nothing, only dipped his chin.

Joseph continued. "I shall not leave immediately. I will need to find someone to care for Jacob until I return."

"Of course," Nathaniel said. "Washington will be all too pleased to have someone as capable as you serving in the ranks."

"You're leaving us?" Thomas descended the stairs,

all but floating, though in his face the solemn look of knowing darkened his eyes.

"Soon, aye," Joseph said.

William stayed back, his arms crossed, considering what they must already know. "Spies cover this land, and I fear if Mr. Wythe has been nearly taken, you may all have been compromised. Attempting another exchange may be too much of a risk for any of you."

The other three men stared in various directions, expressions at contemplative slants.

"We could simply deposit the goods and leave them to be retrieved later," Thomas said.

"Aye." Nathaniel stepped forward. "That way we could—"

"You're wrong."

The men turned to look at William. He neared, resting his palms on the back of the chair. "'Tis not the manner of your exchange that is problematic but who is executing it."

All three sets of eyebrows dipped. William finished. "You are well known here, therefore, further attempts by any of you to conduct exchanges will be fruitless."

Joseph transferred his weight over his feet. "Then 'tis settled. I will make my efforts useful in Boston as it seems I can be of no further service here."

Nathaniel spoke through his teeth. "I refuse to cease this operation when so many are in need." He paused, anger twitching at his mouth. "As I am yet unable to go with the militia, I will do what I can. Risks be hanged."

"You will be hanged, Nathaniel, if you insist on such impetuous behavior." Thomas neared, pointing a finger at Nathaniel's chest, before finishing under his breath. "You've yet to make that weakness a strength."

Nathaniel's face reddened as he strained to keep his voice quiet. "You would have us surrender our mission?"

"I would have us consider what else might be done before—"

"I will do it."

Again, all three pinned their gazes on William.

"You're not serious." Nathaniel didn't ask, he stated.

"I am." William rounded the chair and joined the circle of patriots, his shoulders straight and conviction strong. "I am unknown to the town, and though that will cause some suspicion, 'twill be minimal and allow this much needed work to continue."

"You are mad," Thomas said.

William stepped forward, gesturing as he spoke. "I am unmoved." Stirred by the knowledge that his experience and skills may at last be put to use in a righteous cause, his muscles pooled with zeal. "My understanding of the British army, their practices and so forth will allow me to do what the local patriots never could."

"'Tis suicide, William." Nathaniel looked to Joseph then Thomas. "There are plenty of ways for this to be resolved without you risking your life on a solo undertaking. You know all too well what dreadful end awaits you if you are discovered. Your wife will be made a widow before her time."

Pensive quiet stretched between them. William studied his boots. True. Yet...

He pulled his shoulders to their full height, buoyed by the flooding convictions within. "I am well acquainted with the risks. If my life is cut short for such a cause, so be it."

Anna stared at the door, as if the words were poisonous air and she were inhaling it. He couldn't possibly be serious. The small room—part guest quarters, part storage area—radiated heat from the back of the fireplace that jutted into the space. Somehow, all the same, her skin chilled.

Looking to her friend who sat at her side, Anna whispered, "Have you known of this?"

Kitty nodded slightly. "Aye."

Resolute, calm, her answer jolted Anna to the edge of the small bed, any thought of sleep vanished. "Are you not afraid of what might happen?"

An assured, steadfast gaze overcame her and she studied the ground. When she peered up again, a kind of serenity painted her face. "We live in a time of trouble. And I cannot be one to bow to fear however I am tempted—that spirit is not of God." She looked forward, nodding toward the door. "There will come a time when we will be called upon to act in defense of the cause we believe in. It will not be enough to merely stand by and watch others do our fighting for us." At that, Kitty turned. "Your husband spoke those words to me not too many months ago, and I have pondered their wisdom ever since."

"You believe them?"

Kitty nodded. "I do."

Anna gathered her husband's profound words but struggled to hold them. Kitty would be willing to let her husband jeopardize his life? Indeed, allowing her husband to do so 'twas the same as if she risked her life as well. Anna blinked. It seemed as if such a thing hardly affected her friend at all.

The room quiet, Anna narrowed her focus on the voices misting through the door.

"What about tonight's goods?" Nathaniel said.

Anna looked at Kitty, but her friend stared forward, mouth tight.

"Let me take them," William said. "Is the package cumbersome to transport?"

"Nay," the newly familiar voice answered. "'Tis little, so as to prompt less suspicion. Simply a bag of breads and dried meat, healing herbs, and a small inner-bag of munitions—just what the ailing people are in need of. The other towns offering assistance do the same."

The clomp of boots against the ground made Anna sit straighter.

"If I leave now, 'tis likely the redcoats are still

SO *rare* A GIFT

waiting. But they will be gone by morning."

"Aye, but the man with whom I was to meet is surely gone by now. He's no fool."

"If he was there at all."

"We must determine a system to exchange at varying times and places. Inconsistency will aid in the effort to make our work appear innocuous," William said. "Tell me who is in charge at Plymouth, and I shall deliver both the goods and the report of what has happened."

"You will do no such thing," Thomas said. "Are you really so ignorant to believe you wouldn't be caught?"

"I've never known anyone as reckless as you, William." Nathaniel said. "Nor so courageous. But I will not permit it."

"Someone must—"

"I will do it," Nathaniel interrupted. "I know the man in charge and my work as a physician allows for less suspicious night travel."

The conversation in the parlor quieted and Anna turned as she felt Kitty's gaze on her. "We must not speak of what we know."

"Why would they wish to keep this from our knowledge?"

"'Tis not a desire to keep us uninformed. Rather, I believe they wish to keep us safe."

Anna's palms began to sweat, anxiety jolting through her limbs. How could William do this? She needed him. If anything were to happen...

Just then a soft knock tapped on the door. "Anna?"

It was William.

"Aye, come in."

He opened the door cautiously, as if he wished to find her sleeping. How could she possibly sleep? She stood and Kitty did the same.

His smile broadened when his gaze fell on her, and she scolded her heart for the way it regained its hold upon him.

"Forgive us for needing to stay a bit longer."

Kitty trailed her hand across Anna's arm as she made her way to the door. She smiled as she looked back, leaving the two of them alone.

"I understand," Anna said. But she didn't.

He motioned behind him. "Mr. Wythe will escort you home. You will sleep more comfortably in your own bed. I should like to return with you, but I have other business to attend to before—"

"Other business?" She snapped her mouth shut before she could say more. Had they spoken of something she hadn't heard? More things he wished she didn't know? In a flood of panic, the burden she'd carried since her time at the shop surged like a storm in winter. If he knew whom she had seen in town it might change what he planned to do.

She gripped his arm. "William, I must speak with you. I—"

Joseph peeked around the door then ducked away. "Oh, forgive me."

"We are just coming." William turned back to her, his expression a puzzle of thoughts and emotions she couldn't decipher. "What is it?"

The intensity in his eyes and the way his fingers wrapped her elbow, as if to say he truly wished to know, made her chest pinch. Why must he appear to care so much when he surely did not. Engaging in such perilous activities with the patriots, no matter how valiant their cause, only put their lives in unspeakable danger. Danger he didn't even plan to warn her of.

She pinched her lips, the heat of scorn searing them shut. If he cared so little, what would speaking of her encounter at the shop accomplish? The cutting answer made her turn away.

"'Tis nothing...I've forgotten."

He dipped his head sideways and hummed low in his throat before placing a hand at her back and leading her to the parlor. He whispered to her ear. "Keep the door latched until I return. I should be home by morning."

Morning? That was hours away.

A cascade of unnamed frustrations ran down her back as she neared Mr. Wythe. William would so quickly ignore his feelings for her—if indeed he had such regard—and allow this man to escort her home in place of himself?

"Good evening, Mrs. Fredericks."

Mr. Wythe bowed slightly, his kind features softening her burgeoning frustrations. His height and broad shoulders took away another layer of her concerns. She could be safe with him. Though her traitorous heart wished it were William by her side, the resentments piling in her middle refused even the slightest acknowledgement that perhaps she misjudged him. She continued to refuse his gaze, though she could feel his eyes upon her.

"Good evening, Mr. Wythe." She passed William as she strode toward the door. "I do appreciate you being willing to see me home safely."

"'Tis my pleasure."

William rushed forward and opened the door. He touched her back again as she exited. "I shall be home soon."

The song of his voice curled around her and she looked up. Suddenly unable to move, captured by the swell of tenderness in his eyes, Anna gripped her skirt to keep from reaching for him. Did he care? Truly?

His mouth opened as if he would speak, but he shut it again, snipping the thread of hope she'd nearly used to mend the rift in her spirit. He looked to Joseph, a kind of warning blazing behind his eyes.

Joseph nodded and gestured for Anna to exit in front of him.

Walking into the chilled air, she gripped her arms and rubbed her hands up and down, trying to stay warm despite the chill that ravaged within. She was safe nowhere. Even here in this little town with a husband and friends beside her, her father's ever-expanding influence would uncover her hiding place and snatch her from the only happiness she'd ever known. A bitter laugh reached for her throat but she kept it back. Not that she took any pleasure in burning every meal she touched or enjoyed the ache in her back from the endless scrubbing and digging and washing. A grin lifted her face and she glanced to the sky. In truth, she did take pleasure in such things. She loved this new life. All of it.

Lord, look down on me in mercy. Keep me from being discovered.

She glanced up at her escort and he smiled down at her before turning his attentions to the road with a stern set to his jaw.

Her stomach clenched. Had the look William given him been an unspoken command to be sure he kept her safe? Perhaps she was too harsh in her judgments. With a sigh that cleared the darkness from her spirit, Anna straightened her posture and resolved to rise above her childish sensibilities. William would no doubt be famished when he returned. Well then, he would return home to a feast.

Chapter Thirteen

A strange perfume rested on the air. Dew-kissed autumn leaves, sea mist, and the promise of rain. William trudged across the path from the creek and up to the house. Fatigue cramped his weary muscles. Numerous times in the past he'd stood watch for many intense and dangerous hours. But these last six were more charged than he'd ever endured.

The sun's glow peeped at the edge of the trees, asking how he'd spent his night. His lips stretched in response. Tense as it had been, his body still buzzed with that excited energy he craved.

He'd all but forced Nathaniel to allow him to ride with him to Plymouth. The man had nearly burst a vein in his head, but he'd allowed it. And good thing. The ride there had been easy enough and the meeting with Willis Plains, the leader of the Plymouth patriots, had gone as planned. 'Twas the ride back that still had his pulse racing. He grinned again, recalling the speeds at which they'd ridden to escape the lone rider who followed. Then, like Joseph, the three hours they'd spent lying in the reeds, praying God would shield them. And he prayed God would continue to shelter him with His all-knowing hand. For now, the bulk of the responsibility rested on William to exchange the goods or deposit them, whatever the case might be. At least, until they could discover what else could be done.

Trudging forward, a dusting of orange sunlight rested upon a company of pink flowers, their petals so delicate William stopped to marvel God's creation. Lowering to his haunches, he brushed his fingers against the silken blooms, their yellow centers and circle of slender petals all but beseeching him to carry them away that they might bask in the brightness of Anna's smile. How could he resist? Plucking a handful of the delicate flowers, their lovely hue tempting a grin, William rose and continued on.

He rounded the small bend in the path and stopped when his house came into view. A light flickered in the kitchen window and a thread of smoke drifted from the chimney. Anna must be preparing breakfast. The image of her wounded expression when she'd left with Joseph still pained. Staring down, he questioned his reasoning for the hundredth time. Aye, Eliza and Kitty were both aware of the dangerous task they'd undertaken, but Anna carried fears of which the other two women still did not know. The burden of discovery weighed upon her heavily. If Anna were to have added worries over his safety.... He shook his head. 'Twas better to keep her ignorant, though he despised himself for the secrecy all the same.

Nearing the door, he stopped, a flash of color snatching his attention. Peering through the glass, he paused, a grin at his mouth as he watched the familiar morning scene repeating itself. Hands at her hips, Anna faced the fire then bent and swung around, plunking the skillet on the table. She blew upward at the strand of hair that draped her brow when suddenly she stomped and straightened her arms at her sides. "Mi rifiuto di rinunciare!"

A ripple of affection dashed through him. Whatever it was she said, she said it with passion. A grin etched into his face and he relaxed his stance, leaning his shoulder against the door to stay hidden but continue his pleasurable view. He'd seen this side of her only a few times, but now it seemed deeper, more real. This passion, this tenacity, was at the center of the woman he'd married. Though her courage had always been evident, this vibrant personality she unknowingly revealed sang to him, and he had to fight the powerful urge to rush in and embrace her.

With a quick shake of his head, he dispersed the outrageous idea from his mind. He pushed from the door and started for the barn. Though the flowers in his hand begged otherwise, he continued on, sure that the chickens might have eggs Anna could use, if she hadn't already gathered them. The task would give him ample time to be sure his heart wouldn't replace the entangling feelings from which he'd just freed himself.

A scream pierced the air and he whirled toward the house. The frightful sound came again and he bolted for the door. He gripped the handle and pushed, but the latch was in place.

"Anna! What's wrong? Let me in."

"William! Help me!"

She screamed again, but this time her voice snapped with horror.

Moving back, William kicked the heel of his boot beside the handle. The latch cracked and the door swung open. He rushed in and his chest seized.

Anna writhed on the floor, her skirts aflame.

He lunged for the cloak on the peg and raced forward, beating the flames. His pulse exploded. He pounded again and again until the orange ribbons vanished, leaving only the smoldering black of their handiwork.

Hands at her face, Anna dropped her head back against the floor and sobbed.

William dropped to his knees at her side, his pulse refusing to quit its erratic pace. He trailed her body, examining her lower legs. His throat went hard. A strip of red flesh surrounded by charred fabric stole his breath.

Careful not to touch her wound, he pried at the still-hot petticoat and searched for signs of any other injury. When he could find none, he turned his attentions back to her.

"Come," he said, sweeping his arms beneath her

shoulders and knees. "Your burns need dressing. I'll take you to Doctor Smith."

"Nay!" She resisted with her words but her quivering body gave him the real answer he sought.

Starting for the door, he stopped when she almost jumped from his arms.

"Nay, William, I do not need a doctor."

Still holding her, he stared, his face almost cramping from the scowl. "Of course you do—"

"Please." Tears tumbled over her cheeks and she looked away. Her voice cracked. "Please put me down."

The scowl hardened, but from questions, naught else. She didn't know what she wanted. She'd gone mad with the knowledge she could have met a fiery death. That was all he could surmise. Turning, he rested her on the kitchen table, and crouched at her feet, once more examining where the heat of the flames had nibbled her flesh. Red and swollen, but not black, thank the Lord.

He looked up, a hand on her knee, trying to slay the rising concern that drove up in his chest at the sight of her tear-filled eyes. "If you do not wish to leave, then I will go fetch him and bring him here—"

"Do not leave me again!" Her face crumpled and she covered her mouth, though her weeping gaze refused to leave him. "I cannot bear to be alone."

He stood and cradled her head against his chest. "Then you shall not be alone."

Her hot tears bled through his shirt, as if to seep

through his skin and coat his heart. He'd seen her upset, aye, but never so distressed.

With a gasp she pulled away and gripped his shoulders. Her chest pumped and her expression drooped. "I wasn't going to tell you—I should say, I planned to tell you in the beginning—then I decided against it when I feared perhaps it wouldn't make any difference, but I'm so afraid, and I tried to be brave, I tried to tell myself all would be well and that I should focus my attentions on being a good wife, but—"

"Anna, calm yourself." He would have chuckled at her endless stream of words if the lingering panic in her eyes didn't caution him otherwise. After he'd held her gaze and a measure of the anxiety in her muscles eased, he spoke again, low and loving. "Tell me."

She swallowed. "I saw him."

"Who do you mean?"

Her chin quivered but her voice stayed calm. "The man who attacked me. He was in town yesterday morning with the sheriff searching for me." More tears pooled. "I tried to tell you, but Eliza had her baby then you went to help the men." Now her voice quivered and she turned to look behind her. "I knew you would be hungry when you returned, so I tried to make you a good meal and take my mind away from my troubles, but I've failed again. On both counts." A sob shook her shoulders and she dropped her face into her hands.

That old familiar warning, the one that cautioned against succumbing to a woman's tears blared like a war-cry, but William smacked it away. She could not have fabricated such a story. The grief in her face and the fear in her eyes testified of that. And to think she'd had to keep such a burden to herself for so many hours.

Gathering her close, the weapons in his protective arsenal primed, ready for battle. What kind of demon was this man? That he would refuse to give up his search for her when it was clear she had no intention of ever going with him.

When her tears were spent, he eased her back. "Did you hear anything else? Anything that could be helpful in knowing if they are still in town?"

She shook her head, dabbing at her nose with her apron. "I did not. 'Tis a miracle I wasn't seen."

A miracle indeed. He swept a tear-sopped strand from her cheek and lowered his chin to meet her misdirected stare. "I will keep you safe, Anna."

"Will you?"

He brushed his fingers against her cheek. "I promise."

"I can hardly keep my mind on anything else." Her voice wobbled, matching the quivering of her body. "I cannot release this fear that he will find me and return me to England..." She covered her mouth and looked down, attempting to hide the sob that scrunched her face.

William smoothed his hands over her shoulders and down her arms, holding her tight above the elbows. "Anna, listen to me." He increased the gentle pressure of his grip, putting as much depth, as much strength into his voice as he could. "I give you my word that you will never return to England."

Anna lifted her eyes, those long, lacy lashes flecked with tears. She searched him, her clear blue gaze twining with his. Something tugged within him, tightening the strings that mended the shredded bits of his spirit he believed would remain forever torn. Such trust in her eyes. Such unwavering faith. *What would she think...if she knew the truth of me—knew that I am Henry and not William?*

He released his hold, fighting against the demons that pricked from behind. 'Twas right to keep the truth from her. She was safer not knowing. The reasons for his silence were clear.

Speaking to supplant the inner battle, he took half a step back. "If you ever see him again you are to tell me immediately."

She nodded. "I intended to, but couldn't find you at home, so I went to the Watson's—"

"You are sure you were not seen?"

Her brow crinkled. "I believe so...I hope so."

So she wasn't sure.

"From this time forward our vigilance must be paramount." His mind ground at the facts like a gristmill. They knew her adversary was near—or had been. But the question remained. Where was his? He moved forward, closing the small distance between them. "Speak to no strangers. Go to town only if you must, and never leave the house without telling me."

Swallowing, her head bobbed shallow and quick. "I understand."

He smoothed a hand around her waist. "Can you walk?"

Her slight arm gripped around his back. "Aye." She flung him a quick look as he helped her off the table. "Where are we going?"

"To the Watson's."

She shook her head, pushing away. "I don't need care, William, please. I wish only to—"

"Anna." The finality in his tone stopped her mouth, and he held her before him with his stare. "I must speak to Thomas on some pressing business and I will not leave you here alone."

Her face slackened and she glanced to the kitchen fire, her mind clearly warring against some unspoken ill. "I see."

The way her eyes saddened and her lips pressed together made William's muscles flex with the need to draw her close, hold her against his chest and reassure her that all would be well, that he would be her protector always.

But the truth battered his redoubt of courage.

Until Paul found William—and William defeated him—he would continue the facade of refuge. Forever, if he must.

l

The little town reeked of patriotism. Paul sat taller on his mount and doffed his hat at a woman and child as they passed, pressing the anger to his core, away from the fringes of his exterior. He must, to fully embrace this new identity, though the vile stench of their felonious actions against the crown pricked his skin like a shower of arrows. Several stores had notices in the windows proclaiming their disdain for English goods, vowing to sell only that which was proudly produced by the colonies. He smiled to hide the sneer that lurked beneath. Nothing in these sorry provinces could match the quality of goods from the mother country.

He stopped and dismounted, tethering his animal to a post outside the cobbler at the edge of town. He eyed the townsfolk that mingled in and out of shops and down the streets. How this place had any significance to anyone he couldn't begin to tell. A flash of crimson in the corner of his eye brought his shoulders back and he slowed his pace, feigning interest in the goods of the shop window, when in truth, he studied the reflection of who waited on the other side of the street. Two soldiers. Who, he couldn't tell from such a distance. His pulse rose and he continued on, hoping his look of an overmountain man would make him unrecognizable to any who might know him. Passing another shop window, he glanced again at the reflection and his ride-weary muscles flexed beneath his heavy coat.

They followed.

His fears were realized then. Father intended to find him. He continued walking, keeping his pace neutral despite the rapid charge of his pulse. As he passed an open shop door he turned in, instantly spinning out of view. He peered from the corner of the window beside the door. The two soldiers continued on, speaking back and forth as if they discussed only the weather, not once glancing his direction.

"May I be of service?"

Paul turned, relaxing his shoulders, a grin on his mouth. The man behind the large printing press, tall and well-muscled, looked genuine with a spark of reserve in the back of his expression. Paul's gut soured. He knew that look well.

Patriot.

"Good day, sir." Paul stepped forward, easy charm and warmth at the ready. "I was hoping you could tell me which is the best inn in town."

The man's eyes narrowed before a quick smile flashed across his face. "Fessenden Tavern across the way is popular. You heading to Boston?"

Paul fought the urge to answer the man's question with a question. Instead he smiled. "Aye. Plan to lend my hand to Washington."

At that, the man's face beamed. "Then Fessenden is the place for you."

"Excellent." Paul nodded. "Good day to you."

He chuckled to himself, allowing his spine to

stretch to its fullest. Never could he have guessed such good fortune would smile upon him. Garnering information from an unsuspecting idiot? This time his laugh escaped into the air. The patriot tavern would be "the place for him" and before too long, Donaldson would be his as well.

William had been reluctant to leave Anna at the Watson's, but her smile, the one that showed the depth of her heart, imprinted on his mind and allowed him the strength to leave. Kitty had been there and insisted on tending Anna's wound while the new baby and mother slept. He'd promised to return within the hour—had even kissed her on the cheek in front of Kitty. He ground his teeth to bite off a growl. Fool. Not that it shouldn't be done, but every touch, every allowance of feeling drew him ever closer to the edge of that infinite pit from which, if he fell, he could never escape.

His muscles twitched as he marched from the Watson's toward Thomas's print shop. So. The man Anna's father had hired was at their heels. He scowled. He'd imagined such a thing was possible, but Sandwich was so far removed from any city or town of import, it seemed impossible. But the impossible had happened.

Staring several paces ahead as he walked, William brooded. What should he do? Take her away? It seemed the only option. Their life together was good and seemed to allow them both the anonymity they craved, but if word should spread and the man discovered her...

He lengthened his stride. The thought made the hairs on his neck stand on end. And to think she'd almost not told him?

Once in town he hurried to the shop, entered, and shut the door.

"Thomas, I must speak with you."

Thomas turned and instantly his jaw went hard. "William. What are you doing here? Nathaniel is resting, as should you be."

"Do you remember when I explained that Anna was running from someone?"

"Aye."

William ground his teeth. "He is here."

Thomas lowered his arms from their position by the galleys, a hard scowl across his brow. "How do you know this?"

"She encountered him yesterday. He was with the sheriff, claiming to be her father, but he is not."

"Why does he want her?"

He rubbed his jaw, feeling the prickles of a morning without the blade. "I cannot say with certainty. She is a widow, that much I know. I have also learned that she was not poor, as she would wish us to believe. Though why she would have wished to keep that a secret I do not know." He bit the inside of his cheek, combing through the crumbs of knowledge he'd collected over the past weeks. "She is from England, had a brother—a soldier, actually, but he's dead. As for the rest, I suspect somehow she is avoiding another marriage, but that is all I can tell you."

"She was avoiding a marriage?" A questioning look consumed Thomas's face. "But she married you."

"Aye. 'Tis only a suspicion, of course. But marrying me was an arrangement of her choosing and no one else's. I believe she was to be forced into something she feared somehow, and decided she would rather be with me..." he slowed, "...than with anyone else." His mind quieted as he reexamined their few tender moments as one might a precious jewel. The time he'd first held her against him as they hid in the bush. The moment she'd offered her ring and when she'd tried with such earnest that first morning to prepare his breakfast. And how, not thirty minutes before, she'd clung to him as if she wished he would never leave her side. His mind whirled. She had chosen *him*.

Thomas's jaw shifted. "What do you plan to do?"

William let out a rough breath and pulled the solitary chair from the wall and straddled it. A sliver of teasing laced his words. "That's why I came to speak with you. You have all the wisdom."

Thomas's loud billowing laugh bounced through the small room. His face crinkled as he smiled. "How I wish that were true. I have learned to be wise from the mistakes of my past." By degrees, the muscles of his face dropped. "If I were truly wise, I would have known how to best Samuel Martin before he could do as much damage as he did." His words trailed off and the light in his eyes vanished.

At the mention of Samuel's name, a cloak of black memories draped William's mind. He saw the man's cold eyes, heard his demeaning words and felt the sting of Samuel's hand against his face. Loathing, like foul ocean foam, floated on the current of William's past. He too had become wiser. If only he had known just how to use that wisdom and found a way to overcome Paul's consuming hatred. He pressed a hard laugh from his chest. Some things could never be.

He looked up, resting his elbows on the back of the chair. "Should I take her away? It seems the only option."

Thomas came from behind the press and leaned back against it. "Where would you go?"

William shrugged. "West?"

In a swift plunge, Thomas's forehead creased seconds before his mouth quirked sideways. "You love her."

The statement jolted William upright. "Love her?"

A knowing smile widened Thomas's face as he remained quiet, a considering kind of slant to his head. "'Tis nothing to be ashamed of. Do not pretend you don't feel it."

The scowl was instant. "I do have some feelings for her. I do care, indeed, but I would not call it love."

"In the beginning we rarely do." A reminiscent kind of gaze overcame him before he met William's stare. "Be not surprised if one day you discover you have given her your heart unawares."

Sharp bitterness assaulted him. He knew the feeling all too well. And doing that again...nay. He couldn't. Wouldn't.

"She is a kind woman," William said, "and I could not have asked for a better wife." He stuck Thomas with a look he hoped would drive the conversation into the grave. "I will keep my vows and do all that I can to protect her. That is the end of it."

Thomas nodded with an understanding slope of the mouth. Not even a hint of recrimination in his eye. William took a deep breath and opened his mouth but Thomas spoke before him. He crossed his arms over his chest and his gaze flitted to the window and back. "What did this man look like?"

"Older. Tall, firm build. Grayish hair." He straightened in his seat as both hope and horror mixed in his muscles. "Have you seen someone?"

Mouth quirked in a frustrated slant, Thomas shook his head and his posture eased. "I thought perhaps..." He sighed and again looked out the window in the door. "A man was here not ten minutes ago. Our age. Tall, long face, dark voice. He was dressed as if he came from the mountains of the south, but I have my doubts."

William stilled. "Did he say what he was doing in

town?"

"He *claimed* he planned to join the cause in Boston..."

William stood, straining his heart to keep a regular rhythm. "Anything else?"

Thomas growled and turned back to the press, but instead of preparing the galley as he had before, he removed his apron. "Nay. He said he was passing through. He may stay at Fessenden's for the night, or not at all, 'tis hard to say. But he was villainous." His face went slack. "Do you think him a spy? Someone looking for you?"

Nodding, William wiped a hand over his mouth. "Paul Stockton will find me at any cost." A bitter laugh popped from his chest. "'Tis my turn to be the hunted."

Thomas's expression hardened. "If I learned anything from Samuel, it was to never underestimate and never take for granted."

"Then you are saying I should leave, for my safety and for Anna's."

"Nay. Your life is here now. Be cautious, aye. Be prepared." Resting a hand on William's shoulder, Thomas stepped forward. "Do not let him drive you from your home. Wait until he comes to you, and when he does, you will drive *him* back to the place he belongs."

Paul's words bit at William's heels. *I will find you.*

William met Thomas's strong stare. "Then let him come."

Chapter Fourteen

Mid-day was the most dangerous time for an exchange.

Autumn light blazed above him through the trees, signaling to all his hiding place. William grunted his anger and tapped his finger against the heavy bag of goods in his hand. Ten days of this new subversive strategy and so far only simple exchanges and deposits without a single impediment. But the past two nights with no one coming to the cove was a portend of ill. So when word reached him early in the morning that the man would come when the sun reached its zenith, William hadn't been able to contain the growl that rumbled in his throat. Madness. Secrecy was everything and though the cover of darkness didn't ensure it, 'twas a far better cloak of security than the blazing light of day. Aye, they'd discussed the importance of inconsistency, but such a haphazard execution of their plan was not what he'd meant. And why he couldn't have simply left the goods in the rock-covered pit, he didn't know. A powder keg of rage waited for ignition, but he resisted, refusing the lighted spark a chance to ignite an explosion.

William stood at the edge of his property, his farm just a half-mile beyond, praying with the weight of the earth upon his shoulders. *Do not let us be seen Lord, I pray thee. Do not let us be seen.*

That is, if the man showed up at all. Either he was a coward, lazy, or the soldiers were so thick he couldn't get through.

He ground his teeth. If that man didn't appear in the next—

"Fox."

William straightened at the sound. "Hound." His tension eased, but only a mite, and the words hissed out. "You are two days late."

The man, nay the boy neared, his face streaked with sweat. Any frustration William harbored evaporated at the sight of the skinny figure before him. His red hair and thick spray of freckles seemed to match the friendly, fearless spark in his hazel eyes. How old was he? Eleven? Twelve perhaps? This was far too dangerous work for one whose face was yet to need a blade.

The boy nodded, panting as if he'd run for miles. "Aye, I know, sir. The soldiers are thick around Plymouth."

"Where is your father? Should not he be here?" The question popped from William's mouth as if the boy had been his relation rather than a stranger.

"He must stay with Mother as her time for the baby

has arrived and there's no doctor or midwife to tend to her." He straightened. "I am as capable to serve this cause as any man."

"'Tis true, I can see that." William inclined his head. "But you could not have run all the way."

"Not all the way, sir." The boy pointed deeper into the wood. "I tried to meet as planned these two nights past. The watch has been thick, but I kept making my way here, sir, and I've finally made it." The triumph in the boy's voice clamped William's chest, and he studied the freckles that dotted the young patriot's determined expression. What prompted a parent to send their child on a mission all alone when danger lurked in every shadow? What would possess a mere boy to risk so much for what so many people believed a futile cause?

In that moment, the desire to be connected with this alliance of intrepid men and women consumed him like never before.

"Where is your mount?"

"About three miles back, sir." The boy glanced over his shoulder. "I thought I'd been spotted so I left him there and ran all this way."

"You ran?" Running would draw attention. It was the boy's first mistake. Allowing a grin to ease up his mouth, William extended the large bag toward the boy. Whispering, he gazed down at his freckled friend and placed a hand on his shoulder. "Run only if you must. 'Tis more prudent to out-wit the enemy, than try to out-run them."

The gentle sound of humming filtered through the trees followed quickly by a quiet, dainty footfall against the leaf-covered ground. William lunged for the boy and pulled him behind the nearest tree, shielding the rest of him with his own body.

Who came in the wood this time of day?

He squinted as the sound neared, searching wildly until his gaze found the source and his stomach lurched to his throat.

Not twenty feet away, Anna strode through the trees, holding a basket in her hand as she glanced at the ground. The shawl around her shoulders, strands of hair straying from her cap, the sun on her face—she'd never looked lovelier.

William clenched his fingers around the bag still in his fist and his biceps flexed. If she saw him with the boy she would ask questions. And questions would only bring them closer to the precipice of discovery. Something neither of them could risk.

William breathed slow with long ins and outs, but the boy behind heaved heavy breaths, oblivious to how even a sound could change the course of their future.

Keeping his gaze upon her, William willed her to turn and walk home with every pump of his pulse. Yet she did not. She stopped, a smile lighting her face as she crouched to the ground, tugging at several plants and placing them into the basket.

Go, Anna. Go home.

William glanced behind. The boy flung him a

questioning look and William answered with a finger at his mouth.

"Good day, miss."

What in heavens name?

William's blood went from hot to instant boil. A soldier, tall and well-muscled, stood with cocked hip at the other side of the wood, not ten yards from Anna.

William looked from the boy to the soldier. He'd been followed.

Anna jumped to her feet, face ashen. She clutched the basket to her middle and retreated a step. "May I help you, sir?" Her voice wobbled and William leaned forward. If the man even thought of touching her...

The soldier pointed to the basket with a smile. "What are you gathering?"

She didn't answer and her posture shrunk. 'Twas not the same reaction she'd had to the soldier at the creek, but then again, that had been a thin, weak boy, while this man was a giant. That, and William had been near. Only this time, she believed William was far from her rescue.

Thank the Lord he was not.

From behind, the boy tugged on William's coat. William shot him a pinched look and the boy nodded.

Continuing forward, the redcoat motioned in a wide circle. "Have you...have you seen a boy pass by here?"

Anna shook her head.

"Nay?" The man continued to move closer. "A

beautiful woman like you would certainly not lie."

She froze, stopping even the slight up and down of her shoulders as she breathed. "Nay, sir. I would not lie."

"Of course."

William's legs burned with the urge to lunge and tackle the seething enemy. The soldier was too close. If he reached out he could grab her. Glancing down at his feet, William spied a large stone and crouched to retrieve it. He captured the boy's gaze and mouthed silently as he counted on his fingers.

One, two, three...

With a swift swing of his arm, William hurled the stone to the opposite side of the wood. A loud smack cracked through the trees and the soldier whirled, scanning the opposite side of the forest.

William grabbed the boy's elbow and mouthed the words more than spoke them. "Go. Quickly."

The boy's round eyes spoke his unvoiced gratitude. Gripping the bundle he darted quietly away as William launched to his feet.

"Looking for me?"

"William!" Anna turned to him, her voice filled with relief.

The redcoat turned, his posture unchanged, unchallenged. "Coming to the rescue?" He chuckled. "As you can see, I mean her no harm."

"If you have questions you may direct them to me, not my wife."

"Your wife?" The soldier looked her up and down then did the same for William. "I hardly think you are worthy of someone so lovely."

"Get off my land."

The soldier leaned his head back, a laugh peeling through the air. "All you patriots are the same." He faced William, his grasp tightening around his musket. "You believe simply because you own this land you have license to harass me. But I speak in the name of the king, and therefore you must answer or find yourself in prison."

William pulled his shoulders back and widened his feet, studying his opponent. Short jacket with off-white facings on his cuffs and lapels. From the 47th foot no doubt. Well-trained but not well-seasoned. An easy victory should he be forced into combat.

Playing the part, William raised his palms. "I simply petition for our privacy, that is all."

"Then tell me what you know of that boy."

"Boy?" *Lord, let him escape unharmed.*

"Do not think me an idiot. I followed him here. He was smuggling and you were helping him."

William didn't need to see Anna's mouth drop open to know it did. Her quick gasp testified of that.

She stepped forward. "How dare you accuse my husband."

"Anna—"

"Nay," the soldier chuckled, "I like a woman with a bit of fire." The soldier bobbed his chin up. "Let her speak for you. Perhaps I will find her pleadings adequate enough to let you go."

"I am under no arrest."

"You could be."

William struggled to keep his jaw from ticking. He'd better play this game with his head more than his heart or he could find a rope around his neck.

He flung a glance to Anna. Her wide eyes and pinched lips screamed the questions she could not bring to her mouth before she turned her attention to the man in front of her. "We are gathering nettle as you can see." She held the basket forward and pointed at the greens with her gloved hand. "And as we've only just arrived I can say with certainty there has been no boy here."

Nodding, the soldier took the basket and placed it on the ground. "Perhaps you would like to stay a bit longer with me and watch for him." He stepped closer until his shoes touched the base of her skirt. A sickening hunger in his eyes, he reached for her face but pulled his hand back, sending William a rotten smile. "'Tis a shame your husband had to be here. We could have had such fun."

William lunged a step forward, his fists ready. "Get out."

With a mocking bow, the soldier stepped backward. "As you wish." He straightened and suddenly stopped, the hatred in his face morphing to question. His voice dropped. "I know you." 'Twas more a query than a statement.

William scanned his memory. Though he had been familiar with the 47th regiment, he'd never served anywhere but under Martin and Stockton. How could the man possibly know him?

William ground his teeth. It didn't matter why or how. It mattered that he did.

The redcoat's forehead wrinkled. "I know your face." He stepped nearer, his eyes thinning. "Aye. I have seen you before. But I cannot place it."

A lie sprung to William's mouth. "My brother fought and died at Lexington."

The soldier quirked a brow. "Rebellion runs in the family, does it?"

"Nay, he was a redcoat. Like you. He fought under Smith. We were often mistaken for one another..."

Lord, let him believe this falsehood. If not for me, for Anna.

The soldier stepped forward, lips prepared to speak when a voice called through the wood.

"Pryer?"

The man turned as another soldier joined them. William's inner call to battle drummed his pulse to a pace he'd rarely known.

"You are needed back at camp." The soldier looked between William and Anna then back to Pryer. "Is there a problem?"

Pryer's eyes thinned. William's muscles bulged as his blood consumed his limbs. The soldier had nothing to prove, but that did not always stop them from making examples of those they disliked.

Pryer answered flat. "Nothing more than a patriot and his wife."

"Good." The other soldier motioned behind him. "Stockton has need of you. Now."

Stockton? Which Stockton?

William walked toward Anna, feigning ignorance though within a thunder of cannon fire exploded.

Pryer glared and stepped backward, silent, before turning to walk the way he'd come when suddenly he stopped and spoke over his shoulder. "Do not allow yourself to get casual, patriot. We are watching. Always."

Anna gripped her skirt to keep her hands from shaking as she flicked her gaze from the retreating soldier to her husband. Never had she witnessed William's face become so red and his biceps flex so hard beneath his shirt.

He rushed near and took her arm. "Come, wife." Snatching the basket, he led her back to the house. "We have much to do before sunset."

Anna berated her ignorance. The soldier could still be watching, listening. She did her best to squeeze the lingering panic from her arms and legs. "I hope I gathered enough nettle." Anna peered around him at the basket. "Kitty shared a recipe that I should like to try." She felt the heat go to her cheeks. "It seems simple enough for one with so few skills in the kitchen."

William glanced down as they reached the edge of the wood. His eyes were still rimmed with concern, but the deep blue centers were tender. "You under estimate yourself."

"If only that were true."

They continued their walk in silence and soon entered the house. Anna went to the table and placed the basket beside the chair. William closed the door.

"Tell me," she said, removing her gloves. "Was all that true?" She turned to face him. "About your brother—did he really die at Lexington?"

William removed his hat and greatcoat, hanging them on the peg by the door. He raked his fingers over his head and pressed out an audible sigh. Finally, he met her gaze. "Nay." He went to the fireplace and crouched to add another log. "I needed him to leave, so I said what was necessary. Then, of course, the other soldier arrived and saved us from further scrutiny."

"You lied."

He craned his neck. "You disapprove?"

She smiled and dumped the nettle in an empty wooden bowl. "I can hardly find reason to reprimand when you came to my rescue. A second time."

He pushed up from his haunches, a handsome half-smile on his mouth and started to step past, but she grabbed his arm.

"I know you didn't follow me." A quick breath gave

her the strength to speak the question. "What were you doing there?"

William blinked, his mouth tightening. "There are some things that are best left unspoken."

Releasing her hand from his arm he started for the door. "I must check the garden."

"You were smuggling."

He stopped mid-step and glanced over his shoulder. "You cannot know that, Anna."

"I do."

William's eyebrows plunged to his nose.

Anna summoned her courage and rounded the table. "Why will you not confide in me?"

"I know not of what you speak."

"Please, William. I've heard Eliza and Kitty whisper things about their husbands helping to bring goods to Boston." She knew her husband did the same, but waited, silently hoping, praying he would confide in her as Thomas and Nathaniel had done with their wives. "I should like to hear from you if you are doing the same."

His gaze searched her face, as if he were looking for something that could tell him he could trust her. Could he not see it in her eyes?

The silence stretched long between them. Each remained motionless, waiting for the other to speak or touch or move.

William stared, his mouth hard. "There are things we must be willing to risk for a cause that is just."

"And you are willing to take that risk?"

"I am."

The truth socked her in the stomach, stealing the air from her lungs. Then he would both tell her, and not. Why she was shocked, she couldn't tell. Yet she was. "You are a man of secrets. Yet I know enough about you to know that there is a past you wish to keep hidden. I hardly think engaging in treasonous actions is wise especially if you hope to keep the life we've started."

He closed his eyes and rubbed his head before dropping his arm to his side. His gaze was strained but his tone remained even. "I know the risks."

"Then why take them?"

"There are things—"

"If any of you are imprisoned, what will become of the rest of us?" Her throat began to thicken. "Do you not see where your actions will lead?"

The glimmer of patience snuffed from his eyes. "I see more than you do, Anna."

"You do not see what I see."

"I see more."

"You think that I am closed. That I do not think past tomorrow?"

"I think your fear of being discovered clouds every other thought."

The truth cut. She spun her back to him. Was her fear so wrong? The knowledge that at any moment that man—or any other man her father hired—could take her back to England, threatened to extinguish the very breath in her lungs.

A warm hand on her arm made her flinch until his thumb began tracing small circles on her skin. "I promise that you will not be found." The silken ribbon of his voice twined around her. "I know very well the risks. All of them. And the risks of acting outweigh the temporary safety of not."

She turned, and his hand traveled the length of her waist, gripping her other arm as she stared up at him. "You are not afraid?" she asked.

A brief chuckle passed his lips. "I would be a fool not to have some healthy trepidation."

Anna reached for her throat but her fingers found only skin, not the ring and chain. She closed her eyes, remembering the ring now rested on her finger. She stroked the gold with her thumb and spoke to the floor.

"How do you do it?"

His reply came after a few breaths. "Do what?"

Grasping for her remaining courage, she forced her head up and met his eyes. "How can you continue on...when you could lose so much?"

The soft lines around his eyes deepened, as did his voice. "I do not think of what can be lost." He reached for the hair at her ear and brushed it back. "I think of what can be won."

Her vision misted as his words etched in her mind. *What can be won.* The quiet rush of their breath, the only sound, rustled the air between them and smeared ignorance from her face to her feet. How foolish she was. How low and self-centered.

Shame made her drop her gaze. But what *could* be won? Was helping those in Boston truly worthy of such a risk? Were there not others who could do the same? Others closer and more able?

"Anna." His rich timbre, smooth and draped with caring, urged her to look at him. "I had no brothers. I did have sisters."

This brought her head and eyebrows up.

The way his smile rounded, the way his breath went heavy, told Anna he spoke the truth. The pain he tried to mask behind his eyes whispered of loss. She released her arms and pulled the chair beside her, then sat. "They are passed."

Looking down, his neck flexed and his jaw ticked. "My father died of the pox—we were all taken with it." He pulled his bottom lip through his teeth. "The rest of us recovered, but Mother and Julia and Jane were not quite themselves again, though I never heard a word of complaint from them."

Anna stared, fearing if she spoke or even breathed aloud, he would cease sharing this precious revelation.

He peered at her, moving his eyes only. She offered a small smile to urge him onward.

A large sigh heaved from him. "They mended clothes and I worked at the smithy." His eyes lowered once again, and Anna gripped her hands at her lap to keep from reaching for him. "We had but little, and what means acquired were enough to keep us alive."

Enough to keep alive? She had never known such poverty.

His throat bobbed and his voice scraped the floor at her feet. "But they are gone now, and though I would gladly have gone in their stead I am left to mourn the loss of them until 'tis my turn to breathe my last."

Unable to stop herself, Anna reached for his rounded fist, and stroked his skin. His eyes shifted to hers.

"I am so, so sorry." She could not fully flood the words with the emotion that welled within her. "I know that loss. It is consuming."

He said nothing, but his eyes remained locked on hers as she stood.

"It grieves me that you should so keenly suffer at the memory of them," she said. "I feel the loss of my mother and brother with every sunrise, every sunset." She glanced down, weighing the sudden words that rose to her lips. Pushing aside the thread of resistance, she spoke. "I will strive ever harder to make your days joyful. You were the first person to show true kindness to me since their passing. Despite our secrets, despite everything, I am happy, so happy, to be your wife, William."

Once her lips stopped moving, her skin went hot and pricked. She waited. Would he speak? But he said nothing. Her heart, full and raw, rested with its center to the sky. Did he feel the same? The truth bobbed between them like a rowboat on a choppy sea, ready at any moment to capsize and plummet to the rocky bottom.

Regret began its way up her back. Oh why hadn't she kept such things safe? For now, he would either feel obligated to profess the same, or would be awkward in her presence or—

In a single swift motion he lifted her chin and descended, pressing his lips over hers, so warm, so gentle. So wanting. Tingles of pleasure trailed down her skin as he nudged her mouth apart, his hands cupping and angling her head to more fully accept him. She couldn't breathe, her limbs weightless. The floor melted away and she reached for him, gripping his chest to keep from falling. Never had she felt such burning—a deep powerful yearning to be one—to feel this way again and again and be his unyielding companion until the end of her days.

Was this love? Did he love her? Did she love him? The thought nearly made her pull away, but he held tight, his hands trailing up her back and into her hair, tasting more of her. She surrendered, tilting her head back as he trailed hot kisses along her neck. 'Twas good, was it not? 'Twas more than good. 'Twas natural. As husband and wife, this kind of longing would make them as one, would bring children into the world.

With a gasp she pushed away, her breath heaving. She brought a hand to her lips, feeling the warmth where his mouth had been.

"Did I frighten you? I'm sorry." His heady tone kneaded the air between them.

"Nay, you did not." She swallowed and glanced up, her heart pounding, pleading to finish what they'd begun. The sight of his own mouth, red and glistening, made her long to feel his lips against her skin once more. The truth dragged at her spirit and she looked away. Tears threatened, but she pressed them back. "I...there is something...something I..."

"What?"

Her breath came in quick, sharp bursts. *Lord help me.* She had better speak quickly and end the agony. She opened her mouth then snapped it shut. What would he say? He could leave her, could he not? For not disclosing the truth of her barren womb?

"Anna, what is it?" He neared, crooking a finger around her chin and nudging her face forward. His eyes, large pools of tender blue, swam with longing. "Tell me."

She bit her lip and scrunched her eyes before finding the strength to form the words on her tongue. Once she did, they came fast and pinched with grief. "I cannot bear children."

William stared at her mouth, blinking to clear his clouded vision. He breathed in deep to make way for any other thought than that of taking her in his arms once more, to test his lips against her silken skin and press her femininity against his chest.

And though he wished to, he could not.

I cannot bear children.

The words spoken seconds ago floated on the air and drifted to the floor like feathers, allowing him time to follow them down to his feet and stare in quiet disbelief. Had he heard her correctly? He lifted his eyes to hers and his chest went tight. The agony in her sweet face brought his arms around her before he knew next what to do or what to say.

He cradled her against him, and there, as if in the safety of his embrace she could finally be free, she wept as if years of pain over the loss of something she wanted and could never have was suddenly brought from its grave, still fleshy and pink with life—not long since dead as it should have been.

His chest constricted and he held her tighter. So, she had no child from her first marriage because she could *not* have a child. He had only given a fleeting thought to the question of any children she may have had, as he understood there was much he didn't know of her past. But here was the tormenting answer.

He stroked her hair, memorizing the soft curve of her head as he listened to her choppy breathing and muted cries. Her arms gripped his back and clung to him as if he could relieve the pain within. He cooed in her ear, continuing to sweep his hand over her head and back.

No children? His chest pricked. Never to have a child of his own? Never to hold a babe in his arms, to care for him—or her—to laugh with, love, and train up into maturity? He stopped his stroking and wound his arms around her slight shoulders. Marriage was divine. Though they would not have children, if they could truly love each other, and spend their lives in each other's service then they would achieve in marriage what so many others never did. A life of love and joy. A life fuller than he'd ever imagined for himself.

She lowered her head and dotted her nose with her apron, then pulled away, keeping her head down. "I didn't expect to make such a scene." She sniffed and took another step back. "Forgive me."

He reached for her cheek and moved his thumb against her skin, still wet from her tears. "There is nothing to forgive."

Flecks of light brightened her pleading eyes. "You do not hate me for not telling you?"

"Hate you? I could not. Especially when such a thing is not of your doing. God is over all, is He not?" William neared, closing the growing distance between them. "I understood we both had much within—much that could not be spoken." He trailed his vision around her face and down her neck, lingering on the throbbing pulse at her throat then down to where her neckline dammed her breast. His own pulse jumped and he spoke to keep it from taking his mind to a place he wasn't sure she—or he—was prepared to go. "I do not fault you."

"You do not?" Her voice cracked, weakening his resolve to stay away.

Smoothing an arm around her waist, he closed the remaining gap between them, his body throbbing to fill the sudden void. *Let me show you...*

He lowered, dusting his lips atop hers, savoring the sound of her breath and the feel of her hands as they inched up his chest.

"I don't know what to say," she whispered, her mouth brushing his as she spoke.

He nuzzled her cheek and rested his lips against the tip of her ear when he answered. "Say nothing."

A quick inhale made her chest rise and he could feel her skin prickle beneath his touch. Masculine pleasure surged and he continued on, leaving a trail of soft kisses along her neck and collarbone. She leaned her head back, imploring him to savor her more and he lost himself. Pulling her hard against him, he kissed her open mouth, consuming her with the sudden heat that roared between them. How long they stood there he knew not. How long before they moved upon the bed for their souls to finally and fully entwine, he cared not—only that they did. This moment, so intimate, so pure, so right, would live with him forever.

Anna's dainty fingers cupped his face as she lay beside him beneath the quilt. She dotted a slow kiss on his mouth. "William..." Slowly, she stopped, her whispered words like a prayer. "I love you."

'Twas then the reality crumbled like a rotted wall and the past loomed from his memory, ghostly and dark.

I love you, Henry. I'll love you until the end of my days.

He clamped his eyes shut, but still the memory wailed. *Father has died, Henry, and I have nothing. If I cannot pay the debts I shall be forced to leave for Germany by week's end. Whatever shall we do? Help me, Henry, please.*

"William?"

The quiet sound lifted him from the mire of the past, but his soul was left caked with it. He found her eyes and stared, searching for the same trust he'd seen in them before, seeking for the honest purity to which he'd been drawn. He stared, fighting the consuming battle that warred between his mind and spirit. This was Anna Fredericks, his wife, not the Anna Muhr of the past. This Anna was both gentle and strong as sunshine, resolute like a bud in spring. But what did he *really* know of her? This one painful secret she'd shared seemed so unfeigned, but how could he be sure she spoke true? Then again, how could he not and why should he doubt her?

Even if this one truth were founded, his mind argued, there was much he still did not know of her. And the years of experience, still fresh in the cracks of his heart, admonished him to be vigilant. She too could be a villain—'twas too early to tell. Opening his soul, giving himself fully to her could be his utter ruin. It could mean his death.

"William...are you well?" Anna's sweet sound roused him back to the present. "Do you despise me after all?"

Blinking, he forced a smile on his lips. He moved away, his chest aching as he pulled back, unable to leave the sanctity of their embrace without leaving a kiss upon her head. He cleared his throat. "I...there is something I must attend to."

Her expression paled and he looked away, pained that his sudden change caused her such hurt. For he knew it did—because he hurt just the same. But he couldn't halt his soul from shredding at the memories. He couldn't bring himself to hand his heart to one he knew had the potential to destroy the fragile pieces that remained.

He rolled from the bed, dressed, and left, pulling the door shut behind him. On the other side of the wood he shook his hands at his sides, helpless to forget the feel of her smooth skin and hair, or the way she'd whispered, "I love you." The sun shined in from the window, kneading the knots in his shoulders. *There is too much to lose. You do not know her.* This chance at a new life was too precious to risk exposing himself. He could not let his guard down and confide in her simply for the sake of love.

Love.

He stopped cold and stared at the wall, allowing the word to drift in and out of his vision. Was such a word not equally dangerous, nay more so, than his work with the patriots? As if smuggling goods sixty miles to Boston was not foolhardy enough...

His jaw threatened to crack from clenching. He would remain kind to her, as was his nature. Make her laugh, make her smile, meet her needs—above all, keep her safe. But to fall in love? Nay. That could not be done.

Chapter Fifteen

A flash of approaching red amongst the colored autumn foliage slowed Paul's step. He dashed behind a tree and watched from the safety of the wood. He'd overheard during last night's meal at the patriot's tavern the rumors of smuggling in the wood beside the creek. But as he had not seen Donaldson nor heard tell of anyone that might possibly be him, Providence would be the next place for his search. He *had* to be close. Paul's limbs buzzed. The proximity of the troops was doubtless a sign. For where there were redcoats, there would surely be patriots. And where there were patriots, there Donaldson might be found.

"We've been searching for half an hour already. He's gone, Pryer."

Pryer? Paul squinted to see past the canopy of colorful branches that blocked his view. That shock of bright yellow hair confirmed what he thought. Mark Pryer. He knew him well.

"He was here, I swear it." Pryer looked behind. "Give me another moment, then I shall return to camp."

"Fine then. But don't be long." The other soldier

withdrew, leaving Pryer alone.

When the lone redcoat passed only five feet from his hiding place, Paul stepped from behind the tree. "Lieutenant Pryer?"

The soldier halted and reached for his pistol, face rigid then instantly calm with recognition. "Captain Stockton." He stood straight and replaced the gun at his side. "Forgive me, sir, I did not see you." Questions gave rise to lines around his eyes as he studied Paul's state of dress. "Why are you here sir, and without uniform?"

"I am on assignment." The answer seemed to satisfy his old companion-in-arms.

Pryer relaxed his posture. "Fortunate you are. We're to pick fleas from a dog's back." He laughed. "Patriots are a destructive and elusive nuisance."

"How many have you found?"

"Smuggling? None." He pointed from where he came. "Just nearly apprehended one, but 'twas left empty handed." He sneered. "Did find a lovely pair of lips I would have liked to sample though."

Paul shook his head. Pryer's need for women made him both weak and a second-class soldier. "What do you mean you nearly apprehended one?"

"Been trailing a boy for some time, convinced he was preparing to exchange goods." Pryer gripped both hands on the muzzle of his gun and leaned against it. "But I lost him and found only a farmer and his wife."

"You lost him?" Predictable. Paul resisted the urge

to growl. And his father found reason to scold him when scores of soldiers were disgustingly inept. "Did you not think to follow them?"

Mouth pinched and quirked at one end, Pryer lifted one shoulder. "A fool's errand. Those ignoramuses can waste their efforts all they like, as far as I'm concerned. Our energies are better spent blasting away at those rebels on the hill then stopping something that won't make a hint of difference even if they can get goods into the city."

Paul rubbed his jaw and breathed hard through his nose. A false sentiment shared by many. Every effort must and should be made to end any act of rebellion before too many soldiers were forced to risk their lives in a civil war.

"On your way back then?" Paul turned to look toward Sandwich. "Any soldiers stationed in town?"

"A few I suspect, but I've just come from Providence, so I don't know the particulars here." He straightened and his expression folded with disgust. "I do know 'tis a hotbed of patriotic sentiment, but they're as trivial as all the rest."

"Did you—" A streak of color and a rustle of leaves made Paul jerk. He looked to Pryer, whose eyes were trained on a swaying branch. "Your lost boy perhaps?"

Pryer's eyes narrowed and he lifted his musket. He motioned forward with a quick lift of the chin, but Paul pressed his hand against Pryer's chest. He shook his head and pointed to a strip of white beside a bush of dried leaves not a stone's throw to the right.

He mouthed, "Shoot."

Raising the weapon, Pryer yelled. "Show yourself!"

Nothing. Not even the slightest movement.

Pryer tried again, louder. "Show yourself, patriot."

Paul's patience snapped. "Just shoot him."

"I will not shoot if I don't know who it is."

"What kind of soldier are you?" Paul ripped a pistol from his side and aimed at the motionless spot of fabric. "Come forward, or I will shoot."

No response.

After another beat of silence, Pryer gave Paul a sideways glance, motioning to the taunting piece of white. "Let him be, Paul." His gravelly whisper carried a spark of rage. "Killing him will change nothing."

The racing thump of Paul's pulse thundered in his ears. Was every soldier turning soft like his father? Donaldson could go free after all he'd done, and now this traitor would be permitted to continue his treasonous actions without consequence?

Passion pushed reason to the side. He gripped the weapon harder and pulled the trigger. An ear-splitting crack slashed through the silent forest. Paul raced toward the victim, Pryer close behind.

He slowed as he neared the target and lowered to his haunches, unschooled violence poisoning his blood. A stream of profanities clouded the wood as he tore the piece of white cloth from its perch on a naked branch. A decoy.

He peered up from his crouched position by Pryer, whose raised brows and round eyes made Paul's fists itch to punch the look from his face. "Impressed are you?"

"He fooled us both."

Another slight rustle not ten feet away stole Paul's attention and aimed it with deadly accuracy. Speaking to the concealed offender, Paul kept his voice to a whispering roar. "Show yourself."

No movement.

Paul stood, fury flooding his muscles with every second the patriot refused his commands. "Get up now!"

Still nothing.

He lunged and the figure whirled but ran only a few steps before Paul yanked at his collar and spun him around.

Stunned, Paul spoke to Pryer, keeping his eyes on the freckled face, twisted in fear. "Is this the boy?"

Pryer hurried beside him and answered. "Aye, I believe so."

"You *believe* so?"

"I cannot be completely sure."

Paul rolled his eyes in place of smacking the sorry excuse of a man. "I'll help you tie him so you can bring him back to camp."

"Nay." Pryer's face went slack as he stared at the boy then turned to Paul with narrowed eyes. "Let him go, can you not see he's petrified?" He reached for Paul's iron grip, but Paul jerked away, gripping tighter.

"Have you gone mad?" Paul jammed a rigid finger at Pryer's chest. "This boy is a traitor—a lover of self more than a lover of country—just like the rest of them! If we do not make every turncoat pay we will all suffer." Keeping the boy at arms length he pointed at Pryer's ready musket. "Finish him."

Pryer grimaced. "He's only a boy!"

The lad gasped and gripped Paul's wrist with his thin, cold fingers. "Sir, I beg you! Let me go!"

Paul stared into the youth's round, pleading eyes, his own as unmoved as an island in a storm. Allowing the soft, inner core of his heart to sway in the boy's favor would lead to greater, more grievous betrayals of conscience.

He turned back to his companion and yanked the musket from his grip. "Do it."

"You are mad." Pryer scoffed and retreated a step. "I followed him, aye. But I never witnessed an exchange and my orders were to bring in a man, if I found him. But this is no man and you are not my superior." He paused, his lips tightening. "Let him go, Paul."

The bubbling rage in Paul's gut surged like a boiling spring, flooding his limbs with steaming blood. His father's words rang in his ears. *Let the man go, son. We have more important things to occupy our time.*

Paul hardened his grip, hot air seething as he breathed through clenched teeth. Nay! He would not let him go. He would not let anyone go. Not

Donaldson, and certainly not a boy who would grow to betray the crown. If he had to find every miscreant and bring every deserter to justice, so be it.

He released his grip on the boy and shoved him to the ground. The lad's mouth gaped open as he gasped for air, tears welling in his eyes.

Paul stepped back and strangled the boy with his gaze. "Get out."

Shock seemed to smack the boy into action and he was on his feet, scrambling for the freedom of the wood.

Pryer's shoulders dropped and he released a worried laugh. "You had me scared, Stockton."

Paul looked sideways. "Did I frighten you?" His muscles formed granite under his sleeves. "How foolish of me. I am loathe to think you might believe I had forgotten that every person, young or old, who chooses to fight against the crown is a traitor and deserves a traitor's just reward." He shook his head in disgust and raised the weapon at the boy's receding figure. "I would never..."

With a roar Pryer lunged for the gun. Paul struggled to keep the pistol pointed at the figure as it faded farther from view.

"You...shall not..." Pryer grunted as he strained to pry the weapon from Paul's fingers.

A sudden flash and crack was followed by silence.

Pryer dropped his hands and looked from Paul to where the bullet had flown aimlessly into the wood.

Paul crushed a curse between his teeth. He'd missed.

He pointed the smoking musket at Pryer, growling his words. "You're no better than they."

"Perhaps." Pryer stepped away. "But at least I won't have to answer to God over an innocent life taken."

Paul leaned in. "God and King George are one in the same, and until you come to realize that, Pryer, your life is worthless."

Pryer pulled back with a grimace and strode away, speechless, leaving Paul alone in the curls of gun smoke. Paul turned to stare where the boy had fled. He might have escaped capture. So be it. But Donaldson would never be free. *I will find you. Do not worry. I will find you.*

William knocked at the back door of Nathaniel's home, his stomach at his feet. He released a long breath, wishing the autumn breeze would brush away the lingering pains in his chest. Instead, they only played with his queue, tickling the hairs along his heated neck.

He tapped his fingers against his leg and prepared to knock again but it opened and Kitty stood in the doorway, her smile wide.

"Henry, what a pleasure to see you."

He scowled.

She cleared her throat. "Forgive me, William."

Cheeks a sudden red, she craned her neck and peered side to side out the door. Once she seemed certain her blunder hadn't been witnessed she relaxed and motioned for him to come in. "What brings you here this fine evening? Where is your wife?"

"She's uh...she's preparing the nettles she picked." William entered, closing the door. "She is most grateful to you, for helping her learn some...for sharing some recipes."

"I adore her more than I can say." Kitty made her way to the kitchen and flung a quick smile over her shoulder. "Nettles are the most pleasant in spring, but with good seasoning they should be quite delicious."

She found her place beside the kitchen fire and stooped to place some additional ashes atop a cast iron lid. "Nathaniel isn't here. I assume you've come to speak with him."

"I have." William leaned his shoulder against the doorframe. The storm still bellowed within and he pressed out another breath as he picked at the fraying edge of his cocked hat. He must speak with Nathaniel as soon as possible. If he didn't return within a few minutes, William determined to find Thomas.

"What troubles you?"

William looked up. "Hmm?"

Kitty wiped her hands against her apron, her smile at a tilt. "Did you forget how much time we spent together in Boston those months before I returned?" She stopped several feet in front of him and crossed her arms, her head slightly bowed. "I know something troubles you, *William*. And I would venture to suppose it isn't the farm or the smuggling." She whispered the last word.

Rubbing his jaw, William released a weak chuckle. So, the strain of his home life he suppressed beneath the matters of war was evident. He stared at the floor. The urge to speak the burden and ease a portion of his pain—perhaps gain some wisdom in the ways of women—became so tantalizing his jaw ached from keeping back the words.

He shrugged one shoulder.

Her hands went to her hips. "So, you will not speak of it? Do you not trust me?" The accusation was said with a raise of her brow and quirk of her mouth, nearly bringing another laugh from his throat.

"It seems I am as easy to read as you are."

"Is Anna...is she all right?" Kitty's eyes went soft. "Are you?"

There in the warm, homey kitchen, William's muscles began to soften. Kitty had always reminded him of his sisters, and being near her made him feel as though he did still have family, that he wasn't entirely alone. Though he was, and the emptiness never left him.

You have Anna.

He brushed the thought away, though it lingered when the aroma of lavender brought back the scent of Anna's hair, the feel of her skin. And the need to feel it again.

William shifted his feet and looked down again at his hat. "We are learning how to manage this new life. 'Tis difficult for both of us, but...we'll fit into ourselves in time."

Silence welled between them. Kitty dropped her hands to her sides and her voice went quiet. "You have feelings for her."

He looked up, his eyes meeting hers. So many things he wished to say, but how to say it? *I do, but my past imprisons me.*

She must have seen a semblance of answer in his eyes. Reaching out, she touched his arm. "What happened to you, William? There is much I know you do not speak of. I would hear it. And nothing you say will leave this room, I give you my word."

"I believe that, Kitty." He straightened and put his hat on his head. "Perhaps someday I will speak of it, but for now I should—"

"Speak of what?"

William spun to see Nathaniel enter through the back and plunk his medical bag on the large table beside the door. His grin consumed his face. "Just the man I wanted to see," he said.

"Is that so?" William tucked his hat under his arm once more.

"Aye." Nathaniel removed his coat then looked to his wife, who dashed from behind William to swing her arms around her husband.

She planted a quick kiss on his cheek then spun back to the kitchen. "I shall leave you gentlemen to your conversation. Supper requires my attention."

Nathaniel's gaze followed her away, his expression dreamlike. "I will never deserve her, William. No matter how I try, I shall never deserve her."

"I must say I'm surprised she forgave you so quickly." William moved to the parlor and took the largest chair.

"Well, I'm easy to forgive." Nathaniel chuckled, then grew serious. "But you didn't come to discuss my marriage."

William pulled his lip between his teeth. "The boy I met today, the one for the exchange—"

"Boy?" Every hint of a smile vanished from Nathaniel's face. "You should have met a man. Are you sure you were not duped?"

"'Twas our smuggler, no doubt." William explained the boy's struggle and Nathaniel stared, mouth tight as William finished. "That is not the worst of it. He was followed."

Nathaniel's face went slack. "To you."

"Aye, to the very edge of my property." His stomach churned. "If Anna had not come, I fear what might have happened." He let out a dark breath. "Though her presence there nearly ripped me in half. He was far too close."

Cheek between his teeth, Nathaniel answered low. "What was Anna doing in the wood?"

William flung a quick glance over his shoulder toward the kitchen to be sure they were still alone. "She was gathering nettles for supper." The memory sparked the fear and indignation that simmered just beneath the surface. If that soldier had touched her...

"What did he say? Could you discern if they had any additional intelligence?"

William nodded. "We must be more discreet if we are to continue. Find another route perhaps. Not exchange in the middle of the..." He stopped and bit his tongue to keep from swearing. He growled and finished the thought, "The middle of the day." The anger he'd suppressed since the moment he'd seen Anna bubbled.

Nathaniel's neck ticked. "We must speak of this to Thomas." He hurled from the chair and yanked his hat from the table. "Come. I have much to tell you, as well."

They were out the back door and striding down the road for some minutes before Nathaniel began speaking again. "Thomas and I are feeling the need to do more."

"More?"

"Aye. Our army surrounds Boston in the hills outside the city, but their situation is desperate."

William focused on the ground, forehead pressing down. "I had heard they were in some need." He stopped short as a horse and rider approached. Both men nodded as the rider passed and only when the sound of the hooves had completely passed did Nathaniel continue.

"Thomas knew Henry Knox from his time in Boston and has corresponded with him."

"Knox? I don't know him."

Nathaniel nodded. "He's the officer over artillery. He has pleaded with Thomas to secure any and all weapons, and as much powder and lead as we can."

"So you will switch your attentions to only gathering and supplying the army with more ammunition?"

The Watson's home came into view and Nathaniel picked up his pace. "Nay, not switch them. We shall do both."

Nathaniel knocked twice and strode in without so much as a second's pause. "Thomas?"

Eliza called down from the stairs. "He is just outside, Nathaniel."

"Thank you, Eliza," he answered as the back door opened and Thomas entered, a load of wood in his arms.

"Good evening, gentlemen." He deposited the load by the fire and brushed his hands. "You have told him?"

Nathaniel nodded. "Aye."

"I've alerted Joseph Wythe," Thomas said. "I expect him here any minute."

William went to the fire and stared at the orange flames. Did these men know what opposition awaited? His forehead cramped. They were not fools, not ignorant of the challenge that lay ahead. But the British out-gunned and out-manned them at ratios hard to comprehend. He glanced over his shoulder. Thomas and Nathaniel spoke together in quiet tones. 'Twas possible they were blissfully unaware of the consequences. He gave a quick shake of his head. Nay. Never were two men more astute, more acutely in tune with the realities of life.

A quick knock tapped through the room. "There he is now." Thomas opened the door. "Joseph."

Joseph entered and doffed his hat. "Gentlemen."

Nathaniel spoke first. "William encountered a lobsterback today."

"You did?" Both Joseph and Thomas answered together.

William stepped back and crossed his arms. "'Twas unpleasant but we managed. I gave the boy the package and he escaped, but I fear his passage to Plymouth will be hampered."

"How long ago was this?"

"Not three hours."

Joseph neared, resting his hands atop the upholstered chair. "'Tis becoming too dangerous?"

"Never too dangerous." William shook his head. "We simply need to out-smart them. And that shouldn't be at all difficult."

The door slammed open and Kitty rushed in. "Nathaniel!"

She whirled aside and two men entered, the limp body of a boy in their arms. William's blood went still in his veins. The red hair and freckles were unmistakable. He rushed forward but Nathaniel was there before him.

"Put him down, let me see him."

"Help me, help me!" The boy's broken voice ripped William's heart.

He rushed to the boy's side as the men lowered him to the floor. "You'll be fine, son."

The boy's eyes found William and his quivering hands reached out. "I did what you said—ahhh!" He cried out in pain as Nathaniel ripped open his blood-soaked coat.

Nathaniel's features went hard. "Get me a cloth. Now!"

Eliza rushed into the room. "What's happened?"

No one answered.

Already prepared, Kitty thrust a cloth at the boy's chest and Nathaniel held it firm. He turned to his wife and gave instructions while the boy wailed.

"I can't die, I can't die, I can't die." The boy's entire frame quivered, and his pale face went ever more white until even the freckles began to lose their pigment.

"Son, look at me." William cupped his face and forced the young stranger to look in his eyes. "You will be well—look at me. You will be well. Now, tell me your name."

"Lund...Townsend." He struggled to look down at his middle, but William held his head still.

The boy groaned again, this time with a shrillness that stabbed the air. His eyes went round and his breathing hiccoughed. William's limbs went numb. *No, Lord!*

William threw a frantic look to Nathaniel. The doctor's arms and chest were spattered with blood, as were Kitty's. They worked together to stem the flow talking fast and grabbing at the cloths and bandages that Eliza thrust at them.

William turned again to the boy. "Tell me what happened."

The boy's body shook more now, his jaw tapping his teeth together as he tried to speak. "In the woods...the same soldier... and...another man."

"Another soldier?"

"No, he was..." He stopped as tears poured from his frantic eyes. His young face contorted with fear as he met William's gaze. "I don't want to die."

Dear God, please keep him alive!

William coughed to clear the rock from his throat but it wouldn't move. He spoke deep and low, stroking the boy's head as huge tears continued to fall over his trembling cheeks. "You will live."

Nathaniel yelled something and Kitty responded quiet but with equal urgency.

The boy's trembling began to fade and his voice quieted. "I'm scared."

William forced a smile he didn't actually feel as he stroked the boy's head once more. "You are the bravest man I know."

The panic smoothed from his features and his eyes

went still. It was only when the boy's head went limp that William turned to Nathaniel, unable to breathe.

The doctor swore between his teeth and hurled a blood-covered rag on the ground beside him. Kitty slumped to the side and turned her head away.

William gasped and his lungs raced, meeting the sudden pace of his pulse. He looked again at the boy. A needless death. Rage misted through him like a poisonous fume.

He rested the boy's head gently against the ground and looked to the men who had brought him. "What happened? Where did you find him?" Rising to his feet, he started to speak again, but Nathaniel neared and spoke before him.

"Were you returning from Plymouth?" Nathaniel turned to William. "This is Andrew Cooper and his son Leo."

William nodded as the older one spoke.

"Aye, we were." He looked to the boy's limp form on the ground. "We heard gunfire, then not long after Leo heard him—"

"Did you see anyone?" William interrupted. "Was he alone?"

The younger man answered. "We saw no one else."

William spun and strode from the room, but Nathaniel caught him by the arm. "Where are you going?"

"To get my musket."

Nathaniel's grip went as hard as his look. "Wait." He

turned to Andrew and Leo. "Report your story to my wife, then bring the child's body to his family." He turned to Kitty. "I'm going with William."

Thomas reached for his musket above the mantel then turned to Joseph as if he knew full well his thoughts mirrored theirs.

William exited with the others following. "Meet me at my farm at the edge of the wood."

The men raced from the house and the part of William he could not suppress—the soldier he would always be—surged to the forefront, giving commands as they parted ways to ready their mounts. "If the murderer is on foot, he'll be easy to catch. On horseback, it could be impossible." He looked up. "The sky is darkening. Be ready to ride."

Chapter Sixteen

The front door was locked.

William jostled the handle and rammed his fist against the door. "Anna, let me in."

When the door finally opened, Anna's face was as white as the flour on her hands. "What's happened?"

He rushed in and hurried to the mantel, yanking his musket from its perch, then snatched the powder horn and lead balls he'd made two nights before.

He spoke as he flung the strap of munitions over his shoulder. "You are to go to the Watson's immediately."

Her arms dropped to her side. "What is it? What's happened?"

"I will tell you when I return." Taking her by the arm, he led her outside. "Run and do not stop until you reach their door."

She nodded and turned, but his fingers refused to release her. Anna flung him a look, eyes wide with fear.

He should run with her, make sure she was safe, but his duty was elsewhere. *God, please stay with her...*

Her brow puckered and he finally spoke. "All will be well."

His words seemed to smooth the depth of the creases but not eliminate them. She studied him. "I pray it will."

Aye, pray. "I shall return. Now go quickly."

Grabbing a fist-full of skirt, Anna ran toward the Watson's just as Joseph and Thomas arrived on horseback. Thomas scowled, looking after Anna. "Where is she going?"

William yelled over his shoulder as he raced to the barn for his mount. "To your home."

When he returned, astride his saddled horse, Nathaniel had arrived, two pistols strapped to his chest and a musket across his lap. "Ready?"

"Aye," William answered.

The animals tossed their heads and stepped side to side. William looked to the wood and snapped a curse between his teeth. "This fog will do us no good."

A low mist had begun to blanket the forest with a thick curtain of white. 'Twas just the sort of cover a fugitive praised and a hunter despised.

He yanked on the reins and motioned for the men to follow. "Thomas and Joseph, take the road. Nathaniel, follow beside the creek and I'll take the wood."

Each man nodded in turn and kicked their mounts, disappearing into the gathering fog.

William's chest burst as he recalled the young boy's pale skin, his pleading eyes. A vice-like grip on the reins, William prodded his animal forward but the fading light and heavy white that encircled him made a swift journey impossible. His muscles ached to induce the same fear in the killer's face as he'd seen in the child's. If only he could be found.

William trained his ears upon every snap, every rustle, every scratch that might echo through the trees, but the fog seemed to deaden the air. An eerie silence loomed as the sun stole another bit of its light. *Lord, let me find him.*

The horse's ears perked and William tugged on the reins, bringing the animal to a quick halt. He'd heard it too, a tiny brush against the ground not three yards distant. He barely breathed, praying that the sound was evidence his prey was within reach of his musket's ball.

Sensing a pair of unseen eyes trained on their approach, the hairs on William's neck pricked and his blood charged faster in his veins. A familiar sensation expanded in his stomach, turning it to granite.

He was not alone.

Every creak of leather as he dismounted seemed loud as cannon fire and William berated himself for not having ventured on foot. Ghostly billows of fog drifted round like a haunting apparition.

Utter silence.

William pursed his lips and scanned the dark pillars that surrounded him. He'd heard something, no doubt. But had he—

Another tiny brush made his lungs solid and he readied his pistol, his skin hot with rage. "Show yourself!"

He stepped forward. If it were an animal, it would scamper to safety. A fugitive, however, might stay and pray the fog would prolong its cover.

"I know you killed that boy." He stepped again. Nothing moved.

Slow and deliberate, William took another step. His prey darted and William's instinct consumed. The swift figure raced over the leaf-covered ground and William charged after. Chest heaving, he gripped the ready pistol. Dodging branches and bushes that jumped out from the mist, William's breath matched the desperate pace of his pulse. Deeper into the wood, farther from safety.

Could this be a trap as well? A ruse to lure him away and finally bring him to justice? Nay, that mattered naught. The pace of the one he pursued quickened and so did William. The boy had been killed and this was the murderer. There was no doubt.

The distance between their crunching steps lessened and a muted gray figure began to take form through the fog. William pushed harder, almost feeling the skin of the man's neck beneath his fingers. His legs burned as he strained to close the remaining gap. Though he could run full-out for much longer, the rage pooled in his limbs. Flashes of memory scarred his eyes. That innocent, freckled face. Pain. Fear. So much blood.

With a roar he skidded to a stop and raised his

weapon. A burst of fire and thundering crack snapped against the trees. Even shooting into the fog, he couldn't have missed. Not at this distance.

Silence consumed once more. Only the heavy in and out of his breath echoed in the unearthly stillness. He'd done it.

Racing forward, William hurried to the place the body had fallen, studying the ground as wisps of white swirled around his boots. His fingers twitched against the pistol.

It couldn't be...

He stood motionless, grinding his teeth. How could the man have gotten away? How could he have disappeared with not so much as a telltale footprint?

William's limbs grew heavy and his grip on the pistol turned to iron. The grayish-white fog dimmed a measure as the sun slipped farther down. Staring into the mist, resolve plastered into the tiny fissures of his will. The boy's courage, his fearless sense of duty, knitted into William's soul. More than ever the cause needed him. More than ever the British needed defeat—to be taught they could not demand a person's loyalty. Or their life.

This was not the end. Nay, only the beginning.

Paul's chest burned. Allowing only the thinnest thread of breath to his starving lungs, he pressed his back against the base of the tree. So, the boy had been killed after all. Well then. One less patriot. Refusing even to blink until the sound of his pursuer's boots could no longer be heard, he pressed his fingers against the gushing wound in his middle.

Entombed in silent fog, Paul gasped and leaned his head against the bark of the tree. Staring at the unseen sky, his mind replayed the sound of the voice he'd heard. Could it have been?

He rubbed a hand over his face. It sounded so much like him, Paul would have wagered his weapon. This was Sandwich, was it not? Donaldson could be here, as he'd surmised, so the probability of such an encounter was not without reason. And *good Samaritan* that Donaldson was, meant where trouble could be found, the traitor was not far distant.

Paul winced and breathed hard through clenched teeth to keep his mind formulating the sorry tale he must produce. He pushed to his feet just as it lighted his mind. He'd seen the man who shot the boy. Aye. 'Twas the same man who pursued and nearly killed him as well. The murderer must be caught and brought to justice. A felon didn't deserve to breathe the same air as honest men.

Black hatred charred the edges of his weary mind. Stumbling from his hiding place, he stopped only long enough to catch his bearings and started toward Plymouth. Recovering in Sandwich could put him at risk of being found by the man whom he must find first—and bring to justice. Once he reported to the townsfolk the crime of the murdered child, and the butchering fugitive who was surely abiding in their midst, he would have their loyal support. Donaldson would get a piece of lead in the chest. And Paul would put it there. Today or tomorrow or next week, it mattered not. His pursuit was nearly over.

Chapter Seventeen

In front of the fire, only minutes after returning from the Watson's, Anna stared. The golden glow faded in and out as the flames popped and snapped. She was numb, struggling against the image that continued to plague her. The motionless boy on the floor, covered in blood and with a face so white he looked almost stone-like. The fierce look in William's eyes affirmed he would do more than find the killer. But he had not found him, and the tension billowing from his shoulders caused a pang in her middle.

Her throat ached and she blinked to keep the stray tears from falling. Eliza and Kitty, though devastated, seemed as though their determination against the British now heated instead of cooled. She looked to her hands and picked at the skin around her nail, remembering how at the sight of the boy she'd nearly collapsed and was forced to spend the remainder of the time resting above stairs while the two men took the child's lifeless body away. Shame spilled over her like sap, slow and thick. Where was her courage? These people seemed to be strengthened by trial, not destroyed by it. Was it their ignorance, like her father had always said? Or was it truth that shattered the shackles of servitude, giving way to their unbridled courage? She looked forward again and studied the flames as they licked the far end of a log. Eliza had said the truth had done that for her—given her an understanding that carried her forward in the cause of freedom, despite the difficulties, despite the risks. For truly, there were risks. Today proved that in a way Anna wished more than ever to forget. But she never would.

The door clicked behind her and Anna turned in her seat. William entered and removed his hat, resting it and his coat on the peg by the door.

He flung her a sideways look, "I expected you to be abed."

She looked back to the fire. "I could not sleep."

The gentle stomp of his boots against the wood floor neared until he took the seat beside her. He sat with a humph and rested his elbows on his knees, wiping his hands over his face. "'Twas the soldier, I fear. But impossible to know for certain."

"Will he be punished?"

A curt, quick laugh left his lips. He slumped back in his seat. "The British will do whatever they like, when they like."

"You mean the man who shot that poor boy will never be charged, never forced to pay for such a crime?"

SO *rare* A GIFT

William stared, his eyes lost as if he were still in the wood. "Not in this life it would seem."

A rolling sensation tumbled down her middle. Vengeance was God's. Somehow they must take comfort in that. She sent William a sidelong glance. The light of the flames cast angled shadows along his profile, and not for the first time, he reminded her of Bernini's David—the creased forehead, the determined lines in his jaw.

She looked away before he could feel the weight of her stare. "You did all you could—"

"Did I?"

Anna turned only her head to him. "Will you keep up this dangerous pursuit?"

He questioned her with a look.

She swiveled toward him. "That innocent boy was killed because he was smuggling. The same could happen to you."

William's eyes narrowed. "We have discussed this matter before."

"Aye, but not since a young child was murdered." She stood and turned away from the light of the flame. "If you were to die and if I were forced to return to England—"

"I have already given you my word. Is that not enough for you?" The chair scraped along the floor, indicating he stood. "I will not abandon the fight simply because you choose to cling to your fears."

"Choose to?" She spun around. "Do not I have a

right to be afraid?"

"When we married I made a vow to provide and protect, which I have done and will do. Always."

She spun to the fire once again, praying he didn't see the moisture in her eyes. "I do not wish to argue."

The logs popped, their tiny sparks singeing the swollen places of her heart. This marriage *was* meant to protect her, not leave her a widow in a strange land. Yet the strains that played in her chest were not from that threat alone. She knew from whence they came, but she refused to believe it was true.

You love him, do not try to deny it. She'd even spoken as much aloud. Closing her eyes, Anna yearned to crumple the memory from her mind and watch it curl to ash in the fire. The moment the words had left her mouth, he'd changed. No longer near and warm, but distant, like the sun on a winter's morn—present, but ever so far away.

She shook her head and continued on. "'Tis true that my concerns of being discovered are never far from my mind." Anna braved a look behind and caught his gaze. "But you must know I fear for your safety, William. For no other reason than my desire for you to be well."

William looked down at his hands, rubbing his thumb against his forefinger. "There is more at risk than simply my welfare and yours, Anna," he said, looking up. "People yet to be born will thrive in this liberty we now hazard to give. 'Tis a freedom we have never known."

Anna turned the ring against her finger, studying how the orange flames turned the brown log to black. She looked to her husband, praying he detected the concern with which she laced her words. "You would give your life for such a thing? Something you cannot even be sure will be realized?" She scowled, staring at the ground. "That boy is dead. His future is no more. His parents will learn of his passing and grief will become their companion for the rest of their days. Will they believe his death was worth the pain once they realize this war is waged for a lost cause?"

William sat back against the chair, not looking to her as he spoke. "You believe the cause is lost? I tell you, it is not." 'Twas then he turned to her. "Liberty will be the victor."

Deep within, a swelling began. 'Twas so foreign, Anna stopped breathing to detect its origin. "So you will keep on? You all will keep on, though one of you may be killed?"

"I will keep on at any cost, Anna. I am driven, as all patriots are, by the image of our children—"

Anna froze, his words gripping her motionless. A cutting silence slashed between them. She dared not look at him for the tears that burned behind her eyes. Seeking refuge in the dark of their room, she darted for the door.

William reached out, gripping her arm with firm but tender fingers. "Anna, forgive me. I didn't mean to pain you."

"Nay, 'tis I who am to blame." She lowered her tone, hoping the hollow resonance would dispel the hurt from her voice. "Had I told you before we took our vows, then you would have been able to choose a different wife and have the joy of a posterity to fight for."

She felt the warmth of his stare upon her, but still she hadn't the strength to look up. Her middle pinched with grief and her knees threatened to buckle. "I am tired."

She turned to leave but the grip on her arm tightened and William's voice warmed her like the fire in front of them. "I cannot let you go. Not until you are assured I meant no harm."

Of course he had not. But her bare womb would haunt her, and therefore him, until the day they left this world for the next. She'd endured the pain of this curse since her youth, but he had only just learned that he would never father a child.

Her courage began to lose its grip on the cliff of her grief, the weight of pain pulling harder, but she clung tighter, finding the strength to lift her eyes and meet his gaze. When she did, the pity she prepared to find was not there at all, but something she couldn't name. Compassion? Tenderness? Whatever it was seemed to reach from his fathomless blue eyes and twine around her wounded spirit, bandaging it with the kind of caring she'd never known.

Releasing his fingers from her arm, he reached to her cheek but pulled his hand back before his skin brushed hers. "When I accepted you, I accepted everything—the known and the unknown. I must be prepared for anything must I not?" The last of his words lacked warmth, as if the coals of his charity were extinguished before he'd finished speaking.

Truth, but still it pained, for his words said more than the mere syllables he'd spoken.

"'Tis every man's wish to have a son of his own," she said. "A joy you will never know."

He shook his head lightly. "This liberty we sacrifice for has value for all and is worth our efforts whether our name continues or not." He trailed his vision down her face and neck and arm before reaching to take her hands in his. He stepped closer. "Mankind needs this freedom. We must *live* truth. Fearlessly. Since we are all brothers and sisters in Christ, should we not go on in so great a cause?"

Her heart turned to liquid, spilling out the heated blood in her chest and flooding her limbs. She stared up at him, wonder cascading down her spine. This was not freedom for the colonists alone. Freedom was for mankind. The veracity pricked her spirit, and for the first time, the roots of truth took hold in her mind. But a thought from her center cut its way through the sprouting vines, and the words slipped from her tongue before she could stop them. "But if you are killed...and if I am taken..."

"That is a thought on which I refuse to dwell." His jaw squared and his soft timbre coated her fears like a cloak in winter. "But I am willing to take the risk. Are you?"

In that moment, the valor she gleaned from his rich eyes, the strength that warmed her hands and up into her soul was enough to make her courageous in the face of anything. She gripped her fingers around his. "I am."

The twitch of a smile started at the corners of his mouth. "You are a true colonial then, no matter how your proper English betrays you."

The breath of a laugh eased from her nose as she finished her short journey to the bedchamber. "That and much else betrays the truth of me, I fear." Her words dropped in a heap at her feet and she all but tripped over them. Would he gather her meaning? She plucked a candle from the table near the door and entered the room, her pulse trying to find its calm.

"There is something I've wanted to ask you." William rounded the bed, leaning his shoulder against the tall poster on the side opposite. "How is it, if you were so poor as you claim, that you speak with the tongue of the wealthy?"

Her cheeks grew hot, but she acted untouched. "I was unaware there is a difference."

"Aye, there is indeed." He pushed away and started to unbutton his waistcoat. He eyed her with a sideways glance. His jaw worked as if he chewed on the words he wished to say, then with a large sigh expelled them. "There are many differences between the rich and poor, but those of us in lower ranks will never know all the particulars. For that I am grateful."

Anna sunk back at the anger that snarled between his words.

He sat on the bed and began to remove his boots. "There is still much of you I do not know." He stopped and turned to look over his shoulder, mouth firm, then turned away again to finish with his boots. No anger, only resignation in his tone. "'Tis hard to increase in trust when so much is still left unspoken."

The statement pricked like a stray needle. Aye, there was much she kept within, and with his renewed sentiments of disdain for the status of life she'd left, was not her silence well placed?

Sighing, Anna sat on the front of the bed and looked down, turning the ring against her finger. The barb of his words left a small pulsing wound. How could he say such things when she had not prodded him for the truths he guarded?

Let it be, Anna. 'Twas true that she had shared little. They were married, were they not? Should she not engender at least a spoonful of courage and share with him one small part of her?

Then, without bidding, the words tumbled from her lips. "I had a twin brother."

l

A twin?

William's brow tightened as he watched Anna, her mouth pinching and her throat bobbing as she struggled with emotion, though no tears glimmered in her eyes.

He gnawed on the inside of his cheek, flogging himself for the veiled reprimand he'd spoken. *'Tis hard to increase in trust when so much is still left unspoken?* Selfish coward. His conscience began a deep and thorough castigation. Did he really expect his wife to expose all of herself, when he could never do the same?

"My brother was very kind to me." She continued despite the cloak of hurt that draped her gentle voice. "I could not have endured so much hardship, if not for him."

She continued to stare down, twisting her ring against her finger. "Mother was a saint—our very angel on earth—offering us a haven from our father who never cared to disguise his disdain for us." Her voice went deep and her expression dropped. "When we were ten years old, Mother became desperately ill and slowly, over the course of two years, slipped away from us."

With a choppy sigh, she pressed her hands to her knees and looked forward toward the fireplace. "She always wished for me to marry for love. Something she herself had not done. She made me promise that I would put all else aside and when the time came, give my heart to one that was worthy." At this she stopped and looked again at her hands. "But after her death, my father's disdain developed into cruelty and on my sixteenth birthday he announced he had chosen a husband for me. An older man who wished a companion but didn't want the burden of siring a child."

Oh, dear Lord. What father would do that to his child? William clamped his jaw, refusing to take his eyes from her. The soft muscles of her face tightened and her dainty fingers knitted tighter in her lap. He yearned to reach out. Would she want to be touched?

Releasing a long quiet breath, Anna craned her neck toward his side of the bed, a tight smile pulling at her lips. "All my life my brother was there for me—making me laugh, holding me when I cried—'twas almost as if he knew me better than I knew myself." At this, a bitter laugh escaped her throat. "When he learned what father planned to do, he flew into a rage and promised me I would never be made to endure such a vacant life. That very night he stole me away and we rode toward London, believing that in the vast city we could remain hidden and begin our lives anew..."

Her voice trailed away, as if the memory carried her with it. The color drained from her cheeks and she turned away again to stare at the far corner of the room, the past holding her captive. William could stand it no longer. Standing, he rounded the bed and rested beside her. He cupped her knee and she flicked toward him as if he had pulled her from the edge of a cliff.

"You escaped him?" he gently prodded.

She blinked and shook her head, speaking forward. "Nay. We had not gone ten miles when our father's men apprehended us and forced us home. I was married three days later and lived as Edwin Rone's wife for ten years until he died, leaving me his vast estate and all the misery that accompanied it."

She slammed her eyes shut and covered her face with her hand.

William dropped his gaze, allowing the grievous truth to trickle down him like the cold, stale drip of melting ice. Her marriage had not been joyful. She hadn't loved her husband as he'd thought. Pain for her and regret for ever having believed otherwise swirled into a vortex of guilt in his middle.

"Anna, I'm—"

"So now you know I lived a life of privilege." She turned to him, harbored tears in her eyes. "I never intended to lie to you, I simply wanted to find a way to start anew. I should have told you so much—that I cannot bear children and that I cannot do all the things I led you to believe I could..." Her chin quivered as she held his gaze. "I was afraid, especially when I learned how you felt about the wealthy, afraid you would despise me. I am sorry."

The pain in her words ripped open what remained of his battered shame. He covered her hand with his. "I have known for some time that you did not come from the background you feigned."

"You did?"

"'Twas not difficult to surmise. You..." He stopped, and cleared his throat, reevaluating his tact so his words would not cause unintended wounds. "Your abilities are different than those of a farmer's wife. I have never seen anyone who was so adorably unaware of the risks of cutting an onion." Allowing only the slightest smile, not the chuckle that rose from memory, he pushed up from the bed and pulled her to standing. "What woman of simple means would have occasion to study Italian? Your hands are far too soft, your speech far too—"

"That is enough." Her cheeks pinked and she lowered her head. "I can see now I was foolish to believe I could ever hide my past."

He stroked the back of her hand with his thumb. "Now that I know the truth from your own lips, I want to know more about the real you. With none of the charade."

She lifted her chin, her innocence, trust, and sudden nearness fogging his once clear mind.

"I should like that very much," she said. "Though I must admit I find myself ashamed, disclosing aloud what few skills I have compared to you."

Guilt clawed at his chest. If only she knew they were not so different. His spirit groaned and he clamped his teeth shut to cage the truth that suddenly wished to break free. He stared down at her, the swelling sincerity in her sweet face assuring the suspicious parts of him that she was not like the first Anna. Nay, in every way she was different.

But you believed Anna Muhr sincere until the moment she—

He stepped back and straightened his shoulders to slough off the barbs of memory, but they gripped harder. "We best prepare for bed."

Large eyes blinking, eyebrows slightly tipped, Anna swallowed and spun away. "You may, if you like. I have a few remaining chores that require my attention before I retire."

"Nay, allow me." Passing her to reach the door first, he clenched his fists to keep from touching her. Any slight brush against her skin could topple the precarious wall of defense he'd erected. "I neglected to be sure the latch on the door is in place."

He left, still struggling to free himself from the snares of his past. In front of the kitchen fire, he closed his eyes and took long draws of air. *She has given herself completely to you.* But he could not do the same. Could he?

Staring at the dancing flames, he cursed his cowardice. The longer he withheld the truth, the greater the chance of destroying not only her faith in him, but the life together they'd only just begun.

Chapter Eighteen

The cold early winter wind plumed into the hood of Anna's cloak, biting her skin with its icy teeth. December now, and with it, the shorter days that followed. Six weeks had passed since the innocent child lay lifeless on the Watson's floor, forever marking them. With one hand Anna clasped the fabric around her neck, still clinging to the laden basket with her other. She'd left the Watson's only a few minutes past, but already the sun had started its doleful decent toward the horizon. Anna increased her pace, but the low murmur of nausea she'd battled for several days now forced her speed to abate. Swallowing, she fought the unpleasant sensation with a grimace, steadying her mind upon how she would tell her husband she'd promised Eliza to deliver this basket of supper to Thomas's shop so Eliza and the baby needn't traverse out of doors in such harsh conditions. As he'd made her vow never to venture into town without informing him, she determined to stop home first, despite the waning daylight.

After several minutes more of chilled walking, she

spied their house at the end of the road. A pit developed in her middle and not from mere physical discomfort. It had been so long since she and William had become one. The warm memories of fleeting rapture dissipated like her breath on the wind. William had been so genuine, so real, but the amiable affection he'd shown before they'd shared such intimacies had somehow turned as cold as the coming winter. Still kind, still caring, yet without the nearness or warmth. Without even the hint that perhaps he might once again renew his attentions to her.

She sighed and gripped the cloak ever tighter. Nay, there had been a few times she'd thought she'd seen a spark of desire in his eyes, but it disappeared too quickly for her to detect what true emotions lived there. The house grew closer with each step, as did the sensations she'd struggled to stamp from her mind. The soft touch of his calloused hand on her cheek, the way his lips folded against hers—how he'd shared with her the pleasurable, sacred secrets of husband and wife. She had never known such passion could exist, or that it could feel like heaven.

Anna reached the stoop and stared at the latch as the wind pulled harder at her cloak. If only she had kept the emotions within, not allowing them to spill from her mouth in a moment of vulnerability. Though her heart whispered of love, she refused to grant such feelings residence. Not when her husband had such a visible distaste for the word. Thinking would lead to feeling, and feeling would lead to speaking—and speaking such a word would only lead to more pain. Never could she allow it to take root in her spirit. Not until he did.

Gripping the latch, she pushed the door open and pulled it shut against the driving wind.

William straightened from his crouched position by the fire. "Where have you been?"

"Just returning from the Watson's." She entered and rested the basket on the table before going to the fire to check on a stew she'd started before leaving for Eliza's. Stirring, she continued. "And I must leave once more, but I shall not be long."

She stood and turned to find William resting against the table, his arms crossed.

His eyebrows lifted. "You should have told me where you were going, Anna." Was that worry she detected in his voice? Hope fluttered behind her stays.

"'Twas only to Eliza's. You were busy and I—"

His hard expression stopped her words and he cast his gaze to the basket. Nay, not worry but frustration. She cleared her throat to prove the realization didn't pain her. "The...the weather is too foul for Eliza and the baby to venture out in. I offered to deliver supper to her husband this evening. I do not see how that can be so wrong."

"The sun will be setting soon."

"Aye, 'tis true, which is why I must hurry." The scent of the stew, which at most times would have made her stomach yearn to be filled, instead forced a hand to her mouth as she turned away from the fire. She inhaled a quivering breath, struggling to choke away the bile that inched up her throat.

"Anna?" William stepped near, helping her rise.

"I am well, 'tis only my belly that seems distressed of late." She stood, both hands on the table, still taking slow breaths to calm the quell of discomfort. "It shall pass in a moment."

He paused, motionless, but for the gradual descent of his brow before it crumpled between his eyes. "I am right to believe I heard you cast up your accounts this morning, am I not?"

She shot up, meeting his piercing gaze. He had heard? She'd hoped to have been discreet. Looking away, she bit her lip, unable to answer with words. The flutter of worry that bore in her muscles since the first she felt strangely ill days ago urged her to nestle her head against his chest, while the promise of a comforting embrace beckoned in the center of his warm blue eyes.

He closed the space between them, resting a hand at the small of her back. "You are unwell. I cannot allow you to go out in this storm, no matter how benevolent your purpose."

"Please, William, I must do what I—"

"Nay, Anna. My word is final." His scowl deepened. "'Tis too much of a risk. I'm sorry."

Indignation wound its way up her back, edging out the spinning in her belly. "You leave me home alone nearly every day for hours on end while you make your deliveries and do who knows not what for *the cause.* I cannot see how this is much different."

"It is different because you are ill."

"I am not that ill—"

"It is different because you are a woman—"

"My sex makes me less capable?"

He sighed with a tilt of his head. "You misunderstand me. You are a woman with a price on her head. Or do you no longer fear the reach of your father's hand?"

"It has been weeks, William, weeks!" She strained to keep her voice even and void of the dissonant chords that swirled within her. "I would be foolish indeed to believe my father would cease his search for me, but are we to remain prisoners forever?"

"Anna." William stepped away and rolled his shoulders to their broadest. "I cannot have you venturing into town or going on errands unless I accompany you. We have discussed this before. I promised I would protect you and I will, but you must do as I say. You will not go tonight. That is final."

Ghostly memories choked the air in her lungs and she turned back to the fire. *Do as I say.* Edwin had spoken those very words time and time again until she feared they would be inscribed on her very flesh. Her stomach roiled and she breathed through her mouth to keep back the hurt. "William," she spoke toward the fire. "Eliza cannot bring Thomas his supper before the meeting tonight without risking the health of the child. This weather is far too cold. I offered to deliver the basket, and I will."

Turning, she lifted her eyes and met his gaze, emboldened by the bite of freedom that gave nourishment to her spirit, which until coming to America, had been chronically weak.

His eyes rounded. "You will defy the word of your husband?"

Rounding the table, Anna snatched the basket. "I will return within the hour."

She left just as the winter rains began to fall.

The rain and cold winds mirrored the mood Paul carried within. Marching into Sandwich, he stepped through the widening puddles instead of rounding them as waves of heat undulated through his chest. Four weeks of recovery in Plymouth and two on a mad hunt for Donaldson that had produced nothing, only to be back in this God-forsaken hamlet. Six weeks wasted!

Walking through the driving rain seemed to flood the shallow memories to the forefront of his brain. 'Twas almost as if Donaldson had known who it was he shot, for the ball had grazed to the bone and infection had left him at the mercy of an idiot doctor and unable to move for near a month.

He'd told the sordid tale to the sheriff that night—a peaceful traveler, attacked and nearly killed by a stranger in the wood as evidenced by the weeping hole in his flesh. He'd implored the man for a hunting party to begin and insisted an immediate pursuit of the assailant was imperative, but his pleas were ignored. Paul growled at the biting recollection. Apparently the knowledge of a dangerous stranger meant little to a town filled with simple-minded Whigs. The heavy drops splashed Paul's cheeks and trailed down his neck, all but steaming from the anger that burned through his skin.

"I have little time for such things," the sheriff had said. *"You are not dead, therefore I cannot expend my energies on something that might have happened. But if you are determined to find this man, the best I can do is direct you to someone who also seeks a man that matches the description of your attacker."*

The rain descended in sheets now, but Paul made no attempt to find cover as he once again replayed the words in his mind. *"There is a gentleman in search of his daughter taken by a tall, muscular blonde. The gentleman left town several weeks past, but he cannot be far. He gave me his name and how to discover him should I find her or any information that would aid in his search."*

Paul had polished this promising intelligence, following the trail of this Warren Fox from Providence to Plymouth and here again. Crumbs of knowledge but nothing to satiate his hunger for revenge. Donaldson slipped ever farther from his grasp, but Paul's determination multiplied by thousands with every sunrise. He refused to believe his enemy would forever elude him. Not if this Warren could be found. For though the description the sheriff gave was vague indeed, Donaldson matched the look, and desperate as he was, Paul could not ignore the possibility. Somehow, in the depths of him, Paul believed that in this Warren Fox, his answers would be found.

The rain suddenly fell as if God himself had tipped the very skies on end. What few shoppers remained on the quiet road now scurried to the nearest shops, papers or cloaks shielding their heads as a downpour deluged the streets. Paul continued on, the weight of the rain dragging at both his greatcoat and his spirit.

A hurried footstep from behind made him turn and he stepped aside as another townswoman raced for the shelter of the shops, clutching a basket with one hand and clinging to the hood of her cloak with the other.

That face...He squinted, needing little more than a second before his memory splayed open.

"Miss!" he called, jogging toward her across the road. "Miss Whitehead."

She looked behind but continued on until she'd reached the protection of the roof in front of the print shop.

"Miss Whitehead!"

"Sir?" She paused, her hand on the door handle, lips pulled in a tight line.

Either the question in her raised brow was a ruse, or

she was more a simpleton than he thought.

He bowed slightly. "Miss Whitehead, I fear you do not remember me."

Her mouth dropped open with a quiet gasp. "Forgive me, I—"

"Please." He patted the air, a small smile pasted to his lips. So she had forgotten. He calmed the sudden spike in frustration at the sight of her with a slow deep inhale, keeping every other emotion but friendly concern from the edges of his grin. "'Tis I who must seek your forgiveness. I had not heard from you and began to worry for your safety. How selfish of me to ask you to venture out on your own in search of a man you had never met. I do hope you are well." He stopped, rethinking the forthcoming statement, but it slipped from his tongue before he could chew on it longer. "Finding you here is quite a surprise."

Quite a surprise indeed.

Anna's teeth locked tight. What was this man doing here? Why was he not in uniform? Had he worried over her to such an extent that he came in search of her? She stared, scrambling to find an excuse to escape the forthcoming conversation without answering the pointed questions, but his pleading eyes stabbed through the bewildered exterior she flung to her defense.

"Sir, I thank you for your concern." She gestured to the door. "I am well, I assure you. But if you will excuse me, I really must be—"

"Of course, I do not wish to detain you." His smile warmed, melting the prick of ice in his eyes. "But, pray tell me, did you make it to Providence? Have you any word regarding Captain Martin and the man who knew him?"

Samuel.

The rain that before had only chilled her skin now seeped deeper, and the tears that had burned her eyes as she'd stormed from the house now pricked like needles of a hundred buried hurts. Her departed brother she had risked everything for, the search for answers, all but abandoned. She swallowed and looked up at the man before her. Patience hovered in his pale blue eyes. A memory flashed and suddenly the rich blue of William's gaze arrested her—and the way he'd commanded her as if she were a mere possession, something to be used instead of treasured. Was that his true estimation of her? An admonition whispered from the clouds that lined the sky. *He wishes only to protect, nothing more.* Her throat ached and her gaze dropped like the rain that continued to cry from the heavens. Did he?

"Miss?" The man's tender petition lifted her face and he continued. "I hope no ill has befallen you."

She opened her mouth to answer when a hand from an unseen being clamped around her lips. *Do not tell anyone of me.* William's warning blared in her ears and echoed in her heart. But why not tell this man what had brought her to this place? He deserved an explanation, did he not?

"Aye, forgive me. I am well." She straightened, stepping from the grasp that imprisoned her words. "I had made it nearly half way when the driver of my carriage tried to force me away with him." A shiver trailed down her back and she snapped her mouth closed. Could this man now be in service of her father? His reaches were like ever-growing vines, forever snaking about to strangle her. If she told more, her identity might be known...

His shoulders pulled back. "How did you escape him?"

"I..." Again, she tried to speak, but the words crowded in her throat as if God refused them utterance. She glanced toward the road as an inky shadow crept like smoke through her spirit. *Do not tell anyone of me.*

Her breath quickened and the unease that billowed refused to be abated by the unwavering kindness in his eyes. Pulling the basket closer to her middle, she cleared her throat. "A family found me—rescued me in fact—and insisted I join them here. Since I had no other family, I was grateful to them, and accepted their offer." Not entirely untrue. The Watson's and Smith's had welcomed her, and in a way, had insisted she stay, had they not?

"Is that so?" His chin raised slightly as one eyebrow swooped low. "You no longer wish to discover what happened to Captain Martin?"

Anna swallowed and licked her lips. "I shall always wish to find that truth."

"Then you would still wish to find the man who knew him?"

She squirmed in her stays. "Certainly. But I fear there is little chance of that now."

"I have not given up hope." His mouth quirked before he straightened once more and relaxed his stance as if he'd changed his line of thought. "I must say...I mean, I don't know if you've heard. There is a woman who has been kidnapped—forced away from her father by a man of devious character."

Dear Lord...

Anna's blood slowed and her knees threatened to buckle. "Oh?" Her voice wobbled, but she prayed he saw only the mock surprise she plastered to her expression.

He shifted his feet with a shrug. "Have you heard of this? I ask only because I should like to assist her father in bringing the woman to safety. As now I am on assignment away from the army, it gives me pleasure to help others as so many have done for me."

"How kind of you." The sounds that emerged were thin and flat. She remained frozen, her limbs so cold she could not find the strength to move them.

An easy smile etched across his face. "I shall be in

town for a few days. If you hear of anything, would you be so kind as to send word?"

Anna's strength continued to drain in waves. Her voice no longer worked at all. She nodded, struggling to force a smile at her lips.

He bowed low but his vision remained trained upon her. "I wish you good day."

As he turned and strode back into the downpour, Anna's spirit surged to life. She leaned back to rest her shoulders against the wood and closed her eyes. *Foolish, foolish girl.*

If only she had listened to William. She could only pray this encounter wouldn't pull the thread that dangled between them, threatening to unravel the life they had built. If William knew what had happened he would surely never allow her to leave the house unaccompanied again. Worse, the admission would prove her foolishness and she couldn't bear such a weight. 'Twas enough to admit within she had done wrong. No need to explain or worry her husband further.

With a heavy breath, she whirled and entered the printshop, fully knowing she could never keep such a thing within.

Chapter Nineteen

William gripped the side of the building near where he crouched, squinting against the rain that flicked his face. A keg of rage ignited as he captured the image before him. From across the street he could discern Anna's profile—and that of Paul Stockton's.

William's shoulders cramped. This could not possibly be mere chance. He rose from his haunches and whirled back, pressing against the side of the building. How long had Paul been in town? Had they known each other before or was this their first encounter?

Deep in the far corridors of his mind the whispering call of wisdom beckoned. *You know her better than to believe she would betray you. She knows not even who you are.*

He shook his head to disperse the seductive thought. Nay, never again would he be used by a woman. Not when his very life and the lives of his friends were at risk of being party to the scheme. It would mean death for all of them. Paul would see to that.

Careful to keep well hidden, William peered around the corner and his pulse erupted like a volley of infantry fire. Both Paul and Anna had gone. The street was empty. Doubt collided with fear. What if Paul had taken her in those few moments he'd turned away?

Ignoring the driving need for stealth, William hurled from cover and dashed toward the spot where they had stood, the very sinew in his limbs pulsing hatred. He prayed with every stride his enemy would slink from the shadows, that Paul would show himself so this game could finally be ended. But he halted when Anna emerged from Thomas's print shop.

He stood in the center of the road, puddles at his feet and rain drenching his clothes, while confusion and hurt drenched his spirit.

Anna clutched her cloak at her neck and bolted into the rain then stopped when she saw him, her mouth open and eyes wide. "William." The large drops plunked on her red-cold cheeks.

He stared, fists round, struggling to calm the turbulent sea of emotion before he formed a reply. "Did you think I would let you come alone?"

She wriggled and looked away before answering. "I suppose I did. 'Twas wrong of me, forgive me."

Humility laced her voice as a sheen of relief veiled her expression. What had happened? He expected the same indignant woman that had stormed from the house, but the droop of her shoulders and the peek of her lips read of distress more than deception.

He coiled his scorn around the foolishness she pursued in place of his wisdom, but the thin cords gripped as well as rope around a hill of sand. The recollection of his behavior smacked at his pride while his ever-growing affections for the woman with whom he shared a bed urged him to cease the construction of the redoubt between them. William ground his teeth. Could it be possible her seeming rendezvous was nothing more than an accidental meeting?

He offered his elbow, hoping the gesture would pull him from the depths of his thoughts, unprepared for the intensity of her grip. She glanced to him and waited a breath before initiating the return home, dragging him from the trench of darkness that gaped behind him.

She spoke, keeping her face forward. "Thomas was grateful for his supper as he has only half an hour before he is to meet the other Whigs at Fessenden's Tavern."

William's neck corded, his vision trained on the puddles in the road. "The streets are quiet," he bated, cautiously probing the secret he prayed she would reveal, but in the same thought, loathed to hear. "I suppose you spoke with no one, as I instructed you to do."

He looked to her, noting the quick rise of her chest and the way her neck muscles twitched.

Pray, do not lie to me...

Anna shrugged and turned her head away, yet her

hand gripped harder. The dual message in her unspoken answer tipped his ready accusation on edge. "So you encountered no one, then?" *Tell me all.*

She stopped and spun to peer up at him. Worry pinched her forehead in the middle and pulled her lips to a firm line. "I did see one man. Spoke with him." She slammed her eyes shut. "William, I am a fool. I should have listened to you."

Hope plumed in his chest, pressing his lungs until he could hardly take a breath. "What happened?"

Her eyes darted back and forth between his. Her chest pumped and the words poured like the very rain, drenching him with their cold truth. "He is from the army. He said...he said he is looking to help the man whose daughter had been kidnapped."

William's muscles both weakened and toughened in the same quick pulse of blood. *She spoke the truth.*

Her chin wobbled and he reached for her, ready to speak the comforting words that nestled on his tongue, but she went on.

"I had met him once before—the first day I'd entered New York."

"You know him?" The question came too quickly.

"Nay, we are only acquainted." She shook her head. "I came upon him in my search for someone who could tell me the truth of my brother's death—as that is the other reason I came to America."

William scowled in question and Anna swallowed, penitence shimmering in her eyes. "My father claimed he took his life, but I don't believe it."

Her brother had killed himself?

Looking behind, the prick to continue conversing in the cover of trees almost moved his feet before his legs did. The battle would best be ended now, but sanity brushed past the masculine pride as the thought of Anna being caught in the crossfire consumed every breath. "We must keep moving." He took her arm and led her along. "Tell me more of this man with whom you spoke."

She nodded, walking beside him. "In New York he claimed there was a man who knew my brother and could tell me everything I desired to know. I was on my way to find him when that man—the coachman—tried to force me with him, and you blessedly came to my aid." She clutched his arm harder as grief dripped from her tone like the trails of water down her cheeks. "I must beg your forgiveness, William. I should never have gone out alone, for now not only are my past sorrows resurrected, I have put us both in more danger."

She knew not the half of what she'd done, and yet he didn't care. He looked down at her as they walked, aching to be home, out of the rain and to cover her with his affection. Nothing else mattered to him now but that she'd told him. Everything. Just as he'd hoped, but never dared believe. Her meeting with Paul *was* unintentional and it had left her visibly strained. The knowledge that she was not like Anna Muhr, that she would not withhold the truth and use him for her gain, bound his heart in a balm so powerful the raw wounds healed and the scars all but faded in a burst of blinding light. Love—so passionate and pure, so peaceful yet raging with power—consumed to the deepest part of his lost and lonely spirit. The need to keep her safe, to be with her always, to give her the best of him surged as his heart pumped ever quicker.

He continued the questions as their house came into view. "Did he say anything else to you? What was the name of the man you were to find?"

"I do not recall. Henderson perhaps?" She looked up at him, her thin brows swooped up. "I wish I could have attained the knowledge I sought, but there is a far greater need now."

He nodded. Aye, the need not to be discovered.

They reached the door and William ushered her in front of him, helping her remove her sopping cloak before shaking off his greatcoat.

She moved to the fire and hovered her hands in the faint heat that still radiated from the weak flames. William reached for a log and rested it atop the hungry embers.

He brushed his hands together to keep from tugging her against him and feeling once more the warmth of her body beside his. Only this time, no doubts would peel them apart. "There may be a time when you can learn what you wish to know about your brother. Having been a soldier, there are many who would have known him. Think not that you must abandon what you desire, 'tis only put aside. Allow the Lord to preserve it for the future. Perhaps when this conflict is finished—"

"Nay. I do not believe there will ever be chance of that now." She lowered her hands. The dusty light painting her features in softest orange. "Samuel was my dearest friend and guardian after mother died. He could not have changed as they claim he did. He was sweet and good and kind."

"Do you remember your brother's rank? Where he served?"

William snapped his mouth shut. He must tread with caution or unwittingly reveal what he loathed to keep hidden.

Anna reached her hands out once more, and 'twas only then he saw that she shivered. He spun around and searched for the shawl he had seen before leaving and snatched it from the back of the kitchen chair, draping it around her shoulders and allowing his hands to rest on the slope of her arms.

The smile she offered in return warmed like a summer sunrise. Looking back to the fire, that sad, reminiscent countenance returned. "Samuel served in Boston and had reached the rank of captain, I believe."

Slowly, William lowered his hands and stepped back as the room expanded around him, leaving him suspended in a cold, gray light. Like the flash of a long forgotten dream, the reverend's voice and Anna's reply pulsed in his ears.

"Forgive me, I didn't ask your full name."

"Anna Fairchild Martin Rone."

William choked on his breath. *Dear Lord.*

"William?...William?"

Anna's quiet appeal roused him from the briars, but the thorns remained lodged. He blinked with a quick nod.

"Aye, forgive me." He flicked a look to the clock on the mantel. "I suppose the soup is ready, hmm?"

"Oh! The soup, of course." She snatched a wooden spoon from the table and bent to stir the contents of the pot when she flew a hand to her mouth and lurched back up to her feet. "I am sorry, I cannot...I fear my former pride forbade me from admitting the truth, that I am overtired."

The weight of the revelation made his limbs drag against the floor, but he ushered her to the room. "You should retire early, my dear. Tomorrow is full. I shall fetch my own meal."

She turned, innocence and love radiating through the tiny smile that lifted her mouth before she slipped into the bedchamber and shut the door, leaving William to tread the murky waters of reality alone.

Appetite long since vanished, he slumped in the chair nearest the fire and stared into the crackling fire. His long deceased enemy returned now from the world of the departed to begin again what he'd loathed to part from. Even in death, Samuel Martin would endeavor to dominate, endeavor to demean, and command his every breath.

And now, he must keep himself all the more closed, all the more hidden from the woman he loved.

Paul opened the door to the tavern and stepped in from the rain. The aroma of savory meat and yeasty bread consumed the warm air, and the sudden pang in his stomach reminded him he'd eaten nothing more than stale bread and fatty meat in bland broth for weeks. He pressed a hand to the wound that still pained. Soon, he promised himself, soon Donaldson would have a similar wound in the left of his chest.

He stepped toward the large kitchen fire in the back of the tavern. A tall, thin gentleman poked at a round of pork turning on a spit.

The stranger spoke without raising his eyes. "Care for a room or just a meal?"

Paul cloaked the abiding irritation with charm. "Aye, sir, I thank you. I should like a meal, indeed. "He stopped and pivoted to glance over his shoulder. "But I am curious...perhaps you can help me..."

The man batted the air to quiet him. "Aye, just a moment—Kimball!"

Another man made his way through the crowd, his arm waving. "Coming, sir."

"We've much to attend to and I'll have nothing but your full attention."

"Aye, sir."

The proprietor poured ale into three large mugs. "Take these drinks to the table in the corner."

With a nod the man took the large tray and hustled back from whence he came.

Paul followed with his gaze as the man weaved through the crowd toward a large table in the back. 'Twas the patriots, no doubt. Paul had seen them there before, full of self-righteous zeal. Foolish men. Ingrates—

"Now, how may I help you?"

Paul turned back with a quick shake of his head. "Of course." He took another quick look behind before pinning his gaze on the man in front of him. "I am looking for a gentleman by the name of Warren Fox."

The proprietor's attention turned once again to the spit. "Don't know him."

"I hear he might be passing through. He is looking for his daughter and I wish to help him." Such a sincere overture would not be ignored, surely.

Heaving a breath, the man stood, his forehead and neck glistening from sweat. He gestured to a man seated alone to the left of the patriot crowd. "You'll be looking for him. Been in here several times before."

"Really?" Paul allowed only a single eyebrow to rise, though anticipation burst like black powder. "The distinguished fellow, tan jacket, black hat?"

A nod was the only reply.

Paul bent slightly to offer his thanks before

hurrying to the man he sought, the table a mess of maps and notes. When the fellow didn't immediately look up, Paul readied his charm.

"Good evening, sir."

Only the man's eyes lifted, slowly, as if the intrusion were nearly a criminal offence. "Aye?"

Paul grinned wide. "Forgive me, I do not mean to disturb you, but if I may be so bold, are you—"

The heated patriot discussion cut off Paul's words. Pressing back the scowl that itched to swell across his face, Paul looked up and stilled at the sudden recollection. The man from the print shop stared directly at him, his jaw hard, his arms crossed in front of his chest.

"State your business. I am busy as you see."

Paul turned his attentions once more on the man at the table whose eyes were hard and brimming with suspicion.

Though it had not been offered, Paul took the opposite seat. "Are you Warren Fox?"

The man leaned back against his chair, glare hard and scrutinizing.

After another look around Paul's gaze landed on the printer once more and his muscles jolted. The man still stared. Not only that, he had moved closer. The temperature of the room rose and a string of profanities thumped through Paul's mind.

Clearing his throat, Paul spoke while his gaze lingered on the printer. "I am looking for a man named

Warren Fox." Now, he faced the one who sat opposite. "According to the tale I have heard, this fellow is searching for his daughter that was taken by a man in the wood."

The tight expression on the man's weathered face softened a degree, but still he did not speak. Paul went on. "I believe that the man I seek could well be the same who took his daughter."

Rubbing his hand over his mouth, the man squinted. "Who are you searching for?"

So this was Warren then? The man had not said, but Paul continued as if he were. "Henry Donaldson— tall, dark blonde hair, strong build. He deserted the army and betrayed his country by helping the colonists in their quest for freedom." The last words tasted like gall. "I plan to find him and bring him to justice."

Blinking, the man's stare sharpened. "Who are you?"

Paul shot a look to the patriot table and breathed out when he saw the print shop owner no longer looked at him. Even still, risks could not be taken. Should the patriots know he was a soldier...

He leaned forward, careful his volume didn't carry beyond the table. "I am Paul Stockton. 'Tis my duty to find this man. And I will."

"A similarity in physical appearance means nothing. What makes you think we search for the same man?"

Paul leaned forward. "Then you are Warren Fox."

Folding his arms around his chest, the man lowered

his chin answering only after two slow breaths. "I am."

Confidence seized. "Do you remember anything else about the man that might identify him? Did he have a wound on his arm?"

The man's crossed arms released, his face rounding in shock. "He did."

Paul rested back against his chair, struggling to subdue the childish jubilance with trained solemnity. "Then it is confirmed. Shall we not combine our efforts in search of this man and your daughter?"

The man leaned forward, resting one forearm on the table, his strained tone choking the air between them. "How can I be sure you speak the truth? That you will not take her as he has done? How can I be assured you are not simply looking for a reward to line your pocketbook?"

"Reward?" Paul shook his head. "You will know I am in earnest when we combine our efforts and I speak not once of material gain." He strained urgency through his voice. "I must find this man. I am close, I can feel it, but I believe to find him we must work together."

"Hmm..." That familiar suspicion returned, deepening the shadows around Warren's eyes. A deep command rumbled across the table when he answered. "If we are to work together, you will do as I say."

Irritating, but Paul had suspected as much. He nodded. "When shall we begin?"

"Immediately."

Paul glanced out the window as the rain plinked

against the glass, begging for entrance. "Now?"

"You wish to begin later?"

"Of course not."

"Then let us away."

"Excellent." Paul rose, but the man reached out, gripping his arm with iron-like fingers. "If you betray our agreement, if you harm my daughter in any way, I will have my vengeance upon you. Make no mistake."

A tremor toyed with Paul's spine. This old man was no fool. Then again, Paul was no peasant farmer. He straightened to pull the anxieties from his back. Steeped in the cloak of sincerity he wore so well, Paul dipped his head. "Never fear. I give you my word."

A rapping on the door lurched William from his lounged position in front of the fire. He sprang to his feet and lunged for the pistol that rested on the mantel.

He swallowed, rubbing his thumb against the gun's smooth handle, wishing his vision could penetrate past the planks of the door. Flicking a look to the clock, he frowned. Midnight.

The knock came again, followed after by a voice. "William. 'Tis I, Thomas."

Heaving free his anxieties with an audible breath, William replaced the weapon and charged for the door. Thomas entered without an invitation, spiking the remaining edge of William's worry.

"What's happened?" William clicked the latch shut, his scowl growing heavy as Thomas faced him, his own expression hard, no doubt from the report he prepared to relay.

Only he did not. He stared, his jaw ticking before he removed his hat and tapped it against his leg. His gaze sharpened.

A suffocating mist of confusion and angst thickened the shadowed room. William stepped forward. "Speak, Thomas."

"I have seen your hunter. He is in town."

"This I know."

Thomas's eyes narrowed and he turned his head. "You know?"

Growling deep in his chest, William raked a hand over his head. "I saw him speak with Anna not seconds before she delivered your supper."

Thomas hummed, his head still cocked. "I saw him at the tavern. He spoke with a man named Warren Fox—a man claiming to be searching for his daughter."

A crack of rage shot down William's spine. Then 'twas true, though he'd clung to a thread of hope his fears would prove false. Somehow, in the hours since Anna had retired, he'd almost convinced himself 'twas all some strange ghostly dream, that Paul had been a phantom and their lives were not truly on the brink of utter ruin. He shifted his weight over his feet. "Paul claims to seek the man who pretends to be her father that they may join their efforts—believing that indeed I am the one who took her. Find Anna, and they find me."

Thomas huffed a quiet reply and slung his hat on the chair. Resting against the edge of the table, he pulled his bottom lip between his teeth and folded his arms across his chest. "He cannot be sure you two are together. No one knows but us."

"It matters not how he came to such knowledge, only that he is here and that I must reckon with him."

Tipping his head, Thomas's tone reached to the floor. "You plan to fight?"

"I must." William rubbed his eyes, then his forehead. "I know Paul too well. He will not surrender his hunt until I am found."

"What of Anna?"

William looked to the bedchamber, regrets and wishes pulling against his spirit. His fraud, his lies and deceptions, cackled like demons in the sparks of the fire. She knew nothing of him, of his past and the darkness that followed. Here his enemy waited to ensnare and burn them, leaving ashes of grief where the walls of their joy once stood.

"You could flee."

Thomas's quiet words lured William from the singeing heat.

He shook his head, having already discarded that enticing alternative. "Running would only prolong that which is coming."

A low sigh breathed from Thomas. "Then we shall

fight him together."

"We?" William pivoted, gripping his friend motionless with his gaze. "This is not your fight."

"Is it not?" Thomas straightened, his stare darkening. "Your life is at risk because of what you have done—"

"What *I* have done—not you, not Nathaniel." William snapped his jaw shut and looked behind to be sure his rising tone hadn't awakened his wife. His chest pumped, holding back the edging fury. "'Tis I who acted and 'tis I who must answer for it."

Thomas gripped the mantel, speaking through his teeth. "You acted on our behalf. Without us, you never would have—"

"If it had not been you, it would have been another." William's glare battled Thomas's hard blue eyes. "I joined the army to defend the rights of others, not destroy them. 'Twas only a matter of time before I could no longer give my allegiance to the king."

Thomas turned to the fire, his jaw shifting.

"God led me to you and Nathaniel, this I know. I will never regret the choices I have made on your behalf, nor the bonds that have been forged between us through our trials. But I alone will answer for my actions." William clapped a hand on Thomas's shoulder. "I would not have my friends in the cross fire."

The logs popped, the dwindling flames casting shadows against Thomas's ticking expression. "You placed yourself at risk on our behalf. Are we not to return the favor?"

Teeth grinding, William shook his head. "You do not understand what you offer. I am a soldier, as is Paul—captains both. My quarrel with him is matched equally in the sight of the law. But not you. Your punishment, should you be caught, would be much greater than mine."

"Your punishment for defecting is—"

"I refuse your offer, Thomas."

Thomas released his hold on the mantel and straightened, forcing William to drop his hand. "I respect your stand. You have made your decision and shall answer for it. As shall we."

Thomas started toward the door and William yanked his arm. "Thomas!"

Shaking his head, Thomas yanked his hat from the chair and pointed over William's shoulder. "Paul is coming and I refuse to watch from a distance when so much is at stake."

"Is everything all right?"

William spun and stilled at the sight of Anna, a shawl draped over her shoulders, standing with round eyes in the doorway of the bedchamber.

Concern pinched her forehead in the middle. "Thomas, you are here so late. I hope Eliza and the baby are not unwell."

Bowing, Thomas fit his hat on his head. "Eliza and the baby are well, Anna, I thank you." He straightened. "I am sorry if our conversation has awakened you."

"Not at all."

Thomas inched his eyes back to William. He barely spoke. "We shall resume this conversation tomorrow at supper."

William nodded, anger fogging his throat. "That we shall."

"Good evening." Thomas offered a smile to Anna before seeing himself to the door.

When the latch was once again in place, Anna stepped toward the fire, her hands gripping the shawl at her chest. "William, what's wrong? I have rarely heard Thomas so anxious."

"'Tis nothing." He reached out and she folded against his chest. Stroking her lavender-scented hair, he lied through her trust. "We are smuggling munitions now, as you know, and the troubles mount. But we will overcome them as always."

She craned her neck to peer up at him and the cracks in his heart snapped deeper. Should he not tell her now? End the painful charade? With a sigh he pressed her head against his chest and ground the words between his teeth. Nay, he could not. Watching the love she carried for him drain from her eyes would bring pain beyond his strength.

Her arms twined around his waist. "So long as you are safe." She looked up then brought her hand to his cheek and dusted her fingers against his jaw. "So long as we are together. That is all I shall ever need."

He kissed her head and turned her toward the

bedchamber. "'Tis late. I shall prepare the fire and be with you shortly."

Trailing her hand down his arm, she squeezed his fingers and returned to the darkness of their room.

Blinking, William turned and pressed his palms against the table. Letting his head hang, he groaned as the mountain of his sins angled higher. He could not allow his friends to risk their lives on his behalf. He could not begin to think of what would happen to Anna. Peering across his shoulder, he heaved a weighted breath. After hours of debate, after sifting for the gem in a bucket of pebbles, the only option surfaced like a polished stone.

Pushing away from the table he turned to the fire and poked the ash-laden logs apart, making room for another. If she were sequestered with the Watsons or the Smiths, Anna would question—and her presence would force his friends to risk for him the very thing he would never wish of them. Their lives were in danger enough. William stood, staring down as the fire gnawed at the wood. What if he could trust this Warren Fox to take Anna and remove her just long enough to ensure Paul was no longer a threat? William could at last be free to live as he desired—as *they* desired? But would Warren take her to England as Anna feared?

William reached back in his mind to the attempted abduction. The lack of malice, the sincerity in the man's eyes when he vowed he would do Anna no harm seemed to plead for William's confidence. A war of questions sparked a firefight. Should he risk trusting him? Expounding his secrets to such a stranger could bring down hell upon them both. When Anna learned the truth of who William was would she even wish to return to him? Going to England might be more of a comfort than returning to a man who had lied from the very moment he'd saved her.

Trust him.

William stared into the rounding flames, a prickle darting over his skin. Could he trust his wife to a man who could take her away forever? Could he trust his secrets to such a stranger?

The whisper of God's piercing voice echoed between the doubts of his spirit.

Trust him. And trust Me.

Bowing his head, William answered in silence. *Yea, Lord, I will trust in thee.*

He wiped a hand down his face. Now, if only he could find the courage to bring it to pass.

Chapter Twenty

In the grove of trees just past the edge of town, William clutched the pistol he'd hidden beneath his greatcoat, training his vision on the road ten yards from his position in the wood. The chilled breeze bit William's cheeks. He exhaled a pluming breath that curled white in the air. It went against everything he knew, waiting for Warren in such a place. Far too exposed, within hearing of the townspeople should a brawl ensue. Which it might. Nay, mostly likely would.

He released his hold on the gun and tapped his hand against his leg, the only outlet he allowed for the blistering anxiety that shot like jolts of lightning through his limbs. What if Paul had intercepted the note and came in place of Warren? What if he didn't come alone? Like a wise reprimand, Thomas's admonition to allow him and Nathaniel to help bring down the enemy slapped. But, like a stubborn adolescent, William pretended not to feel the sting. Putting them at risk was unthinkable. He would end it. Alone.

His heart wrenched. *Alone.* Anna must leave.

Telling her now would make her wish to stay and vouch for him, perhaps even fight beside him, and never would he allow that. A ripple of questions lapped against his resolve. Was trusting in Warren—

You are trusting in Me. That is all you need know.

William gripped the bark of the tree beside him, lowering his chin but not his eyes. Aye. He could trust God, he could follow the darkened path, knowing Providence would illuminate all in time.

"Who are you and what is your business with me?"

William whirled, his hand instantly on his weapon.

Warren.

The man's face rounded in recognition then crashed into rage. "What have you done with her?" He pulled a club from his side and charged forward. "Tell me where she is!"

William dodged the in-coming blow and reared sideways, locking his grip around Warren's wrist. In a swift, singular motion he lunged and pressed Warren's back into the trunk of the nearest tree.

"Quiet." He gripped Warren's neckcloth, impressed with the dauntless will that blazed in the man's eyes. "You have come alone?"

"As you see." Warren snarled, this time his volume low, but the hate roaring. "What have you done with her?"

Stepping back, William softened his grip, then released his hand but kept his vision locked with Warren's. "I have married her." The truth he'd not intended to speak sprung from his lips like a captive yearning for freedom.

Silence killed the air between them. Diving to a deep V, Warren's brow carried the weight of a thousand pains. He stared, his expression growing harder and more dark with every rise and fall of his chest. "Where is she?"

William blinked, then glanced behind, both to show direction and to ease his mind that Paul was not waiting in the shadows. He inhaled deeper when only the trees answered his gaze. "She is here."

The man straightened. "Here?"

"In Sandwich."

Warren laughed, a bitter undertone to his words. "So. You have had your fun with her and now wish to dispose of her to me? I see how it is." He stepped forward, fists curled. "You want money. You think I will give you the promised reward—"

"I love her."

Like a blade, the truth slashed through the air, slaying the vulgar accusation. Warren halted, his mouth agape. "You lie."

"I do not." William's own fists clenched. "I am sure you cannot conceive of how such can be true, but I give you my word that I love Anna more than my own life." He swallowed the rise of feeling that soared within. "I cannot explain why I have come to you when I know my wife's fear of discovery—she is terrified of you." Pausing, he strained to decipher the code of thoughts that flashed through Warren's eyes. "But I seek your aid, and despite my misgivings, I feel in my heart that you are the one I must trust with her care."

Not a single muscle twitched, but those on Warren's face. His eyes trailed downward and the tension in his mouth relaxed, replaced by a tender question. "She fears me?"

"You tried to take her against her will—to place a gag at her mouth—"

"I feared if she were heard then she would be taken. If she were I could not protect her, which is precisely what happened."

"Anna claims you were hired by her father to take her back to England."

At this, Warren raised his head and straightened, the motion pulling him nearly as tall as William. His voice was broad and sturdy. "I was hired by a man named Rush Martin, aye. But he is not her father. I am."

"I do not believe you." William stepped forward, speaking through his teeth. "My wife has disclosed everything to me. If you were her father I would know it."

Not a flicker of anger, no hint of irritation in Warren's ice-colored eyes. William paused. *His eyes...*

He nearly spoke but Warren offered a polite rise of the lips and filled the quiet first. "She has not told you, for she does not know it herself."

William scowled and Warren answered the

unspoken question. "Anna and her brother Samuel were the fruit of the love between myself and their mother Catanna."

Dear God, it is true.

Like a flash from heaven, a memory illuminated in his mind. Those striking eyes. He knew he had seen them before. First in Samuel, then Anna. Now Warren. They were *his* eyes.

"Why has she never known this?" William said, his question sharp.

"When Catanna's family learned of our love," Warren answered, "and that she planned to run away with me, they forced her to marry Martin. They did not want her to suffer the life of a gamekeeper's wife. Martin knew she was with child and accepted her—for her fortune." Warren's jaw flexed. "He despised our offspring, knowing they reminded Catanna of me. When she died, he unleashed the fullness of his malice upon them."

The cold wound its icy fingers through William's limbs, but the chill that bit curled more from the inside than from without. *My dear Anna, what you must have suffered.*

"She was forced to marry at sixteen," Warren went on. "A man older than I, who wished not to have a child. Knowing Anna's inability to bear children, Martin arranged the marriage and though she tried to escape it, she was forced to live a life of misery for ten years, until her husband died and Martin arranged another."

William shook his head, recoiling. "Why do you then wish to return her to England?" He balked. "If you truly cared for her then why take her against her will?"

"Any father truly caring for his child would not wish them to remain in such a war-torn land. She is not accustomed to such a life. She never learned the skills needed to survive, let alone thrive, in such a place." Warren looked past William to the road. "I would not return her to Martin. I would see her safely in England, at a cottage I have prepared for us in the north. Far from anyone who would wish harm upon her."

The man's sincerity eased the tension in William's fists, but not fully. "Though your intentions are benevolent, forcing her away with you is no less violent than what Martin intended."

Warren bit the inside of his cheek.

"She does not wish to leave," William said. "She wishes to continue the life she sought here. She is not blind to the dangers. Anna is the most courageous, most honorable, most trustworthy person I have ever known. We wish to build our lives here. Which is why I have come to you for help."

Dropping his hands to his sides, Warren neared. "Anything."

"I must first have your word that you will not steal her back to England."

"You make me ashamed of myself," Warren said. He looked down then raised his gaze to align with

William's. "I have always wanted to protect my daughter but never could. Then when given the chance I..." A longing clouded the older man's face. "I give you my word. What would you have me do?"

Tension rising in his blood like a hot spring, William turned toward town. *I place my trust in you, Lord. Pray, do not let him take her from me.* "We must find a more secure place to talk, for tomorrow I will end the conflict. And I cannot do it without you."

Anna leaned into the large barrel by the fire and scooped the last bit of meal from the bottom when a knock on the door pulled her back to standing.

She brushed the back of her wrist against her forehead. "Come in."

The door creaked open and Kitty entered, brighter than a burst of spring sun. "Good day, Anna."

"Welcome, Kitty." Anna rounded the table, relieving her friend of the basket in her arms. "I'm so pleased you've come."

Kitty glanced through the room. "Is William not here? I didn't see him outside."

"He said he had business. I assumed he and the other men were occupied with their duties for the war effort."

"Aye, the munitions of course." Kitty nodded. "You've already started, I can see."

"Only on the pudding."

Kitty raised her chin, sniffing the air and smiling. She removed her outer cloak before hanging it on the hook by the door. "It smells magnificent."

Did it? This morning Anna's ailments were no less potent than the days previous, and the scent of anything—be it sweet or savory—made her belly defensive. At least she hadn't lost the few bites of day old bread William had insisted she eat to ease his fears of her becoming too weak.

"I'm pleased you think so, Kitty." Anna motioned to the chair nearest the fire. "Warm yourself, please." She quickly turned her attentions to the pudding she'd already placed on the fire. Hunched by the embers, the warmth kneaded her cheeks. "I cannot imagine I am prepared to share my cooking with everyone the way you do."

Her friend giggled. "You are far more prepared than you think. Your beginnings may have been...simple, but you are a natural, dear Anna, and if anyone should know that 'twould be me, surely." She crouched beside Anna, a spry smile in her eyes. "And I should expect that Henry will be remarkably pleased when he learns that you made this evening's lamb."

Anna turned her head. "Who's Henry?"

Kitty's face slackened, a sheen of white pasting her cheeks before they brightened once again the next second. She pushed to her feet and went to take the chair Anna had first offered. "Did I say Henry? How

silly of me, my mind is all a jumble these days."
Clearing her throat, Kitty nodded toward the basket.
"Shall we begin?"

Anna's stomach churned. "Kitty, I fear you put too
much confidence in me."

"Nonsense." Kitty sat straight with her hands upon
her knees. "I shall sit here and give you instructions.
Thus you may say in all honesty that you fashioned this
meal without the help of my hands." She rested her
back against the chair, her dainty mouth swooped to
one side. "And we shall have the pleasure of chatting
while it cooks. If it turns out well, then I shall be sure
to give you the credit. If it does not, the blame will be
mine."

A sprite chuckle bounced through Anna's chest.
"No one would ever believe you capable of a failed
meal."

"There's a first for everything, is there not?" She
smirked then pulled back, a contorted type of grimace
to her face. She put a hand against her chest and
squinted, breathing out the obvious discomfort until
her expression released the folds of tension.

Anna reached for her. "Kitty, are you unwell?"

Kitty looked up and breathed again through tight
lips. "Aye, forgive me."

Anna reached for the pitcher and offered Kitty a
cup, but she waved it away.

"These discomforts come and go," Kitty said. "I only
hope it will not last much longer."

"Discomforts? Surely your husband has told you what ails you."

Kitty looked to her hands then back at Anna, her mouth hiding a smile. "He knows nothing of this."

Anna neared, alarm pricking her center. "Are you not concerned you may be ill? If these discomforts you speak of are something—"

"I am with child."

Anna flung her hands to her mouth as an excited chirp pierced the air. She threw her arms around Kitty. "Oh, Kitty, I am so pleased. Nathaniel will be beside himself, I'm sure." She released her hold and tugged the unoccupied chair near Kitty's and sat with their knees touching. "But how do you know? Can you be sure—you have spoken to Eliza, of course."

Kitty nodded. "I spoke with her this morning and she confirmed my suspicions."

With child.

"I could not be more pleased for you, Kitty." Anna pressed her teeth together. Battling the hurt that charged its way through her spirit, she displayed the years of polished pretend—not a hint of grief would she show, though the pain of it stabbed like a dagger. Such a truth could not mar the happiness of one who had become like a sister to her.

Beaming, Kitty gripped Anna's hand and rose to her feet. "I cannot wait to see his face. I plan to tell him this evening, though I have not determined the best time. I shall know it when it is upon us, I suppose." Her expression softened as a day-dreaminess took ownership of her eyes, as if inwardly she imagined her husband's face, the bewilderment and happy surprise that would brighten his countenance, and how he would take her in his arms, kiss her mouth and whisper low in her ear that he would love her—and their child—always.

Anna stilled, her throat swelling. Though worn soft after so many years of stroking, the silver treasure of her own dreams refused to be forgotten, no matter how deep in the corridors of her heart she secured it. Hope carried it forward, where she, never willing to tarnish such beauty with the pain of truth, would polish the vain wishes 'til they all but breathed. Releasing a pained sigh, Anna once more abandoned the dream in the dark inner halls of her spirit where her grief and pains refused to perish.

Pushing forward, Anna pressed a kiss to Kitty's cheek. "Well, you shall remain seated then, as determined." Removing the lamb from the basket, Anna unwrapped the large leg and rested it on the table. With a huff, she placed her hands on her hips. "I should think William will be heartily surprised to learn I have attempted such a meal."

"All the more reason for him to be pleased he chose you as his wife."

Anna shook her head, staring at the pink mound on the table, trying to focus her attentions on the meat and not the man with whom she shared a bed, and little more. "William didn't choose me. We needed each other for our different reasons..." Reaching for the knife, she sighed. "But I do hope that he will be pleased with me...more than I can say."

Kitty rested her hands in her lap, her head inclined. "Do you not believe he cares for you?"

After a quick shrug, Anna started into the lamb. "I have no way to be sure."

Only that one sacred time, that moment when...She shook her head when an inner voice chimed. *How many looks and touches of his hand, how many smiles has he gifted you? They cannot mean nothing.*

Kitty raised a single brow, a serious slant to her mouth. "I have known your husband for some time. I can say with all honestly I have never seen his smile so warm or his eyes so bright as when he looks at you. A man cannot bestow such devotions without harboring feelings of love."

Anna continued to cut into the lamb, as if her friend's words didn't echo through her silly, hopeful heart. "William is a good man. He offers the same kind smiles to everyone."

"I can assure you he does not." Kitty giggled. She looked off, her mouth pinching for a moment before her gaze went to Anna. "I have known few people as kind and as brave—and as sincere—as your husband." She paused again, that intensity in the back of her blue-green eyes growing deep. "He loves you, Anna. Of that I am certain."

The knife nearly slipped from Anna's fingers. *Loves me?* Curling like smoke from a candle, the words washed over her, but she refused to allow the longing to imprint on her soul. Quickly regaining herself, Anna took the knife once again, feigning indifference. "How do you know such a thing?"

"'Tis hardly a secret." Kitty's expression bowed into a playful scowl. "Do not tell me you cannot see it?"

Anna continued to cut, wishing she could finish the infernal task so the conversation could at least turn to the meal. "He has...he has been more than good to me. If he looked at me as only his helpmeet, a sister even, I should be happy."

A laugh burst through the room and Anna turned.

Kitty shook her head. "Sisterly feelings are what he carries for me, dear friend. A man who sees a woman as a sisterly figure would not kiss her—not the way he has kissed you."

Heat burned through Anna's cheeks. "Well, I suppose a man does have...urges, does he not?"

"Your husband is hardly the kind of man to exercise his rights as a husband simply to ease some natural need."

Anna stared at the half-prepared lamb leg when the truth started fumbling from her lips. "I love him, Kitty, so desperately that I fear I cannot even allow myself to believe he cares for me as well. For if I ever learn that he does not, it shall pain me more than I can endure."

"I promise you, he does care for you. Deeply." Kitty

stood and rested a hand on her shoulder. "He would give his life for you, Anna."

Anna shook her head with a quiet laugh. "Such a romantic thing to say."

Kitty pulled back, as if she were struck by the words. "Aye, romantic indeed, and equally true."

By now the heated longing Anna had fought singed upon the fleshy center of her soul, and she was helpless to remove the scars. She groaned, resting the knife upon the table. "I wish it were so. He kissed me once..." Her mind caressed the tender memory, yearning to relive the pleasures of all they had shared. "Though he continues his kindness, he hasn't appeared at all interested in revisiting such intimacies."

Kitty rested her palms on the table and leaned forward. "Then we must assure him of what he is missing."

"I fear a meager dish will do little to entice him." A soft laugh breathed from Anna's chest. "Nay, Kitty, let us forget we ever spoke of it and—"

"What gown will you be wearing?"

Anna frowned. "You mean this evening? I planned to wear the gown you gifted to me for our wedding."

"You mean the one you wore when speaking vows? 'Tis lovely indeed, but..." Kitty's mouth twisted to the side, before the spark in her eye lit her face like a bonfire. "I have another you must wear. A gown so striking he shall not be able to take his eyes from you." Kitty rested one elbow on the table, the other at her hip. "Awaken his yearning for you until he can no longer resist." Her voice trailed off as she lowered her chin.

The room suddenly heated. "I do not wish him to think I'm enticing him for something I shouldn't."

"You are his wife are you not?" Leaning closer still, Kitty's voice lowered so not even the chopped lamb could bear witness. "Why should you not entice him? Let him ache for you by night's end."

A delightful spray of flutters tickled Anna's chest.

Kitty's eyes sparkled. "A brush of the hand, a whispered word, a look of longing." She moved nearer. "Make him know you want him, and he will be helpless against his need for you. He already feels it. 'Tis your turn now to let him know you do as well."

Like the fire that sparked behind her, tiny bursts of excitement popped within her chest, but her heart refused to allow the sparks to flame. "You believe so?"

Straightening, Kitty grinned. "I know it, dear Anna. I know it."

Chapter Twenty-One

The sun had gone to rest an hour past. William looked back to the bedchamber door, still closed with Anna inside. The clock struck six and he looked to the fire where savory aromas drifted from the pot hovering over the embers, making his stomach growl and mouth water.

He tapped his fingers against his leg. She wasn't one to be late. Was she ill again? William fought the temptation to trespass against her privacy. She'd eaten so little of late. And knowing she'd cast up the small portion of her mid-day meal forced worry up his spine.

The Watsons had expected them by now, but he wouldn't rush her. If she didn't appear in another five minutes, he would enter whether she was dressed or not. The tempting thought brought a pleasant heat to his chest. *Privacy.* He huffed at his foolishness. Why he still allowed her to dress alone he didn't know. He tapped his fingers again. Nay, he did know, but refused to admit the truth of it. Seeing her shape beneath her chemise, watching her remove her dress and stays was too much for him. He needed to keep a safe distance,

SO *rare* A GIFT

which he had done remarkably well—and would continue to do, as long as he had strength. Which he must do even more now than he had before. *Until tomorrow has passed...*

He rubbed his forehead, recalling the meeting he'd had with Warren not five hours past. God had known indeed who to trust, and why. Samuel was Anna's brother indeed—and Warren her true father. The dust of such a revelation still floated in the air, catching the light as it drifted ever so slowly to the ground. She needed to know of this, both for herself and for Warren. And what better man to trust with her care than the one who had always wished to protect her. He exhaled slow, remembering again Warren's humble vow. *I will not let Paul come within her reach. When you are safe, find me, and I will return her to you.*

Covering his mouth, William let out a muffled growl. But would she even want him when his past was revealed? Would he even live past tomorrow's battle?

"William?"

He turned at the sound of Anna's ethereal voice, breathless as she floated across the small room to stand before him. Combing her with his eyes, William swallowed, attempting to moisten his parched throat.

"I began to worry over you." His words came out even, a remarkable feat, considering how his pulse raced with the sudden need for her.

"You did?" She lowered her lashes then raised them again, her crystal blue eyes baiting him closer.

Had he not seen this pink gown before? He traced her with his gaze. Perfection. The alluring color enhanced the subtle shade of her cheeks and complimented the ivory color of her skin, tempting him to touch. Her raven hair curled and stacked atop her head, waist impossibly small, breasts pressed and mounded from her stays. He cleared his throat and reminded himself of the need to take in air.

She neared, a kind of whimsical smile on her full lips as she lifted a string of pearls toward him. "Will you assist me?"

He cleared his throat. "Aye, certainly."

She neared, stopping only inches from him and tickled her fingers against his as she rested the necklace in his hand. "Kitty is letting me borrow these. Are they not lovely?" She turned, a soft lavender scent wafting from her hair.

After a second clearing of his throat, he reached around, securing the article, desperate that his fingers not brush against her skin. Another drifting scent lured him closer and he ignored the previous warning, allowing his thumb to caress her neck as he rested the fastened string along her back. Her shoulders adjusted and she raised her head then looked behind.

"Thank you," she cooed. "I must take the lamb. It should be ready." She looked to the clock and gasped. "Oh, heavens, we're late!"

She rushed to the fire and lowered to retrieve the cast iron, but William followed and halted her with a hand on her shoulder.

"Let me carry it." He winked. "Wouldn't want to spoil your lovely gown."

Straightening, her features went soft. "You think it is lovely?"

Did she not know?

He traced her once more, his insides whirling. "Of course I do. Pink is my favorite color."

"Is it?" She neared, a coy tilt to her smile.

"Aye." His pulse thumped as he took another sweeping glance of his wife. "My sister Julia loved pink, and...I learned to love it because of her."

Anna's full lips rounded into a smile that caressed his heart. "You have spoken little of your family." She neared. "I should like to know more of them. For I believe...by knowing more of them, I will know more of you."

I would tell you everything. If only I could.

He cleared his throat. "Should we not be going?"

That flirtatious grin returned. "Aye, we should, but your shirt..." Reaching for his collar, she tugged and straightened. "I have not seen you wear this before tonight. 'Tis a handsome waistcoat and jacket." Another step closer and she combed her fingers through the side of his hair, her fingers lingering behind his ear, her eyes on his mouth. His pulse doubled.

Her gaze lifted to marry his as her hand trailed down his shoulders and rested on his chest, her voice low and beguiling. "How handsome you are."

Have mercy. He tried to breathe. What was she doing? Whatever it was, he liked it, despite the danger that lurked behind the unopened doors. The need for her clawed at him. And from the way she toyed with him, he knew she must desire him as well.

With a smile she stepped away, removing her hands from their perch on his chest, leaving an empty spot both without and within. The urge to pull her back and test the texture of her skin with his lips consumed him and he reached for her, but she whirled away, a playful spark in her gaze.

"We must leave or we shall be even later than we already are."

Hang the party. He would much rather stay and experiment on the desires that roared inside him.

She walked to the door and took both of their cloaks, extending his toward him. "Come now, we must hurry. Here is your cloak. Will you take the lamb?"

Snatching a towel from the table he grabbed the handle of the pot and stopped in front of her, failing to keep his mind or his eyes away from her. "Shall we?"

"One moment." She reached around him, lifting on the tips of her toes to put the cloak around his shoulders, her chest brushing up against his.

Lord help him. This was too much. In a swift move, he set the pot away from them and pulled her to him, covering her warm lips with his. A small mewing sound escaped her throat and she leaned her head back to accept him as a surge of masculine need heated his blood.

Their friends had waited this long, they could wait another moment. Or longer.

Hands cupping his head, fingers in his hair, Anna raised to her toes and pressed into him, answering her husband's passion with her own. He tempted her lips apart and she submitted, savoring the feel of his mouth against hers. Slowly, as his kisses deepened, she trailed her hands across the breadth of his shoulders and rested them against his chest.

"I must have you," he whispered, trailing hungry kisses along her ear and down her neck.

Her heart throbbed and she tipped her head, allowing him greater access to her skin. "We shall be late." Her voice quivered.

"They can wait. I cannot."

She couldn't help the petite moan that escaped when he returned his mouth to hers. Anna's knees began to weaken, as did her memory. Where had they been going? Why couldn't they spend the evening hours in each other's arms? Unbidden, the scent of the lamb caressed what she'd forgotten. *The party.*

She found a way to speak between kisses. "We must go."

He hummed his protest and dusted his lips up her

jawbone and into her hair, his hands molding her ever more intimate against him. "A moment longer."

He descended, nipping at her collarbone and she struggled for breath as his warm mouth heated her skin. "I feared after our first time...I feared somehow—"

"I was a fool to stay away so long." He pressed a full kiss to her lips and lingered, pulling away slowly as if the action might temper the fire between them. Resting his forehead against hers, Anna savored the warmth of his breath dusting her still-damp lips.

William nudged his nose to her ear and whispered so low, the sound barely passed his lips. "When we return, I shall remind you of all the heated secrets of our love."

Chapter Twenty~Two

"Welcome, dear friends."

"Forgive us for our tardiness. 'Twas my fault." Anna smiled as Eliza ushered them in, William just behind her. "I do hope the lamb has not been overcooked."

Thomas appeared from the stairway and took the heavy pot from William, the two men sharing slaps on shoulders and heading straight for the kitchen.

Anna pointed where the men had gone, speaking to Eliza. "Should not we be doing that? The lamb I mean."

Eliza gave a brief shake of the head. "Ah, nay. Thomas enjoys helping me and I certainly don't disapprove." She chuckled lightly and motioned to the parlor. "I will follow him momentarily, once I know you are settled."

"Do not worry over me. I should like to help as well. Is there anything I can do?"

"Nay, everything is well prepared." Eliza stopped, a pensive twist to her mouth. "There is one thing—you stay here, I shall not be a moment."

Anna nodded, watching as Eliza escaped into the kitchen. A movement out the front window snatched her attention and she whirled to see the cause of the commotion.

'Twas Kitty and Nathaniel. She giggled to herself. Thank heaven she was not the only one to arrive later than planned. She reached for the door but hesitated when Kitty tugged on Nathaniel's arm, stopping him.

Curious, Anna continued to watch, wondering if perhaps she should usher them in or leave them to their privacy. The purple shadows of twilight crept 'round them, snow just beginning to fall. Kitty lowered her head as she spoke, then peeked back up. Nathaniel's forehead scrunched then melted, his entire face drooping in bewilderment. He bent slightly forward and cupped her elbows, mouthing something Anna could not determine. Kitty's face brightened and she answered, placing her hands on her stomach. Nathaniel pulled back, celestial joy lighting his face. He grabbed her at the waist and twirled her once, setting her on her feet before kissing her on the mouth.

Anna spun away from the window, reprimanding herself for not having looked away sooner. Such an intimate scene and she'd willingly stood and watched. She stared at the floor, blinking away pricks behind her eyes. How Nathaniel had looked at Kitty. How he'd kissed her. Never had she seen such adoration in a man's expression. The smile on his face...

She closed her eyes and ground the crumbs of her desires to dust. Such would never happen for her. She must accept what God had allotted her. Clenching her eyes tighter, she fought the imaginations that hovered. What would it be like to have William look at her that way for that reason—to tell him she carried his child and to see the burst of joy in his face?

"Anna?"

She gasped at the sound of William's voice and straightened as he walked near, his eyes darkened in concern.

"Are you all right?"

She brushed her hands in the air. "I was lost in thought."

He shifted his head. "I do not believe you."

A sprite laugh left her mouth, though it was too thin to cover the shape of grief in her tone. "'Tis nothing."

Closing the distance between them, he smoothed his hand down her arm. "You are sad." His eyes narrowed. "What is it?"

Her throat ached and she swallowed to press away the lodging bulge of sorrow. *Not here.* She willed the tears away and took his hand, entwining her fingers with his. "I have no sorrows when you are near."

His eyes grew pensive, the delicate lines around them deepening. Circling his thumb against the back of her hand, he caressed her with his gaze, the depth of it reaching down to patch the fresh crack in her heart. "Then I shall always be beside you."

"We are here!" Nathaniel entered with Kitty close behind. "You have pined for our arrival, I have no doubt."

Thomas and Eliza rushed in from the kitchen and the greetings began to chime like church bells, but even the gaiety could not lure Anna from the cocoon that circled her and William. *Then I shall always be beside you.* His words embroidered themselves in her soul. She looked up and stalled, his eyes still upon her. In that look, that moment, he said a hundred things— assuring and comforting, promising and pleading— before he squeezed her hand and pulled away, joining the choir of happiness that sang in the space beside the door.

"Our plan is working then?"

Anna jumped at Kitty's surprising closeness. "Kitty! I did not see you there." A half-smile half-frown wrestled at Anna's mouth. "Working? What plan do you mean?"

Kitty raised her eyebrows and tilted her head. "With William I mean."

"Oh!" A tickle of delight twirled in Anna's middle, remembering the heated promises they shared before they'd left the house. "It is, and I have you to thank I believe. The gown and pearls are lovely."

"Nay." Kitty hooked her arm in Anna's and started toward the kitchen. "I supplied the means, but you are doing the work."

With a smirk, Anna whispered. "I would hardly call it work."

Kitty's face went wide and she laughed full out as

they reached the kitchen.

"Do share what you find so entertaining."

Nathaniel came forward and took his wife at the other elbow, nodding politely to Anna as he took Kitty to the table and pulled a chair for her.

"We were simply discussing the night's festivities. Perhaps later you would read for us darling," she teased.

He grinned, taking the seat beside her as both Thomas and Eliza took their seats as well. "I think that honor is Eliza's, unless you wish me to entertain you all with my *incredible* talent."

"Oh, please do." Thomas leaned back in his chair, his eyes slanted with humor. "I believe we could all benefit from a bit of laughter."

At that, a merry chortle jostled around the table. Those already seated continued their back and forth teasing and reminiscing. Anna stared, feeling for nearly the first moment, the rich, encompassing love of family. She'd eaten in fine halls, sipped wine from gold plated goblets, conversed with royals. But never, never had she felt her soul float as if it might rise to the heavens. *Lord, my heart is filled to over flowing.* She'd never dreamed of such happiness for herself. Never dreamed she would have a family as she did now. If only her brother could have felt this love.

"Shall we join them?"

'Twas only then Anna realized she and William were still standing.

He placed one hand at her back and pulled a chair for her with the other before sitting in the empty seat beside her.

Thomas gestured across the table then clasped his hands in front of him. "Let us pray."

The candles that framed the lamb at the center of the table waved their amber-light against the white china. Utensils chimed and clanked, goblets were slowly drained. The warmth of the fire circled the room, as if happy to shield its companions from the snow that fell just past the walls.

"This lamb is divine, Anna, truly."

Kitty's compliment made Anna's cheeks grow hot. "I do hope so. I feared such a gathering would be a poor choice for my first attempt at such a dish." She prepared for another taste herself, grateful that the nausea she'd suffered had yet to visit her since morning.

"No one would ever believe this was your first." Eliza dotted the meat with her fork. "'Tis more tender than I've ever tasted. Not a dry morsel to be found."

Kitty hummed in agreement. "You are a natural, my dear."

"Nay." Anna shook her head with a laugh. "You are too kind."

"She speaks the truth, Mrs. Fredericks," William said, a tease in his voice as he spoke her formal name.

"I am pleased to be the one attached to you, so you may prepare this for me on future occasions."

The playful smirk on William's face made flutters start in her chest. The shadows cast by the candles highlighted his sculpted features, accentuating his masculinity. She struggled to swallow the bite in her mouth. The lines around his eyes softened and the smile he offered made her weightless.

"I'm pleased you were willing to venture out when such cold is upon us." Thomas spoke to William from across the table. "Only yesterday the rains fell, but it seems winter's chill was not far behind."

"A little snow will not deter us." William dotted his mouth with his napkin. "We must celebrate your return to Sandwich, must we not?" He shot a look to Anna before his tone captured a more somber thread. "'Twas a deciding time for all of us."

"A deciding time?" Anna prepared a bite. "I recall learning of your coming here when we prepared to celebrate the first time—before the birth of little Mary. But you speak of a return? It would seem I do not know the whole of the story."

"'Tis a long one I'm afraid." Eliza set down her glass, a slow pensive sigh exhaling from her lips. "My father was..." She stopped and flung a pleading glance to Thomas. "I hardly know where to begin."

Thomas reached for his wife's hand as he spoke to Anna from across the table. "Eliza was courted by a captain in the British Army." He sat back against his chair and turned the flat end of his knife against the table cloth, a drawn look owning his features. "He believed himself to be in love with her. But when I took her to safety after her father's involvement with the Sons of Liberty had come to light, this man believed that I had taken her against her will."

"How dreadful." Anna rested her fork on her plate.

"He was prepared to force me to marry him," Eliza said. "If Thomas hadn't arrived, I'm not sure what I would have done." Her voice trailed off as if the memory reached out to capture her.

"How did you escape him?" Anna placed her hands in her lap, the small semblance of appetite she'd had now completely forgotten at the horror of such a tale.

Eliza tossed a look to Thomas before returning her gaze to Anna. "Thomas and Nathaniel risked their lives freeing Kitty and me."

"Do not forget Don—" Nathaniel cleared his throat and dotted his mouth with the napkin. "Without William we would never have escaped. He is the true hero."

She swung her eyes to William, whose expression had hardened, his mouth in a straight, angry line. The mirthful line about heroism died at his hard look.

"You were all there that night?" she asked. "Had you known each other long?"

William took a large bite of lamb, glancing across the table to Nathaniel who obliged to answer.

"I had known Thomas for some time," he said, and

reached for his glass. "I met Eliza and Kitty only when they came to Sandwich to seek refuge from the soldiers. Of course, I couldn't allow Thomas to be the only one to enjoy all the heroics that grand night." He gestured to Thomas with his half-full goblet. "Truth be told, this man needed my superior mind. He was too lovesick to put two clear thoughts together."

Thomas's face swooped in a half-smile as he prepared for another bite. "I won't stoop to reminding you of the time you nearly let Kitty slip from your fingers."

Nathaniel leaned across the table to Anna, not quite whispering. "Do not take your facts from him. I shall tell you the entire story some other time."

A quiet laugh bubbled in Anna's chest and she tapped her gaze on Eliza then Kitty who were reserving laughs of their own.

"Well..." Nathaniel sat back and poked a piece of meat with his fork, a contemplative expression shifting his face. "I must say, God be praised for preserving us from such an enemy. Captain Martin was—"

"Nathaniel, how did the meeting at Fessenden's go last evening?"

William held both fork and knife above his lamb while all eyes questioned his sudden interruption.

Anna latched on to Nathaniel's words, the very sound of them seeping through her skin. Nathaniel answered and the conversation ensued once more, but Anna's mind refused to surrender. Had she heard him correctly? The man's name was Martin? Anna stilled. A coincidence no doubt. The name was not so uncommon. Yet...

"Did you say his name was Martin?"

She didn't realize she'd interrupted until it was too late.

Thomas peeked up as he cut another bite. "Aye," he said, before mumbling the last. "A man I shall not soon forget."

"Anna, would you please pass the pudding." William pointed toward the dish just out of his reach.

Anna handed it to him and prepared to speak again, but William did before her.

"All this talk of the past will unearth too much grief, will it not? We should talk of more pleasing times."

Nathaniel grunted. "Those were difficult times, indeed. And though I do not wish to be one to speak unkindly of the dead, I will be forever grateful we no longer suffer under his—"

"Nathaniel..." Kitty pinched her lips and widened her eyes before taking a quick sip of wine.

"He could not have gone without accusal for treating you all in such a way." Anna lifted a dainty bite to her mouth.

"Not in this life, but perhaps in the next," Thomas answered, before taking another bite.

Eliza shot him a look, but he answered with a quick jostle of the shoulder as if the words he spoke should be more accepted than they were.

"So...so he is dead?" Anna asked.

Eliza sighed, resting her wrist against the edge of the table. "He is." 'Twas then she looked to William. "William offered us protection that night. We will forever be in his debt."

Anna reached for her glass. "William never said he was in Boston. What were you doing there?"

He locked eyes with her, the sudden pleading, almost apologetic sheen in his stare formed a pit in her stomach that deepened with every breath. Was he angry with her? Had she said something wrong? His jaw hardened and he shot a quick glance to the others before returning his gaze to her. Why were his eyes so dark? Anna rested her fork on the table and clasped her hands in her lap, her limbs suddenly cold.

"I will say one thing about the trials of the past," Thomas said, luring Anna from the darkening hall she had begun to traverse. "Without Samuel our lives would not be so tightly woven. So in that, we should give thanks."

"Forgive me, did you say, Samuel? Samuel Martin?" The air died in her lungs. She shot a look to William before facing Thomas, but 'twas Nathaniel who answered.

"None other." He raised his glass before draining the last of its contents.

She moved as if her limbs were slowed by tar. Blinking to keep her vision clear, she rested the utensils on the table and put her hands in her lap. Her voice came out as a sad thread of volume. "How did he...how did he die?"

Thomas cleared his throat. "He, uh...he took his own life."

Dear Lord, no!

The blood drained from Anna's head. The room faded in and out. She gripped the edge of the table, the sound of her name swirling in the darkening space around her. Her breathing hastened as the sculpture of dreams she'd treasured all these years crashed against the unforgiving ground of reality. Father had been right. Samuel was not the man she thought him to be. Why had she never seen his true nature?

"Anna?"

She looked up, unable to force her mouth to form words. Breathing through her mouth, she stared at her plate. What had God done? Sending her here amongst the people her brother had treated so ill? If they knew who she was they would hate her just the same.

"Anna. Anna!"

Jostled by a hand at her shoulder, Anna swung away from her thoughts to see William crouched beside her, but the momentum of grief threatened to pull her down again.

She opened her mouth and struggled for breath as a familiar wave of nausea returned. "Forgive me, I need a moment of air."

A clank of metal and glass split the air as she pushed away and raced for the door, desperate for the solitude that might ease the choke around her spirit.

Once outside, she stumbled to a stop. The snow, tiny shimmering specks, shook from the clouds like salt, stinging the fresh cuts in her heart. She inhaled a gasp of frigid air. Hand at her chest, Anna tried to calm the sobs that stacked in her chest. Her eyes burned and she covered her mouth as a single cry burst from her mouth. *Samuel. Why? Why?*

"Anna." The sound of William's baritone voice tempted her to turn but her quivering frame refused it.

His boots crunched over the cold ground but she waved him back to the house, refusing to face him. "Leave me."

William grasped her from behind and turned her toward the house. "You should not be out in this cold." She offered a cursory glance as he slipped the jacket from his shoulders and draped it around her. The tender act nailed the humiliation in place.

Her legs refused to move and he stopped beside her. Wiping a stray tear from her cheek with the back of his fingers, he lowered his chin. "Are you ready to go back in?"

"I..." Her voice cracked her words apart. "I cannot go back in."

"Speak to me," he whispered.

The tender command urged the truth from her throat but she clamped her teeth, refusing it utterance.

Again he brushed his hand against her face, his words so tender they all but melted the flakes around them. "I ache to see you grieve so. Will you not confide in me?"

She grasped hold of her remaining strength and used it to flood her thin voice. "I do not wish to speak to anyone." A lie. The tears streamed freely now. She struggled to keep her tone even as the trail of sobs erupted. "I wish...I wish to be alone." Another lie, but the humiliation of creating such a scene before her friends was too much.

"Anna," he pleaded, swerving to stand in front of her. "I accept your wish to stay silent, but I cannot leave you to bear it alone."

Hot tears poured from her eyes and she collapsed against him, the realities of what she'd learned consuming the wishes of her past like flame. She melted against his strong chest, his solid arms enveloping her, holding her as the years of pain and longing flooded with the knowledge that she'd lost Samuel all over again. The memories of him, once so bright and sustaining, now charred to lifeless black.

She could hardly speak. "I...I want to go home."

His head bobbed above hers. "Of course, my love. As you wish."

Chapter Twenty-Three

William helped Anna into the seat facing their kitchen fire and made sure the logs roared before he kneeled in front of her, his concern at his throat.

"Can I get you something? Anything?"

She shook her head, her lips pressed tight, chin quivering.

He squeezed his fingers around her knee, looking away, hoping to find some semblance of thought in his frenzied mind. A whipping began on his spirit. There were not harsh enough ways to punish his foolishness. He should have ceased the conversation long before it had taken such a turn. He knew the revelation of their connection would need careful consideration—had thought about little else since he'd learned she and Samuel shared the same blood. But now, the worst had showered on them like a sudden summer rain, drenching the thoughts he hung out to dry.

Blinking, Anna inhaled a choppy breath. "I dislike keeping things from you." She glanced to him then back to the fire. "I realize telling you what I have just learned, that which causes my grief, may force you to change your feelings about me, but I cannot keep it within."

One hand still on her knee, he reached up to her cheek with the other, tucking a curl around her ear. Praying his sincerity would cut past the vines of despair that choked the light from her eyes, he whispered. "Nothing you can say will alter my feelings for you."

She shifted her gaze to align with his. "Samuel was my brother."

William searched her eyes, frowning in question. "Your brother?" Did she believe his act? Was his surprise both as sincere and convincing as he hoped?

Anna blinked, keeping her face toward the fire. "When word reached us that Samuel had died, that he had in fact taken his own life, I refused to believe it." Her voice compressed, emotion replaced with a flat, soulless sound. "I knew, *I knew* with everything in me that the reports were false."

A report I had given.

William bowed his head and stroked his thumb against the back of her hand. Agony impaled his conscience. He could give her more, quell the questions these revealed truths had unearthed, but they would only injure her further. Knowing her brother had abused and threatened to the point of death might slay her tender sensibilities too deep. Would God condone his silence when done to keep the woman he loved from such pain? Either way, he deceived. Either way, she would suffer.

He peered beside him to where she sat. Tears still streamed from her red-rimmed eyes.

"Samuel was never that kind of person—not cruel and unkind," she said, the next words spoken to herself. "Not when I knew him."

William's response flowed even before he could weigh their veracity. "It matters not what he was, only how you remember him."

A bitter laugh breathed from her nose. "It does matter. When I first came to New York, I was determined to discover what had happened." She lowered her eyes and studied her fingers in her lap. "I was determined that no one should know who I was or why I sought after him, believing that indeed I may have been followed." She dropped her gaze to her hands. "But I was. And 'tis as you said, God has granted the wishes of my heart even though I had believed them abandoned." She sighed. "Perhaps if I had delivered that note, if I had found the man who knew Samuel so well I could have...but nay, I have all the knowledge I need now, I suppose."

"Note?"

Anna glanced to him then away again. "I was to deliver a note to a man who would assist the soldier and I in locating the one who had known him."

All sound faded. "You and this soldier were looking for the *same* man?"

Had he missed something? Had she said this before? But no, she'd said the man she sought was

Henderson. "What happened to the note?"

She looked to the bedchamber then to him. "I...I think I still have it."

His heart thrashed against the prison of his ribs. "In your Bible?"

Not waiting for more than a slight nod, William raced to the room and snatched the book, flipping through the pages as he returned. At the back, the note and a likeness slipped from the cover.

Samuel. William stilled. 'Twas her brother's face then that she'd looked at those many times. William glanced up, his pulse running once more. Their fates whirled too fast and too close for him to find safety. She had sought the truth of her brother, and now she'd found it. God's doing. She had sought the only man who'd known him...

Without asking permission he unfolded the letter and the words yawned before him like a menacing cavern.

> *Find Captain Henry Donaldson and a large reward will be yours. Bring him to me. Alive.*
> *P.S.*

William raised his eyes, staring to the farthest, darkest corner. *Dear Lord...I should have known, should have seen this long ago.* He could feel the disgust contorting his expression. Breathing out, he forced the emotion from his face though his mind was not yet ready to release it. Only Paul would assist himself under the guise of assisting another.

"I am a fool." Her voice grew heavy. "I should have known that there was nowhere I could go where he would not follow."

"What do you mean?"

Anna shook her head. "I believed coming here, immersing myself in the search for Samuel, I would escape my past—but I have only brought it closer to me." She swallowed. "That man I saw in the street, even he knows that there are those who search for me. 'Tis proof that I can never escape. Somehow my father will always find me. I am a fool."

"You are not." William released the articles on the table and once again took the seat beside her. Cupping his hands around hers, he inclined his head to meet her gaze. "Your past will not touch you here. I will not let it."

The words had not the reaction he had hoped. Anna pulled her hands from his and stood, stepping toward the fire, her back to him. The small distance between them stretched like miles of battered wilderness.

The fire spit and popped, casting warm shadows across her straight nose and long lashes. She stared, motionless, as if willing the undulating ribbons of flame to pull the fitful thoughts from her mind and turn them to ash.

He rose and stood beside her, dusting his fingers along the curls that draped her neck. "I give you my word, Anna, nothing will happen. To either of us."

Such a lie. So easily spoken, so easily broken. He bit his lip to fight off the edge of anguish that cut through his chest. Tomorrow he would at last execute the plan he'd set in motion. The only way he knew of to end this mad hunt. To end the demon that haunted him.

'Twas then she glanced up, her eyes oceans of pleading. He ground his teeth, battling the need to grant her what she'd given him. Her trust, her future. Her very life. Would he not grant her the same when she had offered him so rare a gift? Torn, he pulled her to him, cupping her head against his chest.

In his arms, the tension in Anna's muscles eased as her breath timed with his. "You say such lovely things." She sighed and pulled from his embrace. "And never have I been given cause to disbelieve you."

"As you should not."

"I *do* not." Turning her back to him she stared at the dark wood at her feet. "I have expounded to you everything—almost from the start, though not as quickly as I should have, I suppose."

"Do not think yourself less because it took some time to trust."

At that, she faced him, scanning his eyes with furrowed brow. "Do you?"

He reached forward, curling a hair around her ear. "Do I what?"

"Trust."

Lowering his hand, he stilled. The spear of her

words plunged through his crumbling shield. "Of course I trust you. Do you believe that I—"

"You know all of me, William. Yet I know nothing of you." Anna's dainty features scrunched with hurt. "What of your family—where are you from? Why do you refuse to share with me the way I have shared with you?"

He turned to face the fire, more able to clear his thoughts away from the pained stare in her ever-faithful eyes. "William." The yearning in her voice toyed with the neglected parts of him that cried out. "I would know all of you. As you now know all of me."

A quiet sigh escaped him before all the years of grief spilled from him like wine from a severed cask.

Turning his head, he caught and held her gaze. "My family...I told you before we were all taken with the pox." He motioned to his face. "I still bear the scars."

She neared and brushed her warm fingers against his cheek, examining the remnants of the battle he'd nearly lost. "How old were you?"

"Sixteen."

"I'm so sorry." Lowering her hand, Anna's gentle voice coated the boyhood sorrows that had never left.

Again, he kept his attention at the fire. "I took over Father's smithy. Though I was young, I was strong and worked harder than I ever had to keep food in our bellies." The memories loomed, some shadowed from time, some clear as present day. "Mother, Julia, and Jane brought in extra by laundering when they had the strength and mending when they did not."

When *she* appeared in his mind, the bitter palate he'd tried to forget began to singe his tongue. "'Twas four years later when I met Anna Muhr."

Anna's dainty eyebrows peaked.

"Aye, she carried your given name." Exhaling the memories in a heavy sigh, William continued. "I imagined myself in love from the moment I saw her. She was from far too wealthy a family to ever be courted by one of my station, but somehow she made me believe such things meant little to her and that only her father refused our union." Flowered memories turned brown and brittle. "She carried my heart for three years until the day she came to me weeping, claiming her father had died, leaving her with his debts she had never known of and saying if there was no way to pay them, she would be forced to leave England forever."

As clear as the moment itself, her deception burned and his chest grew tight. "She begged me through her tears to help and in my innocence I believed she wished my assistance so we could finally be wed now her father was gone."

The pain of his regrets stabbed and ran a hand over his mouth. "Of course my mother and sisters knew of her, they knew how much I loved her and how I would have given anything to make her my wife. When I explained to them her need, not even considering that what few pounds we had could never make a difference, they insisted I take our savings and give it to her. They believed, as I did, that it would assure our future together."

Darkness lurked in the corners of his soul. "When I offered all I had, she took it with hardly a word of gratitude and left. No mention of where she was going or when she might return. But in my youthful ignorance I believed she would come to me within a few days at least, and report that our painful wait was over and that at last she was free to follow her heart and be my wife. But she did not."

"She did not?" The sweet shock in her face tightened the binding of her soul to his.

"Nay." He moved away from the fire and rested his back against the space between the mantel and bedchamber door. "I searched for her for three months, frantic that something had happened. I knew she would never simply leave without telling me, unless something dreadful had befallen her." He stalled, the cold rain of that misty October day drawing him away from the warm kitchen fire, to the dank London street. "But then I saw her in town, leaving the market, clinging to the arm of another man."

"No..."

The memory, so thick, chilled his skin. "I rushed forward and questioned her, fearing perhaps she had been taken against her will, but the smile on her face spoke otherwise." He pulled his bottom lip between his teeth. "She smiled as if she hardly knew me and introduced me to her husband of two months—a man who stared at me as if I were unworthy to shoe his horse." The rage and shame he'd wrestled still thumped in his pulse. "She said nothing of the money I had given, spoke nothing of the grief she had caused. Only offered my mother and sisters her best." He pressed a hard laugh from his nose. "I had never been so ashamed."

"But how were you to know? 'Tis she who must be ashamed for doing such a wretched thing."

"'Tis I who am to blame. I *should* have known. I should never have fallen for her charms." He ground his teeth. "Of course mother and my sisters were grieved for my sorrows, but they could never know how deeply I felt it. My deepest regrets were not over a lost love, but for what they had sacrificed for me. I had taken our money—their money—and given it to a woman who cared only for herself. The medicines they needed to ease their discomforts were..." The ache in his throat thickened. "We could hardly earn enough to pay for them as it was, and now with everything gone, I knew I must do something. My skills as a blacksmith were poor at best, despite my efforts, and the shame I felt every time I saw their pains—their suffering from what I had done—I could bear it no longer. Knowing I could regain my honor and provide more for those I loved by going abroad, I joined—"

Every bit of him stopped, his tongue still waiting at the back of his teeth to finish the words he'd started.

Slowly, William closed his mouth, berating himself for what he had nearly revealed. He closed his eyes. *Tomorrow. Tomorrow when the shadows are past...*

"My love?" Anna craned her neck to view him from her spot at his side.

William blinked, grasping for an answer that would save him from the edge of the cliff he clung to. "I joined with those coming to the colonies in search of fortune. I sent my family everything I earned..." His mind lost hold and he fell backward into the cold, haunting dreams he'd tried so hard to forget. "'Twas last March I learned of their passing. My efforts had not been enough to save them."

Anna rushed to him, filling the space between them, her innocent, pleading eyes darting back and forth between his. "You must not think that, my love. What a terrible burden you place on yourself."

"I would have forever labored under the belief that the desire for the things of this world were at the root of a woman's heart, but for you." He kissed her forehead, needing to free himself from the pain of the pity that pooled in her eyes. "For that, I will praise God all my days and pray that with the passing of years the grief of my actions will not haunt me as they have."

She took his hand in hers, holding him motionless with the sudden strength that owned her soft features. "And for those years I will be with you. I—" She lurched and flung one hand to her mouth, the other to her stomach.

William reached for the nearest pot and she yanked it forward, retching the meager contents of her stomach.

"Forgive me," she said, panting. "This nausea comes in waves..."

Worry gripped as William helped her to sit. Relieving her of the pot, he crouched in front of her. "Give me your word that you will see Nathaniel tomorrow. If something is truly wrong—"

"I am well, William."

"Nay, you are not. This has gone on far too long."

She nodded, her shoulders slumping. "I shall visit Nathaniel in the morning."

He helped her to her feet and wrapped an arm around her as he walked with her to the bedchamber.

She patted his arm as she sat on the bed. "Tomorrow everything will be well. Nathaniel will tell me everything is well, I am sure of it."

He bent and kissed the top of her hair. *Aye, tomorrow. Tomorrow.*

Chapter Twenty-Four

Anna pressed a hand to her stomach, the constant rolling of the past weeks replaced by a nervous tumbling. She stared at the panels of the Smith's back door, the chilled air biting her ears. If not for William's prodding last night and again this morning, she would not have come. 'Twas nothing. Just a small irritation, soon to be recovered from, surely. Anna swallowed, a low throbbing of anxiety pulsing in her chest. Her mother had not been much older when her fateful illness began. And 'twas only two years later it finally closed her eyes forever. She clutched the cloak at her throat. *I could not bear such news, Lord.*

Somehow, as if without her bidding, she reached forward and knocked against the wood. Her arms and legs quivered, but not from fear, she promised herself. When the door didn't open immediately she breathed out a white-cold breath and prepared to leave just as the door opened. "Anna?"

Nathaniel's kind tone reached out to stop her.

Anna smiled, her cheeks hot. "Forgive me, I didn't mean to disturb you."

His face softened in a welcome smile, his manner as warm and inviting as the air from the house. "Never a disruption. Come in."

She hesitated, but the thoughtful way he gestured into the house eased the tightening in her shoulders, if only a little.

When she entered, he spoke, closing the door behind her. "If you've come to see Kitty, I'm afraid you may have to wait. She's gone to town, but I don't believe she'll be long."

"Nay, I...I, thank you, but..." She glanced around the study before dropping her gaze to her fingers. "I came to see you."

When he didn't answer, Anna looked up. Her rising pulse stilled at the understanding slant of his brow and the way his mouth lifted at one end. "Of course. Please sit down."

Anna sat on the edge of the seat he offered by the fire while he rested against the table.

"I'm so pleased at the news you and Kitty shared last evening before dinner," Anna started, delaying the reason for her coming. She smiled. "She is radiant with joy. I could not be more happy for you both."

"Thank you, Anna. I am a blessed man, indeed." Nathaniel's eyes beamed and he glanced somewhere past her, his mind carrying him away. "She is a remarkable woman. I hardly deserve her." With a quick shake of the head, he lowered his chin. "But I must assume you didn't come to speak to me about that."

SO *rare* A GIFT

His pointed gaze and the somber strain in his tone made Anna grip her hands tighter in her lap.

She licked her lips and flung him a fleeting smile, but the words refused to leave the safety of her mouth.

Nathaniel tilted his head in question. "Please know that I will not share what you tell, if you do not wish me to."

A mite of her disquiet drifted from her shoulders. "I...I uh..." She shrugged, allowing a quiet laugh to take with it more of the tension in her chest. "Forgive me, I don't often speak of...I don't quite know how to—"

"Of course, I understand. It is often difficult to share troubles of a private nature." His eyes squinted in polite concern. "What troubles you?"

"I don't exactly know." She sat rigid to keep from squirming in her seat. "William insisted I come because...I have not been able to eat much and he was concerned."

He nodded with a quiet hum. "I'm pleased you heeded his wisdom. Any good husband would be concerned if his wife could not eat. Do you feel pangs of hunger or simply do not wish to eat?"

"'Tis difficult to say—I know that sounds strange." She looked down to her hands. "I can only eat small portions and when I do my stomach rebels."

"I see. You suffer from nausea?"

"Nausea, aye."

"How often do you feel that way?"

She almost laughed. "Nearly all the time."

Nathaniel took the chair opposite her. "You are vomiting?"

She nodded. "Aye."

"How often?"

She raised a shoulder, slanting her head. "I don't quite know...one to three times a day sometimes."

He straightened, his eyes rounding. "Anna, that is concerning indeed. Are you able to keep any food in your belly?"

She nodded. "Enough."

"Have you any fever?"

"Nay, nothing like that."

"Flux?"

She shook her head.

"Fatigue?"

"Aye." She relaxed her knotted fingers, grateful she could finally look at him while she spoke. "I find I must lie down mid-day or I cannot finish my chores come supper. That's never happened to me before."

"Hmm." He pulled his bottom lip between his teeth, leaned forward and rested his elbows on his knees. "I feel I should ask you a few questions of a more personal nature."

Her skin burned. Were these questions not already personal? "Of course."

He must have sensed her anxiety, for his eyes somehow softened even more. "I do not wish to make you uncomfortable. I simply must know if my understanding of what you're experiencing is correct."

She nodded and he smiled. He motioned to his chest. "Are you having any tenderness here?"

Her breasts? Merciful heavens. Her voice refused to work so she nodded her answer.

He was silent a moment and she looked back to him. His forehead creased. "Have you missed your monthly?"

The question shoved her upright. She blinked. Come to think of it... "Aye, I suppose I have." Her shoulders dropped. "What do you think that means?"

Nathaniel pushed up and sat back, a knowing, almost teasing-like smile lifting his features. He raised his hands as if she should know exactly what it meant.

Still, her mind was blank. "What's wrong with me?"

"Wrong?" He leaned back in his chair, a grin widening his face. "I would not say anything is *wrong*, Anna."

"But what is it?"

He sat straight, a kind sort of frown owning his expression. "You really do not know?"

Nerves bubbled and her voice escaped more pinched than she'd wished. "Nay, tell me."

"'Tis very likely you are with child."

Anna's breath stilled as the words whirled around her, soft and beautiful like the scent of a spring bouquet that lay just beyond her grasp. "Nay, 'tis impossible."

His smile vanished, replaced by a drawn concern. "You have not been intimate?"

Anna opened her mouth but any sound lodged in her throat. She shrunk back in her chair and cleared her throat to dislodge the embarrassment. "We have...but..."

"You have." His statement held enough question to require confirmation.

Her face was surely crimson. "Aye."

The mirth in Nathaniel's kind face returned ten fold. "Then I do believe 'tis possible that you are not ill in the least. Rather, quite healthy indeed."

"Nay, Dr. Smith. You do not understand. When I was young I was very ill. The doctors attested I would never have a child, and after ten years of marriage I never did, so you must understand that—"

"How long have you experienced these symptoms?"

She counted in her mind. "About a week."

"And you've missed your monthly. Has that ever happened before?"

"Nay."

He leaned forward once again and reached out, resting his hand over hers. "Then I do believe you have some very glad tidings to share with your husband."

"You think it possible? Truly?" Her throat began to ache, but the thought was so precious she hardly wished to cradle it at all. If she allowed any hope...

Nathaniel's angled features grew soft. "There is a very strong possibility that you are with child, Anna. It will be another month or two before you will know for certain, but I believe the chances lie in your favor."

Her breath caught and she turned her face to hide the hot tears that flooded. "Forgive me."

His kind grip tightened. "The Lord delights to give good gifts to His children. He wishes for you and William to have joy, Anna."

She tugged a handkerchief from her pocket and dotted her eyes. *Lord, could it be?*

Nathaniel stood and she followed suit.

"I am pleased you came to see me," he said, motioning to the back door. "I hope you will feel comfortable to confide in me at any time."

"Of course." Looking up, Anna's gratitude nearly caused her to reach out and embrace him for his goodness. Kitty was a fortunate woman indeed. As was she.

She walked through the parlor to the back. "I wish I could express the depth of my gratitude. I feel foolish for not discerning such a thing on my own."

"Nonsense. 'Tis understandable, indeed." He opened the door, that same congenial smile on his mouth, the same generous depth in his tone. "I do believe in time, we shall be offering our congratulations to you and your husband as you have for Kitty and me."

She nodded her thanks and stepped from the house. "You will keep the news to yourself? I should like to be the one to tell William."

He gave a quick bob of the head. "You have my complete silence."

She turned toward the road with a grin that reached

through her middle. Then, as if the knowledge were melting the frost of disbelief from her mind, Anna's heart burst. Striding home, eyes wide, breath quick and shallow, she half-laughed, half-cried.

With child? She could hardly think the words without weeping.

The emotions spilling from her eyes weighed at her feet and she stopped. Closing her eyes, she prayed. Joy, so rich and deep she felt it clean through her soul as the tears spilled over her cheeks. She clasped her hands in prayer at her chest. *How is it done, Lord? I am unworthy of such goodness.*

The winter sun warmed against her cold cheeks and she opened her eyes, her gaze landing on her ring.

Forget not He who loveth thee.

Paul marched through the snow-flecked center of town, the mid-morning sun shining bright above him, his limbs pulsing with ravenous need. Warren had expounded their good fortune this very morning—only an hour past—that he had found the man they sought. It hardly seemed real, but it was. *He will be mine.* After all this time, Donaldson would finally be brought to justice.

Passing the last shop and heading toward the grist mill, Paul increased his pace. Everyone believed Donaldson was so virtuous. 'Twas almost blasphemy, when the man worked against the very thing he swore to uphold. Was not following through with the old man's request to take his daughter away first not proof that he himself was more righteous than the benevolent Donaldson?

He reached for the gun beneath his colonial coat. The urge to shoot at first sight of his prey twitched in his fingers.

Turning up the road to the right, he paused, a motionless figure in the road, her back turned to him. As he neared the stranger's visage found place in his memory and he stilled.

Dark hair, petite frame.

His curiosity pricked. It must be her. But why was she alone?

Before he could retreat from the thought, he spoke. "Miss Whitehead?"

The woman straightened and turned, the color draining from her face when she saw him.

He smiled. *Excellent.*

The clock on the mantel struck noon and William's shoulders cramped. Anna should have returned home by now.

He glanced out the front window before returning to the table where his pistol rested. Snatching it up, he scorned the anxieties that bit at his heels and checked again to be sure it was loaded. Warren would be here any moment. Had he done as planned?

Inform Paul you have found your daughter and the man who took her, William had said. *Propose that you desire to rescue your daughter and do not wish for me to follow you, and for this you will require his aid. Have him hide in the wood and wait for the moment you take Anna away.*

A rustle outside stole William from his memory. Again, he went to the window, this time, gripping his pistol. Blast. 'Twas no one. He stood, staring past the garden into the wood. Was Paul there now? Would he wait as planned? William stepped to the fire where he checked on the lead he heated to mold more balls for his gun. Paul wished an easy fight, thus waiting would be to his advantage. But such knowledge did little to temper the rising heat in William's body. Perhaps he would find others and bring them with him? Perhaps his rage would drive him to disregard their plan and come after William before Warren could take Anna to safety.

Bowing his head, William rubbed his temples, praying through the fog of fear that threatened to choke him. *Protect Anna, Lord, I pray thee.*

The latch to the door clicked and William whirled.

"William?" a voice whispered.

Exhaling a plume of tension, William went to the door. "Come in, Warren."

The man entered, removing his hat. "I peered in the window and saw only you. You said to enter so—"

"You did well," William said, glancing left and right in the yard before shutting the door. "Is he here?"

He nodded. "Aye, though I do not know precisely. I told him where to go but he was still at the tavern when I left."

A fear he'd harbored since the moment he'd presented Warren with his plan bolted William into action. He turned and hurried to the fire, plucking the tongs from the table and removing the small pot of molten lead from the fire. "I must be prepared. Something tells me he will not come alone." He poured the liquid into the mold, cursing himself for not having done this the night before, instead of allowing himself the pleasure of blissful sleep next to Anna's warm and perfectly feminine frame.

Warren neared and knelt beside him. "Who might he bring with him?"

Glancing up, William noted the worry that folded into the creases around Warren's wise eyes. "He wishes me dead for defecting." He grabbed his mallet and tapped the bullet into a bowl already half full. "Bringing others would mean not only an easier capture, but witnesses of my death."

"Tell her." Warren gripped his shoulder, halting William's arm. "Anna is no simpleton nor is she fearful. She will understand why you have done this, I am sure. We *must* tell her what is coming. She could run to the safety of town—if you do not wish to implicate your friends—and I could help you fight—"

"Nay." William held the man's stare. "I refuse to put anyone at risk." Warren removed his hand and William continued with pouring another stream of lead into the mold. "I will not rest until this is ended—at my hand alone." He kept the next thought in his teeth. Truly, he craved the appeasement that 'twas he alone who had brought an end to his predator's hunt.

Warren stood. "Where is she?"

William spoke but kept his attention on his task. He grabbed the mallet and tapped another ball free. "She should have returned a quarter hour past." He poured the lead for another while the stab of worry cut deeper. Why hadn't she returned? "I insisted she see the physician. She hasn't been well."

"She is ill?"

William looked up from his crouched position. The sincerity in Warren's strong features, the concern in his voice, fitted beside William's. A father and a husband both pained with concern over a woman they loved.

"I do not know." He tapped out the last ball and returned the lead to the fire before grabbing the bowl of newly formed bullets and setting them on the table. "I pray she will return with an answer."

"I fear God does not hear your prayers, Henry."

William stilled at the sound of the voice, though his muscles flicked to the ready. He shot his gaze to the door then to Warren whose stance showed he too was prepared to fight.

"I told you to wait," Warren growled.

Leaning his shoulder against the doorframe, Paul shook his head, clicking his tongue in mocking disapproval. "Nay, old man. You told me I could have him only when you had taken the girl to safety. But how can she be safe when she walks the road alone." He motioned as one would to coax a timid child, a smile so relaxed it poured rage down William's spine.

Anna entered, her face white, her hands clutched at her middle.

Rushing forward, William reached for her, but Paul yanked her back with a flash of the devil in his eyes. "No, no. You should not touch her. How can a woman trust a man who has lied to her? You must make amends, Henry."

"I will not have you playing games." Warren spoke calm, but a roar of warning rumbled in his tone. He stepped forward. "Let me take her away and you two men can finish what you began."

Laughing, Paul tilted his head back. "Nay, this has all become far too amusing." He quieted and struck William with a glare. "I should like us all to hear this confession. Tell her Henry, who you really are and what you have done."

Anna quivered, her complexion slipping to gray as she looked from Warren back to William.

This could not be happening. Inside, a call to battle drummed, but William reserved the urge to attack while Anna stood between him and the man who would have him dead. He kept his eyes on Paul but spoke to Warren. "Take her away. Now."

Warren stepped forward and Anna jumped back with a strained cry. "No!"

Warren stopped and glanced to William, tension tightening his mouth. The unvoiced question of how to proceed shouted in his eyes.

"Trust me, Anna. Go with him." The command came out with more bite than he'd wished. "I will not have you—"

"You will not have her learn the truth of you, is that it, Henry?" Paul pushed from the door and stepped behind Anna, inclining his head to her ear. "He is not what you believe." He stood and spoke louder. "Will you tell her or shall I?"

William's limbs turned to stone at the sight of Anna's quivering hands and white lips. Groaning under the weight of his deceit, he opened his mouth but Paul's bellowing sound emerged first.

"He, my dear, is none other than the honorable Captain Henry Donaldson." Paul looked to him, then Anna, a surprised grin matching the laugh that followed. "How remarkable, is it not? That the very man you had wished to find made you his bride." He tisked and shook his head. "But I must believe he did not tell you of his past. No...for the name he offered is not his at all." Paul stalked forward, his wicked stare trained on William. "Henry Donaldson. A man able to deceive many into believing he is *good*."

Fists quivering from the exertion not to employ

them, William growled his reply. "That's enough, Paul—"

"It is not enough!" Paul yelled, his face crimson and his arms rigid as the charade of civility vanished. He snarled and spit when he spoke. "You are a traitor! You are not worthy to live!"

He reached for his weapon, but William drew his first. Warren raced to Anna, grabbing her around the shoulders and pulling her away. The men stood motionless, pistols aimed, hatred already warring in their eyes.

"William!"

Anna's cry pulled William's vision toward her and worry stole a measure of his strength, but Warren tugged her nearer to the safety of the door. "Come child, you are not safe."

"Nay! I will not!" She struggled against him. "Let me go."

"Anna, please!" William kept both his stare and his weapon on Paul while his soul reached for the woman he loved. "Go with him now."

"Yes, go with him," Paul said. "You would not wish to see this traitor trembling in fear, begging for his life like a child."

Child.

"You!" Rage jolted through him, his outstretched arm rigid as iron. "You killed that boy!"

"I did what had to be done! More rebels only means more war and suffering for us all." Gun still pointed at

William's chest, Paul's face twitched and he yanked at his shirt, revealing a circular red scar. "You did this to me!" he yelled, his face contorted. Clamping his jaw shut he inhaled through his nose, but the even tone belied the undercurrent of loathing. He released his shirt. "As you see, I cannot be killed. But you can."

William's frame went solid when Paul's finger reached for the trigger. Time slowed, like the strained motion of a disquieting dream. Anna pulled from Warren's grasp and hurled herself against Paul as both guns exploded the same instant. With a pained cry she gripped her side and William yelled for her. Dropping his weapon, he lunged for Anna as she tumbled backward, hitting her head against the bench and crumpling to the ground.

The room faded around him, all commotion no more than a tinkling bell compared to the blaring shock that numbed him. Darkness shrouded all but her motionless form and the blood that stained her bodice. *What have I done? Dear God, what have I done?*

Paul charged through the gun smoke and the speed of life returned like the shot of a cannon. He tackled William away from his wife and into the ground. A blow to his jaw shot a blinding pain through William's head. With a giant heave, William thrust Paul to the side and scrambled to his feet, vaguely aware that Warren knelt beside Anna.

Paul sneered and pushed to standing. He flicked aside his coat and gripped the dagger at his hip. "I enjoy a bit of sparring." He snapped the weapon forward. "Let us finish this."

William lunged and grabbed Paul's wrist, gripping and twisting. Paul's eyes blackened, his hot breath heaving as he struggled against William's resistance.

"If she dies, I will make you pay with your life." With a heave strengthened by hate, William shoved Paul back.

From behind, Warren's voice cracked through the air. "Dear God, I fear she is dead!"

No! William's vision wavered. *Lord, she cannot be gone from me!*

"You have killed your wife!" Paul laughed, straightening. "How that must pain you. Allow me to end your suffering."

He spun the dagger in his hand and lunged. William dodged as a flash and boom came from behind. Paul's features went flat and he fell at William's feet. William stumbled back, staring at the body of his enemy. He turned and stilled. Arm outstretched, face ticking, Warren lowered the still smoking weapon.

A breath of relief followed by a wind of pain stormed through William. He rushed to Anna's side, his heart clutching when his hand brushed against the blood that dripped on the floor. His throat tore with emotion. She had risked her life for him—his own bullet doing the work against her that his enemy's could not against him. He pressed his trembling fingers against her neck. Nothing.

Panic battered like a dominant foe. "Are you sure she is dead?"

Warren crouched beside him, his own voice uneven. "I could not feel a pulse."

Trying his fingers at another spot, William exhaled a choppy breath when a small throb beat against his touch. "She lives." He scooped her into his arms and raced through the open door.

"Come. And let us pray we are not too late."

Chapter Twenty-Five

William called for him even before he reached the house.

"Nathaniel! Nathaniel!"

Anna groaned and he looked down, the sight of her white cheeks sending his pulse to ramming speed.

The backdoor burst open and Nathaniel hurried out. "What's happ—" He stopped, his mouth dropping open, voice deep with command. "Bring her in." He swung back toward the house. "Kitty!"

Kitty rushed to the door just as William hurried into the small surgery. She thrust her hands to her chest. "William! What's happened?"

"I shot her." Speaking the horrid truth made his limbs weaken.

"What?" Nathaniel jerked to a halt.

William didn't answer until he'd rested Anna on the table. "My bullet was meant for Paul—he was readying to fire at me and Anna...she...she pushed him aside to save me from—" He couldn't finish.

Nathaniel's firm look answered without the need to voice it, and he raised his shears preparing to cut through her clothes. "Kitty, prepare the bandages and needle and thread."

She whirled to the cupboard when Nathaniel began to cut. Though the shears snipped through her fabric, 'twas William that felt the cut of the blade. *It should be my flesh that is torn, my blood that is spilled.* Ropes of guilt twined with fury and tightened around his neck as he stared at his wife's limp form.

Nathaniel flashed a quick look to William. "Tell me all."

William swallowed to ease the lump that lodged in his throat. "The force of the shot propelled her backward and she hit her head." His voice wobbled and he wiped a hand over his mouth. *Dearest Lord, do not take her from me.*

Nathaniel frowned and released his shears. Reaching for her head, he dotted his fingers around her skull. "A large lump but no gash or crack in her skull." Returning to his previous task, he pulled away the fabric of her stays to reveal the chemise beneath.

Glistening red soaked through the small gash in the fabric. William curled his fists and clamped his jaw to keep from speaking the stream of panicked questions that flooded his mouth.

Kitty neared with the supplies just as Nathaniel tore open the fabric to reveal the wound in Anna's flesh.

Nathaniel and Kitty spoke in quiet tones as they worked. William's nerves were shattered. How long would this take? He tossed a look to Warren who waited outside the surgery door. His arms were crossed over his chest, his mouth hard and eyes soft with pain for the daughter he loved.

Nathaniel straightened, touching his wife at the small of her back. "Take these to the basin to be washed."

"Aye, my dear." As Kitty passed, basket of blood-covered cloths and instruments in her arms, she offered William a tight, reassuring smile before hurrying to the kitchen.

With a sigh, Nathaniel turned and cupped William on the shoulder. He opened his mouth to speak but stalled when his eyes landed on Warren.

Warren uncrossed his arms and glanced between the two as if he understood the need for husband and doctor to discuss matters in private. With a curt nod he started for the backdoor, but not without allowing himself one last glimpse of his daughter. He exited and closed the door behind him.

William yanked Nathaniel's arm. "Well?"

Nathaniel glared after Warren, not answering quick enough to satisfy William's anxiety. Gripping harder, William strained to keep his voice even. "Will she be all right? Will she live?"

"Calm yourself." Nathaniel clapped William on the shoulder, smacking him back from the edge of the crevasse of despair that threatened to consume him. "She will be well, God be praised," he said, releasing an audible sigh. "The ball grazed her ribs, broke one of them, in fact. I believe the blow to her head caused her to lose consciousness, but she will be well."

William gripped the table as relief blew through his muscles like a spring wind—chilled, but edged with a promise of warmer days to come. "I thought I had lost her."

"Nay, my friend. Praise the Lord for that." A reverent smile etched across Nathaniel's face before he once again turned solemn. "'Tis dangerous for any person to be wounded as she, but most especially for a woman with child. Not to worry, they are both—"

"With child?" William froze. He couldn't have heard right.

Nathaniel's expression folded, his response frayed with strands of both surprise and remorse. "I...I thought she had already told you. Forgive me, I would never have said anything but, under the circumstances—"

"But Anna cannot bear children." William shook his head, grappling for the bit of truth that swung just out of reach. "You must be joking."

Nathaniel slanted his head, not a hint of mirth in his tone. "You know I would not jest about something of this nature."

William looked to Anna then back to Nathaniel, and the doubt he carried slipped through his fingers as the grin on Nathaniel's face widened. William stepped toward the table, speaking to his friend but looking at his wife. "You are in earnest. She is...she is with child."

"I have not been more earnest in all my life. Her

discomforts of late make it difficult to believe 'tis anything else." A slight smile, one fringed with regret tightened his mouth. "I am sorry. I know she had wished to be the one to tell you."

William glanced over his shoulder with a nod then looked back to his wife. The slightest pink had returned to her cheeks, and the up and down of her chest allowed his own lungs to take in air with less strain. His throat, constricted with a swell of emotions allowed only the slightest sound when he spoke. "How far along?"

Nathaniel nodded. "Early. Another month or so and you will know for certain."

Like sunshine on a hillside, the realization washed over William, warming him with its light. "I cannot believe it." He stepped beside the table and stroked his fingers against her cheek. "So that has been the cause of her discomforts."

From behind, Nathaniel gripped William's shoulder. "Our God is a God of miracles, William, and I do believe the two of you have been given one."

Slowly, the blood returned to his limbs and he turned to his friend. "She will be all right then?"

"Aye, indeed." He pulled a blanket over her and motioned to the door. "She is stable enough to travel. Let us take her back home in our wagon. There she can heal in her own surroundings."

The memory of Paul's body on the floor of his home surged to the forefront. "But I've a body there."

"What? Whose body?"

William didn't answer but continued with his thought. "I don't know what to do..."

"Let me take the man's body to his father."

Both William and Nathaniel turned to see Warren standing by the study.

William inclined his head. When had he come back in? How much had he heard? "You would do that?"

He raised his eyebrows. "Why would I not? I will tell them he told me his name before he died and that he wished his body to be returned to his family."

"How can you be sure they will believe your tale?"

He only smiled. "Your wife's estate is vast. I do not need to tell them from whence I came to such funds, but I suspect any concerns they have regarding the man's untimely demise will find a quick end when they are made aware of the expanse of my pocketbook."

William pushed a quick breath from his lungs. "Sir, how can I properly thank you? You have saved both our lives this evening."

A deep smile widened his face, erasing the grief-stricken years that had before lined his eyes. "And it seems, from what I hear, another life that is just beginning." He neared and rested a hand on William's arm as he looked to Anna. "You will soon know the depth of a father's love."

Turning, he went to the door and exited, stopping briefly on the stoop. "When I have attended to this obligation, I shall return, if you are agreeable."

"Aye, of course."

He gave a quick nod. "I too, do not wish to return to England."

Anna blinked, the pain in her side owning her attentions before the low throbbing that thumped in her head. She raised her arm and rubbed her eyes, once more blinking to focus her blurry vision. The bluish hue of winter daylight dusted in from the window and the fire sputtered. As her vision cleared, the familiar surroundings of the bedchamber calmed the sudden rise of fear. She was home. But where was William? What had happened—why was she abed?

She gasped and her throat seized. Tears burned her eyes as the still-sharp memories cut through the fog of pain. Shouts. Gun shots. Burning in her side and a strike against her head. Then blackness. She bolted rigid and pressed her hands to her belly. *No, no, no, no! Please, Lord in heaven, no!* A low, moaning wail ached its way through her chest, echoing her grief through the lonely room. The child was lost. It must be. How could something so small and precious survive something so grave? Sobbing, she kept one hand on her middle, covering her face with the other. She had lost everything. The man she loved and the child she'd hoped might be living within. Both things more precious than her own life, stripped from her forever.

Again William's biting words and hard eyes nipped at her torn spirit, and she moaned as a wave of anguish crashed over her. She gasped through her tears before another storm of grief assailed her, hot tears running past her ears to the pillow.

"Anna?"

Someone rushed in and she turned away, heedless of the pain that slashed through her as she rolled to her side.

"Kitty, bring the broth. She will need to eat."

Anna stilled, moving her hand from her face as the sound of the voice whispered through her like an unbidden memory. Nay, it could not be true.

A figure dented the bed behind her before a warm hand touched her hair. "Anna, I am here. Tell me what pains you, my love."

She gasped and turned, disbelief plating her pains in gold. This could not be. It was too wondrous.

Blinking the moisture from her eyes she stared, unsure if she should allow such a vision to take hold should it be no more than a dream.

"William?"

He nodded, his mouth bowing in a soft smile, but 'twas only when he touched her face that she knew 'twas not a mere wish of her heart.

"I—" She put a hand to her mouth to cover her quivering face. "I thought you had left me—that you had that man take me away—"

"Never would I leave you." William's forehead

pinched and he leaned forward, cupping her cheeks with his hands. His expression crumpled, his words fissured with pain. "Why? Why did you do it? You could have been killed, and I would have died of grief knowing 'twas by my hand. If I had lost you..."

Lost.

Like a wave in a tempest, the grief assailed her again and she covered her mouth, the sudden wails she could not suppress contorting her face. She gasped between sobs as William gently gripped her shoulders.

"What is wrong, my love?"

"I have..." She hovered her trembling hand over her mouth as she struggled to speak. "I have lost our baby." The very sound of the words ground through her spirit like a millstone against grain, grinding to dust the longings she'd carried so many years.

"Nay, Anna." William scooted closer on the bed, bending toward her and speaking over her cries. "Hush, my love, please. Nathaniel assured me our baby is well."

The next cry stalled in her throat, but her hiccoughing breath still chopped through her words. "He did?"

Could it be true? Nay, she dared not believe it.

She blinked the moisture that still flooded her eyes and William's smile stroked the quaking in her spirit. "Aye, he did." William reached in his pocket and retrieved a handkerchief, dotting it against her cheeks. "'Twas of great concern to him, to be sure the babe was not in danger." He leaned closer still, his own eyes misting. Stroking her tear-streaked face with his hands, while his words stroked her spirit. "You are with child, Anna. *We* shall have a child."

Tears pricked again, but no longer from grief. She took his hand from her face and held it against her chest. "I can hardly believe it."

A reverent sparkle lit his eyes. "I can. 'Tis a miracle indeed and I could not think of anyone more worthy." He lowered his gaze, pulling his lip between his teeth before meeting her stare once more. "I know you had wished to tell me. I hope you do not—"

"Is she all right?" Kitty's voice burst through the room as she entered, when she stopped abruptly. "Oh, forgive me, I didn't mean to interrupt." She rested a tray on the table, love stretching from her eyes and embracing Anna from a distance. She paused and touched William's shoulder. "There is someone who wishes to see you."

She nodded to Anna then William before turning for the door.

William pivoted, allowing Anna a clear view of the doorway, and the man who stood in its shadow. Her neck tensed as if the very hand of fear wished to strangle her, but William's gentle touch and his welcoming gesture to the stranger eased her tensing muscles.

The man neared, standing at the end of the bed. William then turned back to Anna, brushing a hand down her arm and twining his fingers with hers. "My love, you must meet Warren Fox."

The man stepped forward, gripping his hat in his fingers in front of him. His face warmed, tenderness coaxing an unfamiliar longing in Anna's soul.

He opened his mouth then closed it, the lines around his eyes deepening. "Anna..." The man stopped again, looking to William and back again before the words streamed from him like a mountain brook. "You do not know me, but I know you—*have* known you since you and Samuel were born."

Anna stared, motionless. He spoke her name, and Samuel's, with such familiar care it lured a memory to light. Or had it been a dream?

"Your mother and I were desperately in love and our passions over came us. When she learned she was with child, we planned to flee, to live our lives free from the demands of society that held her prisoner. But she was forced to marry the man who claimed you and your brother as his own."

The words smoothed over her like soft cloth. "You are my father."

"Aye." Moisture pooled in his eyes and he rounded the bed's corner. Stopping beside her, he glanced to her hand and motioned to her fingers. "I gave that ring to your mother the day before she was married, and she vowed she would wear it always."

Anna's eyes burned. "She did. I never saw her without it."

Warren's throat shifted, emotion welling in his face. "I know."

A tear blinked free and she brushed it away, the words of the ring glowing in her memory. This man had loved her mother—and she him. *This* was why she had so insisted that Anna marry for love, because she herself had been denied the choice.

"I have never loved another woman in all my life," Warren said. "And I have loved you and your brother more with every sunrise, though I was not free to show it." Bowing, he kissed Anna's hair. "Forgive me for not providing for you and Samuel as I wished, for not being at liberty to protect you from so much sorrow." He swallowed, as if struggling against a rise of pain. "Forgive me, as well, for frightening you that day." He looked to William then Anna. "It seems God has turned our chaos into harmony. I will be your servant the rest of my days."

More tears threatened, her throat thickening. "I...I don't know what to say."

"You need say nothing, my dear." He kissed her again. "When you wish to speak more, you need only call for me." Retreating backward, he turned and exited, closing the door behind him.

Staring, Anna fumbled with the beautiful weight of such a shocking revelation, praying with a gratitude she had never known. *Thy goodness is unbound, Lord. How can I even be worthy of such happiness?* When again His quiet words returned to her, filling her soul as only the God of heaven can do. *Forget not He who loveth thee.*

She closed her eyes, the simple expression embracing her like the very arms of God. *Thank you, Lord. Thank you.* She turned to William. "How long have you known?"

"I learned this only yesterday when I sought his help in protecting you from..." His lips pursed and he lowered his gaze. "From Stockton."

"He is gone?"

"He is dead." After the last word, William's eyes shot to hers.

The weight of their past tribulations hovered between them and she yearned for his nearness. Pushing herself up, she grimaced, the stabbing pain in her ribs protesting the movement. William reached carefully around her shoulders and pulled her against his chest as he leaned back against the pillows. No sound between them. Just the rustling of Kitty and Warren in the parlor, the comforting accompaniment of the popping fire. Anna closed her eyes, and in the silence, could feel their hearts beat as one.

She exhaled a soft breath from her nose and gripped her arms around him. "I despise that man for speaking such slanderous lies. I am so sorry, William."

A slight groan rumbled in his throat. His chest rose and fell. "My name is not William. It is Henry."

1

Henry stared at the ceiling, hearing the words he'd just spoken spin through the room again and again.

Anna pulled away. "What do you mean?"

Inhaling to fill his lungs more with courage than with air, he prayed for strength. "What Stockton said of me is true. I am Henry Donaldson and I knew your brother. I was there the night he died."

What little color had returned to her cheeks seemed to deepen. "You were there?"

"Aye."

"You knew him?" Her eyes rounded, a slight peak of her eyebrows signaling the question before she spoke. "Why did you not tell me, my love?"

My love? She would still call him that? Henry stilled, the beat of his pulse stalling. Where was the anger, the hate? Would she not pull away and call him the vilest of men? She did not. Not the hint of enmity. Just shock. And hope.

Henry shook his head. "I have not known long. And I did plan to tell you, but I wanted the time to be right—"

"I am sure you wished not to say it," she said, resting her head against his chest, "knowing how it might pain me to know how he killed himself."

"You may put your mind to rest on that account, Anna. He did not take his own life."

She jerked away, her mouth agape. "He did not?"

"Nay. But 'tis true he had lost his honor. He was a selfish, angry man."

Her stare drifted down. "How did he die?"

Should he tell? The details of Samuel's death would be startling to anyone. "He was stabbed."

"By whom?"

He studied her eyes, the way their crystal depths ached for the answer. But some things were best left in the grave. "'Twas an accident."

"An accident." Her whispered echo floated up and she rested her head on his chest once more, her arms tightening around him. "I suppose that is all I am to know."

"Aye."

"Hmm." She breathed against him before breaking the silence. "You defected. Why?"

Again, her unmitigated forgiveness cradled his fears like swaddling bands. He breathed out, unburdening his spirit from the weeks of forced silence. "I believe I have sympathized with the patriot cause for some time." He allowed his memory to journey through the past, gathering the bright moments, the ones that sparked his allegiance to shine on a more worthy cause. "I lived here for three years before the war began, watching the patriots persevere against stronger and more stringent laws. I heard their impassioned speeches in the streets, and their cry for freedom pricked a cord in my heart. It was not until Stockton's treatment of Kitty that I knew I was fighting for the wrong side."

Anna pushed up, a twisted grimace on her face. He

rushed to help her, not removing his hand until the peace in her expression was restored.

Once seated straight, she held her gaze against him and cupped her hand against his jaw. "I do not condemn you for choosing not to tell me."

What manner of woman have you given me, Lord? "I give you my word, it was only to protect you."

"This I know." Her eyes shone, wisdom and love shimmering in their crystal depths. "God has given me more joy than I ever could have wished for, answered every prayer, blessed every pain. I sought you and found you. The love I craved I have been given. The child I have dreamed of is ours. All because of you."

Gratitude swelled until it forced his eyes to moisten. "How will I ever be worthy of you?"

"You are already. Everything you are, Henry—" She stopped, a smile slanting her mouth. "Henry."

The sound of his name, the one he had abandoned but never forgotten, hung in the air between them as Anna's smile widened. "We owe God all we can give," she said. "We owe our child's future all we can give."

The sudden drop in her lilting sound, the somber veil in her features forced his head to tilt. "What do you mean?"

She kept her gaze plaited with his, her voice carrying strength far beyond her feminine tone. "You are a soldier. You must fight."

He reached for her hand. "You would be alone."

"Nay." She shook her head. "Eliza and Kitty and I

shall be together. God will provide."

A flash of warmth spilled over his skin. "I do wish to go."

"I know."

"But I do not wish to leave you."

"I know. My heart aches at the thought." She leaned forward and pressed a kiss to his mouth. "But you must go, and I must let you."

Henry pulled her against him, willing the love that burned in his chest to carry through his embrace and warm her to the depth of her soul. Finally his mouth could form the words his heart longed to speak—words he believed he would never again have been able to utter, but for her. Now, he whispered their tender sound, savoring the perfect feel of them on his lips. "I love you, Anna."

Chapter Twenty-Six

Warmth from the blaze radiating in the fireplace filled the Watson's parlor while tension and woe weighted Anna's body like lead. The morning had not heeded her beseeching, and had come far too soon. She finished preparing Henry's bag, tucking the letter she'd penned deep in the safety of the pouch. Kitty stood beside her, doing much the same. Peering over her shoulder, Anna spied Eliza and baby Mary, both wrapped in a blanket, standing beside the door while the men finalized the plot of their journey.

She turned back to her task as a spike of regret readied to pierce her gut. Why the men must leave so early, she understood, but struggled to accept. Henry was a soldier and liberty was a cause more valiant than any on earth. She would not dissuade him no matter how her grief threatened to tear her to pieces. She nestled another cake along side the others, deflecting the incoming blow of fear with the shield of courage she'd fashioned since the moment the men had declared with certainty their intention to help Henry Knox at Fort Ticonderoga. That had only been three days past. And now, the dreaded moment was upon them.

Anna glanced at Kitty, whose light freckles had lost a shade of color. She must have sensed Anna's stare for she looked sideways, her gaze gripping Anna's.

With a tight smile, Kitty directed her vision to the men before fussing with the knapsack once more. "I want to go with them," she whispered.

"We all do. But you know we cannot."

She looked at Nathaniel, the sound of her pinched voice little more than a breath. "My heart will break if I should lose him..."

Do not speak it, Kitty. Anna raised her chin and fought the emotions that clawed at her chest. "That fear plagues us all."

"There are times despair threatens to overcome me. The future is so dark, so unknown, and the enemy so vast I feel I cannot move right or left. I try to be brave, but..."

"You are not alone in your feelings." Anna reached beside her, gripping Kitty's hand. "As they shall be courageous, so shall we."

"Aye, we shall." Kitty peered once again to the men, their conversation beginning to find its benediction, signaling the time of their departure. "Fear comes to us all, but we must not submit to its cries." She looked back to Anna. "I've known that, of course, but Nathaniel reminded me of it last night. He said submitting to our fears is the same as submitting to our foe." A healthy pink returned to Kitty's cheeks as if speaking her husband's words infused her blood with tangible courage. "I may shed a tear, but I will never submit. I know well the cause for which we sacrifice so much. It is worth every effort."

"You are a remarkable woman, Kitty." Simple words, yet not strong enough to carry the weight of their veracity.

"Nay, not at all, but I thank you." Kitty looked up and smiled to Eliza who turned just then to motion them from the table. "That praise is reserved for my sister. 'Twas she who planted the seed of liberty in my heart and for that I will be forever grateful." With a quick exhale and smile that failed to cover the emotion in her face, Kitty squeezed Anna's hand before making her way to the others.

I am not ready.

Anna reopened Henry's bag. Had she included enough cakes? She recounted and scowled. That would hardly be enough for such a journey. She looked out the window and removed the scarf she'd stuffed near the bottom. 'Twas far too cold. He would need it now, not later.

A pop in the fire burst to light the memory that gripped since its birth not ten hours past. Henry's wisdom embraced her, just as he had in the dark of their room. *We are few in number, those of us who strive for liberty—and you are one of them my darling, though you do not fight with ball and powder. But though we are few, we are strong in purpose, and our cause emboldens us against our enemy.* Anna closed her eyes, reliving the feel of his strong arms at her back, his breath on her cheek.

"Anna."

Henry's hand brushed her elbow, the pleasant remembrance dispersing like smoke in the wind. *Nay, I am not ready.* But she would never be.

Swallowing, Anna turned, gripping to her threadbare courage, praying it would not rip until he had gone. He could not see her cry. Not now.

She looked up. Except for she and Henry, the parlor was empty. "Where are the others?"

He glanced to the door then back to her. "They are saying their good-byes. We must leave now if we wish to travel in daylight." His eyes, like the sky on a spring day, lured the bud of hope to bloom.

"You will return to me."

"Dear, Anna." Reaching for her cheek, his warm, masculine smile widened his face, while his eyes reserved a strand of pain, refusing to give voice to the worries that pricked his soul as well as hers. He pressed out an audible breath. "You and Warren will get along well."

She studied his face, straining against the ache that clawed her spirit. "We will."

"I am pleased he will stay and look after you." Henry's jaw shifted before he spoke again. "He is a good man, and I trust him with your care."

Anna glanced down. Warren had told her everything, and though she was pleased—nay, overjoyed—to learn the truth of her birth, she would have Henry at her side over any man.

"Anna..." The depth of Henry's timbre brought her gaze back to his. "Should I...should anything happen to me, I want you to—"

"Oh, I nearly forgot." She snatched the scarf from the table and reached to fasten it around his neck. She could not allow him to speak such words, or her tears would stream from her eyes. "I would not have you worry. Of course Father and I shall keep watch over the garden and be sure our home is well cared for until you return." The last word wobbled and she coughed to cover the sound of it.

Henry traced her with his gaze, as if memorizing her every feature, capturing every memory that lived between them. "I will send word to you when I can."

"I shall treasure every letter." Anna smiled, the pain of sadness so sharp in her chest, she could only breathe in quick, short bursts. "You mustn't forget your bag." She thrust the small pack at him. Her throat strained and she smiled broader. "I do hope what I prepared is sufficient. There is a letter I penned for you near the bottom, and I—"

"Anna." He swept her against him and lowered his mouth to hers. All warmth, and depth and yearning. All grief and hope and faith together. His muscles tightened against her and she lifted to her toes, pressing against him and willing every ounce of her love to seep from her soul into his.

Groaning, he pulled away, resting his forehead against hers, allowing their breath to slow. He trailed his hands down her arms, finally knitting his fingers with hers as he raised his head. "Come."

He lead her away from the table and stopped just inside the door as the other couples stood in twos, speaking and embracing in the cold of the gray December morning. Three mounts stood ready, prepared with blankets and gear to carry them through the travails that awaited.

The ticking of Henry's jaw refused to abate. "You will be sure to have Kitty and Eliza assist you when your time approaches." He faced her, his gaze dropping to her belly then rising again to her eyes. His throat bobbed. "I will pray for you. That your pain will be minimal and that you will—"

"I will be fine." Anna reached for his face, brushing her fingers against the few faded scars on his jaw. "If our child is a girl, I shall name her Louisa, after your mother." His eyes misted and he swallowed, urging the lump in Anna's throat to swell. "If we are given a boy..." She inhaled and raised her face, gripping Henry's biceps. "I shall name him William."

Henry's eyes rimmed with red and he tugged her to him again, pressing her head against his chest and whispering into her hair. "I love you."

Holding to him, Anna gripped fistfuls of his coat at

his back. "I shall always love you, Henry."

"Henry, we must away."

Thomas's voice pierced the frosted air and Henry nodded. "I am coming."

No! Lord, help me be brave.

Henry eased Anna away, grinning as he reached for his pocket. "I have something for you."

"Oh?"

He took her hand and opened her fingers, resting a ring in her palm. Anna flung a look to him, gratitude and joy nudging back the weight of sorrow. "'Tis lovely—nay, 'tis more than lovely. 'Tis perfect."

"I know you have your mother's, but..." Smiling, his gaze lingered on the ring then rose to her face. "When I learned I would be leaving—"

"Come, Henry. No more dawdling." Anna looked to the source of the voice and found Nathaniel with his arms around Kitty, his face not carrying a hint of the jest that played in his voice to cut the sadness that stretched between them, no doubt. "I fear if we stay too much longer we shall not leave at all."

"I am ready."

Give me strength.

Anna rested against him and he tugged her close as they walked to the others. He faced her one last time, speaking low and gazing at her as if he could buoy her faltering strength with his faith alone. "I shall think of you always. I shall pray for you, just as I shall need your prayers."

"I shall pray for you with every breath." Smiling with more sincerity than she knew she carried, Anna reached to hold his face. "Kitty told me you once said that there will come a time when we will be called upon to act in defense of the cause we believe in. That time has come, and we were made for it." She rose to kiss him again, wrapping her arms firm around him, then stepped back, pressing the ring to her chest. "This shall hover over my heart while you are gone, and I shall put it on my finger in place of my mother's only when you return to me."

His mouth tightened, his gaze straining, it seemed, for one more touch. "I love you."

Lord, help me. She nodded, holding a strong smile on her mouth to fight the quivering of her chin. "I shall see you again, Henry. Promise me."

The low baritone of his voice wavered ever so slight. "I promise." After a quick smile he stepped to his horse.

A melody of heavy farewells played through the group as the women found comfort beside each other, while the men they loved mounted, preparing at last to leave them.

Though there were others beside her, though there were trees and sunshine and cold winter air, Anna could see and feel nothing but the last look that reached from Henry's eyes to embrace her, before finally he turned and kicked his horse to a gallop.

He was gone. All three men, so noble and good, had left them. And so they should, Anna reminded herself.

Eliza turned first, her cheeks stained with streaks of tears. "I am honored to have them go. I would have nothing less." She released a wobbled breath. "Do not think my tears mean I believe they should stay."

"I do not," Anna said first. She placed a hand at Eliza's back. "As I told Kitty, we shall strengthen each other."

"Aye, we shall." Kitty took Eliza's arm and motioned to the house. "Come, let us find the warmth of the fire. I believe the bread I prepared should be ready now."

Anna paused and Eliza took her hand. "You are coming, Anna?"

"Aye, I thank you." She peered toward the road where the men had gone. "Forgive me, I beg a moment alone."

Both women nodded and started for the house.

Praying, Anna closed her eyes, painting in her mind a vision of days yet to come—Henry riding back just as he had rode away, whole and strong, with Thomas and Nathaniel riding beside him. They would tell of their victory and how freedom was theirs, just as they'd hoped, and sacrificed and prayed. She squinted her eyes tighter and bowed her head, pressing her fists to her mouth. *Lord, protect them. Carry them home, I pray thee. Grant them victory and carry them home.*

Blinking her eyes open, Anna exhaled and turned toward the house when the feel of the gold circle in her grasp halted her steps. She released the protective fist around the ring Henry had given her. *Oh, how I love you, my dear Henry.* Lifting it to the light, she turned the precious gift in her fingers and gasped in reverent surprise, her eyes misting, as she read the engraving etched in scrolling letters.

> *Tho' the world hath striv'd to part,*
> *God hath joined us, hand and heart.*

Author's Note

The historic Siege of Boston lasted nearly a year, from April 1775 to March 1776, when Washington finally drove the British Army from the city. Boston's harbor had been closed since March 1774, isolating the city in an attempt to make the citizens submit to British authority, but it only fueled their growing anger over continued atrocities. By mid-to-late 1775, the city was in great distress. Starvation, disease, and poverty were rampant. Many of the civilians had left the city, but many were unable to leave and subjected to the terrible conditions.

The colonists in surrounding areas wished to help their fellow patriots and did what they could. Though I know of no documented instances where smuggling goods into Boston occurred (literary license there...), smuggling was a very real part of the Revolutionary War era and extremely dangerous for those involved. But danger, it would seem, did not deter the tenacious colonists from living fearlessly.

Thank you for taking the time to read Henry's and Anna's story. It was a joy for me to write, and I hope, a joy for you to read.

39458017R00296

Made in the USA
San Bernardino, CA
27 September 2016